LEE MATTHEW GOLDBERG

THE GREAT GIMMELMANS

LEVEL
BEST BOOKS

Everybody needs money. That's why they call it money.

-Danny DeVito, Heist

Prologue

The road is empty because where we're headed no one wants to go. My son Roark sits in the back, earbuds blasting, tuning me, the hell out. He's not happy about this four-hour drive, and neither am I. If someone told me a few months ago that I'd be making this trek, I would've slapped them across the face and shouted "Lies," but life is a tricky one, and I learned early on it could give you whiplash with how much it changes. I'd been rich, I'd been poor, I'd been wanted by the F.B.I. at the tender age of twelve. I've seen death and someone's guts oozing out of their stomach. I've shot a person, been shot at, all in another lifetime that feels like a nightmare. I worry that Roark is traveling down this same dark and twisted path.

He started with smoke bombs, fireworks, innocent kid stuff. Aren't we all mischievous as teens? We only crave a rise out of adults. So what if he left a live crab in the bathroom that pinched a boy's ass? Or a whoopie cushion under a teacher's chair? Or mutilated a frog as a present in a bully's lunchbox? That was the first instance his mom Melinda rang me up. She and I are—well, now we're far from fights where dishes used to be flung. We've been divorced longer than we've been married, and Roark mostly lives with her. It's for the better. Writers don't make great parents. We're too devoted to our characters as surrogate children. And crime writers especially. I spend my days, conjuring up fifty ways to hide a body. Makes it difficult to find sympathy in wiping away tears when a toe gets stubbed.

So this trip was her idea. A bonding experience. The open road before us with nothing to do but impart my wisdom because dead frogs in lunchboxes had now turned to grand theft auto . He broke into his Earth Science teacher's car. Don't even know how. She had a dinosaur of a sedan, and he hotwired it off a TikTok video he saw and went joyriding around town. The cops got involved. How he managed to avoid juvie is a mystery. But the next time he won't be so lucky.

"Aaron," she said, pushing him toward me in her front yard. A strand of hair had escaped from her bun, and I longed to put it back into place, but we were far from that ever happening again. "He's all yours." She threw her hands up, her face pinched like her nose was being used to juice a lemon and retreated inside slamming the screen door. If Roark didn't get his act together he wasn't welcome in her home anymore.

He shoved his fists into his hoodie pockets and bumped into my shoulder as he passed by.

"Jesus, you got old," he said.

My fingers traveled to my newly-whitened beard, that seemed to have sprouted overnight. It began with a phone call a few months back. An inmate at the penitentiary. A return to my past. I'd kept my hellish upbringing at bay for many ignorantly blissful years, but I always knew that one day I'd be forced to confront it again. And so here we are on this empty road passing by cow farms without another car in sight while I think of what to say because it's been so long.

He was eight when I fully left. My latest thriller was primed to blow up and they sent me on a massive tour. Not Stephen King levels but close. Enough that my publisher paid my way. I never came back. Things had already turned sour between Melinda and I, and my relationship with Roark was non-existent, even when he was young. I fell in love with my publicist and we got drunk off of life spreading our carnage through Europe. Then she left me for a new, hot debut author, and now I find myself back in the States with Melinda telling me that it's "my turn to parent for once."

I catch his eyes in the rearview and point to my ear, gesturing for him to remove the buds. He looks at me like I'm sewage and plucks one out.

"What?"

"What are you listening to?"

"What The Fuck?"

"Roark, work with me. That's a normal question."

"What The Fuck? is the name of band."

Touché, I nod.

"I was thinking we could listen to something else."

He raises one skeptical eyebrow. His sigh clogging up the stuffy car. He plucks out the other bud.

I'm taken aback by how much he looks like my father Barry. His curly hair, like a helmet, wild eyes, and a smile that seems to forever drip toward a smirk. Fucking Barry, making his generational mark in appearance and in criminal deceit, his DNA just too strong.

"We could listen to my first book," I say, my fingers hovering over my phone where the audio version is ready to play. "The memoir."

"What the fuck?" he says, that smirk tormenting me.

"You could be in juvie right now."

His eyes glide over to a cow in the distance, mooing away. I bet he wishes he could trade places.

"Stealing your teacher's car. *What* the fuck were you thinking?"

He rolls those eyes. "She deserved it."

"No, no one deserves it."

He rips off a cuticle as I wince. "She was always calling on me in class."

"Yeah, Roark, that's what school is."

"No, like, when she knew I didn't know the answer. To make me look stupid."

"You gotta do your homework," I say, the words foreign on my tongue. "You gotta study."

I know I sound foolish. When I was his age, I was casing banks, far from a good pupil in front of the class leaving an apple on my teacher's desk.

"Being bad, acting out," I say, tripping over these gems I manage to unearth. "It may seem *cool*—"

"No one says 'cool'."

"Okay. It may seem fleek."

He forms his fingers into the shape of a gun and mimes shooting himself. The goosebumps along my arms go into overdrive.

"It won't get you anywhere," I cough, quieting my chills. Guns—even imaginary ones—have a tendency to do that. "What do you want to be?"

"An outlaw," he says, that smirk in full force. Silence eats up the air, a sparkle in his eye. "Like you."

Now my guts are seeping out of my stomach. I'm crawling through broken glass begging for a reprieve. That's how it feels.

"What do you know of that?" I ask, carefully observing his reaction.

"Wikipedia," he says, and that ends that.

"But you don't know the whole story," I say, struggling to swallow.

"I got the gist." A lightbulb clicks on in his head. "That's why you're taking me today. To see—"

"Your mom thought we could bond."

He makes a gagging motion and for once I agree with his assessment.

"She's afraid of me," he says, like he's proud.

"You're damn right she is."

"So now you're stuck with me."

There's a quiver to his voice, as if deep down, he fears being unwanted. He's loved unconditionally, I'd take a bullet for this kid. But do I like him...? Jury's out on that one.

"My book," I continue, beaming. I can't help it. My first baby, the one that shot me to the bestseller list. That paid for a beach house in Miami, even his ridiculous private school in Texas. My others had been minor successes, all fiction. None quite hit the zeitgeist like that nugget of truth, readers salivating for a window into what made my family tick. How I'd been paid by my publisher in innocent people's blood. "I think you could learn from it."

He makes a jackoff motion and spews imaginary spunk my way.

"Jeez, Roark. C'mon."

He's laughing now, a rare occurrence, so I'll let his crudeness slide. He likes to poke the bear—and I get it, I was the same. My genes, my blood, in so many ways too.

"Will you stop talking if we listen to it?" he asks, his laughter sounding now like a machine gun. *Rat, tat, tat. Ha, ha, ha.*

"Yes, Roark, yes I'll stop talking."

"I lied," he says, sucking at his thumb now where he ripped off the cuticle.

"I never read your Wiki page. You're a mystery to me." He turns back to the cows. "You're not that important."

"I deserve that," I say, meaning only to think it, but honestly, he deserves to hear it out loud. When things got rough, I fled. I was a coward.

"Well…" he says, stretching out the word. "I know what *he* did."

The chills come back. *He,* meaning Barry, my father, my scourge.

"How can you forgive him?" Roark asks. No smirk anymore, dead serious. It's good to see he at least has an intact soul.

I never stopped loving Barry, that's the truth. Even when I swore him off. Even when so many years passed that we'd be unrecognizable to one another. A boy's first hero can never fully fall from their high. They were worshipped too greatly. At least that's what I tell myself, even after he shattered my heart a thousand ways.

I couldn't answer Roark. I'd never fully forgiven Barry, carrying around that anger like an extra limb all through adulthood. Middle-aged with grey in my beard still with daddy issues. Staring at Roark, I pray he won't be the same.

"Your great-grandmother," I say. "My mother's mother lived most her life as an Orthodox Jew. Everything the woman did revolved around Hashem. I remember sitting with her on a plastic-coated loveseat after all the shit went down, after my family…" I took a deep breath, exhaled a cloud of sadness. "'*Boychick*', she'd said. She called me that. '*Boychick*, Judaism teaches that because humans have been given free will, they are responsible for their own actions'. She wagged her ancient finger at me. 'If they commit an action which is wrong, then they must seek forgiveness. Forgiveness can *only* be accepted from the victim. This is *teshuva*, repentance. According to the *Talmud*, God created repentance before he created the physical universe."

For this, Roark stays listening, something I've said keeping him rapt. His mom's a Christian, so I hope there's something magical to hear about Judaism, this other half of him.

"I believe we become whole once we accept *teshuva*. I'm seeking this ability, Roark, I'm trying." I choke on the last word, a budding tear waiting to spill. "I can't carry it with me anymore, this cancer—you get it?"

"What The Fuck?" he says, about to pop back in his earbud, fooling me all along that I thought he could care.

"Hand it over," I say, reaching for the buds. I leave them on the dashboard. "We got over four hours to go, best get comfortable. This is my cautionary tale."

Through the rearview, he crosses his arms, but it's an act of show. That glimmer in his eye has come back. For he idolizes outlaws, and none held a candle to us, the great Gimmelmans.

I push play as my voice from thirty years ago fills up the car, since the publisher tapped me to narrate the book to bring in all the possible dough.

I steel myself as he and I travel on the way-back machine to hell, keying in the coordinates to our final destination: United States Penitentiary, Beaumont, Texas.

1

When I was a little kid, like eight or so, I'd stand in front of a mirror and ask myself, "Who is Aaron Nicholas Gimmelman?" I knew I was me, of course, and that I loved basketball and the Knicks, specifically Patrick Ewing who won NBA Rookie of the Year despite his injuries. I hated milk with the passion of a thousand fiery suns after being forced to squeeze a cow's udders on a school farm trip. I thought Hebrew school was definitely the worst, since my bar mitzvah seemed a million years and a shit ton of work away. I always had a cow lick that no amount of gel could tamper, and my ears curved out enough for my Grandma Bernice down in Florida to shame my mother, into taping them back when I was a baby. I listened to my cassette of "Walk Like an Egyptian" over and over that I bought from Nobody Beats the Wiz and was gobsmacked when I learned Boy George was actually a boy. When my older sister Steph got boobs, she had a rotation of paramours I liked to call "stray cats waiting on our doorstep for scraps," and my little sister Jenny tortured animals in her spare time. I once threw up spaghetti and meatballs and the meatballs looked like eyes and the spaghetti a smiling mouth. A goat sneezed on me at the Westchester County Fair, and I became convinced I was dying. Sometimes I touched things in threes for fear that God would strike me down if I didn't. And my dad worked on Wall Street, making a boatload of money, and we lived in a big house in New Jersey, close enough to see New York City across the Hudson River.

But who was Aaron Nicholas Gimmelman really?

It took only one sperm to fertilize my mom's egg, but there'd been two hundred million other competitors. Two hundred million alternate Aaron Nicholas Gimmelmans who maybe gorged themselves on milk and hated the Knicks. But somehow, I won the lottery.

I was thinking of this a few years later at the ripe age of twelve while we raced away in the RV we dubbed "The Gimmelmans' Getaway Gas-Guzzler" with the FBI on our ass, about a million bucks stuffed in the cabinets, Steph's Debbie Gibson tape blasting "Electric Youth" while Jenny surfed in the "living area" with a taxidermy opossum she called Seymour, my mother Judith weeping like mad into her pashmina, and Barry Gimmelman, my dad and the most notorious bank robber of the 1980s, flooring the Gas-Guzzler through the Mojave Desert.

We'd taken a pivot, both with the RV off the highways, and in our lives. The 1987 Stock Market Crash left us worse than penniless, in debt to banks and loan sharks that would take multiple lifetimes to pay off, but the Gimmelmans were a resourceful bunch, descendants of Holocaust survivors that never gave into defeat. I leaned out the RV's window with a Bren Ten stainless steel gun that had become an extension of my hand, all Sonny Crockett cool, wearing my pastel jacket and Ray-Bans that Barry gifted me after a successful bank job. I was gonna fire on those FBI fucks when my mother let out a scream so bone-shaking that I nearly dropped the gun on the road.

"This has gone too far," she yelled, snot dripping from her nose, her face red and beating, hair in a tizzy, and her eyes dull. They used to go wide with exhilaration, now they blinked vacant like the seedy motels tucked behind interstates that we hid out in on our spree across America when the Gas-Guzzler became too tight quarters, and Mom and Barry wanted to bump uglies without abandon. I saw our faded neon-sign pasts in her sad pupils, but her throat became too sore from crying to hear over "Electric Youth."

Zappin it to ya. The pressure's everywhere...

Barry cackled over the dance-pop, usually blaring songs that took him back to Woodstock '69, when he and Mom fell in muddy love over a bottle of Jameson and Janis Joplin in the air. But today he catered to Steph because she was going through a tougher time than any of us at the moment and prone to sobbing uncontrollably—he even sang along to the Debbie Gibson tune.

I idolized him, proud to be the Aaron Nicholas Gimmelman from his loins that conquered all those vying sperms. He'd been a successful stockbroker and an even more successful robber, we all were, but none as great as Barry Gimmelman, a mensch who was tan even in the winter, had black curly hair he'd try to slick back and a laugh that could pierce your heart, teeth so white and glowing you thought he was lit from within, tough but fair, and quick for a joke or a light of your smoke, as he used to say. He made us into the Bonnie and Clyde of the late eighties, our Dillinger from New Jersey, who believed in keeping us accustomed to the lifestyle we knew. The reward worth the risk. Anything but to be ordinary. His parents, Avraham and Ethel, didn't survive Treblinka and the Nazi scum to flee to America for their offspring to eke out a paycheck-to-paycheck existence. Barry would be immortalized—*we* would be immortalized. Despite any misgivings creeping into my brain during those times of silence the Gimmelmans rarely experienced, I'd convince myself of our king and swear my proven loyalty.

I saw his eyes fan over to me through the rearview mirror, not dull like Mom's, but spinning with hope, winking at me to do what I needed to do...

Who is Aaron Nicholas Gimmelman? they asked.

So, I pulled the trigger and watched a bullet spiral toward the FBI's flashing car, the front window shattering upon impact, and a "That's my boy!" escaping from Barry's lips as the Gas-Guzzler flew into the sun spreading across the barren landscape.

I could feel the heat as we plunged into its burning abyss.

2

Rewind. Our new lives on the FBI's Most Wanted ultimately began on Black Monday, October 19, 1987, when the Dow Jones fell 508 points, 22.8% of the market, the largest one-day drop in history. Twenty-three major world markets experienced a decline that day with losses estimated at 1.7 trillion dollars. People feared another Great Depression. But the writing had been on the Stock Ticker. I could explain about the House Committee on Ways and Means introducing a tax bill that would reduce the tax benefits associated with financing mergers and leveraged buyouts. And that unexpectedly high trade deficit figures announced by the Department of Commerce had a negative impact on the value of the dollar while pushing interest rates upward, but let's be honest, the crash was the impetus that got us on the road to thieving. And because all our assets and funds were tied to the market, the Gimmelmans, once popping Champagne corks from our surging portfolios, were about to get fucked seven gazillion ways come Tuesday.

Thank God for office windows that didn't open from the inside.

While watching his Monday turn from this-ain't-so-good to complete-toilet-overflow, Barry Gimmelman pondered a *splat* against the pavement. He even crawled up on the window sill, checking for a way to unlock what he conceded as his inevitable destiny. Coworkers wandered past his office, shrieking and wailing, banging their heads against the walls, attempting to slit their wrists with tie clips. He worked for one of the biggest firms on the Street. Not only had he lost a fortune in a matter of hours, but he lost the fortunes of some very powerful people who would be rightfully pissed and looking for a target to blame.

His superior Edina shuffled inside, hair zapped like it had been electrocuted, grinding her teeth so hard he could hear the shards whittling off the bone. Her zombie eyes told Barry she might not ever recover. She pleaded with him, arms outstretched as if begging for alms, morphing into a bag lady in mere minutes.

"What am I to do?" she asked, in the voice of a child.

Edina, one of the toughest women he knew, who rose the ranks in a boys' club operation of pinched butts and misogyny. Who looked like a shark with her prominent forehead and poof of hair like a fin and proudly thought of herself as one, hovering in circles around the office searching for blood.

She left his office without getting an answer. Like everyone else in this field, his job prospects tomorrow would be slim. He also had invested all of his money in stocks because they were doing well enough to get him a palatial home in Jersey, close enough so his commute wasn't a ball killer, and a Maserati in fire-engine red. For his daughter Steph's bat mitzvah four years ago, he'd booked the band Men at Work to perform "Down Under" for her friends. He liked to only wear Armani suits, have steak tartar at the 21 Club, despite it being far from Kosher, foie gras in a baked eggy dough at Lutece, (also not Kosher), and martinis at the Odeon with clients. Growing up, his parents squeezed pennies and owned a Jewish bakery down in the Lower East Side. They all lived above in an apartment with a bathtub in the kitchen and sheets to partition the bedrooms for he and his older brother Morty. Adult Barry believed he and his offspring deserved a rich life after an ancestry filled with plight and suffering. No more fighting with the household mice for a piece of babka that caused his mother to have carpel tunnel from the repeated twisting and braiding. With his blinding smile and knack for utilizing market trends, New York City became Barry's playground to prosper.

He could see visions of that sad bathtub in the kitchen. His family, forced to look the other way while hearing the *splash, splash* of one of them simply wanting to get clean. A mouse going to town on a nub of babka and the growls of his children's stomachs. The growls turning into a voice that would ask, *Why couldn't you get a more stable profession? You could've been a doctor,* like his mother would've loved, God bless her, *or a lawyer,* like his father pushed, Hashem bless him too, even continue running their bakery on Elizabeth Street rather than going to Columbia. The market had been going up-up-up, it was bound to cave. He had been too blinded by foie gras and Maseratis to see it.

And Judith, what would she say? He had avoided his brick of a cell phone, even though she knew not to call during work. His hippie moon goddess turned lady-who-lunched at the Four Seasons. The amount of hats she owned, was enough to keep the country of India dry during monsoon season. Their home in Tenafly was not close to paid off. Those sea of hats would soon be repossessed like everything else they owned. And the kids in private schools. They had just started the new school year in September! Little Jenny in the plaid uniform she hated but with teachers who kept her from becoming a true terror. Yours Truly so smart, and Steph starting to think about colleges. We'd be torn apart in public school, forced to wind up at community colleges, then bagging groceries. And since Barry would be out of a job too, he'd be bagging groceries right beside us.

"Goddammit, there's no lock on these windows," he shouted, beating against the glass, hoping against hope for it to shatter so he could plunge. His boss Oren roamed by, high on cocaine and sputtering nonsense. Conspiracy theories out the wazoo, a bloody line dripping from the man's honker.

"Oh no, death is too easy," Oren said, wiping away the bloody line only to rub it under his eyes like a football player ready for war. "Kinda luck we're having, you'll bounce right on the sidewalk and land back up here in Hell."

Oren shuffled away, the last time Barry would ever see the man. Apparently, death did come easy for Oren that night with a coke binge that exploded his heart.

Barry tossed his computer screen at the window only for it to boomerang back and knock him over to the ground. With shaking fingers, he found his giant cell phone and called his love Judith.

"Baby," he said, squeezing out tears.

"Oh Barry, my Bear-Bear," she said, a nickname due to his furry chest. "Is it as bad, as the news is making it out?"

He had crawled under his desk, gripping the giant cell phone. The melee happening outside kept to a din in his new secluded cave where only he and Judith existed.

"It's worse," he said, having trouble swallowing. "There's nothing left."

"There's always *something* left." He imagined her in the kitchen, curling the cord around her finger, telling herself to keep him hopeful, to be his rock. "You and I, the kids, we're not publicly traded."

"I looked out my window," Barry said, in a daze, the words spaced far apart as if he had to search through the fog to find them. Something was burning, a crackle of flames down the hallway. Had they finally reached a place where the devil reigned? "I've ruined us."

She let him breakdown for a second, only a moment of self-pity before continuing in the authoritative voice of a dominatrix.

"Listen to me, Barry Gimmelman." Her tongue clicked like a whip. "When I met you, you were high on acid without a coin in your pocket and clawed your way up from nothing. Now we have a swimming pool I do laps in every morning, and a maid, but it's just a bonus. I grew up in Sheepshead Bay and my mother sewed clothes after my father died. I never realized I was poor until we became rich."

"What about your hats?" he blubbered, wiping his snot on the inside of the desk.

"Pish. So, I won't have hats. So, I'll skip the beauty parlor. 'So buttons,' as my mother used to say. Are we rich in health?"

"You say this now..."

"*Are* we rich in health, Barry Gimmelman?"

"Yes, yes, our kids, you, I—we have health."

"Feh, that's all I need."

"I don't want to tell you what I thought about when I looked out of the window, Judith."

"Then you don't have to."

"My biggest fear is of failing."

"Barry love, you're certainly not the only failure today. The world failed and we got caught up in it. Now come home, baby, we'll put on a record, open a bottle of red, and defrost a roast we shoulda eaten last week."

"You cooked?"

"It's leftover from when we breaked fast after Yom Kippur."

As Judith enticed him to come home for old meat, a body flew past Barry's window—tie flapping up, face mashed into a final scream, toupee left in the clouds. Barry scooted out from his desk cave to watch this man's ungraceful fall, his arms flapping in an attempt to fly. A thud at the bottom of the street so soft it was barely a whisper. If he hadn't seen this man's horrible descent, he never would've known it happened. Even peering out of his prison window, only darkness could be seen at the bottom of the building along with a guess of how many lives that day had taken.

"Barry? Barry, are you there?" Judith squawked, for my parents had a psychic bond and she could read his stress levels tilting to maximum from far away.

"I'm here," he said, and then repeated it definitively. Black Monday would not be the end of Barry Gimmelman. He would rise from the stock chit ashes and defrost that roast, chasing it down with a bottle of red and his family by his side until he figured out his next move.

He ended the call and breached out of his office into the chaos of the hallway, past souls pulling their hair from its roots, and onto the street where the city was both loud and eerily quiet at the same time.

Got in his Maserati to floor it to New Jersey, searching for songs on the radio to avoid the news and settling on the oldies station where Janis Joplin sang, *And if you ever feel lonely, dear I want you to come on, come on to your mama now.* The song from when he first held Judith in his arms and tickled her ear with tales of their imagined futures, laying her down in a mud-splattered field, and tasting the acid tab on her pretty pink tongue, and then her pretty pink self, until the future laid out in all its glory like a great Smorgasbord of a feast.

He'd find it again, in whatever nook and cranny it hid, he'd hunt for that sweet paradise he so deserved.

3

While on the phone with Barry, Judith found her calling—that of Soother
with a capital S. It was a role she knew well. Mother of three children, the
amount of booboos, she cleaned and bandaged obscene. Except for young
Jenny who relished cuts and scrapes and lived for the sight of blood. Beyond
booboos, Steph required solace on a constant basis due to her dramatic flair.
Everything, a crisis for a teenager. Her socks not crimped enough—God
forbid. Not the right scrunchie for her hair—suicide. The on-again, off-
again tragicomedy of her relationship with Kent, a boy who Judith found
decidedly not Jewish enough, more like the type who ran singalongs at a
Christian camp. Then there was me, the middle child, whose wheels were
always turning like a cat. Smarter than her, mischievous but sensitive like
the rest of the Gimmelmans, except Jenny. No matter how much trouble I
got in, Mom always forgave her favorite "little cub" and wouldn't let me
feel bad for behaving like a shit.

But what to do with Barry now, who she'd known and grown up with since
they were sixteen and took charge in a way that sometimes took her breath
away. Barry always had a plan, then a backup one, and a third lingering
around just in case. When as teens, he said he was going to make a lot
of money and give her everything she desired, he was right. Every goal
reached. She liked to think she was a part of the reason for that success,
holding together a strong home while he shone, but she wondered if that
was really true. Barry so bright that he outshone everyone around him, the

need for others dimming in his light. And yet now, *now*, he needed comfort, assurance. She had it in spades to give.

She focused on what was truly important. Health. Family. But when she got off the phone, she poured a hefty glass of *vino* and wandered into her walk-in closet of hat boxes galore. Each of them, a friend. How could she possibly say goodbye?

If you would've told young Judith that this would be her life, she would've spit in your eye and laughed at the tall tale. The fact that jewelry dripped from her body when all she planned on that day was going to the grocery store. A family vacation in the Seychelles where she swam in water so clear it was like a mirror and they had a private hut on the edge of the world. That she devoted Tuesdays to shopping with a gaggle of other rich girlfriends and that those Tuesdays were now in the past. No more bottomless credit cards. She closed the walk-in closet door.

And yet, she had told Barry she didn't care. She'd grown up with little. Things, tough for her from the start. When she was a child, her father had a swift battle with pancreatic cancer, dead in two months. She watched him disintegrate. The hospital bills left her and her mom with nothing. Bernice took work as a seamstress, the only skill she had without even a high school degree, while Judith rebelled. By fourteen, she smoked a lot of pot. At sixteen, she followed bands around on tours living in the back of VWs. She grew her hair long and never wore bras, found psychedelics and hitchhiked to Woodstock. It was there she met Barry, whose crazy hair stood out like a bush, and even though it wasn't burning, it was the first time she believed she saw God. Bernice had become borderline religious. They kept Shabbat, not even allowed to turn on a light. Nothing unkosher was allowed inside the house once her father got sick. Bernice went to temple whenever she wasn't working and it was open, but Judith never bought what Judaism was selling. That was until she met Barry, her own spiritual Torah in the body of a five-foot- nine Jewish kid from the Lower East Side.

He had a crooked nose that she wanted to honk and these doofy glasses, swaying to Joplin's "Cry Baby." She popped an acid tab and glided over as if a force linked them. Like a wraith she appeared in his line of vision. They danced together before they even spoke. He had a couple of friends with him, and she had gone there with Jeanie and Ruth, two girls she knew since grade school, but she couldn't remember their names anymore, or even her own. His breath smelled like Rheingold beer, a tongue probing her soul as they Frenched, his shirt unbuttoned and a carpet of chest hair she clung onto. He scooped his hand in hers as the acid kicked in and pulled her away from the crowd to a tree that looked like an enormous spider.

"I'm Barry," he said, and thankfully she remembered her name.

"Judy," she said, because that was what she went by at the time.

With the music making history in the background, they talked over one another, telling the story of their lives. He had just graduated high school, got accepted at Columbia. She dropped out, following music wherever it took her. He was going for a business degree because his parents owned a bakery that was always struggling and in danger of closing. He never wanted to live that way. She told him of her own tough ride: burying her father, a newly religious mother who'd given up on her. He asked what she planned on doing with her life and she had no idea. She honestly had never thought about it. She wanted to simply float. And then the acid really kicked in and he made weird, swirling love to her up against the spider tree, both of them going in and out of their bodies, and afterwards she nestled in his chest fur and thought of it as home. When fall came, she moved into his dorm room even though he had a roommate. By senior year, she was pregnant with Steph, and his parents had passed. Surviving the Holocaust together, one could not exist without the other, they were too enmeshed. When his mother got very sick one winter and died of a mysterious infection, his father was gone before spring arrived. Barry sold the bakery, and they lived in Colombia housing while he went to B school. When he graduated, he got a job, and by the time they had me, he'd saved enough to buy their first home in New Jersey. Bernice had moved down to Florida at that point to live in an Orthodox community. If on a random day you would ask if my mom was happy, she'd definitely say yes. Beyond her wildest dreams, even though she'd never fantasized about them specifically. She simply floated into this existence.

But now she knew of the Gimmelmans' inevitable decline, the state of their finances. Their first home upgraded for a bigger one, impossible to pay off. The mortgage piling up. And did they need his and hers Maseratis? Neither paid off either. Everything on credit. Barry always assuring her they were earning way more than they were spending, but not after today. The plunging market, a halt to their parade. She didn't know how much they had actually lost and what Barry meant by *everything.* It was impossible to lose everything, they had too much. But she'd never heard him speaking the way he did on the phone. A scared undertone reverberating in his voice, as if he had given up. She'd coax him back to reality. She couldn't lose him. She had not an iota of skill that could put food on the table and as a single mom of three would be lost. The only thing to do was soothe. Ease him off the edge. Pull him away from the nightmares. On the news, there had been images of men flinging themselves off of high buildings on Wall Street and she couldn't watch for fear of seeing him. And then his call. His nervous, babbling call, and a commandeering voice bubbling in her she never knew she had. He'd provided for her for over twenty years, now it would be her turn to help him rise again.

She knocked back her glass of wine as the front door slammed open and the kids burst inside, oblivious to the sinking universe around us.

4

Swish. I was shooting hoops in our front yard. The school bus had left Jenny and I off and she hopped around trying to catch squirrels. I feared for the one who would finally get caught, since Jenny had torturous plans. They say you can spot psychopathic tendencies, well, we all knew we might be on the news in a few years talking about early signs with Jenny. First: the goldfish she would take out of the bowl and watch flop around. Next: the tiny bird whose feathers she plucked. Our old cat Tuxedo whose tail she'd grab and whip the poor thing around like a tornado. When Tuxedo finally went to cat heaven, we all breathed a sigh of relief.

Other than worrying about animals' fates, I rarely paid Jenny any mind. She was eight and I eleven. We'd pass each other at school with at most a nod, if we were being generous. She had zero friends and kept to herself, usually singing quietly, always seeming content in her budding serial killer mind. Besides, I wanted to make JV squad that year. Usually, Drake and Liam would come over after school and we'd play H-O-R-S-E, or I'd practice free throws until dinner.

Our house was at the end of a cul de sac, big and white, our closest neighbor hidden by a line of black spruce trees. Even late at night I could shoot hoops without bothering anyone. And not to pat my back, but I was fucking good. Maybe not Patrick Ewing level yet, but hey, I was five foot zero and lean like a switch. Give me time.

Basketball was an escape because other than that, I pretty much shat the bed at school. Barry would defend my toilet grades as me being too smart. A brain like mine needed to be challenged constantly, and even though my private school was one of the top ones in the county, I was bored, bored, bored. I didn't want to learn Earth science or read a book called *Watership Down* about a group of bunny rabbits. Snore. I wanted to be like Barry, make a fuck ton of money, and buy a house even bigger than the one we lived in. If I wasn't good or tall enough to play for the Knicks, I could buy the goddamn Knicks.

Steph's car pulled into the driveway blasting "I Think We're Alone Now," by her hero Tiffany. She'd started to dress like her, teasing her hair and dyeing it off-red, wearing big plastic hoop earrings and a jean jacket with a thousand flower pins, a black bowler hat and knock-off gold chains around her waist. She jingled as she shut off the radio and exited the car Barry recently bought for her Sweet Sixteen.

Like she was in an MTV video, she leaned against the car and lit a Malibu 100. She smoked to be cool because she'd barely take a puff before exhaling like a poser.

"Gimme one, bimbette," I said, tucking the basketball in my armpit.

"They're lady cigarettes."

"Like I care."

I snatched one and she graciously lit it against hers. We smoked like two divorcees drunk off Boone's Farm strawberry wine.

"Are those two mustache hairs I see?" she asked, pointing at me with the cherry of the cigarette.

"Uh, like ten."

She laughed, and it echoed. "Baby's all grown up. Is Mom home?"

I shrugged, since I hadn't even gone inside yet.

"Kent was gonna come over," she said.

"So you could swap spit?"

"Yeah, so we can swap spit. Not like you would know."

"I've kissed before!"

"That pillow you call Sheila doesn't count."

"The girls at my school are like, so Jersey."

"*We're* so Jersey."

"You are, with your mall hair. Seriously, you spend every waking minute at the Tenafly Mall. At night, you and all of them turn into the mannequins so you won't have to leave."

"I love *Mannequin* the movie."

"You would, it's spoon-fed garbage. Like Tiffany."

"Bite your tongue."

"And Debbie Gibson."

She whacked me on the side of the head, hard enough to knock me over.

"If you didn't spend most of your time trying to act cooler than everyone else, you might actually have a life."

"I have a life."

She flicked her cigarette to the curb, put it out with her pointy toed white boot.

"Not one I'd care to live."

I thought about flinging the basketball at her head but let her walk into the house unscathed.

Jenny emerged from the forest of trees behind our backyard, leaves in her wild hair, dirt on her face like a chimney sweeper. A squirrel clenched in her fist, the squirrel's eyes bulging from its sockets.

"What the fuck, Jenny?"

She saw me and lost her focus for a millisecond so the squirrel could squirrel away. It bolted off to freedom. She leaned back and growled at the heavens like a feral beast. I took a step back out of fear. Wiping the spittle from her lips, she barreled into our house leaving mud-prints behind, the little psycho.

I landed a hook shot like *swish* and followed my nutjob sisters inside.

* * *

Mom was acting rather squirrelly. I went to watch a *Night Court* repeat I hadn't seen when she jumped in front of the TV and turned it off.

"Hey!" I snapped. "Roz enrolled in anger management and the group was taken hostage. Now I won't know what happened."

She put her hands on her hips. "We're going to sit down to dinner."

"I wanted Gino's Pizza Rolls."

"I'm defrosting a roast."

I must've made a face because she scolded me not to make one.

"Your father is joining us and we're going to have a family meal *away* from the television."

An hour later, after the roast was defrosted, Barry hadn't returned home yet, and the unfrozen meat sat gray like Rhinoceros skin on my plate. Jenny had devoured hers, typical for a hungry wolf, while Steph chewed grape Bubble Tape.

"I thought you said Dad was joining us?" I asked.

Mom glanced at her watch for the thousandth time with a sad frown. "Must be traffic."

Steph had her Walkman on, "Photograph" from Def Leppard pumping.

"Stephie, not at the table," Mom said, indicating Steph's ears.

Steph shut off the tape and hid the headphones in her nest of hair.

"You're acting weird," she said.

"Who? Me?" Mom replied, like a perp who was totally guilty.

"Like, you never cook," Steph said, poking at her gray dinner.

"I cooked this when we breaked fast after Yom Kippur."

"That was weeks ago and none of us ate it then."

"Jenny likes it. Don't you, doll?"

Jenny gave a *grrrr* that none of us could tell was a positive or negative review.

"Jenny would eat a tire," Steph shot back. "Are you guys getting a divorce?"

"What? No. No, definitely not."

I didn't like to see Mom getting the third degree. I pictured coppers circling her with a spotlight in her face. The sweat on her top lip, clenching and unclenching her fists.

"If it's not a divorce, then what is it?"

Mom let out a deflated sigh. "The stock market crashed."

Dim bulb Steph blinked in confusion, and Jenny was off in Jenny land, but a knot formed in my stomach. I knew what this meant. Honestly, I'd been following the news recently that predicted a storm.

"How bad?" I asked, and Mom looked over at me like she'd forgotten I was in the room.

"I-I don't know, but I don't want to cushion things for you kids. That's not right."

She rose and turned on the news on our thirteen-inch where some old anchor gave us the rundown. Almost a quarter of the market was in decline. Steph twirled the grape gum around her finger and Jenny licked her plate, both oblivious to what this meant, but I knew. It was easy to see we lived beyond our means. A grand foyer that led to a grander staircase, fancy modern art and sculptures, the twin fire-red cars. Christ, that boat Barry just bought, sitting on the edge of the Hudson, losing money as we spoke. How much had been saved that didn't go up my father's nose? I wasn't stupid. I knew his vices. Both of theirs. She with her wardrobe. The woman was a hat factory. Even now, the dress she wore to dinner, extremely inappropriate, like she was going to the Kentucky Derby, all poofs and polka dots. His collection of Rolexes. Did anyone need more than one Rolex, let alone, *even* one? Steph's new car, summers at basketball camp for me, the lawyer we'd likely have to retain to keep Jenny out of the clink.

"How much do we have saved?" I asked Mom.

"Saved?" she questioned, like it was the first time she ever thought about it. Fuck, I realized it was. Barry earned the money, she spent it, and had no idea how much was in reserve.

"What about college?" Steph asked. "You know I have my eye on NYU."

"Like NYU is waiting with bated breath for you to apply," I said.

"Fuck you, Aaron," Steph yelled back.

"Fuck, fuck, fuck, fuckery, fuckayou," Jenny said, in the voice of a grizzled war veteran.

"Now you got her started," Mom said.

Even the plates we ate on, fine china, all of this might belong to our old lives.

"Sell the house," I said.

"What?" Mom asked, barely able to pay attention to all of us. She looked tired. The first time I think I'd ever seen her look tired.

"This house, we could get about a million for it, right?" I asked.

She nibbled at her fingernails. "I–I dunno."

"Is there anything you *do* know?"

I'd caught her off guard and she shrank in place, reevaluating her own worth.

"Jesus Christ, how much is mortgaged?" I asked.

"I…"

She left the table. Steph gave me a look signaling what an asshole I was. I found Mom in the kitchen having a cigarette by the window. She went to put it out when she saw me come in.

"It's okay, I know you smoke."

She inhaled a giant suck. "I feel foolish."

"Why?"

"Because at the age of eleven, you seem to have more knowledge about our financial affairs than me."

"I'm gifted."

"You're something all right."

"Look," I said, hopping up on the counter. "Like, I'm sure Dad has it all figured out."

"You should've heard how he sounded," she mumbled.

"What was that?"

"Nothing. I want to be able to protect you. You and your sisters."

"We're pretty resourceful. Throw Jenny into the woods and she'll come out alive. Toss Steph in the mall and she'll come out with the best discounts. And me, I just need a hoop and a ball."

"You all have been spoiled rotten. You won't be able to cope. We've made things too easy."

"Markets recover."

She reached over and patted me on the hand. "You're a good one when you want to be."

She put out the cigarette, and I made a mental note to take the unfinished nub for later. It had started to rain, and we watched the back lawn get drenched, a quick burst of a downpour. When it ended, she seemed relieved.

"I wish your father would come home."

"Why don't I make some pizza rolls? No one ate that roast."

"Okay, cub."

She pressed down her beautiful dress and left a kiss on the top of my head. This moment in this kitchen, likely one of our last. Mom may have been worrying about how us kids would handle a mega shift in finances, but she and Barry would have the hardest time adjusting.

The rain started up again, harder than before, pummeling against the window and leaking inside. Shutting the window only seemed to make it angrier.

5

Before he'd head back across the George Washington Bridge home, Barry would need a drink. More like six. After getting in his Maserati and hearing a Joplin song, he spied Henry and Julien exiting their building and managed to wrangle them for whiskeys at Fraunces Tavern, a nearby haunt that opened in 1719. The bar had weathered many generations of high times and catastrophes, which he hoped would put today's climactic events into perspective. An hour in and they were already four drinks deep and had snorted a few lines in the can.

Julien, with his thin cheeks that always seemed concave, and Henry, the Hardy to Julien's Laurel, were bound to cheer him up. Except the coke was wearing down and the other suits in the place had already vomited and left. The old bartender Sammy cleaning a glass with spit and a rag, telling him about the crash of 1929.

"Holy fuck, you were alive?" Barry asked, doing the math of how old Sammy could be.

Sammy gummed his lips. "A teen. Saw them spilling from windows like Olympic divers, although without the graceful landing."

"I just saw one too," Barry said, as it all came back. The guy's tie flapping in the wind, his mouth locked in a forever scream.

"No shit, you did?" Julien asked, picking at his nose.

"Uncanny," Barry continued. "And I even...well, I had climbed up on the window sill."

Sammy spat into another glass, half listening. Barry knew how bars did great business in times of boon and decline. Barry should've been a barman.

"Those windows don't open," Henry said, gorging on peanuts.

"I know. I mean, I had forgotten at the moment. Scares me to think what could've been if they had. It was my wife, she talked me down."

They toasted to their wives and signaled Sammy to pour another round.

"She's defrosting a roast for me right now."

Spit. "So why ain't ya home with her?" Sammy asked. "Why you drinking with these two knuckleheads?"

Barry took a moment to ponder this. He had every intention of running home to Judith and us kids, opening a bottle of wine, watching some *L.A. Law*, maybe shooting hoops with me in the front yard. But the Barry his family once knew, this grand persona who gave us everything we wanted, he wouldn't be walking through the door that night. And nothing made him sadder.

"Cause I'm fucked so hard my ass'll hurt for eternity." He turned away from Sammy. "Lemme ask you, fellas, and be honest, how much you have in savings?"

Julien's eyes rolled to the back of his head as he counted. "'Bout a hundred grand. Mostly for the kids' educations, college and whatnot. Andrea made me put aside a chunk of my paycheck since I started earning."

"Yeah, about the same for me too," Henry added, moving from a bowl of nasty peanuts to French fries that a waiter brought over. "You?"

"Put it all back into stocks," Barry said, cackling now, loud enough for glum faces along the bar to look over. What kind of whack job was laughing on a day like today? "Nothing's paid off either. I mean, nothing."

Henry and Julien made faces like they'd sucked on Sour Patch Kids. Their stools inching away, as if being so close to him, meant their own funds would deplete even worse. Only Sammy had enough of a heart to reply.

"Stocks," he said, blowing a raspberry. "An easy fix. Money made the worst way. And yeah, I'm happy all you Wall Street boys tip so well, but I've never put a cent in anything that wasn't a guarantee. Saw how it ripped apart everyone in the thirties. You don't know what it's like to not have food on the table. To wait in lines for bread. We did. I came back from the Navy to a horror I wouldn't wish on anyone."

"You think we're in for another Depression?" Julien asked.

Sammy shrugged, his whittled-down shoulders hanging up by his ears.

"Things happen in cycles. That's history. The gas crisis and the recession of the seventies, this could be another big earthquake. And don't get me started on Reaganomics. Man wasn't even a great actor. Yep, you boys may have seen America's peak in your youth, and it's all downhill from here."

"Well, my coke high is fucked," Henry said, gorging on a final French fry drenched in mayo.

"At least you have savings," Barry said, suddenly hating both Henry and Julien for their savviness. Even ol' Sammy the spendthrift. Like a gambler, Barry had been addicted, never knowing when to get off the pedal, believing the road to be never-ending.

He wandered into the bathroom, well, more like swam through a sea of whiskey waters to get there. Stared into the mirror at a thirty-eight-year-old disappointment. He wanted to return home with new ideas of how to regain their fortune, but beyond predicting market trends—and evidently, being barely good at that—he knew how to do squat.

Another man barreled inside. Designer suit. Tie tossed over his shoulder. A drunken nod. The man pissed a never-ending stream at the urinal, humming Bon Jovi's "Livin' on a Prayer." Barry needed a prayer. And then, like it was tempting him, the man's wallet popped out of his back pocket. Black leather against the piss-stained bathroom tiles.

Don't do it, an angel said, floating down. A righteous prick that only showed up to nag.

Take that money. Buy a final gift for your Gimmelman brood, the devil sang, emerging from a fiery pit below.

Barry picked up the wallet, opened it to find about two hundred dollars in cash. Pocketed it all.

"Jews don't believe in heaven or hell anyway," Barry said.

"Whatwasthat?" the man slurred.

"You dropped your wallet. It's on the sink."

Barry left it there and spun out of the bathroom before the man could ID him. He said goodbye to Julien and Henry with slaps on their backs, knowing their friendships weren't enough to survive if they wouldn't be coworkers anymore. He had no real friends. Just a family. A goddess who loved him and three wonderful children, well, two-and-a-half counting odd-duck Jenny. What could two hundred dollars buy that would make them all happy, at least to cushion the news?

An hour later, he had downed a few cups of coffee, speeding back to Jersey with a Cocker Spaniel puppy in the backseat he picked up at a shelter nearby, searching for Joplin on the radio but finding nothing on the oldies station but Johnny Cash's "The Devil to Pay."

He and the new puppy howling along.

The puppy stopped howling, only Barry singing at the incoming rain.

6

The repo men came swiftly. When the market didn't recover over the next few months, Barry maxed out the credit cards to pay the mortgage and once he defaulted on the payments, they swarmed our house taking everything that wasn't pinned down. Steph cried when they took her stereo and VCR. She managed to hide her Walkman with a few cassettes under a loose floorboard in her bedroom. Mom's clothes all went out on hangers as our cul de sac neighbors who we rarely saw came out in droves to observe our punishment. It took four repo dudes to carry all of Mom's hat boxes, stacked high in towers like spinning plates about to fall in some vaudeville act. Barry cringed once they got his Rolexes, too valued to stealthily hide under the floorboards. The walls barren with white-squared stains of where art used to be. Memories of furniture we had. Only the tire tracks remaining of the Maseratis. They even nabbed my basketball hoop.

The final blow, was when they came for our home, forced us to vacate. After Barry got axed, the bank took one look at our finances and refused any loans. We were given the money Barry had spent on the house, a measly five percent of its value, used to pay off the rest of the credit cards that thanked us by canceling Barry's account with about a thousand bucks remaining. I watched as he cut up his MasterCard, Amex, Visa, Carte Blanche, and Diners Club cards and tossed them in a tin garbage can, which he lit on fire. We had twenty-four hours now left to vacate the premises and all huddled around the flames because it was cold outside, and the creditors had turned off the fucking heat.

With the few clothes we were left with, we bundled up and roasted Hebrew National hot dogs over the fire.

"Bear-Bear, what are we gonna do?" Mom asked. She had grown fretful in the past few weeks, a shell of the woman I knew. Running her fingers through her hair searching for a phantom hat.

Barry gave her a look like, *don't breakdown in front of the children.*

She gave him a look back like, *you got us into this f'd up situation and I'll do what I please.*

"It's either your mother down in Florida or my brother and his family," he said.

All of us made a sour face at those propositions. Both parties, already notified of the situation, each of them grudgingly offering a place for us to stay. That being said, plane tickets for five and a puppy were too pricey now to consider.

"What about the RV?" Jenny asked.

It was like a ghost had spoken. We all whipped our heads in her direction, the flames licking her dirt-caked face. Jenny spoke so infrequently, usually responding with the grunts and swears of a cave girl.

"Right, the RV," Mom echoed.

Barry had purchased an RV for the lone road trip our family had taken to Yellowstone National Park. The year was 1984, "Born in the U.S.A." blasted from every speaker, and Barry was in his Americana phase. We had even hoisted a flag by our front door that was taken down after being ripped to shreds during a blizzard. Now the RV sat in the back woods because there wasn't enough room for it in the garage with the Maseratis. It hadn't even been on the repo men's list.

"We could drive the RV down to Nana in Florida?" Mom asked, as a question.

"Nana is the absolute worst," Steph said, biting into a hot dog. "She's mean and pinches us."

"That's just her way of showing love," Mom said.

"And she's *so* into Judaism," Steph added. "It's, like, we get it lady, you and God have a bond. We won't be able to use electricity on Saturdays."

"We don't have electricity now," Barry said, and we all nodded at that.

Johnny Cash ran inside barking his head off. Barry had named him, refusing any of our suggestions even though the puppy had been a gift for us. A way of softening the blow of that fatal Black Monday. But Johnny Cash wasn't so great. He howled at all hours, shat everywhere, and had a lazy eye. Jenny seemed to take to him, which wasn't surprising—unless she was contemplating a way to turn Johnny Cash into a cooked hot dog.

Steph yanked at her hair and let out a shrill cry. This had become common over the last few weeks and usually ignored, since it involved moaning about her stupid boyfriend Kent. Kent, with his parted hair and Lacoste shirts, his apple-scrubbed cheeks, and his Christian words of wisdom. The only reason Steph wanted anything to do with him was to piss off our parents by finding the biggest *goy* out there.

Sure enough, she went into a diatribe about how her and Kent's love knew no bounds.

"Great," I said. "Then we can leave, and you won't have to worry about breaking up."

She attacked me by strangling my neck, enough for Barry to get involved by pulling us apart. Jenny watched and licked her lips, thrilled beyond belief.

"Seriously, Aaron," Steph sniffled. "You want to go to Florida where everyone is a thousand years old and it's like totally humid? Ever heard of swamp ass?"

"I'm a realist. We can't afford our schools anymore and we've become pariahs here."

"Piranhas? I never know what the fuck you're saying."

I gave Mom and Barry a glance like, *What are we gonna do about these ridiculous children we have to deal with?*

"We are the talk of the cul de sac," I said. "They all watched with gaping mouths as our possessions got hauled out on a truck. Besides Jesus-y Kent, all your friends are calling you poor behind your back."

"I haven't heard that."

"That's what 'behind your back' means. Everyone feels sorry for us. Drake and Liam won't come over anymore because I don't have a basketball hoop, which shows me how good friends they were. Mom, your ladies-who-lunch crowd dropped you."

"Yes, they have," Mom said, into her hands over the flame.

"At least in Florida we can start over," Barry said, joining in as if we were gathering our troops. I liked this closeness with him, being in sync. The Gimmelman men holding down the fort. He worked so hard and kept such late hours in the city that we rarely had time together. I imagined an RV trip filled with Punch Buggy and I Spy games. A radio tuned to his favorite songs and us all singing along. Poor but rich in spirit.

"It's not like Florida has to be our destination," Barry continued, scooping up Mom's hands and kissing her fingertips. "We can lick our wounds there, get back on track. We could go anywhere. I can put out job feelers far and wide. And even if I'm not in stocks anymore per se, I could find something adjacent."

"Stephie?" Mom said, bringing her into the huddle. "I know you think you love Kent—"

"I don't *think*, I do."

"But," Mom said, singing the word, "you must learn that family is the most important thing. We need to stick together. We all have to be on board. And maybe we'll wind up back in New Jersey..."

We all gave each other a look like, *None of us wants to wind up back in New Jersey.* The state of big hair and fake-tanned skin, Guidos and Guidettes, and views of a better land. We had put in our time and were done.

I wasn't sure if Steph actually agreed, but she at least shut the fuck up so we could eat our hot dogs in peace. Even Johnny Cash was acting all cute and trying to catch his tail. And Jenny left the dog alone and was humming and munching, always weirdly content.

I hadn't seen Barry smile since the crash, hiding his pearly whites, but now they grinned wide, a beacon in the dark.

7

Kent gave Steph a lame serenade as we departed. Right before, we stuffed whatever we could in the RV. Quarters would be tight, with Barry and Mom having their own wing, the girls sharing a bunkbed in the back, and me sleeping on a pull-out couch in the living area that doubled as galley kitchen. And the lone bathroom whose door never shut properly. The Gimmelmans would be getting to know each other very well.

We piled in everything left we'd hidden from the creditors. Mostly a suitcase full of clothes for each of us along with a few possessions like cassette tapes, a basketball (not the one I had signed by the Knicks squad in '85, that went to the repo men) so I could at least practice my dribbling, and a taxidermy opossum named Seymour that Jenny used as a stuffed animal. Barry kept a suit, Mom a lone hat that was the kind one of the *Golden Girls* would wear sunning on the lanai, and we were off.

Well, not before we were treated to a rendition of "Jesus on My Mind" from resident God-boy Kent, who strummed in the snow while Steph wept with goo-goo eyes. The song was about finding Jesus when things seemed most grim, and all the Gimmelmans in the RV groaned at the chorus.

"Stephanie Naomi Gimmelman, I love you more than the holes in Jesus's hands," Kent said, when he finished strumming. They kissed. Not a sloppy French kiss like I'd do to my girl if I had one and we were parting forever. They kissed like old farts pecking at their fiftieth anniversary. Also, didn't Jesus have other holes, one in each hand, his feet, and somewhere else? Guy

28

made no sense. I'd keep that dig in my pocket for later.

Barry gave a solid honk of the horn. Enough was enough.

"I'll call you whenever I can," Steph said, getting on the RV.

"I'll make sure to never be away from my phone. I'll sleep with it curled like a baby lamb in my arms."

Dude was so creepy.

"Steph, get in the RV," Barry yelled, starting the motor as an indicator.

"Bye, my ray of light," Kent said, waving like a fool.

"Bye—" Steph began to say, but Barry had already put the RV in first gear and was driving away. Kent becoming a small dot in the snow, the last memory we'd have of the home we made for the past few years.

Steph turned into a ball of tears, using Mom's shoulder as a handkerchief, who was happy to soothe. Now that we had some type of purpose again, Mom continued trying to be a woman on a mission at all times to uplift our spirits. She brought as many packets of hot cocoa she could find in the back of cabinets, as if marshmallows could make up for being broke.

I grabbed Steph's Walkman to tune them all out. Luckily her Def Leppard CD had been left inside. I'd take "Pour Some Sugar on Me" to the twin cloying princesses Tiffany and Debbie Gibson any day.

The road rushed by as I imagined myself in spandex leather and teased hair, screeching to an arena filled with girls climbing over one another, all hot and sticky sweet, to be sung to by famous ol' me, the throngs of fans spilling so far back they seemed to encapsulate the entire world.

* * *

Halfway into New Jersey and we'd already spent two hundred bucks on gas, enough for the RV to earn its nickname. Gas-guzzling it certainly did, causing Mom to question if we even had enough dough to make it down to Florida, especially if we wanted to eat.

"We'll figure it out," Barry said.

Figuring it out so far meant our first lunch on the road would be from a gas station around Hazlet. Slim Jims for all, I'd never felt so white trash. Jenny loved them, unsurprisingly, to me they tasted like spicy lips and assholes. We also got to share a strawberry fruit pie like it should be a prize. Already I was souring to the trip and wondered if Mom was right that we would have a hard time adjusting to our burst upper-class bubbles.

Once free of Steph's blubbering—Mom had found a Xanax she gave Steph who went down hard, snoring like a kazoo—Mom found her stride. She undid the clips in her hair, let it roam wild and free, and found sixties music on the radio she and Barry sung like that drunken couple no one wants to talk to at a wedding. We were treated to CCR's "Who'll Stop the Rain," Van Morrison's "Brown Eyed Girl," to which Barry substituted "Brown Eyed Judith," thinking it hilarious because she had green eyes, and Buffalo Springfield's "For What It's Worth." Jenny was in Jenny Land scaring Johnny Cash with Seymour the taxidermy opossum, so I was forced to be up front with my parents, hearing tales of their youth that sounded like big, weird orgies.

"Forget about the key parties, those were fun, but there was that one time we all got that house together in the Catskills," Barry began, his eyes dancing to the past, "and your mother, this was before she got pregnant with Steph, she had bought these stamps from this guy on my dorm floor who dealt LSD..."

"I see where this is going," I said, trying to act like I couldn't care less but I loved being included in his youthful tales of debauchery.

Barry continued: "She was mailing Rosh Hashanah cards, her mother was big on that, so she licked all the stamps."

Mom put her face in her hands, removed it tomato red.

"I thought I was a glass of orange juice, and I was afraid of your father because I thought he was a straw that would sip me up!"

"Hilarious."

"Remember the dead babies?" Barry asked.

"What the fuck?" I asked.

"No, it wasn't a real dead baby, it's those dead baby jokes. Judith and I would try to offend each other by telling the worst dead baby jokes. Like, how many dead babies does it take to screw in a lightbulb?"

I shrugged.

"None! Because dead babies can't screw in lightbulbs."

My mother laughed louder than I'd ever heard her laugh before. Tears streamed from her eyes.

"This is nice," she said, running her hands through Barry's curls. "It's like we're taking a break from life. I'm gonna take off my bra."

"Oh Jesus," I said.

"Calm down, Aaron," she said. "You sucked from these nipples many times."

"That's not something I ever need to be reminded of."

"And what fine nipples they are for sucking," Barry added, kissing her palm in an indecent way.

"A child is present," I said.

"Nuh-uh, you're not a child anymore, Aaron. I see those mustache hairs."

"Really?"

"Don't think I haven't noticed. Also, that you helped sell the idea of this *trip*. To the girls."

"I was on board," Mom said.

"I know, sweetie. We have to get Steph feeling happy again. Jenny's a..." Barry looked at the mirror as Jenny tried to get Johnny Cash to kiss Seymour. The dog, wasn't having it. "Well, Jenny is Jenny, but Steph's at a tough crossroads in her life."

"I met your father when I was sixteen."

"Right, her life can go in many different directions. Just be nice to her is all I'm saying. Treat her with kid gloves."

The dashboard caught Barry's eye and he frowned.

"Fuck me three ways, we're out of gas again. C'mon."

Sure enough, the tank read almost empty. I could see him calculating the money we had left versus what we needed to make it to Florida, his brain not telling him what he wanted to hear.

"At least we're not being hounded by creditors, or bigshots whose money

I lost," he said. "Couldn't have gotten out of Dodge soon enough, right?"

"Ri–ight," Mom said, making me believe that there were more reasons for jetting as fast as we did other than being kicked out of the house. But no one would find us if we weren't using credit cards. Right? *Right?*

"You look constipated, son," Barry said. "Stop worrying so much."

I must've been doing that thing I did where my nose scrunches and, a dent forms between my eyes.

"Let me do the worrying. That's what dads are for."

But when he turned back to the road, his face was doing the same thing. Like father, like son.

I swore to myself that I'd figure out a way to take on some of the burden.

8

I made my first theft at a rest stop off the Garden State Parkway near Brick. That wasn't really true. I'd stolen baby things before: a pack of Score baseball cards, Pop Rocks, the occasional wine cooler. Not that I couldn't afford them, but for the thrill. How my heart thumped like mad when I'd leave a store with my stolen prizes. The Pop Rocks that burst in my mouth with even more flavor than they would've if I'd paid. Chalked it up to suburban blahs. The curse of Jersey. Nothing to do outside of the malls, and I hated the malls.

So, I knew I had quick hands and was good. Little unassuming me with my nice face. I could look as innocent as they come. The Gas-Guzzler having to make another refuel while I staked out the 7-Eleven. Told my family I wanted Gummi Bears and would be back. Barry slipping me a dollar, like he was afraid to part with the money. That was when I made a decision that we needed more to survive.

An old man was manning the cash register barely able to stay upright. He blinked his rheumy eyes when I walked in and the bell dinged. I decided to buy the Gummi Bears and then ask to use the bathroom before I'd figure out a way to distract him from the register.

Paying for the Gummi Bears, I sang the cartoon theme song over and over in my head to quiet my nerves.

Gummi Bears, bouncing here and there and everywhere.
High adventure that's beyond compare.

They are the Gummi Bears.

They are the Gummi Bears!

He rooted around for the change, handing me a dime and a quarter.

"Thank you, sir," I said, turning on my kid charm. "And do you have a bathroom?"

He handed me a key and pointed toward the back.

Inside the bathroom, I stared in the mirror psyching myself up. *Your family needs you. Get that money. Get that money, chump.* I turned the faucet on hard so the water would spill to the floor. Then I flexed a puny muscle and marched out.

"Excuse me," I said, to the old guy. "Would you be able to give me ten pennies for a dime?"

He cocked his head to one side, eyebrows sloping down.

"My little sister loves pennies, collects them."

He pushed the register button, the tray springing out.

"I was a coin collector too," he said, gumming his tongue like it was a foreign object. "Got some from the eighteen hundreds back home, they were my Grandpap's."

I widened my eyes. "Wow. Oh, I apologize but I think the toilet is overflowing."

"What?"

"I flushed and flushed, but water is spilling everywhere."

"Well, what—why didn't you say that first?"

"I was embarrassed because it was from my pee."

"Oh jeez." He closed the tray and exited the booth, locking it behind him before grabbing a mop and rushing to the bathroom. I knew there were cameras watching, but by the time they'd review the tapes, we'd be gone. In the glass partition was a hole big enough to exchange money and goods. I plunged my thin arm through and hit the no sale button to open the cash register. Grabbed two fistfuls full of dollars and ran out of there so fast you'd have thought my hair was on fire.

Stuffing the money into my hoodie, I jumped into the RV and told Barry to drive out of there, since I saw a weird man in the 7-Eleven and was afraid he might try to follow.

"What did he do to you?" Barry asked.

"He had no nose," I said. Once while in New York City on a class trip I passed by a man who had no nose, only a hollow space where it used to be. It gave me nightmares ever since.

"No nose?" Mom asked.

"Drive! Can we just drive?"

Barry shrugged and stepped on the gas. I looked out the back window wondering if I would see the old man come outside. But he was too withered and slow. He had probably only turned the faucet off by then and was mopping the spill, cursing at me, not even realizing yet what I'd taken. I sat on the bottom bunkbed shadowed in the darkness and counted. Tens and twenties flipping before me, about three hundred bucks in total.

Now I needed to figure out how to tell Barry what I'd done while making him realize this was a good thing.

* * *

My chance came at night, Steph and Jenny already sleeping in their bunkbeds, Mom crawling up top to the bed in the nook she and Barry shared that was basically above the driver and passenger's heads. I'd gotten in my pjs and curled into the shotgun seat. Watched the dark road before us, the headlights illuminating the yellow lines. Barely any traffic in sight. We must've been in Delaware.

"I want to make good time," Barry said, wiping the sweat from his upper lip. The heater had been on full blast. "The faster we get to Florida, the less we'll have to spend on food."

I laid the three hundred bucks on the dashboard between us. Not a word spoken as he took in the magnitude. Where could I have possibly gotten that kind of money? I had an allowance of ten bucks a week, but these tubular funds would've meant that I never spent anything. A suspicious eye glanced in my direction.

"Where did you get that?" he finally asked.

I cleared my throat. "Dad." This was when I still called him Dad. Soon enough, he would become Barry, only Barry. But back then, I'd never think to consider him anything but a father. "I know that money is tight."

He exhaled through his nose in two powerful spurts.

"You didn't bring that money with you?"

I shook my head back and forth. He raised his eyebrow.

"The last gas station?"

I nodded. The RV quiet with the girls all down and no music coming from the radio. The road, so empty like we didn't exist anywhere. Nothing permanent, which frightened and exhilarated me at the same time, us Gimmelmans as ghosts.

"How much is there?" he asked, wetting his lips as he reached over and pocketed the cash.

"Almost three hundred."

"Well."

"Are you mad?"

"Why did you feel you needed to do this?"

"I want to help."

"I don't need you to help."

My shoulders slumped forward, face going hot. "I'm sorry."

He tousled my hair. "Nothing to be sorry for. You're figuring out ways to get us out of a tough spot. Can't knock you for that."

"Are you gonna tell me stealing is wrong?"

The words simmered, prickled in the air. His hand moved from my hair to my shoulders, kneading the muscles like I was dough.

"What do you think, bud?"

I carefully thought of my response. "Haven't we been stolen from? They took all of our stuff."

He chuckled. "That they did. Hey, cheer up," he said, because I probably looked glum. "We'll keep this between us. And we're too far away from that gas station to turn back and give you a lesson. What's done is done. And the extra dough means I don't have to drive through the night."

"Oh, okay."

We passed a rest stop and Barry pulled off of the highway, parked the RV amongst a field of trees. We were the only ones resting there.

"Pretty shitty I put you guys in this situation," he said, as he was about to head up to the bed with Mom. We were whispering so as not to wake anyone. The lights turned off, only lit by a thin moon.

"I'm thinking of it as an adventure."

"Ha, yeah okay. Not quite like the adventures those *Miami Vice* guys go on that you like so much."

"No, but that doesn't make it any less of one."

"I'll get us back on track."

If the lights had been on fully, I would've seen him tearing up. I was glad they weren't. No one should witness their dad crying—turns him into a regular person. I heard him sniffle some, but imagined it was the heater puffing.

"I will," he declared, with one last tousle of my hair. Then he vanished up to bed.

I didn't sleep that night like I'd taken a drug. The adrenaline coursing through my veins, heart pumping to the Jan Hammer *Miami Vice* theme running through my head and the word "adventure" flowing from my mouth like a wonderful secret.

9

Barry and Mom tried whispering in their bunk, but I could hear everything they said. If you listened close enough, the Gas-Guzzler held no secrets. I'd never been a part of their private conversations before, since our house was so big. You could spend an entire day without running into one another. They existed to us at dinner, well Mom did, Barry only if he got home early. Occasionally we'd shoot hoops in the front yard, talk about my toilet grades, or if there were any girls I liked. How to maximize my b-ball potential despite my height. "They don't make us Gimmelmans big," he'd say. "But we're scrappy, and that goes a long way." As for my folks' pasts, they were revealed in snippets, memories of when they met at Woodstock, their courtship, all those remembrances polished with sheen, never the hard times, never what I heard that night.

As they snuggled in their cramped nook, a tiny window with a sheer curtain providing the only light, Mom questioned what he and I had been talking about.

"Promise not to be mad," Barry said. He was combing her hair with his fingers, something that used to help ease her stress.

"Why would I be mad?"

"Do you remember right after you had Steph, and my parents had passed—we had no money?"

She pecked him on the nose. "Yes, Bear-Bear. We were happy then—"

"Were we? I think you're seeing it rose-colored. We survived it, but we almost split up."

"We were—I don't know, twenty-one, twenty-two. I had given up being a roadie, and Steph was a colicy baby."

"So colicky."

"But you had graduated from Columbia, and with honors—"

"You don't need to boost my resume, it was cum laude, but not summa or magna."

"Pish."

"Anyway, your mother wanted us to come to Florida. She was gonna put us up in her guest room, and we entertained it. I was job hunting, but it looked slim. And Steph was going through diapers like—we were dealing with a lot of shit, to put it mildly."

"I know what you're gonna say."

I peered through the shadows to see their facial expressions. Mom was smiling, a big moony one that defied her age. As we get older, it becomes harder to be so happy, so free. Back then was the last time I knew I could smile so purely.

"What is it, love?"

"Those diapers, that corner store, the one up by Columbia. With that nasty man who owned the store and shouted racial slurs. And you went into the diaper jar one day and there was nothing, just a piece of lint. And I told you—"

"What did you tell me, baby?"

Mom sat up, bonked her head. She went to rub it but Barry was faster. He kissed it all better.

"I said for you to take a box of diapers when he wasn't looking, when he was being extra cruel."

"And I took two."

Mom laughed, a titter that tapered off. "It beat using cloth ones, or asking Ma for help."

"Like we're doing now."

Mom hugged her legs.

"I hate being beholden to her," she said. "You know she has been waiting for something like this to happen, so she can feel necessary. When I talked to her last, she asked if I was going to divorce you."

"Are you serious?"

"Calm down, Bar. I would never even entertain. It's me and you till our last breath. But she looks for cracks, like a spy. She'll do it when we're down there."

"You know I hate my brother more than you hate your mother."

"He's truly awful, and like her, he's been waiting for your fall. His sick competitiveness. He only strives to beat you."

"California is out of the question. My brother and his family—we would have to be so desperate, a last resort. So, listen..."

I heard him unraveling the bills I'd stolen.

"What's that?"

Mom was quieter now, my ears having to reach Superman-like powers to hear.

"Aaron took it."

"Took it from where?"

"Ssshh, don't let them hear us. That last gas station."

"*What?*"

"Judith, this could be our way out of this."

"Out of what? This is what..." She flipped through the bills. "Three hundred dollars? And, you told him it was okay?"

"I told him it didn't do anyone favors for me to get mad. We should be happy he shared this with us."

"I'm anything *but* happy right now."

"Judy—"

"I will get a job. Yes. That's the solution. We deal with my mother to avoid paying a rent, get jobs down there, take a year to earn some money and get us straight. Then we go wherever we want."

"A year? You'll be at each other's throats. You won't survive this. *She* won't survive it either. I have people who—"

"What, Barry?"

"I owe some money."

"I got the feeling you did."

"It's more like, I lost some money to people whose money you don't lose. Like ever. And they'll be patient, thank God, because they understand what's going on with the market. But they won't be patient forever."

She must've been crying because Barry told her not to cry.

"Should we be scared?"

"No. Absolutely not. It's not like the Mob or anything. Nothing so... It's simply investors, and investors understand that money fluctuates. But I need to get right with them before the Gimmelmans can get right . I tried to get some bank loans."

"When were you gonna tell me this?"

"I'm telling you now, Judy. So, what if we take a little, here and there?"

"How much do we need?"

"Nothing astronomical. We can pay, over time, I made sure of that. But we *will* need to pay."

Even darkened by the shadows, I could see how intently he was looking at her. Like she had no other choice but to go along with his scheme. The telepathic bond between them. This was not a time to refute. In sickness and in health, for richer or for poorer. The vows had been cast, and she nodded, shedding tears, trying to keep as quiet as possible. She tucked into his chest, searched for solace there, and he held her through the night, whispering that everything would be okay.

When the sun rose, Mom had fallen asleep still in his arms. He was sitting up, watching her as she lightly snored. Making sure she was worry-free, if only in her dreams. I kept myself up all night as well so I wouldn't miss anything said between them. I left my couch/bed before Steph or Jenny woke. Honestly, those two could sleep through a battalion marching by. I went to the fridge to pour a glass of OJ and caught his eye. He gave the slightest nod, as if our plan had worked, the first gaslighting of a Gimmelman. And I nodded back like we had a code between us, a shared understanding of what needed to be done.

The die was cast, neither imagining what horrors would come, but knowing our new lives as thieves were inevitable.

10

Barry showed Mom the gun only after they left us behind in the Gas-Guzzler at a rest stop in Smyrna, Delaware. We were given change for three candies of our choosing, something Jenny and I warmed to while Steph stayed indifferent and defiant. Still mourning her separation from Kent, she used the quarters to call him, disappearing for long enough to give us some time off from her sobs. But anyway, the gun. The spy I was becoming saw Barry pull it out of the glove compartment early in the morning while I was sipping OJ and listening to the snores of the rest of my family. He knew I saw him take it out, part of the bond we were creating. It always helped to have one family member firmly on his side. I'd been waiting for that kind of invitation for twelve years.

While not a Bren Ten like I'd later acquire, a Beretta Pico at 0.71 inches wide was the best option for concealed carry. The biggest question was how Mom would react. I could only imagine.

Barry didn't want to rob the convenience store at the rest stop. That would require doing it in front of us, revealing his hand. Too soon. With Steph, even though the elevator didn't rise all the way to the top, the tricky part would be her very un-Gimmelman like moral code. Protesting acid rain. Saving the manatees. Striving to give herself a purpose. She'd take longer to coax.

Barry and Mom were walking along the shoulder, cars rubbernecking as they passed by, wondering why two non-crackheads were without a car along a highway, when he whipped the gun out. A cute little Beretta to start us on this zigzag journey. She pretended to be offended.

"Oh, Barry. No. No."

She made him put it back in the elastic of his sweatpants, which caused them to droop. He'd taken to wearing sweatpants now after a lifetime stuck in a suit.

"Listen, it's only for scaring. We won't use it."

"I want to go back."

She began heading in the other direction. He shouted over cars zooming past. Hugged her from behind. She used to think there was no safer place than in his arms. She tried thinking about that now. How if she didn't trust him, she might as well walk away for good.

"Give me your bra."

"*What?*"

"Judith, we'll use it as a mask."

Mom, a pro at slipping her bra off without removing her shirt, a fact I hated that I knew. He ripped it in half and showed her what he meant. A padding over their mouth and nose, the strap holding it in place behind their heads.

"Until we get more sophisticated ones."

"This is a joke, right?" She said it in disbelief that their lives had devolved in such a cosmically weird fashion. "Our kids clueless while we—"

"Not Aaron."

"Last night, when you first broached this idea. I don't know, it was a full moon, and I was feeling witchy, deviant."

"You've always been witchy and deviant."

The morning sun had picked up the light in her eyes, those green jewels. Sometimes they changed color depending on what she wore. While Barry's crazy hair had been one of the first things Mom noticed, he'd been taken by her eyes, so green, reflected by the grass they rolled around in, when he telepathically told her they would marry one day. Later when they came down from their acid trip, he asked if he took her virginity and she laughed, not to be cruel, but because she had done it a few times by then, enough to know what she liked and that she very much liked him.

"I'm a mother, first and foremost."

"And a very good one. One of the best. We don't have the easiest children. Each one is a handful...in their own way."

"Okay, we rob this store. We get maybe five hundred bucks from their register. And, if we get caught we go to jail. Who takes care of our handfuls?"

"We won't get caught."

"How can you know that? Even if everything goes off as smoothly as possible, there are variables, Barry."

"I'll be fucking damned if I crawl to your mother licking my wounds. Begging for change like a commoner. It's embarrassing and I refuse."

"So why are we going to Florida?"

"We're not! We're going on an adventure, and this is where it starts."

"When you bought the twin Maseratis, I thought, *this is Barry's mid-life crisis, and I'm gonna support him through it.*"

"That was the old Barry's mid-life crisis. There's a new Barry in crisis now."

"Does he still clip his toenails in bed too?"

"I'll tell you why it will work. We are the most mild-mannered-looking squares on the planet. The kids, the RV, my hair, your fanny pack."

"You know a purse hurts my back."

"*No one* will suspect us."

"Barry, this is... a lot all at once."

"Baby, you gotta trust me. We try it once, here in nowhere, Delaware, and we talk our way out of it if it doesn't work. Look, there's no bullets, I left them back in the glove compartment."

He showed her proof. She believed him, mostly, a shred of her wondering if one bullet had been lodged in the chamber where she couldn't see. She fought back against this accusation, already hating herself for not trusting.

"I need you to trust me," he said, as if reading her mind. An audible gasp left her mouth.

"I think robbery is something I'll be really good at," he said.

This she didn't doubt, his unwavering belief in his abilities. How he promised he'd make a million before the age of thirty, and when he did, with little kids in tow, he took the entire family—Jenny included because Mom was pregnant—to the Four Seasons because Mom had mentioned one time that it was the epitome of class in New York City. How she saw a picture of it in a magazine as a little girl and never imagined she could be eating there. After they finished dinner, the bill was over five hundred dollars with bottles of wine. And she drank even though she was pregnant, because back then no one thought twice about negative effects, and even if she had, the Château Lafite Rothschild was worth it, according to new budding oenophile Barry.

"I think robbing is something I'd be good at too," she said, the taste of that wine hot like acid in the back of her throat.

* * *

A sad liquor store in a little strip mall off the highway, the L in the sign about to fall. Barry wanted a liquor store over a convenience store, since there should be more cash in the register. He wanted to scope it out first. See how many people went in and out. A parking lot that housed a few cars, a nail salon and a restaurant of indeterminate cuisine on each side of the store. A forest of trees to get lost in after they'd burst out with the money.

Scoping for a half hour from far enough away not to be seen, only one person had entered. The guy spent ten minutes there and came out with a paper bag full of liquor. It was still early enough in the morning that a rush wasn't about to come through.

"Let's go now."

Mom got yanked before she could even say no, taking double as many steps as Barry to keep up. Outside of the store, he tucked her hair behind her ears and placed the left side of the bra over her mouth, cinched it behind her head.

"Is it comfortable?"

Her heart beat fast and she wondered when was the last time it beat like that. Maybe when Jenny was born? She found herself remembering that in Dutch there was no word for excitement: sad, but also, relatable. When you had everything, you lost the importance of goals. The allure of the Four Seasons had worn off long ago.

"Very," she said, even though it was a weird thing to say.

He put the right side of the bra over his face, snapped it in place.

"Let me do everything, you watch the door."

"For what?"

"Anything, variables."

"Okay."

She was shaking like she got caught in a downpour.

"Don't be nervous."

"I'm..."

He kissed her, bra padding to bra padding.

And then he took her hand and pulled her inside. The bell dinged. The clerk looked up, older man, former hippie with wild gray hair like a lion, a mustache and a beard, leather jacket. His eyes perked up and he went to reach for something.

"Hands, lemme see those hands."

She didn't even recognize Barry's voice, he gave it more of a deep bass rather than the squeaky high pitch that always sounded like he was going through puberty. This Barry held authority and she could've orgasmed right there, turned into a puddle of goo.

The clerk raised his hands.

"Cash, empty the register," Barry ordered.

She swiveled around, making sure there was no one in the store. Only rows and rows of empty aisles. No one in the parking lot either. She could breathe. One deep breath at a time. In and then out. She could do that. Because she was getting lightheaded. She couldn't let that happen.

Barry was yelling at the clerk, ordering him to move faster. The money didn't seem like a lot.

"Safe, go into the safe!"

46

Barry moved closer to the clerk, the gun pressed between the clerk's eyes. The man squeezed them shut, his face beet red.

"I have to turn around," the clerk replied.

"Then you're gonna do it nice and slow, easy does it, old-timer."

"Okay, okay." Spit flew out the clerk's mouth, trapped in his beard, and Mom found herself embarrassed for the man. She wondered if he had pissed his pants too.

"I gotta bend down to get to the safe," the clerk said, blubbering.

"Then do it, quickly. I have the gun on you."

She looked out in the parking lot, a car pulling in, her heart dangling.

"Bear," she said, being smart, not saying his real name. "Car."

"What are they doing?" Barry asked her.

"They're parking."

"And?"

"Getting out, it's a lady. She's..."

Mom said a prayer to God so the lady would walk into the nail salon or the restaurant. She thought of herself as a little girl in Hebrew school learning about Hashem, who delivered the Israelites from slavery in Egypt and gave them the Law of Moses at biblical Mount Sinai. Would He even listen to her selfish, and frankly, law-breaking pleas?

But the lady fixed her purse against her hip and went in the direction of the nail salon. Mom said a prayer of thank you to Hashem for listening.

"She's in the salon next door, baby," she told Barry, grinning through the bra padding.

"Faster," Barry said, leaning over the counter to poke the clerk in the back.

"I'm trying, I was off one digit with the lock—"

"You think I give a fuck. Go, go!"

The clerk finally opened the safe. Over Barry's shoulder, Mom could see stacks of cash, the liquor store probably only emptying the safe at the end of every week to transfer to the bank. With trembling hands, the clerk handed over the cash to Barry in a plastic bag that said, *Thank You for Shopping.*

"Now get in the back room."

The clerk waddled out of the counter area. Sure enough, he had wet his pants like Mom suspected, a pee trail snaking all the way down his leg. Somehow that thrilled her more than anything. Barry poked him with the gun toward the back room, then shut the door and propped it closed with a folding chair.

"How will he get out?" Mom asked.

"Someone will come in eventually, he'll be fine. A story to tell his friends."

"Okay," she said, tasting her breath in the bra padding, thick and toothpaste-like since she hadn't had any breakfast. Then Barry took her hand and whisked her outside. Nothing in the parking lot except for that one lady's car. They ran into the forest, removed the bra padding from their faces, and made dirty love against a tree like they did over twenty years ago at Woodstock when they first explored each other's bodies. She tilted her head to the sky while he lifted her up and she wrapped her legs around him: the overcast clouds, a formation of birds in a V pattern, calling to one another. It was cold out but she didn't feel cold at all, her blood hot, this new Barry inside of her, a duplicate she slightly feared but enthralled her in a way that no one else could, even the old Barry, her mensch, her husband, who now, bare-assed to the world with his sweatpants around his ankles, and his gun caressing her cheek, made her chirp in sync with those bird's calls who headed south for the winter like they always did. Like the Gimmelmans had planned, but she knew wouldn't be enough of a destination now. Nothing reaching the heights of pleasure she just experienced until the next liquor store would reveal itself along the roadside in all its enticing glory.

"Bear-Bear," she moaned to the sky, her eyes rolling to the back of her head as the birds became long gone, only phantom images remaining of their flight.

11

Mom and Barry's rendezvous had been the first time they left us kids alone since we began our trek. We'd gotten good at avoiding one another in the Gas-Guzzler. Jenny barely spoke so she was easy to ignore, and Steph was still pissed at all of us, so she kept her headphones clamped over her ears humming Heart's "Alone," Whitney Houston's "I Wanna Dance with Somebody," "Only in My Dreams," by Debbie Gibson, and "(I've Had) The Time of My Life" from *Dirty Dancing*. It was a mix tape Kent had made her before we left that she clutched to like a lifeline.

Once we entered the rest stop, she made a beeline for the pay phone. Jenny went for the candy aisles, but I was more interested in eavesdropping on Steph. I grabbed my basketball and pretended like I was practicing my dribbling skills. The rest stop was pretty empty, so I used my superhuman hearing to listen to God-boy's side of the conversation too.

"Stephie, is that you?" he asked, the tears apparent from the treble in his voice.

"Kent, I can't stand it without you here."

Jesus, it was only a day and a half. What was wrong with these two nutbars?

"I hate my family, all of them," Steph boohooed. "My mom and dad are so selfish to do this to us. Like, how did my dad not prepare for a bad stock market, or whatever is happening? And my mother, she sticks beside him no matter what, it's gross. And with Grandma Bernice, her whole house smells like soup and she has a ton of old cats that just lick themselves all

49

day. *And* she's Orthodox."

"Stephie, God places challenges in front of us so He can see how we deal. He never gives us tests we can't overcome."

She spun a blonde curl of hair around her finger, and let it bounce.

"My perm is falling apart."

"If I could, Stephie, I would collect all your tears and feed them to you, so you'd never be thirsty again."

"Aww, you're so poetic, Kentie."

Steph saw me staring and gave me a death glare back. She spun around so the phone was cradled into her chest. Talking softer, I couldn't understand what they were saying.

"Mallomars," Jenny said, appearing like an apparition and giving me gooseflesh.

"Holy shit, Jenny, don't sneak up on people like that."

Jenny shoved a Mallomar in her mouth, her lips crusted with chocolate.

"Sorry."

She had dirt all over her face like she was raised in the woods.

"C'mon," I said, tucking the basketball under my arm and yanking her back to the RV. Inside, I picked her up and sat her on the kitchen counter, wet a towel, and began to scrub her face.

"I like the smell of dirt," she said.

"Yeah, I'm not surprised you would. But it's not good to be dirty, there's germs in dirt."

"Actually, dirt is really clean."

"Just try not to be so weird all the time."

I finished cleaning her face, and she looked cute again. Her hair was a goddamn mess, but she had these little kid freckles she was embarrassed about all over her cheeks and a button nose. I found a rubber band in a drawer and tied back her hair, so it wasn't in her eyes.

"There, now you can see."

"Who said I wanna see?"

The door swung open, and Steph moped inside. She frowned at us and lay on my couch/bed that had reverted back to a couch for the day.

"You guys, love is *so* complicated," she said, flinging her arms in the air.

"Steph, no one gives a fuck about your boyfriend," Jenny snapped, jumping off the table and punching Steph in the arm.

"Oww, Jenny." Steph glared at me. "She's strong."

"I would put money on her in a fight between the two of you," I said.

"God, where are Mom and Dad?" Steph moaned. "It feels like we've been at this rest stop for an eternity. They could've at least dropped us off at a mall."

"But you have no money to spend," Jenny said.

"Jenny, I don't even recognize you with a clean face."

"I don't recognize you without a giant log up your ass!"

"Ladies, ladies," I said, as they were about to go to blows. "I think we need to set parameters."

Steph scrunched her face in confusion, so I clarified, "We need to have rules. Steph, none of us can hear about Kent anymore."

"But..."

"All right, once a day you get to cry and be a pain in the butt. And Jenny, it's a tight space, so you got to bathe."

"Fuck bathing."

"And that mouth of yours. The art of using a word like 'fuck' is to place it at the right time. Sparingly. It can't be your entire vocabulary."

"If we're making promises, Aaron, you can't walk around like you're the king of shit," Steph said.

"What does that even mean?"

"Like you're better than all of us with your two-dollar words and the fact that you *think* you're Mom and Dad's favorite."

"I don't think, I am. Like, Jenny's not even in contention, and you... Mom and Dad are intellectuals, and I'm the only Gimmelman they've got in that department."

The RV door slammed open, and Mom and Barry stumbled inside, entwined. Giggling like they had a secret between them. Drunk on each other. I wondered if Barry had convinced her of our new thieving ways. His eyebrows slanted in a lecherous way, leaving me to believe that he had. Mom was carrying a big plastic bag stuffed with something. She unraveled from Barry and disappeared into her nook. When she returned, she didn't have the plastic bag.

"Could you both have taken any longer?" Steph whined. "I've been in Delaware long enough for this lifetime."

Mom fell into Barry's arms, and he rubbed her tush while kissing her neck.

"Gross, stop it," Steph said.

"Your father and I are very connected right now."

"Are you on something?" Steph asked.

Mom took Steph's face in her hands. "Sweet Steph. We're on the path to happiness. I hope, truly hope, you'll sojourn on that path too one day."

"You smell like pot."

Mom's eyes were a guilty red.

"Not around the babies," she whispered.

"Judith, if you got some, pony up," said Steph.

"Family," Barry said, attempting to gather us together. He spread his arms and we inched closer. They really did smell like they'd gone swimming in a pool of marijuana. "Yes, your mother and I partook in the wacky tobaccy, street name *reefer*. Since we're in cramped quarters, there's no reason to hide it from you all. But we are grownups making a decision to inhale, not for kiddos."

Jenny gave a piquant belch filled with candy scents.

"We all have our vices," Mom said, squeezing Jenny tight. "And we were celebrating."

"Celebrating what?" Steph asked, but I knew. The plastic bag in their nook, holding evidence of how much they were celebrating.

Mom gave moony eyes to Barry, wanting to share her delight with their brood, but he shook his head. We weren't ready yet. I'd have to find the time to be alone with him so I could pry.

"Celebrating our freedom," Mom said, and then nodding as if she'd convinced herself. "Were we really free before? Your father was a slave to his job, I was a slave to ennui—Steph, that means being listless."

Steph scrunched her face for the second time.

"That means your mother had no purpose," Barry said. "Living in the shadow of her hats, and myself. You three gave her purpose, but is that enough? Beyond the idea of being your mother, what had she produced?"

"I never had a job, never earned my keep," Mom added.

"That's all gonna change." Barry showed us his bright teeth. I'd learn that this was a defense mechanism. A game-show host's grin. A soul lacking underneath. It said to the world, *Trust Me*. And the world usually agreed, and followed. We sure did. Like lemmings. Like he was a prophet.

"I have a theory," he began, still engulfing us in a hug. "Once someone is able to acquire a good deal of money in life, even if they lose it, they possess an uncanny ability to acquire it again, even more. We have the power to tap into that oil well, and despite one pipeline drying up, the Earth will bleed slick black for us, amiright?"

"Are we still going to Florida?" Steph asked.

"Not right away," Barry said. "We can take our time. A vacation, of sorts. Get to know one another."

His eyes found mine, nudging me for support.

"Yeah, when was the last time we were on vacation?" I said. "Yellowstone?"

"Lucerne last summer," Mom said.

"But we had separate hotel rooms," I replied. "And you guys did your own thing. We did too. I don't even remember Jenny on that trip."

Barry winked. "Exactly, I want to know my kiddos, beyond the surface. Jenny, when was the last time we had a real heart to heart?"

Jenny burped again, this time bringing up the Slim Jim binge from yesterday.

"And Stephie..." He patted her shoulder. "I want to be your rock. You can cry all your sorrows right here about Brent."

"Kent."

"Who?"

"My boyfriend," she screeched. "Kent."

"Precisely, I didn't even know the lad's name."

He unraveled his arms from around us all and put his hand in the center of the circle.

"Can I get a...Whoa Gimmelmans?"

We all stared back blankly.

"C'mon, Whoaaaaaa Gimmelmans."

Mom gave a smirk and put her hand over Barry's, I placed mine over hers, Steph rolled her eyes but eventually did the same, while Jenny stood on tiptoes to place her little grubby hand on the top. Even Johnny Cash scurried over—we'd been making him sleep outside of the RV, so as not to keep us up at night—and jumped up on hind legs to join.

"Whoaaaaaaaa Gimmelmans," we all sang, some more half-hearted than others, but all of us contributing, Johnny Cash as well with his howls.

"Steph, gimme one of your mixtapes and I'll play it," Barry said.

"Really?"

She took her Walkman out of her jacket pocket and popped out the cassette tape.

Of course, of all songs, "I Want Your Sex" by George Michael came on. I had to give God-boy more credit than I initially thought for his not-so-subliminal masterplan. Mom looked like she wanted to turn it off, but Jenny started dancing with Johnny Cash, Barry was doing his Batman-eyes thing, and I was tapping my foot, so she let it slide. Steph was also laughing like a hyena, which none of us had heard since we revved up the Gas-Guzzler in New Jersey, so we turned up the beat and gave Smyrna, Delaware a rightful show.

"My wonderful brood," Barry said, clapping to the beat. "I love you all so."

12

We didn't make much headway that day, Barry and Mom being high and all. Once we hit D.C. by taking some less traveled roads, they wanted to go sightseeing. We left Johnny Cash behind and did a full tourist's spin: the White House, Lincoln Memorial, and Washington Monument. It was like we were toying with the government after our separate robberies, dangling our crimes in Uncle Sam's face. I didn't mind the detour. We'd given up on Florida for the time being and none of us had ever been to D.C. before.

There'd be too much fuzz around, so we wisely took a break from thieving. Best to keep to little convenience stores tucked away off highways. It was nice to see my folks enjoying themselves. The last few months had been fraught with stress, for all of us. They were able to relax, crack jokes, be the best versions of Barry and Judith (the pot likely helping). The Barry we knew back in New Jersey usually sweating, worrying about the market, always with one eye on the stock ticker. The Gimmelman kids coming second to his first love, money. I probably took it hardest, Steph busy with Kent, Jenny occupied with roadkill. But today, he threw his arm around me, and we took goofy pictures all over D.C.: him giving me a noogie in front of a statue of Abe, both of us throwing up bunny ears behind Steph as she posed along the National Mall. By the time we got back to the RV and let Johnny Cash out to pee, I was wiped.

Steph and Jenny had the luxury of a curtain separating their sleeping area. I was forced to hear Barry and Mom's continued celebrations. I wondered how they could be so wide awake. It didn't smell like they'd taken any more hits of grass. They made loud love, and I stuffed my ears with pillow covers to drown out their moans. But it never seemed to end. The whole RV rocking. I couldn't sleep. I figured I'd take a looksee at the gun.

I didn't even have to tiptoe to the glove compartment. They never would've heard anything over their own blanketed thrusts. I once saw my gym teacher Mr. Flanders and the art teacher Ms. Jacee getting it on in the locker room. I'd forgotten my striped tube socks and went back for them, since it was a Friday, and I wouldn't have them for the weekend. They had no clue I was there. He bent her over his table, slapping her butt and pushing into her from behind. She kept saying "Oooo, oooo, oooo," over and over, twisting her face like she was having a stroke. Mr. Flanders looked like someone squirted Lysol in his eyes. Ms. Jacee was wearing a muumuu that he draped over her head, both of their underwear hugging their ankles. He squeezed her little titties too. The whole shebang was over in about three minutes after a groan from him. She shimmied up her panties and kissed him on the cheek. As she was leaving, I hid behind an open locker while Mr. Flanders whistled "Give Me the Beat Boys" by Bob Seger.

Mom and Barry were different in their lovemaking. While I didn't want to pry, I couldn't help but to watch. Thankfully they were under the covers to spare me from too much damage later on and resembled some weird organism not of this world that morphed into various shapes and sizes. When I saw a foot kick out of the covers, the toenails painted dark red, I ran to the glove compartment.

Not sure of what I'd do with the gun, I figured I'd wing it once I had it in my hand. Should I shoot and stir them from their never-ending sex session? My answer came swiftly when I found no gun in the glove compartment. Wise of Barry to keep it close to him away from us kids.

What I did find was a lot better. A small vile that held white powder. I'd seen enough *say no to drugs, I'm not a chicken you're a turkey,* commercials to know what it was. When Barry used to sport a mustache, he'd return home from work with a white dusting around his nostrils. Also, I could quote every *Miami Vice* episode verbatim and usually cocaine seizing kept

Sonny and Crockett active. But what to do with it? I unscrewed the cap. Took a sniff. A drop shot up my nose like a million tiny firecrackers. Rad. Me likey already. I had a thousand thoughts I wanted to express at once, but no one was available to hear them. My heart felt like a hockey puck ready to shoot out of my chest and start its own life solo on the road. I wished it well. Deciding I hadn't had enough, I took another snort, this one more in depth, the coke like liquid in my nasal cavity, hot and viscous. The RV walls closing in, my parents' wails reaching a full tilt, the universe overwhelming. I burst outside, waking up Johnny Cash who lunged at me only to be snapped back by his leash. I wanted the stars. I ran from civilization, till the RV was barely a speck. Surrounded by trees, I lay in the cold dirt shivering. It wasn't as freezing as in New Jersey, but still cold. I didn't care. I was chasing revelations. I found them in the twinkling lights overhead. I would tell Steph and Jenny about my successful robbery. We would prove that we could have as much to contribute to our burgeoning spree as Barry and Mom. They wouldn't have to keep their bounty a secret anymore.

When I got back to the RV, Johnny Cash was howling. Barry stepped out in Mom's pink and frilly bathrobe with a newspaper in hand to whap him on the nose.

"Aaron," he said, peering into the darkness. "What are you doing outside?"

"Couldn't sleep." I was talking faster than I could think. "I don't know... Big deal? Uh, uh... What's it to you?"

He led me by the back of the head. "I think I know what this is about. You have no privacy."

"No. Yes. Yes, that's true. You and Mom have your nook. Steph and Jenny have their sleeping area."

"What if I constructed you one?"

"I wanna help you rob too."

He put a finger to his lips.

"You wanna tell the whole Earth?" He poked his tongue into his cheek. "I'm formulating plans right now, bud. Our next steps. A kid could be useful, but a kid has to be used in the right way."

"No one would suspect me."

I didn't know why, but I was crying. Maybe it was the coke. This being exactly what they meant by *coming down hard.*

"Hey, hey there."

He tucked me into his armpit, the smell of sex still oozing from his pores.

"I'm not saying no, bud. I'm saying let's just wait. Your mother, she was a find yesterday, held her own. Lemme use that angle for the time being, keep you kids, clean."

"You never would've done it if I hadn't first."

He nodded. "Possibly. Can't lie, though. It's something I pondered before. I'm enjoying not being chained to a desk, the stresses of a boss hanging over you, insane demands. I never wish that for you. I've thought about money in the wrong way for too long. As something I needed to earn. They say it doesn't grow on trees, but that's a lie—it's only that those trees might not belong to you in the literal sense. But who's to say what belongs to any of us. Stocks are the same. The idea of money rather than the tangible. It never really existed. Cold, hard cash, though, I can feel that. Truly makes my dick hard."

I cocked my head to the side.

"Sorry 'bout that, just an expression. Didn't mean to burn your sensitive ears. So, the tears are dried up?"

"Yeah."

"Good. And we'll continue this discussion. For now, your job is to keep your sisters naïve to our new business. Let them roll with this idea of a vacation. Okay?"

He tousled my hair and went inside before I could answer. I sat down with Johnny Cash and let him lick my wounds, his breath like an asshole, but I didn't care. I was still sniffling even though I'd told Barry I wasn't, and the dog's licks were at least making me feel a little less shitty.

When I eventually went back inside, everyone was sleeping, everyone except wide-awake, coked-out-of-his-mind me.

13

It was nearly sun-up when the coke wore off enough to get some sleep. Horrible, nightmarish dreams. The Gas-Guzzler, chased by an evil presence, a force intent on taking us Gimmelmans down. Two headlights in the midst of a dark expanse. The faster we'd rev, the closer those lights became, blinding us so we couldn't see anything but its pursuit, hot on our tail, sparks flying as it scraped our rear, as we screamed until our throats bled, as it drove us off the road.

I woke clutching my heart that burned, mouth gummy and dry, and an alien drip down my throat. A sheet had been erected around the couch/bed like a cocoon. Barry must've put it up the night before, nailing it to the ceiling. I looked out the window. We weren't moving. Stopped again at another rest stop, this one alive with massive tractor trailers and truckers milling about.

Pulling the sheet to the side, I was greeted by Jenny combing Seymour's fur with her fingernails. Mom had gotten her a taxidermy friend so she would leave the real animals alone. While not a complete success, Seymour did keep her busy. Sometimes, I'd hear her telling it stories in her old room, long, intricate tales about fantasy worlds with vague similarities to our own. Even now, she was whispering in its furry ear and stopped once she saw me.

"Coffee," I said, like a divorced, middle-aged manager who had to get to work early for a meeting.

Jenny reached over and turned on the coffee maker that still had about a cup's worth left in reserve.

"Where is everyone?" I asked.

"Mom and Dad left. Don't know where. Steph is in the lot trying to get change to call her dumb boyfriend."

"They didn't leave us any cash?"

"They were gone when I woke up."

"Jesus, what are we supposed to eat?"

"They left us breakfast."

A giant box of Dunkin' Donut holes sat open on the counter.

"Works for me."

I mashed a few glazed chocolate holes in my mouth. Put on some pants and a coat to go find Steph. I caught her over by a phone booth showing a fat trucker her tit, the skin snow-white, the nipple apple-red. The fat trucker, *huh, huh, huh-ing.*

"What the fuck's going on here?" I asked.

The trucker spun around, eyes agog. Head like a watermelon, stammering.

"She's sixteen," I said.

Steph covered herself with her jean jacket that had a pin of Tiffany over the once naked boob.

"And who are you?" the trucker asked.

"Her brother. And our father's a police officer."

"Oh shit."

The trucker scurried away, waddling because of his boner.

"You could've at least let him give me some change!" Steph shouted.

"You were flashing him for spare change?"

"No doy."

She slapped a cigarette out from a pack and lit it, blowing the smoke in my face.

"I turned over the whole RV looking for change and nothing. Mom and Dad are gone, and I promised I'd call Kent."

"Where are we?"

She shrugged. "Nowhere. Just like where our lives are all headed...*nowhere.*"

It surprised me to realize Steph would do something like this. Yeah, she smoked cigs and occasionally drank and smoked pot, but other than that, she was pretty chaste. I was fairly sure she'd gone all the way with some guy before Kent—there had certainly been enough suitors on our doorstep—but definitely not with Kent. And she usually had such a morally superior attitude over our family.

"Stop judging me, it's just a breast. I wasn't gonna let him touch it or anything."

My nose itched. I'd forgotten I'd done rails of coke last night.

"What's wrong with your nose, Aaron?"

"Nothing."

"Whatever. Are you gonna stand there watching me smoke?"

"I have a proposition for you. A guaranteed way for you to get cash."

"Nothing's guaranteed."

"Okay, not a guarantee, but a really good shot. I stole three hundred dollars from a convenience store a few rest stops ago."

"Bullshit."

"*Au contraire, mon frère.* Gave it to Dad. And what do you think he and Mom are doing right now?"

"I don't give a fuck."

"Thieving as well."

I let my words sink in. She kept sucking the cig.

"Thieving what?"

"Our little detour to D.C., where do you think they got the money for that? They robbed a liquor store. There's a plastic bag filled with boatloads of cash. Last I saw it was in their nook, but I'm sure they've got a real hiding place for it now."

She cackled. "Mom and Dad? Robbers?"

"Uh yeah because I did it first."

"You must think I'm so gullible."

"I think you're a moron, but I'm not kidding. Why don't we try to find it?"

She flicked her cig at a car. "I'll play along because I'm bored."

Back in the RV, we ignored Jenny and tore the place apart. Every cabinet opened, every drawer overturned. Under the mattresses, the glove compartment, every nook and cranny, but *nada*.

"They have a gun too," I said.

This got Jenny's attention. Oblivious to the tornado we created while in her own universe with Seymour, this perked up her ears. She danced over, practically drooling.

"Who has a gun?"

Steph and I looked at each other knowing what this little monster would do if she had bullets in her possession.

"No one, Jenny," Steph said. "Go back to playing pretend."

"I heard everything you said. You think I don't listen, but I always am. Mom and Dad robbed a store with a gun and you're trying to take that cash."

"I just want to prove to Steph that it exists," I said.

She tossed Seymour aside. "I want in."

We heard Johnny Cash barking from being tied up outside.

"We've checked everything inside the RV," I said, "but what about...?"

A few seconds later, we made Jenny go flat on her stomach under the Gas-Guzzler where she found a plastic bag taped to the bottom filled with about two thousand dollars.

"Holy cannoli!" Steph said, rubbing the bills all over herself once we dumped it out on the table inside. "You were right, Ar."

"Told you."

"I'm gonna buy so much candy," Jenny sang, grabbing fistfuls.

"Hold on. Before we go buck wild, this is what I'm proposing."

Both girls crossed their arms in a pout.

"We want in on Mom and Dad's game. Here's why. Dad shat the bed with the stock market. We lost everything. We need nest eggs of our own, in case things go south again. Steph, I have to say I'm baffled that you're not morally objecting to this."

"My morals went out the window along with my Aiwa boom box that the repo men took."

"Candy!" Jenny said, gritting her teeth.

"Jesus, Jenny, bring it down twelve notches. So, here's what I propose. We, as in the three Gimmelman kids, do our own bit of robbing to prove to them that we can be a part of their operation. Jenny, I already stole three hundred smackers that I gave to Dad the other day, but I think I can do even better with two partners."

"Okay, we're listening," Steph said.

"Steph, as much as I hate to admit it, you're the looks in the operation. Bat your eyes, show your tatas, whatever it takes. You were gonna do it for quarters, let's up it to get some real cold hard cashola."

"And me?" Jenny asked.

"We all know you're crazy. And crazy can come in handy. Cute freckles on the outside and a bomb that could explode, at any time, on the inside . You both are the distraction and I'll do the stealing."

"Right here?" Steph asked.

"Why not? If we need to, Steph, you'll drive away, and we'll figure out how to find Mom and Dad later. What's the situation at this rest stop?"

"Convenience store, a magazine shop, some kiosk selling garbage."

"We scope out all three and make a decision on the best one to hit."

"Yeah." Jenny nodded. "Let's do this."

"Can I get a Whoa Gimmelmans?" I asked.

"You can get a Whoa Gimmelmans once we have cash in hand," Steph said.

She pocketed a few bills and swiveled out of the Gas-Guzzler for us to follow.

* * *

The kiosk sold tchotchkes, manned by a dorky teenager with a butt chin. Steph could work him, but honestly, how much would that stupid kiosk really give us, a hundred bucks max? Same with the magazine store run by an old woman. Jenny could distract her with cuteness, but how many truckers bought the kind of magazines sold there?

Convenience store, all the way, baby.

The guy manning the register wore a Redskins cap and had a long mustache and a mullet. A few truckers wandered the aisles stocking up on Corn Nuts and tall sodas. The three of us pretended to get slushees by the fake Slurpee machine.

"So, what's the plan?" Steph asked.

"We need to get that guy away from the cash register," I said.

"I can fake an emergency," Jenny said. She removed a nail file from her pocket and slashed it across her inner arm. "There, I'm bleeding."

"Jenny, what the hell?" Steph shout-whispered.

"No, this is good. Jenny, stay right here and yell bloody murder. Make the clerk come to you."

I grabbed Steph and whisked her toward the front counter. From behind us, we heard an eruption of tears, a wailing so loud my eardrums felt assaulted.

"I'M BLEEEEEEEEEEDING! HELP!"

The few truckers craned their necks over to Jenny, who had tucked herself into a ball and spread the blood all over the floor. One of them made their way over to her and the other followed.

"Hey, the little girl's hurt."

I swiveled around and saw two burly truckers hovering over Jenny.

"What happened? How did you hurt yourself?" they asked, in tandem.

"I DUNNO."

The clerk was standing on his tiptoes so he could peer past the aisles to see what was going on.

"Band-Aids, do you have Band-Aids?" I asked him.

The dim bulb registered what I said and connected it to the chaos erupting in his store.

"We got a first aid kit," he said, his Adam's apple bobbing like crazy.

"Well, use it," Steph said. "Where is it?"

He blinked once to absorb the question, then another time to try to remember.

"Back office," he mumbled.

"The first aid kit's not gonna get itself," Steph said.

He eyed the cash register, telling us he couldn't leave his position.

"She could be dying," Steph yelled, pounding on the counter. "I'll help you." She reached out her hand like a temptress, bewitching him. Like putty, he exited from behind his station, gave her his hand.

With Steph in control, they picked up their pace. I waited until they disappeared into the back office, hoping Steph would use her wiles to stall for time. With the truckers busy with Jenny, I hopped over the counter, adrenaline pumping like I'd swallowed a rocket ship and was raring to take off. The cash register had a zillion buttons in different colors, so I started pushing them all until the tray *zinged* with a small fortune. I grabbed all the bills, stuffed them in my waistline, and slammed it shut. Hopping back over the counter, I landed as Steph and the dim clerk ran outside from the back room. The clerk seemed on a mission, not even paying attention to me. I caught Steph's gaze, gave a precise nod and she did the same.

Steph took a big step to follow the clerk toward Jenny, but then reeled back, watching them all closely as she continued toward me.

"How much?" she asked, when she'd gotten close enough.

"A good amount, lots of bills."

"What do we do about Jenny?"

"We can't wait around."

"We can't leave."

"These people haven't connected us to her."

"What if they want to take her to the hospital?"

"Steph," I angry-whispered. She jumped in place. "Okay, I'm gonna go and you extricate Jenny from the situation."

"What does that mean?"

"Figure out a way to get her outta here."

Like a ninja, I slid out of the store. I saw Steph going over to Jenny, tugging on her lip with her fang tooth, meaning she was in deep thought. I ran out of the electric doors of the main entrance. The outside wind hit me like a brick and some bills loosened from my waistline, scattering all over the parking lot. I scurried around, catching them in my fists, letting a few fly away.

Back in the Gas-Guzzler, I waited, dripping sweat. I turned on Steph's mixtape, which had been left in the cassette deck and listened to Michael Jackson's "Bad." *Who's bad?* I asked, tapping my foot like a junkie, begging for my sisters to emerge. An outpouring of love for them both immediately overwhelmed. Steph could be a pain in the ass, but as big sisters went, she could've been a lot worse. Sometimes she drove me to the mall with her friends so I could get greasy Hardee's sandwiches. Her friends all like her, Tiffany rejects with big hair and valley girl voices. This was before she started dating Kent and lost everything interesting about her. Once after the mall, I was in my room, deep in an X-Men comic I'd bought and she said one of her friends thought I was cute. "Which one?" I asked. "Gross, Aaron," she said, "Not to date you or anything, she meant cute like a younger brother." She stood in the doorframe and slurred her next words, "You're not like the worst younger brother is what I'm saying. Like, you're not great, but not completely embarrassing either."

I thought of that day as Steph and Jenny still hadn't emerged. What if they were being arrested? Would they narc on me? Should I floor the Gas-Guzzler out of the rest stop and start a new life on my own? I had a good chunk of money between what Barry and Mom had taken plus our recent stolen bounty. I was about to do it when my first memory sprang to mind. I was probably three years old when Jenny was born. Not quite understanding when Mom told me she had my little sister in her belly, I would kiss her stomach waiting for her arrival. Jenny was born with a full head of dark hair and these little squished eyes, her face red and a cry that stopped when Mom allowed me to pet the top of her head. She blinked away the goo, keeping her eyes shut, and looked up with wonder.

"Hi, Mommy's belly," I had said, kissing her tiny nose.

"This is Jenny," Mom said, laughing.

"Hi, Jenny belly."

I hadn't called her that in a while.

Materializing back in the RV, I wiped my eyes, not realizing I was welling up like a little bitch.

Who's bad? Michael Jackson finished with a final *Shamone!*

I had taken both my sisters for granted, but I would be a better brother if we reunited again. And just when I'd given up any last hope, Steph and Jenny exited the electric doors of the main entrance, Jenny licking a ridiculously large lollipop with a bandage wrapped around her arm.

Once they got inside, I nearly tackled them both to the ground with the force of my hug.

14

Barry and Mom took us all to a steakhouse later that night for dinner. They'd obviously scored big to be able to afford one. They knew I knew where the money was coming from, but had no idea I told Steph and Jenny as well. They also knew I'd stolen the first time, but not about our last bounty. Which meant that the Gimmelman kids held the best cards. Not that we would, but we *could* turn them in, as a threat if needed. My goal was to merge all of our talents, since Steph and Jenny proved to be naturals. Both surprising in their own ways. That Steph could leave her morals behind, and Jenny could tame, her wild beastly ways and use them for good.

The steakhouse was located in an unfortunate town called Lynchburg. Not a good first impression of the south. But it was the fanciest restaurant we'd been to since we started the trip, excited to eat something other than Slim Jims and Gummi Bears. Had the feel of entering a Civil War-era haunt, but with modern touches. The seat cushions and backs of booths made out of cowhide, smooth to the touch. Waitresses dressed with bonnets, waiters with gold pocket watches and powerful mustaches. A jaunty tune over the sound system. A nice break from the 1980s, which had toyed with our emotions. Psyching us up by making us mucho money and then skull-fucking us to pieces.

But things were looking up! The last convenience store netting five hundred smackers. Steph wanted to know how much that left for each of us. I had to remind her of the plan. Rob as a family. Hit even bigger targets. Score the kind of money we'd gotten used to having.

Barry and Mom thankfully put the weed pipe down for this meal. And I re-hid the cocaine vial so Barry wouldn't know I partook. All of us clean and sober.

Lula, the waitress with a bonnet, brought out our appetizers: blue crab cakes, Waldorf salads, potatoes au gratin, raw oysters, which Jenny said looked like giant dead boogers, and shrimp cocktail.

While Barry was slurping giant dead boogers, I decided it was time to utilize the knowledge I held.

"This meal is gonna be pricey, huh?" I asked, spearing a shrimp.

Mom shot Barry a worried *look*.

"I told you guys, we're on vacation," Barry said, pinching Jenny on the ear with a loving gesture. She swatted his hand away. "The Gimmelmans won't be reduced to gas station dining anymore."

I arched my eyebrows. "And why is that?"

"We're not as financially unstable as I once thought."

Like a two-year-old I continued, "Why?"

Barry choked on his oyster. Mom had to slap him on the back.

"Bear-Bear, do you need the Heimlich?"

His face was turning purple, but he waved her away with his napkin, then coughed up a dead booger into it.

"Aaron, just enjoy your shrimp," he managed to say, after getting his choking under control.

"We stole five hundred dollars," Jenny said, then covered her mouth.

"Damnit, Jenny," I said.

"What-*what*?" Mom said, squawking.

Barry glared at me.

Steph hit Jenny on the back of the head. "Jenny, that's not how we said we were gonna do this."

Barry thrust his pointer finger. "Stephie, don't hit your sister."

Lula came by with a cherry pie smile.

"How's everythin' tastin' so far?"

"It's fine, Lula," Barry growled.

The smile still stained her face, but she backed away.

Barry turned his attention to me. "Talk."

I lowered my voice. "We found your stash. There's no reason for the girls not to know what you've been doing."

Mom started petting Steph's hair. "Sweetie, it's not what you think."

"Mom, it's like, fine."

The restaurant was loud and boisterous enough for our conversation to remain at our table. The only reason Barry allowed it to continue.

He kept eyeing me. "The last rest stop?"

"Yup, convenience store."

"Five hundred dollars?" He shrugged, feigning being impressed. "What did the girls do?"

"Dad, they were amazing. Steph flirted with the clerk and Jenny cut her arm, distracting everyone so I could grab the loot."

Mom picked up Jenny's arm, inspecting for wounds.

"Baby, are you okay?"

"I'm not your baby," she said. "I've taken an animal's life. No baby can say that."

We all left that alone, Mom receding in her seat.

"What was *your* last score?" I asked, crossing my arms.

"Okay, here's all the cards on the table. At the last two rest stops, your mother and I went off on our own. I'm sure you noticed how long we were both gone. First was a liquor store. And lemme tell you, your mother impressed me so much."

Mom hid in her hands, coming up bashful.

"She was my eyes and ears."

"So was Steph," I said. "And she made sure to get her and Jenny out of the store eventually."

"Second time, we stuck to liquor stores. We use the padding of your mother's bra as a mask."

We all made a face at that.

"But I'm thinking we need something more incognito. Less self-made. Girls, we were gonna tell you. We were just trying to figure out the right time."

"We don't care," Steph said. "Like, we're all obviously good at this."

Lula returned with a mustached waiter carrying our steaks. It took a minute to figure out who had which steak at each temperature, from Jenny liking it bloody to Mom preferring shoe leather.

"Thank you, Lula," Barry said, the tremor in his voice veering toward menacing. Telling her to leave us alone.

Once again, Lula stamped on a smile and backed away slowly.

"You think no one will suspect you two?" I asked. "We're the better cover. A family with a little girl with freckles in an RV? No one will see us coming."

Mom grabbed the edge of the table. "I don't want... I don't want to put any of you in danger."

"What your mother means—"

"I'm serious, Barry. This ends if I ever feel like my babies are in trouble."

He threw up his hands. "Yeah, of course, of course, babe. The kids come first."

"We're doing this for you kids," Mom said. "We gave you a certain style of living and it's unfair to expect you to settle."

I let her think what she was saying was true. But they were doing this for themselves. At least Barry was. Mom maybe doing it for him.

"We do need a getaway driver," Barry said, ending the discussion of the reasoning behind it all. This was a fact of our lives now, no need for explanations. "The last score, your mother and I running away as fast as we could. But if there was a cop close, we would've been done for."

"You've now robbed twice with bra padding over your faces," I said. "You can't do that again. Between Delaware and Virginia, the cops might be looking for a couple, who robs liquor stores. You used a gun. That's armed robbery."

"So, what do you suggest, smarty pants?" Barry asked.

Lula returned, "And how's the temp on all those steaks of yours?"

"Lula!" Barry snapped, enough to make her jump in place. "We're having a very sensitive family discussion. If you would please..."

Lula seemed to curtsey with an apology. As she walked away, I swore I heard her say, "Jews" under her breath.

"Did she just say...?" I began to ask.

"Aaron," Barry said. "Focus. I man the gun. I'm the only one who can. I will *not* let my children handle one."

Mom nodded in approval.

"I'm there to put the fear in whoever we're stealing from." He shifted his eyes around the table. "Judith is lookout. Steph you're wheels, since you're the only other one with a license. Aaron, you're good cop. You make sure everybody does what we say, hands over the money. We rob a place, we go after customers too, not just the cash register. And Jenny, you collect the money in a bag. Each of us with clear defined roles that we don't deviate from—"

"What's deviate mean?" Steph asked.

"Honey, you should be glad you're going into this line of work because school was obviously not meant for you."

Mom patted Steph's hand. "It means we stick to our roles."

"We're only as strong as our weakest link," Barry said. "And you best believe we'll be doing trial runs before we test out the real thing."

"But we've all robbed successfully before," I said. "Liquor stores, convenience stores."

Barry tucked his napkin in his shirt, let it flow across his chest.

"Oh son, we're done with those beginner slopes."

"So, what are we hitting?"

Barry carved into his steak, cut a juicy piece that he shoved in his mouth. Gnawing the meat with bloody juice coating teeth he said, "Banks, my boy. The same son-of-a-bitches that took what was ours."

He devoured the bite, washing it down with a gulp of red wine and a satisfying *aah.*

15

Barry wasn't kidding about those trial runs before we hit a real bank. This meant playing different roles to make sure we were utilizing our strengths. We found an empty lot somewhere in Virginia, hidden by thickets of trees where no one would spy on us. Steph played the role of bank teller before we practiced her getaway skills. Barry had seen her speeding away in her car many times while trying to avoid hearing about a curfew, so he figured she'd be capable.

"All right everyone, this is a robbery," Barry shouted. He still used the bra-over-his-face mask until we figured out a better disguise.

"Judith," he continued, dropping his threatening robber voice. "You must always man the front doors. There will be a security guard. We're not attempting a big bank yet, and the small ones won't have more than one guard. First you must disarm him, then use the gun on him. Likely he'll be heavyset, old, or at least inexperienced. If he was anything else, he wouldn't be working as a security guard in a mom and pop bank."

"How do I disarm him if you have the gun?" Mom asked.

"Good point. You need a gun too, at least a fake one. We can pick that up. For now, use your hands."

Mom made her hand into the shape of a gun, pointing it at a garbage can.

"Tell him, 'No one will get hurt. Don't be a hero. Hand over you're gun.'" Mom repeated, trying to sound as forceful as possible.

"And tell him not to try anything funny," I added. "No tripping the alarm."

"Right," Barry said, winking at me. "We make it clear that there should be no alarms. The minute one gets tripped we need to be Audi Five Hundred."

Steph scrunched up her face.

"That means we need to jet," Barry said. "An alarm gets tripped, and we only have a few minutes to get out of there. These are small towns without much going on. A bank alarm goes off and we'll have the entirety of the local force on our asses."

"Okay, I've got the security guard's gun," Mom said. "He's detained."

Barry turned to Steph. "Put all the money in the bag, fast as possible. I don't want to hurt you."

Steph recoiled from Barry raising his voice, looming over her.

"Sorry," Steph said, shaking her head. "It just felt real for a moment."

"It *is* real," Barry said.

"What am I doing?" Jenny asked, sitting on the concrete and crossing her legs Criss-cross Applesauce style.

"Honey, you go around asking for people's wallets, jewelry and watches. We'll pawn anything that isn't cash."

Jenny jumped up, yelling at the air.

"Gimme your fucking purse, asshole."

"Simmer down, Jenny," Barry said. "Only if they're resistant. Folks'll be afraid. They'll respond better to kindness."

"Please gimme your fucking purse," Jenny said, in a sweet voice.

"And me, Dad?" I asked, giddy. Even though we were practicing on a concrete lot, I could visualize the entire bank, the players in our robbery, the successful haul we'd obtain buzzing in the near future.

"Good cop, like I said. You reiterate the mantra to everyone. NO ONE should be a hero. If everyone complies, NO ONE will get hurt. We need to stress that over and over."

"What if someone doesn't go along with it?" Steph asked.

It was what we all were thinking. Humans being unpredictable. In these small towns we'd hit, there'd be those searching to give their lives purpose, for a heroic moment to boast to their family and friends. I knew it would happen. Hopefully, we would be seasoned enough by then.

"I'm not shooting anyone if that's what you're getting at," Barry said.

Mom wiped the sweat from her brow.

"Anyone who gets out of line will be hit over the head with the gun. If we do that, they'll stay quiet and fall in line."

"What about using one of us as a hostage, a plant who's already in the bank?" I asked.

"This is good," Barry said. "You all are thinking of the what-ifs. Not necessary for a small bank, Aaron, but for a big one maybe. We'll keep it on the backburner. Let's continue with the improv."

Steph mimed putting the money into the bag and handed it over to Barry. Jenny took the pretend goods from the pretend people in the lot.

"Okay, now we make a break for it. Judith, I'll give you a signal—"

"What's the signal?" she asked.

"Uh, Woodstock. When I say 'Woodstock,' Judith, you'll hold open the door for us to run out. Steph, you always need to park a little bit away from the entrance so we're not on any cameras. We'll cover the license plates too. The RV should always remain running. Once we're in, Steph, you put pedal to the metal. Gun the shit out of the Gas-Guzzler until we're roaring. Let's practice that now."

Steph morphed from bank teller to getaway driver. Hands on ten and two at the wheel as we burst out of the pretend bank and booked it to the RV. I grabbed Jenny's hand to help her run faster, her little legs having a hard time keeping up. We all leaped inside, slammed the door, and Steph floored it. The RV tilted, sending all our stuff to the left as we rolled on the floor, but Steph gunned it until we were headed toward the nearby highway.

"Turn back," Barry said. "Do it again."

Five times later, we were confident in all the steps, getting from the fake bank to shooting away from the scene in a minute and a half.

"We can do a little better," Barry said. "But once the adrenaline kicks in, it'll help."

We had everything down except for the masks. Back in the RV, we switched out Steph's mixtape and were listening to one of Barry and Mom's odes to

1969.

"Woodstock," Barry said, with a smile. "We use masks of the greats."

After calling an operator at a pay phone, they directed us to a shop for masks in Charlottesville. Barry had Jenny and I go inside to make the purchase, just so he and Mom wouldn't be identified later.

We were instructed to get a Janis Joplin for Mom, Jerry Garcia for Barry, Jimi Hendrix for myself, Joan Baez for Steph, and Mama Cass for Jenny, even though the Mamas and the Papas didn't play Woodstock.

"It was still the same era," Mom said, and hummed "California Dreamin'."

"No one needs a sixties history lesson," Steph said. "I still think it would be cooler if we wore current singers."

"Fine, if you wanna get that redhead or blonde you love so much, be my guest," Barry said. "You're hidden in the RV anyway."

So, Debbie Gibson was purchased for Steph and she shut the fuck up.

Once we got the masks, we laid them out on the RV's floor, our new personas. Shiny plastic idols staring back. I put on the Jimi Hendrix one, felt his soul merge with my own. He died in bed, puking up and choking on the alcohol he'd consumed in the middle of the night. Now he'd be reborn. Each Gimmelman picked up their incognito mask and transformed. Barry had gotten Mom a fake gun too from a toy store and the two of them posed like Charlie's Angels. Debbie Gibson smiled, and Mama Cass laughed her Jenny laugh, a sound that resembled a string of hiccups.

"Now it's time to case out a joint," Jerry Garcia said, a wise troubadour and our fearless leader. "Someday, everything's gonna be diff'rent when I paint my masterpiece."

It would be years later when I discovered Barry was already quoting the Dead, and the last vestige of the old him was long gone.

16

In Horse Country, Virginia, we found a tiny town of under five hundred people. Historic with American flags shooting from every house. The streets scrubbed clean. The town was sheltered and innocent. Ripe for plucking. The Middleburg Bank sat off of Main Street, a three-block radius that boasted a goods store, horse riding equipment, and an inn from the eighteen-hundreds. This bank would be small but have money due to its wealthy clients. No point in robbing a hee-haw operation that would net us less than a liquor store.

We scoped it out the night before. Barry liked that it was at the end of the street. Right around the corner was a line of old homes that ran for four blocks before feeding into an exit that would lead to the highway. The police station was past the other end of the Main Street, four blocks away but bisected by a different street, meaning the police cars didn't have a straight shot to the highway.

We debated whether to rob in the morning or afternoon. The afternoon, having more customers but also more variables. Ideally a customer or two would be best, in case the bank didn't have a lot in their safe and we could grab what was on them. It was night by the time we cased the town so we went to bed early to get up first thing. We had parked in a spot on the edge of town, near a horse farm. We could hear them neighing into the night.

The light pierced through the window at six a.m., but Barry was already frying bacon and eggs. I pushed aside the sheet he had constructed. Mom,

Steph, and Jenny were already eating their breakfast, each with a cup of coffee.

"Early birds," Barry said, passing me a plate of breakfast I ate in bed.

By seven o' clock we were already parked across the street from the bank. Barry had carved into the license plate, making the numbers and letters unrecognizable, but from far away it wouldn't be suspicious. We watched the bank. At seven thirty, an older gentleman opened the doors and went inside. Barry pegged him at about sixty, neat suit and glasses. Nothing screaming hero about him. Likely the manager. At eight, a woman with big shoulder pads and a bouffant hairdo opened the doors, likely a clerk. An hour passed and no one else showed up, meaning the outfit had one teller and one manager, not even a security guard. At nine thirty we saw a man and a woman go up to the bank. They came from separate ends of the block but seemed to know each other and had a short conversation at the entrance. He looked to be a horse farmer with his cowboy hat and boots. She was dressed in a blouse and skirt, likely headed to work. He held open the door for her and they went inside.

"Now," Barry hissed.

Steph put on her Debbie Gibson mask, clenching the wheel, a steely gaze peeking through the eye holes. My family morphed once the masks were donned. We filed out of the RV, a fake gun poking out of Mom's back and a real one in Barry's grip.

"Aaron, you hold the door open for us," Barry said. "Then you go inside."

All other sounds seemed to shut off except for my pulse. My breathing heavy and deafening. The sweat on my upper lip was metallic to the taste. My hands shook so I jammed them in my pockets until we got to the door, and I flung it open.

"Hands in the air! Hands in the air" I heard Barry yell, as Mom and Jenny ran inside, and I followed. The bank, no bigger than our living room back home. The one teller behind a plate of glass, the manager's office to the side.

The teller let out an audible gasp, sounding like a deflated balloon. Tears already building in her eyes. "Oh Jesus, oh Jesus," she whispered to herself like a benediction.

"Hands to the sky," Barry yelled louder, leaping closer to her.

Her shaking arms slowly rose.

"Please, sir, don't..."

"Quiet!"

Jerry Garcia turned to the man and the woman on line.

"Down on the ground, pockets emptied, hands behind your back."

They were frozen.

"Now, now!" Barry said, pushing the woman to the ground. She fell with a thud, her pocketbook skating across the floor. Jenny ran over and stuck it in the garbage bag she carried.

"Get the manager," Barry said to Mom.

The manager poked his head out only for Mom to stick the gun in his nose.

"We don't wanna hurt you," Mom said, her voice rising at the end.

"Keys to the safe," Barry said.

"Yes, keys to the safe," she repeated to him.

"Take care of them," Barry said to me, pointing the gun at the man and woman down on the floor.

"No one wants to hurt you," I said, because the woman was shivering and sniveling. The guy dead silent. "Empty your pockets. Wallets, jewelry..."

"My wedding ring?" the woman asked, blinking at me through tears.

"No, no, not your wedding ring. Just everything else."

A bubble of saliva emerged from her lips. She seemed to want to say *thank you*.

"Your wallet, sir," I said.

He mumbled something under his breath.

"Don't be a hero. The faster everyone listens to what we say, the faster this is over."

"What are ya, some kid?" the man murmured.

I leaned down until I was level with his face. I could feel him gazing through the Jimi Hendrix mask, as if he could actually see my soul. I nearly scooted back in fear. But I kept cool.

"Jerry Garcia over there with the gun," I said. "You don't want to piss him off."

I must've said it threateningly enough because the man nodded and shifted in place while wrestling the wallet out of his pocket. It slid across the floor for Jenny to scoop it up.

"Open the drawers," I heard Barry say to the teller.

"Okay, okay," she said. She had a strong Southern accent. With a key, she opened up the drawer.

Mom had pushed the manager over to the action. The guy, nearly tripping over his feet.

"Anyone near the door?" Barry yelled.

I leaped up and rushed to the front, a sleepy block staring back.

"We're good."

"Hug that door, Hendrix," he said. "Anyone comes down that block, you let us know."

"Yeah, yeah."

"Baby, get the rest from the teller. I got the manager."

Mom switched over. The teller yelped as a different gun went on her. She was stuffing stacks of bills into a bag with a tie.

"Any more drawers?" Mom asked.

"There's one," the woman said, her voice shaking.

"Open it too." Mom looked over her shoulder, caught Jenny's eye. "Take this."

Jenny whisked over, grabbed the bag from the teller, and dumped it in her big garbage bag.

I could just make out Barry pushing the manager down the hallway. "No one wants a hero, sir. You're not a hero, are you?"

"No, I'm not," the manager said.

"Good. Last thing we want to do is shoot someone. Don't make us do that. Where's the safe?"

"That room," the manager said pointing, and he and Barry disappeared inside.

"Faster," Mom said, to the teller.

"I'm going as fast—" the teller began, but I got distracted from listening to them.

Down the block, a car pulled onto Main Street. The town so bare, it took just a car to jolt my nerves. It crawled down the block at a sloth's place.

"Car," I said, out loud. Mom whipped her head around.

"Is it stopping?"

I watched it creep toward us. A light blue Chevrolet, big as a boat. An old lady from World War I era wearing driving gloves and thick glasses piloting the thing. The car pulled into a spot. The old lady slowly took off her driving gloves, placed them in her purse.

"Is there any more cash up front?" I heard Mom say to the teller.

"No, ma'am, that's it. We're a small bank. Whole town is about five hundred people."

"You did really good," Mom said.

"Jesus loves all," the teller replied. "I *hope* you really need this money."

"Grab it," I heard Mom say. She must've been talking to Jenny. I knew the last thing she wanted to hear was this lady's Christian guilt. I wondered if Mom would've been able to rob a bank had it been owned by Jews in Borough Park, Brooklyn. But then I thought about this teller. Could she see that we weren't Christian? Did she already have a prejudiced idea of Jewish people? In a town like this, she couldn't come across many. I wondered if she could hear it in our voices? That nasally Noo Yawk twang, our *cawfees* and *chawcolettes,* our *basebawls.* She'd go home to her husband and tell him, "And these *Jews* from up north just bust into that bank and robbed us. I pray for their souls." But she wouldn't pray. She'd add this to her reasons to hate us, like we'd been hated for thousands of years. I thought of my grandma and grandpa who I never met, who survived the terrors of concentration camps to start a family in America. Would they be proud of us?

"Fuck," I said, spinning back to reality because outside the old lady had gotten out of her boat of a car and was locking the door. If she came in, I would have to grab her, as gently as possible because I worried saying "boo" would send her into cardiac arrest. I quickly checked on the customers on the floor. The woman sobbing into her hands, the man still like he was dead. I didn't like him quiet.

"You two doing all right?" I asked.

The lady responded with sobs.

"Stop crying okay? Just calm down."

This seemed to make it worse.

"Lady, stop your goddamn crying!" Jenny yelled and stamped her sneaker by the lady's face.

"Je—" I began to say, almost giving away her cover. "Mama," I continued, referring to her mask. "Easy, okay? You don't have to be scared, ma'am," I said, and she nodded into the floor.

From down the hall, I heard Barry raising his voice. The walls trapping what he was saying, but the sound sharp in the air.

"Everything okay there, baby?" Mom yelled.

The guy on the ground wiggled a little. He still had his hands behind his back, but I could see a bulge on the far side of his hip.

"Shit," I said, running over. I couldn't worry about the old lady or the boo-hooing one. "Did you empty your pockets?" I asked.

"What's going on?" Mom yelled.

On instinct, I dug into the guy's far pocket and found a tiny gun shaped like a big elbow macaroni. Holding it in my hands, the steel felt cool.

"Give me that," Mom said, swooping down on me. She gave me her fake one instead, the heft lighter, empty. I had the urge to take the other back. I kicked into vigilante mode.

"You didn't say you had a gun," I said, pointing my fake one at the guy.

"I wasn't gonna be a hero," he said, starting to blubber, less cool without a piece. A mental note for later. Any cool customers in the future needed to be pat down for weapons. The blubberers crying because they had no protection.

Barry came out of the room pushing the manager down the hallway. He didn't seem happy. The manager still tripping over his feet as Barry thunked him to the ground. The manager's glasses flinging off. Blind as a bat, he patted around him looking for them.

"Practically nothing in the safe," Barry said. "Says they have a main branch a town over where they keep the bulk of the savings. This one's just for regular transactions."

I'd forgotten about the old lady outside when the bell on top of the front doors jingled and she pattered inside, purse clutched to her neck.

Barry slung a small bag over his shoulder.

"We done?" he asked Mom.

"Yeah."

"Woodstock," he said, making for the door.

The old lady, not expecting any of this and whirling around as Barry knocked past her. She pitched forward on her feet, falling into a desk off to the side.

"Sorry," Mom said to all of them, whisking past me for the door.

Jenny close behind, dragging her bounty.

I was the last out, getting one last look at the melee we caused. These people's mornings shattered, the teller miming the cross across her chest, the other lady weeping, the guy on the floor and the manager simmering, the old lady spinning on the floor like a turtle on its shell. I hated to admit it, the truth like a wedge of food I was choking on, but these last ten minutes were the greatest of my life. It didn't matter what my ancestors had to go through so we could be alive, us Gimmelmans actually being great at robbing was a wonderful sight to behold. The sun outside hitting me like a warm caress, a buttery golden path to the RV where Debbie Gibson sat at the wheel. The door swung open, Barry tossing Jenny and the bounties inside, Mom diving in right after, all of their arms reaching for me, pulling toward their salvation. The tires rolling as I leaped inside, skittering into my bed/couch.

"Go!" Barry screamed, shutting the door. We all were tossed back as the RV revved and shot out of its parking space. Under my ass, I could feel it pick up speed. I got to my feet as we reached the exit off-ramp to the highway. I jumped on my couch/bed and stuck my head out of the window seeing only quiet streets rolling into the distance. No one after us. An empty highway we tore down.

"We did it! We did it!" Barry cheered, jumping up and down with Mom.

"Holy moly!" Jenny said, diving into her bag with money.

But I kept eyes on the road, watching out for any possible heat on our tail. My fake gun in hand, wishing it was real in case of a problem. I kept watch even as Debbie Gibson's "Out of the Blue" poured out of the speakers dwarfing the sounds of my family celebrating.

Only when it seemed we were far enough away that I could breathe again did I join in their cheer.

A pipe full of weed had been lit and no one noticed it got passed my way.

17

We flicked back and forth from news stations on our thirteen-inch TV searching for any buzz about our bank raid. It wasn't until we reached North Carolina when we emerged on the screen as a story of the day. Crowding around the tiny tube, we watched with bated breath about how we'd be immortalized.

A reporter with giant red Sally Jesse Raphael glasses and frizzy hair stood outside of the Middleburg Bank.

"Joan Danchen here with a wild story of four criminals—"

"Criminals," Barry repeated, blowing a raspberry.

"—who robbed the Middleburg Bank this morning. The manager and the teller had just opened, and two customers were witnesses to this frightening act."

The reporter went over to the manager who pushed his glasses up his sloping nose.

"Like bats outta hell they came after us," he said. "All of 'em wearing Halloween masks."

"Could you identify the masks?" the reporter asked.

The Christian teller butt into the shot, lunging for the microphone.

"They had us at gunpoint," she said, tears welling. "Saw my life flash before my eyes. And I prayed to Jesus that he'd get us through this. And He listened, sure did."

"Praise Jesus," the reporter said. She then turned to the farmer and the woman who were on line.

"You, sir, said you had your gun taken?" the reporter asked.

The farmer cleared his throat. "Well, yes'm. Tiny pistol I always make sure to carry. But then the little one—there were two small ones, like a little person or I dunno, well, one of those little people, he—he saw me reachin' in my pocket and was too fast. Grabbed it right from me."

"I was *so* scared too," the woman said, squeezing a wet tissue and then tucking it in her sleeve. "And the littlest one with the high-pitched voice, that one the meanest of all. Swore at me—F this, and F that. Horrible to hear at such an early hour."

"I'm sure, ma'am," the reporter continued. "And you, Ms. Mae Welling-ton, the town's oldest resident..."

The camera panned over to the old lady we left spinning like a turtle on the floor. She had an arm in a sling and was shaking.

"They knocked me over on their way out, lucky I didn't hit my head. Hurt my arm, though. Shame what the world is coming to."

"Did you get a good look at the masks they wore?" the reporter continued.

"Devils that's what they were."

"The mask you mean?"

"You can infer what you want from that."

The farmer poked into the frame. "Jerry Garcia, that's what one of them was called. He was the leader."

"Again, you mean the mask?" the reporter asked.

"Yes, he wore a Jerry Garcia mask."

Barry picked up the Jerry Garcia mask and tilted it in the light.

"I believe we're famous now," he said.

Jenny giggled.

"Do we need new masks now?" Steph asked, over her shoulder as she drove the RV.

"No way," Barry said. "This is how we're identified. This way the second we enter a bank, they know what's up."

The reporter turned the microphone back on the manager and teller.

"Anything else you can tell us?" she asked.

"Camera got a good look at them on the way out," he said. "But not after they turned the corner."

"I think we have footage of that," the reporter said. "Roll it."

In grainy black and white, we watched us dart from the bank, Barry picking Jenny up as we rounded the corner and disappeared.

"If anyone has any tips about the robbers, please be in contact and call the police. They are armed and dangerous. Don't try and bring them in on your own."

Barry snapped off the TV.

"Dangerous." Barry blew another raspberry. "It's all a show. And it seems like we put on a good one."

He tickled Mom's ear, who finally smiled.

"You okay, babe?" he asked.

"Just surreal to see it played back."

"Kids, give us a second."

He shooed us away behind the sheet divider, but I could still hear them quietly.

"What's the plan?" Mom asked.

"Find another bank."

Mom sighed audibly.

"What is it, Jude?" he asked, smooching her neck.

"I think we should lay low. They'll be looking for us."

"Who?"

"The police."

"We're out of Virginia. Their state troopers won't cross the border."

"What if we went to my mother's?"

"Your...*what*?"

"To regroup, Barry. That man on the line had a gun. If Aaron hadn't taken it away—"

"But he did."

"But what if he didn't? I just think everything was too rushed. What if we went to Boca and cased out a bank there? We can stay at my mom's and really plan the next one. A big one. That holds a lot of people's savings. And

Boca is rich. Really rich."

"That's true."

"If we're gonna do this, we can prepare it right. Besides, I haven't had a good shower in days now. And Ma was expecting us."

"You didn't tell her otherwise?"

"I wanted to leave it open, in case. She knows we're stopping along the way, and it could take a few days."

"You're not chickening out, are you, Judy?"

"No. Never. It was exhilarating. But scary too. I need a minute. Catch my breath, Barry. Don't you need to catch yours?"

"Aaron, get over here," he called out.

I parted the bedsheet separating us and went to the front where Barry and Mom had huddled up. Steph had her eyes on the road, humming along to Cyndi Lauper's "True Colors" over the radio.

"Your mother wants to take a break in Florida with Grandma, scope out a place there. What do you think?"

"Me?"

"Yeah, you son. What do you think?"

"Whatever you guys want to do."

"On one hand, we've got adrenaline on our side that could fuel us for the next take. On the other, that same adrenaline could make us sloppy. Do you think we were sloppy, Aaron?"

"I...think there's things we could improve on."

"Like what?"

"Like the fact I didn't have a gun."

Mom jumped in. "You are *not* using a gun."

"Now hold on, Judy, hear the boy out."

"At least the fake one," I said. "If I had that on the farmer guy, he would've given up his real gun earlier."

"That's a good point," Barry said."

"It was almost a fatal mistake," I said.

"All right, you use the fake one, Mom and I will use the real ones. Jenny still collects all the loot. You okay to wait to Florida for the next hit?"

While I had no desire to deal with Grandma Bernice, it would be nice to be in a home with an actual bed surrounded by walls. Now that Mom had mentioned wanting a shower, I could visualize the stink lines rising from my body. The RV only had hot water for a short amount of time, so showers tended to be bone cold, a quick leap in and out.

If I was honest, though, the glaring error with our crew was being one man short. I had to monitor the people in line and the door. And what if there was a security guard? With one extra person, we could have one of us solely watching the door to avoid any other old ladies coming in last minute. I was about to pipe up and say something when Barry shouted,

"Boca Raton it is!"

He started massaging Steph's shoulders.

"Steph, you hear that? Head directly south."

Mom let out a steady breath. We locked eyes. I wondered if the breath was because she had put off our next robbery for a while, keeping us as safe as she could.

Or I could've been reading too much into things. I did that sometimes. The born writer in me. Like I'd always been preparing to put our crazy adventures to paper from the start. At least we'd also have some time in Florida to figure out what to do about adding an extra man to our crew. It wasn't the right time to bring it up.

Besides Steph had turned up "True Colors" and Johnny Cash was howling along, bouncing on his hind legs and leaving a trickle of pee in his place from getting overly excited. We all laughed, deep Gimmelman laughs that brought tears to our eyes. I can remember this, when we were happy, if only for a moment of time.

18

Barry chose to stay up and drive through the night. I figured he didn't want any distractions that might shift us from the plan. Use Grandma Bernice as a roof, while we plotted our next score. All I saw of South Carolina and Georgia was the highway. Steph and Jenny were asleep, but I snuck into the glove compartment where Barry's coke vial had been hidden. Once we reached Grandma's, he might choose a different hiding place, so I needed to maximize my potential last toots.

Ah, the familiar drip. I wiggled my nose and watched the headlights of cars give off their own laser show. We hit Florida before dawn. The sun purple like a bruise peeling over the edge of the highway. Jacksonville and St. Augustine, onto Daytona Beach, and a turnoff to Orlando that we didn't take. Years ago, we'd done a fam trip to Disney World. I was about seven, Steph already twelve and too cool for school, Jenny just out of diapers. We had a nanny at the time. A rotund woman who was all bosoms with a monk's haircut. She smiled a lot, called us "sugar boogers." She always smelled like pies, her whole face eaten up by rosacea. Barry and Mom disappearing for most of it, leaving the nanny with her hands full. God knows where they went. Why they chose a family trip to Disney World when they weren't even gonna show up for most of it was beyond me. But that was typical of them. They likely figured we'd be too distracted by Mickey and Minnie to care. I had a little arcade football game that bleeped and blooped, tiny little dots in place of the players, and all I remember on that trip was playing it while on one of the many lines. And, Jenny getting an ear infection. Even then Barry and Mom didn't return from their own vacation. When they finally did at the end, tanned in a way that seemed as if they laid on a beach for four days, I broke my football game in front of them. I had no interest in ever playing it again.

Melbourne, to Port St. Lucie, and then to West Palm Beach. With the window cracked, I could smell the salt, taste it on my tongue (although that might've still been the coke drip). Jenny and Steph had woken, fighting in their quarters over some inane thing. I heard Seymour's name spoken as a hiss from Steph. Johnny Cash started howling. I heard Mom coo-cooing the dog, asking Barry if we could stop so he could relieve himself. But Barry wasn't having it.

"We're making great time," he said. "Just a few more miles to Grandma Bernice."

This elicited a groan/shrug from everyone. The threat of Grandma Bernice more palpable the closer we got. Her evil little pinches. Only matzo in the cupboards. The never-ending parade of cats licking their own assholes. The creepy shrine to her late husband Herb. The fact she was the only woman in all of Florida not to use air conditioning. Fans swirling dust around and little else. The varicose veins mapping her legs. Her Nescafe breath.

We'd been to Boca a few times over the years. Palm trees and pink condos. The depressing Boca Town Center mall. Sleepy Atlantic Avenue. Just breathing made you sweat fountains. Old Jewish ladies with fanny packs and track suits power walking. Grandma Bernice lived in the Boca Jewish Center condominiums, the hub of the Orthodox community with a supermarket, restaurants, and bakery all within a mile or two. A tiny white bus would chauffeur around the men and women of the community a few times throughout the day. A pool and lounge chairs in the center of the condominiums. Sometimes the women did calisthenics wearing a ridiculous amount of clothing for swimming. When we pulled up it was still early in the morning and the pool was being attended by a pool boy with his shirt off.

"Hubba hubba," I heard Jenny say. I left my cordoned-off area and saw her sticking her face against the window, licking the glass.

"Jenny, stop," Steph said, but she lingered to watch, tugging on her bottom lip with a fang tooth. The further we got away from Kent, the more she seemed to forget God-boy. The pool boy, as if he knew he was being drooled over, shook the water out of his floppy hair and went back to retrieving dead bugs with his net.

We parked the RV and stretched as we exited, the sun hot and pools of sweat already oozing from our pores. Jenny was pulling Johnny Cash's tail, and he was snapping at her playfully. Steph still had eyes on the pool boy, who hadn't taken his laser focus off the bugs. Barry and Mom were psyching each other up for the inevitable Grandma Bernice onslaught, the woman like a Yiddish freight train. He was whispering in her ear, nibbling on the lobe, while she pushed him away and then brought him back for an embrace. Colors were dancing in front of my eyes, and I realized I was still high on coke.

Grandma Bernice lived on the second floor in a three-bedroom, two-bathroom spread. A pink door with a doormat that said, *Hashem Sleeps Here.* The doorbell played a rollicking version of the Dreidel Song. We had to listen to it three times in a row before the door swung open, whapped us with a kiss of soupy heat, and Grandma Bernice stood there in her housecoat and fuzzy slippers, curlers in her hair, makeup half on, the saggy skin on her legs melting like a candle.

"You're here already?" she shouted, hands on hips, lips twisted into a grimace.

"We made good time, Ma," Mom said, moving toward her herky-jerky for a hug that Grandma Bernice welcomed with a quick pat on the back.

"I just didn't expect you *so* early," Grandma Bernice said, as if she wanted to close the door on this reunion before it even began.

"We made great time, Bernice," Barry said, even more herky-jerky as he danced toward her for a kiss on the cheek that she seemed like she wanted to wipe off with varnish.

"Can we come in, Ma?" Mom asked, in a baby voice. She always diminished around Grandma Bernice, turning into a child again, seeking

92

her own mother's love and affection that the woman never gave.

"If you must."

She waved and directed us inside a dark, dank room where fans coughed and whirred, sending dust particles up our noses. Jenny let out an *achoo* that Grandma Bernice responded to with an even more twisted grimace.

Like we were in the musical *Cats*—which my parents took us to last year, giving me nightmares ever since—Grandma Bernice's feline brood made their entrance like they were fighting to be the star of the next Jellicle Ball. A fat orange tabby rolled around and showed off its stomach. An uppity white one curled against my leg and gave it a shock. A black-and-white shot one foot in the air and proceeded to lick itself clean. A Siamese followed suit by licking itself even harder.

"Pussies," Grandma Bernice said, causing Jenny to snicker as all the cats took in their new roommates.

"Ma, open some shades," Mom said, as she pulled up the shades and the yellow eyes of the cats disappeared in the light. They hissed at the sun like vampires and darted into the other room.

"It's just early for guests," Grandma Bernice said. "Let me get myself presentable."

She vanished into the bathroom as we reconvened in her kitchen. A floral Formica table and chairs made for a child. The soup smell the strongest. I opened the cabinets to find only egg matzo.

"Yuck," I said, closing the cabinets and opening the refrigerator. I was thirsty as ever. Sure enough, I found a pitcher of cold Nescafe and poured out glasses for everyone.

"We can still make a run for it," Barry said, peering through the blinds at the street outside. Two Grandma Bernice lookalikes power walking away.

"Can I shower?" Steph said, pinching her split ends. "The thought of using shampoo with hot water..."

"Mmmm," Mom said, like we'd been stranded on a deserted island for months. "Nana's in her bathroom, so use the hallway one."

"I never need to shower," Jenny boasted.

"We know," Steph said, hitting her on the back of the head as she skipped off.

"Jenny, why don't you walk Johnny Cash?" Barry asked.

Johnny Cash had taken to mewling in the middle of the linoleum floor, a trickle of pee left in his wake.

"C'mon," Jenny said, tapping her thigh. She grabbed the leash and left with the dog.

"Not too far," Mom yelled, as the front door slammed.

Grandma Bernice emerged in the foyer looking like she'd dipped her face in even more makeup, the oldest living hooker. Her wig crooked until she fixed it by pinching it down, the curlers removed. She wore a black top that looked made out of felt and a black skirt with stockings and hard shoes, dressed for the coal mines.

"Bernice, aren't you hot?" Barry asked.

"Feh, it's good to be hot," she replied. "You want me to be cold and catch my death?"

"It's actually refreshing," Mom said, always trying to keep everything nicey nice between Barry and Grandma Bernice. "We had our heat turned off back...home."

She struggled with the last word, knowing that *home* didn't exist for us anymore. A twinge of regret. This would be the closest thing we had to a home now, a hot-as-Hades-abode with licking cats aplenty.

"*A bi gezunt*, as long as you're healthy," Grandma Bernice said. "Me, I have Raynaud's disease, blood doesn't go to the tips of my fingers. Look," she said, displaying her fingernails. "They're white and blue, the color of the Israeli flag. That was a joke, Barry."

Barry gave a solid bark of a laugh.

"Still got it, Bernice."

"Let me see my *boychick*," she said, directing her glasses to the tip of her nose. "So thin. He has no *tuchus*." She pointed to my backside and gave it a gruesome pinch. "You need to feed the boy!"

"Ma, we do."

"You're far from a *berryer*. Very little homemaking skills. I failed you at that. The last roast you made tasted like a leather suitcase."

"That is true, Judith," Barry said.

"Such a *punum*," Grandma Bernice said, pinching Barry on the cheek and leaving it reddened. "But not a lot else."

We followed her out of the kitchen into the living area where couches and chairs were covered in plastic wrap and squeaked when you sat on them. Steph danced out of the shower in a towel up to her boobs and came over to kiss Grandma Bernice on the cheek.

"Hi, Nana."

"This one," Grandma Bernice said, and then erupted into a coughing fit. "Comes bouncing in like a *nafka*."

"What's that?" Steph asked.

"Snow-white breasts out for show," Grandma Bernice said. "I have neighbors!"

Steph retreated back to the kitchen.

"Ma, you can't call our daughter a whore."

"Feh, she'll be knocked up within the year, I guarantee. Hashem whispered it to me in my sleep."

She lay back in her Barcalounger and, kicked up her feet. Two cats fought to be the one to nestle in her lap. She welcomed each by kissing them on the nose.

Jenny returned with Johnny Cash, causing the cats to fly off Grandma Bernice, likely smushing her groin area. She responded with a tired moan.

"Oh no, not a mutt," she said. "He'll have to stay in that RV you clanged up in."

Jenny growled in contempt.

"Jenny, could you take the dog out?" Barry said, rubbing his eyes. I bet he could use a bump like I'd had. It definitely made Grandma Bernice easier to absorb at such an early hour.

Jenny continued growling, dragging Johnny Cash out of the condo. We could still hear her outside.

"Ma, be a little kinder to the kids," Mom said, as Grandma Bernice waved her away. "They've been through a lot."

"Feh, so they had to move from New Jersey. Did they lose their husband to pancreatic cancer? Did they come from the old country with nothing but a pair of stockings and dried beef in their suitcase? Or get whooping cough that almost put them in the ground—God bless Hashem for saving me."

"Just mind yourself," Barry said, still rubbing the hell out of his eyes. Driving through the night couldn't have been easy. Nor agreeing to stop in Boca and deal with his monster-in-law.

"You're careless," Grandma Bernice said, almost spitting in his direction. "No savings, no nothing. I know where all your money goes. On *narrishkeit*, foolishness. Pastel suits like on TV and flashy cars. Pish. In my time, we saved for inevitable tragedies. We prepared."

"Well, they cracked the mold when they made you, Bernice," Barry said, squeezing his fist.

"All right," Mom declared. "Barry needs his nap. He's been driving through the night."

"Your bedroom is made up," Grandma Bernice said, not even deigning them with a look.

Mom lifted Barry from his chair and directed him down the hallway with his arm around her neck like he was a wounded soldier.

Now I was left alone with Grandma Bernice, staring each other down like mortal adversaries.

"Too, too thin," she chided, with a *tsk tsk*. "Bubbe will fatten you up."

"Okay, where's my room?"

She tittered. "The girls will be sharing the third bedroom." She glanced at the plastic couch. "You'll have the couch."

Nothing much changing since the RV. I'd almost rather hole up with Johnny Cash in there.

"And don't scratch the plastic," she said, with a blue-and-white finger in my face.

19

Tension in the air from the get-go. Mom cordoned off in a room with Grandma Bernice admonishing Barry while he napped. Steph and Jenny were getting their bedroom ready, but since I didn't have a room to set up, all I could do was listen while practicing spinning a basketball on my finger like a Harlem Globetrotter.

"He's a *fershtinkiner*," Grandma Bernice said. "Always was. Eyes of a jeweler."

"I don't even know what that means. And can you lower your voice?"

"In my own house? The nerve. I'll talk as loud as I want. I won't be on this Earth much longer and then you'll miss my voice."

"Barry was a good provider all these years."

"I lost you at sixteen. You went in the opposite direction of God, just at the time you needed him most."

"I still believe in God."

"Do you? You have a funny way of showing it. A daughter in flimsy clothing—who you said was dating a *goy*—"

"It's only a teenage romance."

"Your father and I met when we were sixteen and had thirty years of marriage before Hashem took him."

I stared at an enormous photograph of my Grandpa Herb, a man I never met, who'd been born in the late eighteen-hundreds. Cars hadn't even been invented when he was alive. It was a later photograph, Herb not an old man but still looking old. A close-up of his bulbous nose with nose hairs peeking through. Bushy eyebrows that needed to be combed and no hair on the top of his head. A smile that appeared as if he was concealing a fart. One of the many pictures on the walls, dedicated to this fine prince.

"He will lead you into sin," Grandma Bernice said.

"What does that even mean, Ma?"

"Always has. You think I don't know what he shoves up his nose. And has he been faithful?"

"Yes, Ma, despite any other faults, Barry is unequivocally devoted to me."

"*Gelt*, that's what that man's devoted to. He thinks in dollar signs."

"Good, then we should be back on our feet and out of your hair soon."

Mom bolted out of Grandma Bernice's bedroom, roaring past me, too angry to care that I was eavesdropping. I found her in the kitchen at the Formica table smoking a cigarette and not blowing the smoke out of the window.

"I don't care if she smells it," Mom said.

"She likes to push your buttons."

I made eyes at the pack of cigarettes, and she shrugged. I slipped one out of the pack before she might change her mind.

"Oh, so now you smoke?" she asked, with a laugh that turned maudlin. "I'm losing it."

I gave her shoulder a squeeze.

"You're a better mother than your mother," I said. "Think of it that way."

"Have you checked the news?" she asked.

"No."

I got up, and turned on Grandma Bernice's tiny white TV on the counter. Repositioning the antennae until a signal came through. *The Young and the Restless* was on. My go-to when I was sick. Nina and Cricket in a fight over Nina's bad boyfriend. I didn't see this ending well. I switched over to the local news. Our escapades in Virginia certainly wouldn't make that.

"I think we're in the clear," I said.

"Until we rob the next bank," Mom replied.

She ashed out the cigarette in a glass with a chipped decal, then got up to run the cigarette under the faucet and toss it in the disposal.

"Why don't you take your sisters and go swimming? It's depressing cooped up in here on such a nice day."

"You could join us?"

She tousled my hair.

"And leave your father alone with Beelzebub? I'm not that cruel."

* * *

"Cannonball!" I yelled, as I dove into the pool, splashing both my sisters. Jenny had brought out Seymour, combing his hair on a lounge chair and feeding herself Starbursts. Steph had changed into a two-piece bathing suit, likely in the hopes that the pool boy might return. We drank Pineapple Crush and brought out a tiny stereo tuned to the radio. The condo was a ghost town, all the kids at school, the adults probably praying at temple.

"How's Kent?" I asked, trying to be a decent brother for once.

Steph painted her toenails. "I haven't called him since we got here."

"Why not?"

"Remove yourself from my ass, Aaron. It's none of your beeswax."

"Trouble in paradise?"

"Distance is *not* making the heart grow fonder..."

She stopped in midsentence because the pool boy had emerged from a tool shed with a leaf blower. At a high decibel, he cleaned the area as Steph got her toenails just right. He apologized when he got closer to us because it was impossible to have a conversation over the noise.

"This thing is the worst," he said, tossing the locks of hair out of his eyes.

"What was that?" Steph asked, posing on her lounge chair.

"There's not many leaves to blow either."

"Have a cool drink," Steph said, passing over her Crush.

He took a swig, wiped his lips with the back of his hand.

"Have you moved in?" he asked. "You're not typical tenants. Like, you don't seem Orthodox."

"It's our Grandma," Steph said, rolling her eyes. "We're staying with her."

"Troy," he said, shaking Steph's hand and nodding at me. "I'm not Orthodox either. Not even Jewish, but they pay good, and I've been taking some time off after graduating and doing odd jobs before I decide if I want to go to college. I live in Delray Beach."

"We're from New Jersey," Jenny shouted.

"And who's that you got?" Troy asked, pointing at Seymour.

"None of your fucking business, Ken doll," Jenny yelled back, and whispered something in Seymour's furry ear.

"I'm Steph and that's Aaron."

Smart Steph redirecting him from Jenny's crazy. I gave a cool wave.

"Yeah, it's an easy job because no one really uses the pool. Sometimes a few of the older ladies wade early in the morning, but that's about it. I upkeep the area around the condos."

"Wow," Steph said. "So much responsibility."

I nearly gagged.

Troy looked left and then right, procured a joint from his T-shirt pocket. "Wanna get high?"

He lit the joint, took a puff, and passed the dutchie to Steph, who coughed like a newbie.

"*So* strong," she said, giggling.

"That's the point," Troy replied, lying on a lounge chair and supporting his head with the back of his arm. He wore Umbros and his T-shirt said Super Bowl XIX. "Mr. Brownstone" came on the radio and the whole thing felt like an afterschool special.

"Pass the dutchie to the left," I said to Steph.

"Uh, you're too young."

"Hey lady, I've done coke twice."

The world got silent. A seagull flapping overhead even seemed to stop and listen.

Steph lowered her voice. "When did you do coke?"

"Last night and a few days before. Dad has a stash in the glove compartment."

Steph thrust the joint back at Troy.

"That's so not okay," she said, really softly.

"Sounds like a pretty rad family," Troy said.

"Does Dad know?" Steph asked, her eyebrows angry lightning bolts.

"No, of course not. But, in the grand scheme of bad things we've done..."

"Aaron, you are a child, like you're twelve years old."

She was shaking.

"Hey babe, chill. Your brother's okay," Troy said. "Right, bro?"

"I'm fine," I said, leaping up. "I'm holding this family together, by the way. You all should be kissing my feet."

I did another cannonball, the pool water stinging my eyes. I sat at the bottom of the turquoise waters, thinking I'd hang there for a while. When I resurfaced, Steph and Troy were gone.

"Where'd they go?" I asked Jenny.

"Probably to swallow each other's tongues."

Sure enough, I found them around back swapping spit. He cupped her chin his hands, his tongue poking into her cheek. She hummed softly. "Mr. Brownstone" had changed to Madonna's "Lucky Star" and I could hear it faintly through the breeze.

Steph pulled away from Troy.

"God, Aaron, creepy much?" she said. "Stop staring."

She gave me a hard push and I almost fell over.

"Hey, hey," Troy said, jumping between us. "Your sister said you've been cooped up in an RV. I'm picking up my little sis at the bakery in town, she's about your age. Why don't you come along?"

"Ugh, can I get a minute off from him?" Steph asked.

"There's a park they can play in." He smirked. "And then we can play too."

"Fine, we won't even tell Mom and Dad we left," Steph said. "Let 'em worry." She cupped her hands. "Jenny, let's go get cupcakes."

Jenny raced over before Steph could even finish the sentence.

We headed over in Troy's yellow Pontiac Trans Am. He was the type to steer with only one hand, the other curled around Steph. The remaining half of the joint lodged behind his ear. Scorpions' "Wind of Change" on the radio.

"I'm so into the hair metal bands," he said. "Cinderella, L.A. Guns, Whitesnake, Poison."

"Me too," Steph said, batting her eyes.

"No, you don't, you like Debbie Gibson," I said.

Troy made a face at that. "Too poppy for my taste. A cheese sandwich."

"Yeah, I've been thinking that lately about her too," Steph said.

"Tell that to the shrine you had of her in your old room," I said.

Steph whipped around and knocked me on the head.

"So, you guys have off from school?" Troy asked. "A winter break?"

"Uh, yeah," Steph said. "And we hadn't seen Grandma Bernice in a while. So, here we are."

"Tubular."

We pulled up to a Kosher bakery where young Orthodox girls sat outside wearing blouses up to their neck and heavy skirts down to their knees with white stockings underneath. Hats with pins over what looked like wigs, the hair color not matching their eyebrows. Each of them pushing a baby carriage with a child.

A younger girl around my age with a ponytail ran over. She wore busted sneakers and different sized socks. One went up to her knee, the other sagged over the sneaker. Her T-shirt was pink and faded, the picture of whatever it was flaked off. Short shorts and a Walkman in her hand. She put the headphones around her neck.

"Hey asshole, I've been waiting for, like, forever," she said to Troy.

"This is my sister Heidi."

She gave us all a cool, detached look, then kept talking.

"The Orthos are all giving me stink eyes."

One looked up from her plate of rugelach and did, in fact, give Heidi a stink eye.

"Let's drive," Heidi said.

Wedged in the backseat between Heidi and Jenny (and Seymour), the windows were open, a hot breeze mussing up our hair. Troy played a Poison cassette, "Every Rose Has Its Thorn" pouring from the speakers. My leg touching Heidi's, our skin fusing, my breath trapped in my throat. She stuck a hand out the window, letting it glide, devouring her Ring Pop, her tongue painted grape purple.

"Want one?" she asked, as Bret Michaels belted out the chorus.

She procured another Ring Pop for me, strawberry. Undid the wrapping and tossed it in my lap. I put it on and cheesily clinked hers like we were toasting. Up front, Steph had closed in on Troy, her head on his shoulder as they talked quietly, laughing occasionally. Sun-buzzed Jenny was out like a light, drool escaping from her lips and sticking to Seymour.

"So, you're Troy's sister?" I asked Heidi.

"Yeah, duh."

"I'm Steph's brother."

"Yeah, I get how everyone is connected."

I recalibrated, since this wasn't going smoothly. I had liked girls before, but all of them at my school were so Jersey. It was like they existed in a different world with a fight to see who could have the biggest hair and biggest shoulder pads and loudest cackle. This girl Jackie who Drake said liked me and snapped her gum like a cow chewing cud. For six of the Seven Minutes in Heaven with her, she snapped away and then placed the gum on the back of her hand so we could kiss. I'd practiced on the pillow I called Shelia before, did some nasty things to Shelia mind you, but when the real shebang reared its head, I chickened out. I ducked and weaved from Jackie With the Big Hair, did a roll away out the door. Heidi seemed like the type of girl I'd want to stay trapped with forever.

Part of it was her fuck-all attitude. Maybe that was how they grew them in Florida— full of sarcastic shrugs, a rough edge that only made her sexier. She licked that pop until it was just a plastic nub and shifted as our skin pulled away from one another.

"It tastes really good," I said, indicating my strawberry Ring Pop.

"Do you say everything that comes to your mind?"

"I…"

"I'm kidding, close your mouth before you let in Palmetto bugs. Seriously, they're everywhere here."

Sure enough, when we got back to the pool Heidi pointed out one darting across the pavement. I still had "Every Rose" in my head, imagining myself serenading her.

"See ya," she said, with half a wave before she was back in the car waiting for Troy to finish his goodbyes to Steph.

"You're such a rad girl," Troy said, rubbing Steph's shoulders. "Awesome meeting you. I'll be back tomorrow to dig out more bugs."

"I'll be here sunning."

They swapped more spit, so I turned away. When I looked back, Troy was roaring off with my first love.

Barry stepped outside.

"Where the hell have you all been?" he shouted, hair sticking up in an Einstein 'do. "We need to go case the bank in town. The more time we spend here, the greater chance I'll drown your grandmother."

He whistled for Jenny to come over too.

"C'mon, we'll take your grandma's car. Your mother needs out of that house before she commits matricide too."

20

In Grandma Bernice's shit-brown Nova, we patroled the streets searching for a bank. Like a beacon, one called to us, the sunlight gleaming off its glass doors. Midday and busy, Hassidic men and women going in and out. Some with many children. One carrying a zipped bag that held a *tallit*, the Jewish prayer shawl. I would get one when I turned thirteen at my bar mitzvah, passed down from Barry. Little did I know, I wouldn't be having a bar mitzvah.

"I can't rob that bank," Mom said, fear in her eyes.

"Judith, it's perfect," Barry declared. "It's on the corner of an avenue, we have easy access to a street to get away, which leads directly to an off-ramp—"

"I can't rob our people," she stammered. "It's just—not right."

We parked with the bank in our sights, Steph was tasked to count how many people went in and out in an hour's span. Jenny had been woken up from one nap and was down for another, Seymour curled in her arms.

"Judith—"

"Mom—"

Barry and I said it at the same time, then laughed and gave each other a look like we were in sync. His eyes said, *allow me to do the swaying.*

"Everyone's money is insured, honey," he said. "No one will lose anything."

"But the bank will." She fiddled with a Jewish star around her neck. I'd never noticed it before. I wondered if she had put it on since we arrived. If Grandma Bernice placed it as protection against Barry's ways.

"Who cares about a bank?" Barry said. "They have millions."

"I feel like God won't understand."

"Two minutes," Barry yelled, his glasses going askew on his face. "You've been back with your mother *two minutes,* and she converted you."

Mom got smaller, her voice barely a peep.

"It feels wrong."

"Well, let me break the news to you, we are in Boca Raton, every bank here is owned by Jews with Jewish customers."

Judith went to speak but he stopped her.

"And we're not going anywhere else. We came to your mother's, to scope out a bank that could give us a big score."

I put my hand in Barry's face so he'd stop talking. He did, but seemed taken aback. He used it as an opportunity to fix his glasses.

"Why do you think it's wrong, Mom?" I asked, in the sweetest voice I could muster. One that told her she was being heard. She gave a slight smile.

"We're so few, Aaron," she said, and that smile faded. "We barely exist. Go outside of New York and Florida, big cities, there are no Jews. There are places where we'd be spit on. Your Grandma Bernice has been spit on, in the old country before she came over as World War Two was brewing. A baker. The man across the street from the one she used to go to. After that bakery closed, she had no choice. But a Jew in his store? He would not let that happen."

Barry pinched his nose. "I'm sorry that happened to Bernice a thousand years ago, but what does that have to do with this bank now?"

"Why should we give any ammunition?"

"To who? That argument doesn't make any sense, Judith. I'd understand it more for a Christian run bank."

"It's what I've been thinking recently." She took Barry's hands. "You heard them on the news, that old lady, she hated us because we're Jews."

Barry went to speak, but she interrupted him this time.

"But I get it, they'll hate us whether or not we rob them. It's a lost cause.

The Orthodox, they already think us doomed. We're not devoting our lives to God and it sickens them. That a Jew could have the chance to follow the traditional beliefs, but strayed."

"Your mother got in your head. This has nothing to do with you straying from her cult-like mentality."

"I am *not* judging what the religion means to her. When my father died, it spoke to her, it comforted her. There's nothing wrong with that."

"I'm still not seeing the connection."

"She'll never forgive me, Barry." Mom nodded as if this revelation hit her sharply; she even winced. "She never has, but this will be the final nail. And I don't know if I can live with that."

"This means you think we'll get caught," Barry said. "Otherwise, she would never find out."

"Seven people," Steph said, spinning around. "Seven people over the last hour."

"Good, Stephie," Barry said, changing his tone. "Keep on it."

I leaned forward from my middle seat in the back, so my head was between them.

"Look, we're not getting caught. Right, Dad? You wouldn't be doing this if you thought we could get caught."

He opened his mouth, but nothing came out. A hard silence that bent and weaved through the air, goosing our flesh.

"Of course we're not getting caught," he said, but it had taken him too long to respond. Steph hadn't noticed, busy counting people, Jenny still napping. But Mom and I felt the absence of an assurance. She swallowed it and let it fester. It bubbled in my own belly as pressure that needed to be released. It was the first time she and I eyed each other since this crazy adventure started, separate from Barry. He and I had plenty of shared glances, winks delineating the men from the women in the family. But Mom and I hadn't shared that yet, not until now.

Hard to remember who broke their gaze first. Who had the stronger desire to remain Barry's number two. Regardless, it should've been her to veer toward reason. She was the parent. I was just the child. The definitive argument until the end of time. After what would happen, I could not be blamed. I didn't know any better. My brain, still developing. Hers formed, firmly understanding right from wrong. She should've held that gaze, ended the whole charade. Not bowed down to him. Not made him into a God because she gave up on her own a long time ago. Barry was not a God, a mere mortal, fallible. Capable of plunging us all into the abyss. A needy man led by the desire for *gelt*, like Grandma Bernice had said. There was no dying child whose life this money would save. There was no justification for our sins and future transgressions.

"They'll never catch us," he said, kissing her worries, the tiny tears that emerged. He held her close, knowing that was her weakness, his arms.

"We're superheroes," he said, and this elicited a laugh. The laugh had to wade through thickets of Mom's snot to be heard, but it came. Mom smoothed over, like always. And I laughed too, because it wasn't hard to turn me to the dark side.

"Now, let's go in and case the joint from this inside," Barry said, in a baby voice, coaxing us into delusion.

21

Steph stayed in the car while the rest of us went inside the bank. She was to remain counting how many people went in and out in the time it would take us to return. We entered under the guise of a family opening a checking account, three hundred dollars in twenties stuffed in an envelope, using the last bit of cash we had before the robberies just in case. Jenny wasn't allowed to bring Seymour, since it would make us memorable. We wanted to be as unmemorable as possible. I was tasked to hold her sweaty hand.

The bank was bigger than our last job. Four tellers separated by glass windows. Three partitioned cubicles to the right with advisers at their computers. A security guard sitting on a fold-out chair at the door, overweight and looking bored. He had a gun in his belt loop, almost hidden by a belly that lopped over his waist. About a dozen customers, half of them in line, a few sitting down with advisers. The advisers all men with yarmulkes. A hallway past the cubicles led to the managers' offices.

We signed our names and waited to be called. Next to us sat an Orthodox man in a very heavy overcoat. He had a long gray beard that held crumbs from his last meal. Dandruff spilled from under his black hat. He winced every time he shifted in place. He eyed us through his thick glasses. We definitely stood out. Barry and I not wearing yarmulkes, Jenny in shorts, Mom showing off her bare arms. You could tell he wasn't pleased. He got called before us and his knees cracked as he stood. In his hand, a crumpled check.

"He smells like pudding," Jenny said, louder than she should have. If he heard her, he chose to ignore it.

"The security guard doesn't seem like a problem at all," Barry said, quietly out of the corner of his mouth. "Doughy and listless."

"Hmmm," Mom said, as if she had checked out completely.

"Four tellers," he said, pointing out each one. "We make them empty their registers and then it's crucial they come out from behind the glass. Each of them has a button under the counter that spells out our doom."

"What about the yarmulkes working at the cubicles?" I asked.

"First, Judith, you'll disarm the guard," Barry said. "Make him lie down on the floor. Once that porker goes down, he'll have a hard time getting back up. I'll go for the tellers. Aaron, you get the yarmulkes to come out of their cubicles."

"What about me?" Jenny asked.

"There's the managers to think about too." He peered down the darkness of the hallway. "Hard to say how many other offices. I'm guessing two, maximum. No way there's more than two."

Jenny looked up with pleading eyes, waiting for her defined role.

"Once I corral the tellers, Jenny, you could monitor them while I go after the managers."

"What if one of the managers rings the alarm in the meantime?" I asked.

Barry rubbed the burgeoning stubble on his chin.

"A pickle certainly. We could really use another member to the Gimmel-man gang."

"I was thinking the same thing," I said, enjoying our telepathy.

"Right? Someone to go after the managers and bring them out front. Especially since the safe is what we really care about."

He turned to me, pupils going wide behind his glasses.

"Aaron, what if you bring the managers out with your fake gun?"

Mom swallowed hard. I could see the veins in her neck strain.

"What is it, Judith?" Barry asked.

"What if one of the managers think it's a real gun?"

"No one would shoot a child."

"You heard those people from the last bank on the news, they thought Aaron and Jenny were little people," Mom said.

"Okay, I'll go after the manager. Judith, you disarm the security guard. Aaron, you take care of the tellers, and Judith, you take care of the yarmulkes."

"What about me?" Jenny asked, raising her voice. We'd been whispering the whole time, but Jenny caused some Orthodox heads to swivel over.

Barry leaned in close to her. "Okay, Jenny, you can take care of the men in the cubicles. Direct them out of their offices, tell them to lie on the floor with their hands behind their backs."

"Gimmelmans?" we heard. It caused a pinch in my gut. Like we were exposed.

It had been one of the advisers in the cubicles. I followed Barry and Mom with my head down like I'd already done something wrong. When we entered his office, there were only three chairs surrounding his desk.

"I can get you another," the guy said, but Mom just sat down and placed Jenny on her lap.

"What can I do for you?" he asked. He wasn't too old but had already gone bald, only a few wisps of hair under the yarmulke.

"We're staying with my mother-in-law," Barry said, taking charge as usual. "I wanted to open an account while we're here."

Barry slid the envelope with three hundred dollars across the table.

"How safe is this bank?" Barry asked, as the pinch in my gut grew sharper.

"Come again?"

"The area...vagrants?" Barry continued.

"Your money is entirely safe here. I can assure you."

I tuned them out. The adviser got the paperwork ready for Barry and Mom to sign. I spent the time counting video cameras. There was one by the entrance, one by the teller windows, and another pointing toward the cubicles, looking directly at me. I couldn't remember which movie, but I had seen one where the robbers sprayed the cameras with spray paint in a bank heist. I knew Barry would appreciate that intel. After I finished traveling off into space, the papers had been filled out and Mom was lifting Jenny off her lap and getting ready to leave.

"Thank you for your time," Barry said, shaking the man's hand. He tapped me on the shoulder as a signal to go. Jenny scooted to the front, but I felt dizzy as we passed the security guard. He gummed his lip, scrutinizing me with tiny, beady eyes. I nearly took a dump in my shorts as I flew out the doors into the hot Florida sun.

Back in the car, Barry was going over the lay of the bank with Steph, but Mom was super quiet.

"I want to go to temple," she finally said, once we started driving.

"What?" Barry asked.

"Tonight, for Friday night services with Nana," she said.

"Have at it," Barry said.

"*All* of us," she continued, more forceful than I'd seen her be thus far. "We need to talk to God about what we're doing. I need a sign to know that it's okay."

"What kind of sign do you expect?" Barry asked.

She didn't respond. For was there really an answer? Did she need to go through these motions so she could talk herself into what we were doing? Or was she more concerned that even if Hashem gave her a warning sign, our barreling train had long left the station and there was no chance of pulling the brake.

22

Grandma Bernice had a conniption over what we would wear to *shul* that evening. My T-shirt from the Young People's Day Camp with a smiley face and short-shorts with knee socks wouldn't cut it. She found an old suit of Grandpa Herb's that I, surprisingly, didn't swim in too much. It did, however, smell like moth balls and old booze. She literally had to blow dust off a striped tie. My feet did swim in Herb's shoes, and I looked like I'd been zapped by a shrinking laser while my shoes stayed the same. Being a tiny old woman, Grandma Bernice found a dress of hers that Jenny could wear while Steph borrowed one of Mom's. Barry was given Herb's duds too.

We walked to temple. Florida better at night. While still hot and humid there was at least a relieving breeze. Because I was in a heavy wool suit, I remained as hot as before, but it would've been unmanageable during the day.

"The men and the woman are separated," Grandma Bernice said. "A *mechitza* divides us."

"Why?" Jenny asked, scrunching up her nose.

"Because it means division! Women should be so lucky we're allowed inside to pray."

Of course, Steph had an opinion about this.

"This takes the women's movement back a hundred years," she said. "What did we burn our bras for?"

She was looking at Mom for support.

"Stephie, be respectful," Mom said, off in another world. I wondered if Mom was on something. She was set to have a heart-to-heart with God and would *not* lose that focus.

"Don't you want a break from me?" Barry asked, giving Steph a side hug.

"Yes. You're right, I do."

Upon entering, everyone seemed to be a thousand years old. The room was separated by a white partition with only tiny slits to see through. The women on one side, men on the other. Women with wigs, mournfully praying, not looking up from their hands. The men boisterous, praying loudly, huddling together and bowing up and down. Barry and I broke off from the ladies and found a spot in the back. He looked at his watch.

"Gonna be a long night," he said, to the watch.

Through the tiny slits I could see the women in my family take their spot. Grandma Bernice nodded to a few of her friends, picked up a prayer book while Jenny picked her nose, digging hard for gold. Mom didn't flinch, just let Jenny pick away. Finally, Steph smacked Jenny on the back of her head, and Jenny wrenched out a dangling booger, leaving it on the divider.

Everything was in Hebrew. Men ran the show. The women dutifully stayed in their place while the men ranted and raved, getting called up, huddling together over the Torahs, chanting and speaking so rapidly you would've thought they'd been fast-forwarded by a remote control. Barry closed his eyes and leaned his head against the divider. I knew he wasn't here to hear anything from God. He'd given up listening long ago. He always said his parents did as well. I guess the concentration camp had caused them to lose faith. Some might come out of that with a renewed faith because they survived, but I was more in line with my dead grandparents' feelings. I would be super pissed at God to put me through something like that. Just the idea of a person like Hitler alone makes me suspect that God even exists. How could a god create such a monster? It didn't make any sense.

Through the slits, I saw Mom with her head down moving her lips. At the time, I knew she was asking for God's blessing. It was crazy to think He would listen, what with a war going on in Iran and Iraq that left over a million dead. But sure, Judith's problems should take center stage. Anyway,

I would learn later on what she was asking of Him.

She had been too exhilarated to feel guilty about our last bank jobs or the liquor stores. Barry had the kind of power to sweep you up into whatever he was excited about, and I didn't know this at the time, but their marriage had been going through a strain. Ultimately, they had an infatuation with one another, which seems great on paper, but in reality—not so much. As hard as it might be for me to say this—remove sex from their relationship and they didn't have much in common. In fact, Barry worked such crazy hours on top of his commute that my parents rarely spent time together. They barely did "couples' things" beyond work events he was required to bring her to. She had a spate of friends in the area, ladies-who-lunch pals, that she told herself she actually enjoyed, but Mom was very much alone. Us kids away at school all day and now we were all old enough to have a ton of after-school activities. Beyond lunch and shopping, what did Mom really do all day? I never thought about it, being a kid and seeing the world with tunnel vision, but her days were rather sad. A big house to bat around in and Barry rarely home before nine or ten at night, usually so tired he ate a heated-up meal, watched Johnny Carson, and went to bed. She didn't even cook. She had no passions. So here, this opportunity came along where she was a part of something, a contributor. Who could knock her for that?

So, this was a sliver of the dialogue she was having with God. Explaining the situation first, in case He hadn't been paying attention. Now came the hard part. She never thought twice about robbing Christians, she'd made that perfectly clear. Why should Jews be any different? Here were the questions she came up with:

1. Jews had been through so much adversity for thousands of years. How could she live with herself by adding to it?
2. The Hassidic community already looked down on her. Would robbing one of their banks cause them to hate regular Jews even more?
3. While Hashem may not have been paying attention to the Christian bank, He would *definitely* be focused on a Jewish one. So, would it be like stealing from Him, in a sense?

Unless... the Gimmelmans had been led down this path—by Hashem!—to this bank in

Boca Raton. All of our own trials and tribulations to be rewarded. Hashem understood our pain and suffering, the tragedy of the market collapse, and offered up this guiding light as a means to pull us up by our bootstraps.

She only needed a sign.

Through the slits, I did see her look upwards. The expression on her face muted until it blossomed. Not a smile, for that would have stuck out, the congregation praying around her very serious and somber. She seemed relieved, as if she'd been waiting for news she finally received. I'd later learn that there'd been an air conditioning vent—thank Hashem these Jews used air-conditioning unlike Grandma Bernice—and the vent had been slightly broken and fixed with duct tape. The end of a piece of tape hung down, getting blown from the exhaust, and to Mom, looked like it was waving at her, even more like beckoning her, telling her that no matter what she would still be welcome in *shul* under God's eyes.

"Hashem forgives me," she would say to me, when she was ready to reveal this life-altering revelation. By then, she had become as religious as Grandma Bernice, mostly as a way to atone.

I did not have a revelation while in *shul*. Barry was snoring and I nudged him awake only for him to fall right back under. I didn't care whether the banks were Christian or Jewish, Muslim or Mormon. Each presented a break for us. So, I used that time to meditate and get into robber mode. Our upcoming act was like a dance, a synchronized choreography where one wrong move spelled disaster. We would be victorious, we would move on from Florida, but then I thought of Heidi.

After dealing with disastrous girls from Noo Joisey my whole life, I'd never been as interested in a girl as with Heidi. That smart sass. It made my nether regions stir, in temple nonetheless. And sure enough, I began saluting in *shul* surrounded by old Orthodox men. I prayed for my boner to go down, but it rose even stronger, a full tent in Grandpa Herb's suit. Barry woke with a snort, eyed it, and then gave me a strange look.

"Might want to calm it down, bud," he said.

I crossed my leg over the boner in an attempt to mask its forcefulness, but that hurt so I just shifted to the side, exposing the tent to a man so old he looked as if he could be blown to dust. I tried to think of anything but Heidi, but unfortunately, she was locked in.

Dead babies, dead babies, dead babies, I told myself, working my brain to imagine the worst possible thing. A baby impaled by a spear right through its eye. A tiny coffin. I looked up and it seemed like every Ortho in the room was scrutinizing me, judging this reform Jew mucking up their holy prayers.

"Excuse me," I said, to no one in particular. I pigeon-toe walked out of the room, booking it toward the bathroom. Inside was thankfully empty. I went into a stall, balled up some toilet tissue and came for the first time to Heidi on my mind, with the congregation outside breaking into song and reverberating through the walls. Part of me thought that nothing could be worse than jerking off in the bathroom of an Orthodox *shul*. From here on I'd no longer toe the line between right and wrong, the devil caught hold and managed to corrupt.

There'd be much more corrupting from here on out.

The devil was just getting started with me.

23

Steph had plans with Troy after services. She let this slip on the way back, forcing Grandma Bernice to have another conniption fit. The woman basically only existed in different levels of shrill. She clutched her purse so hard her knuckles turned white.

"After holy services, you are going on a date?" Grandma Bernice squawked.

Steph twisted a lock of hair, let it bounce. "Yeah, with the pool boy."

"That *goy*? What-what-what?" Grandma Bernice nearly fell to her knees. "Hashem, take me now. There's no reason to go on."

"Ma, it's fine," my mom said, with a renewed spirit. Barry could tell. They walked closer to one another, the electricity sparking between.

"A *shanda*," Grandma Bernice said, as if she was ready to spit. And then she kept saying it over and over.

"I'm gonna play with the cats," Jenny said, rubbing her hands together and slipping into the condo before we could realize that meant doom for Grandma's "pussies."

"I give up," Grandma Bernice cried, and followed Jenny inside.

Barry and Mom had put their hands in the backs of each other's pockets.

"I love you, Bear," Mom said, her head on his shoulder.

"Hey Jude," he said, and started singing the Beatles song through a wide smile.

"So, you're seeing Troy again?" I asked Steph, batting my eyelashes to

118

mock her.

"You're coming too," she said. "He has to watch his little sister."

"O...kay," I said, thinking of the wad of toilet paper getting flushed down the temple's toilet where I professed my love.

After we changed back to normal people attire, we waited for Troy's car to pull up. When it did, he rolled down the window so Steph could lean in and they could make out. He practically swallowed her face. Getting in the back with Heidi, she barely looked at me.

"Hey," I said.

"Yeah. Hey."

"What you got there?" I asked, since the car was dark, and she had cards in her hands.

"Garbage Pail Kids," she said, and showed me one named Adam Bomb of a baby-faced kid whose head was exploding in a mushroom cloud. I could relate.

"Yeah, cool I know those."

"I like fucked-up shit," she said.

"Who doesn't?"

Steph finally got in and swiveled around. "So, this is the plan. We're going to a drive-in movie, they actually have those here. You two can watch from the top of the car."

"Why the top?" I asked.

"Because we'll be getting it on inside," Troy said, winking through the rearview mirror.

"If you're lucky," Steph said, swatting him playfully.

The movie was *Gremlins.* I'd seen it before and loved it, so I was cool with seeing it again. I knew the parts when the Gremlins turned bad could be scary, and I told myself to be there for Heidi if she needed me. Barry had given me some cash so I bought Heidi Sno-Caps and Sour Patch Kids and a small tub of popcorn we could share. We climbed on the roof of the car and could hear Steph and Troy bumping uglies below with an "oh yeah, oh yeah," moaning from them both through the crack in the window.

The moon was almost full, a perfect backdrop to my first date, not just with Heidi but with any girl. I situated the popcorn between us so our hands could have a buttery meeting.

"I hate popcorn," she said. "The kernels always get stuck in my teeth."

"Yeah, me too." I tossed the popcorn over the side.

"That was actually pretty rad," she said, and I caught her first sorta smile.

"I will eat those Sno-Caps, though," she said.

I passed them over and she munched as the movie started with the little old shop in Chinatown and the old Chinese man with a translucent eye. The father, finding Gizmo and buying him as a gift.

"Gizmo looks like my ex-boyfriend," Heidi said.

"Ex-boyfriend?" I gulped. How could she already have *ex* boyfriends?

"He had these big eyes and was fuzzy all over."

"And you couldn't get water on him."

"That was funny." She took off her bracelet and snapped it against her arm as it coiled back around.

"I heard a kid died from one of those, the metal fell out and sliced his wrists," I said.

"You are a morbid fucker, aren't you?"

"Uhh..."

"Don't worry, I like, deface tombstones and stuff. I'm as morbid as they come. Happens when your parents die."

She said this staring at the moon, as if it was nothing.

"You don't have parents?"

"Car accident," she said, reaching for the Sour Patch Kids. "Like, I was really little. Troy remembers them. I have, like, hazy images. So, yeah, morbid."

I was aware of my beating heart, afraid to say the wrong thing.

"Who do you live with?"

"Grandfather, hence being in Boca. He's... I mean, he's really old and doesn't leave his TV chair very much. But it beats a foster home and Troy looks after me. He's... I mean, he's like mental, but he's not so bad."

"I can't imagine not having parents," I said, which I knew was exactly the wrong thing to say. "I'm sorry, I—"

"No one knows what to say. Like, it's awkward. I usually like getting it out of the way as soon as possible and moving on. Hi, I'm Heidi, I have dead parents. I should just wear a name tag. So, what's your story?"

"Uh... I dunno. We're visiting my grandma."

"Yeah, I got that."

"My dad lost all his money in the stock market, and they took our house so we're down here while we figure out our next step."

"Didn't expect that."

"Neither did we."

We felt a foot banging against the ceiling, bouncing us.

"Looks like the passion is ramping up," Heidi said, rolling her eyes.

"Can I have some Sour Patch Kids too?" I asked, and we touched fingers as she passed them over.

I will kiss this girl. Maybe not tonight, but before our time in Florida ends. I will know what a kiss from Heidi is like.

I inched a little closer and we stayed that way for the rest of the movie, our bodies lightly touching. Her breathing going heavy at the scary scenes, and me having the courage to reach over and hold her hand.

* * *

When we got back to Grandma Bernice's condo, Barry was outside in one of the lounge chairs by the pool. He was wearing Herb's old slippers with a bathrobe, not a great look.

"What the hell is Dad doing?" Steph asked, putting her face in her hands.

Barry shot up as we approached, pivoting from foot-to-foot. He was jittery, rubbing his nose, likely from a line up there.

I turned to Heidi before Barry's inevitable onslaught.

"I had a great time."

She'd been looking out of the window. "Yeah, me too," she said, not averting her gaze.

"Maybe another movie sometime?"

"Maybe."

One of her shoulders shrugged. She seemed sad. I wondered if it had to do with her parents. If she forgot about them most of the time and then suddenly a memory snuck up. It was too dark to tell if she was crying. When we held hands at the movie it had been brief, sweaty—I counted the seconds. Made sure to do it with Mississippis, as if that could draw out the time even longer. She had painted her fingernails, but they were chipped like a little girl's. After she pulled her hand away from mine, she chewed on them like they were a saving grace.

"Bye," I said, racing out to avoid any more awkwardness.

Barry grabbed me by the collar.

"Hold on," he said. "I need you to stay."

He patted the hood of the car and stuck his head through the window.

"Want to talk to you for a minute, son," he said, while Troy remained looking cool. This wasn't the first time a girl's dad wanted to have a "talk."

Steph slinked out of the car, her face burning red.

"I'm *so* embarrassed," she hissed at Barry, before running inside.

Troy turned back to Heidi. "I'm gonna leave the radio on for you."

Heidi shrugged her other shoulder.

Troy turned it on, "Here I Go" by Whitesnake cutting through the night. When he got out and closed the door, only the hum of it could still be heard.

"Yeah, Pops," he said, flipping back his hair.

Barry beckoned him away from the car and we reconvened by the pool.

"Your daughter's a cool girl," Troy said, making sure not to show any sweat. "I've been treating her well, swear."

"I don't care about that," Barry said, and Troy's eyes went wide. "I mean, obviously I care about my daughter—lemme explain."

He pointed for Troy to sit and paced back and forth.

"What kind of man are you, son?"

"Man?"

"I mean, morals and such."

"Dad?" I asked, trying to save him because it seemed he was coked out of his gourd.

"I told you, I'm treating your daughter well."

"You eighteen?" Barry asked.

"Yeah, but just," Troy said. "Steph's sixteen. Is that what this is about?"

"It has nothing to do with Stephie," Barry said, exasperated. "Aaron, explain to him what we do."

"Uhh..."

"Go on, lay it all out there."

"Ev-*ery*-thing?"

"Ever break the law, son?" Barry asked, getting in Troy's face. We were standing over him now, watching him squirm. I could see an element of his put-on cool evaporating. He reached into his front pocket, pulled out a pack of cigarettes, lit one up.

"Old man, I'm not sure what you're getting at," Troy said, inhaling hard.

"What if I said I had a job for you?" Barry asked.

"Dad," I said again, yanking at his bathrobe but he didn't budge.

He swatted me away. "No, no, Aaron, this is good, trust me."

Troy flipped his hair back. "What kind of job?"

"There you go," Barry said, shaking his shoulder. "Now we're cooking. A marvelous opportunity." He lowered his voice. "What's your situation at home?"

Troy told him about his grandfather who took care of them but basically sat in his TV chair all day, his parents who died.

"You want out of Boca, don't you?" Barry asked.

Troy exhaled through his nostrils and gave a nod.

"Then I'm your fucking golden ticket."

Barry launched into a diatribe about how we wound up in Florida starting with the stock market crash, then me robbing a convenience store, the two liquor stores he and Mom hit, and finally, our pièce de résistance, the bank in Virginia.

"No fucking way," Troy said, shaking his head in disbelief.

"Way," Barry answered him. "But here's the sitch, we're one man short to really pull it off on a bigger level. With Steph as driver that only leaves three of us to take care of all of the variables, since little Jenny won't have a gun."

"Of course not," I said, catching his eye that refused to stay focused.

"Right. Of course not. So, we need an extra hired hand with a gun."

Troy took one last puff and put out the cigarette on the heel of his Converse.

"What's my cut?"

"I knew," Barry shouted, a little too loud so I shushed him, "I knew looking at you exactly who you were." He clapped his hands. "You're in, aren't you?"

"I'm listening," Troy said.

"There's six of us, you get one sixth of the cut."

Troy shook his head and started to get up. "One fourth."

"That's highway robbery!"

"I'm supposed to get the same amount as a little fucking girl? Hell no."

This had already unraveled too fast, the idea of a non-Gimmelman joining our gang suspect, even though I knew it was inevitable and first had the idea. How could we trust Troy yet? I barely trusted any of us.

"One fifth," Barry said, extending his hand. "Take it or leave it."

Troy didn't shake. "Leave it."

"Wait, wait, wait," Barry said, scurrying after Troy because he started to walk away. "One fourth, one fourth, but...you gotta get your own gun and afterwards you forget we ever existed. Steph included."

"That's cold, man."

"Can't take the chance."

I wanted to pull Barry aside, but he was too full of fuel to be deterred. Did we really want to give this schmuck a fourth of our take?

"Holy shit," I said, out loud, not meaning to. If Troy broke ties with Steph that would mean I'd have to do the same with Heidi.

Barry and Troy glanced my way, but were too in the heat of an argument to pay me much mind.

"Sure, Pops, you'll never hear from me again."

Barry's white teeth gleamed from the reflection of the moon.

"All you need now is a mask," he said.

I wandered away from them back to where Troy's car was idling. Whitesnake changed to Cinderella's "Don't Know What You Got (Till It's Gone)," the lyrics fusing with my soul's yearnings. How much more time would I have to kiss Heidi before we'd be roaring away in the Gas-Guzzler?

I mimed for her to roll down the window, the music streaming out. She had been crying, her face wet. She rubbed her eyes, made them redder. I burst forth, planting a kiss on her lips. Did she kiss back? Hard to say. I was too overwhelmed by my sudden actions to process. It may have lasted a second, it may have even been minutes. She tasted of cherry Chapstick. When I pulled away, the sky greeted me with a thousand stars, more than I'd ever seen in New Jersey. Twinkling just for us. The song ended and the DJ started talking, a commercial for auto parts. How everyone should get their mufflers checked. This perfect first kiss. We didn't say anything to each other, as I backed away. She seemed less sad. Not quite a smile but no longer a frown. The commercial still blaring. A deal on hub caps too. Two for one. Moshe's Auto Mart. Two twenty-two Northwest 2nd Avenue. Open every day from eight to eight. Refer a family member and get a coupon. For all your automotive needs.

Barry and Troy came back, arms slung around each other's shoulders.

Heidi rolled up the window, frosted from the humidity.

24

We planned the robbery for Monday, since the bank was closed Saturday and Sunday for *Shabbos*. While Grandma Bernice was at morning services, Troy came over so we could fully assign roles. I was hoping he'd bring Heidi, but he showed up solo. Probably better off since I would've been distracted. Mom and Steph had been clued in on him joining, Steph obviously excited, Mom wary. I heard her and Barry arguing while I tried to sleep on the couch in the living area. It was difficult because of the plastic covering that kept cutting into my skin. Mom wanted to keep our gang small, only Gimmelmans, but Barry said we were expanding. That this was a mid-level bank and we'd be taking too much of a risk with one less man. Finally, she agreed, but it sounded like she did because she was tired and wanted to go to bed.

Barry woke up early to draw diagrams of the bank. Since I barely slept, I was up with him. On a big sheet of paper he found, he mapped out the floorplan. I pointed out where I remembered video cameras set up and, mentioned about spraying them with paint. He thought that was a good idea. While we were drawing, Grandma Bernice woke up, shuffling into the living room with her army of cats. She went right to the TV and watched some local Jewish channel, sitting in her Barcalounger with her feet up and a steaming cup of Nescafe. She turned the volume up louder to drown out our voices, which was fine with us.

"Doing a little early morning father-son bonding," Barry said, but

Grandma Bernice didn't ask so she didn't respond either.

Once all the Gimmelmans were awake and Grandma Bernice was gone, Barry corralled us since we only had a few hours before she returned. Steph on the couch with Troy, leaning close. Jenny with Seymour in her lap. Mom passing out fresh Pop Tarts to get our sugar levels going.

"Steph, your job stays the same," Barry said. He had placed the marker behind his ear like a professor and propped up the bank diagram against Grandma Bernice's old piano.

"Can I just say how cool your family is?" Troy said, giggling. He seemed high.

Steph gave him an Eskimo kiss. "You're cool."

"All right, all right," Barry said, waving his hands. It sure hadn't taken Steph long to get over God-boy Kent.

"We know the street where Steph'll be parked is a direct shot to an off-ramp and a highway," Barry continued, gnawing at a Pop Tart.

"Monday morning that street will be dead," Troy said.

"Good," Barry said. "Okay, now we need to maximize our potential. Me, Troy, and your Mom have guns, so we'll take care of the security guard, the tellers, and the managers with offices down the hallway. The managers will be opening the safe, so I will handle them. Troy, you get the tellers to empty the registers, and Judith you'll disarm the security guard like we talked about before. Aaron will make sure the three advisers exit their cubicles without ringing any alarms, and Jenny, you collect wallets and jewelry from the people in line. Does this feel too easy?"

"Too easy?" Mom asked.

"Like is there anything I'm missing?"

"I got a mask," Troy said, pulling one out of his waistline. Elvis Presley.

"Not from Woodstock like the rest of us, but should be okay," Barry said.

"Spraying the cameras?" I asked, glad to contribute.

"Right." Barry whipped out a bag of spray paint cans from under the couch. "Aaron mentioned that to me this morning, so I picked some up. Judith, that'll be your job after you disarm the security guard." He pointed to the three video cameras on the diagram. "These are the ones Aaron noticed during our stakeout, but there may be others."

The only thing he definitely didn't mention was how we'd be breaking ties with Troy after the robbery. Steph would throw a fit, but better she did it once we're on the road with Boca in our rearview.

"What happens if someone causes a problem?" Troy asked. He had his arm around Steph now, pulling her close. He caressed the gun in his inside pocket. Mom's eyes went alert, the realness of the steel overwhelming.

"We're *not* shooting anyone," Barry said. "The guns are only to get them to fall in line."

"What if I'm shot at?" Troy asked.

"Yeah!" Jenny shouted. I almost had forgotten she was even there. "What if I'm shot at?"

"No one's shooting at you," Mom said, joining Jenny on the love seat and hugging her close.

"We heard on the news that they thought we were little people," I said, wanting a real gun. Not this toy bullshit I was forced to pretend with.

"This discussion is over," Mom said. "There's no way in hell I will arm my eight-year-old child."

"What about your twelve-year-old one?" I asked.

Mom made a show of going around and taking everyone's half-eaten Pop Tarts. She gathered them all and dumped them in the trash.

Troy caught my gaze, gave me a look that said, *I got you.* I nodded back, Steve McQueen cool-like.

Barry and Mom started arguing and Jenny joined that fray while Troy rose and blinked at me to follow him into the kitchen. No one noticed we had gone. Well, Steph did, but I didn't care about her. Troy opened the fridge, frowned at the options of food, took down some egg matzo from the cupboards and crunched.

"It tastes like wallpaper."

"Pretty much," Steph said, taking it from his hands and kissing him on the mouth.

"I'll get you a gun," he said, opening more cupboards.

"Really?"

"Oh yeah, easy, man. No sweat. Your parents don't have to know."

"Cool."

I could see Steph wanted to say something, but probably didn't want to be seen as uncool.

"Ever shot a gun before?" he asked.

I shook my head.

"We can do it tomorrow in my backyard."

"Yeah, awesome. Uh...will Heidi be there?"

"Will Heidi be in her own house? Yeah, she will, man."

"It's a double date," Steph said, wrapping her arms around him, swallowing each other's uvulas.

Out the window, I could see Grandma Bernice walking up the stairs.

"Fuck, Grandma Bernice is back," I said, and ran into the living room. "Grandma Bernice is here!"

I got out the last word just as the lock turned and Grandma Bernice shuffled inside. Barry dove for the diagram, quickly folding it up into squares. Mom yanked the garbage from the can and tied it up—the Pop Tarts not being Kosher—while Jenny yanked a cat's tail.

"*Vus Machs Da?*" Grandma Bernice asked, suspicious.

"Nothing's up, Ma. We were playing Pictionary."

"I don't know of this *potchka*."

"How were services, Bernice?" Barry asked.

"Feh, like any day. Praying for one's soul and such."

Troy and Steph came out of the kitchen.

"Oh good, the *goy*," Grandma Bernice said, sarcastic as ever.

"Grandma Bernice, this is Troy," Steph said, as Troy extended his hand.

"Very nice to meet you," he said. "I can see where Steph gets her looks."

Grandma Bernice eyes went to the sky, and she didn't bother to respond.

"I'm soaking my feet in salt."

She shuffled to the bathroom, and we heard her turn on the bath.

"We're all good to go," Barry mouthed, and we all agreed. "Nine a.m."

He jutted out his hand.

"Can I get a silent Whoa Gimmelmans?"

We stuck our hands in the circle and mouthed a cheer.

"Fucking aces," he said, chomping at the air, his teeth sparkling and scary.

A Jack-o'-lantern grin that seemed like it was growing larger and larger, consuming his face.

25

Barry needed out of the condo, so he took Jenny for breakfast while Steph and Troy went off on their own. I was left alone with Mom and Grandma Bernice. I wasn't sure that Grandma Bernice realized anyone except Mom was still there because she bathed with the bathroom door wide open. Mom had gone inside, sitting on the toilet. She must've thought I'd left with everyone else too because they had a deep conversation while I listened from the living room.

"We might be leaving after the weekend," Mom said.

"That was fast."

"This was just a stopover."

"Judy, I don't have the patience to *noodge*. Like knowing whether or not the kids are even in school anymore."

"We took them out of school in Jersey."

"*Oy vey*, and you plan on just driving around?"

"Barry has family in California."

"Oh, so I'm not good enough family. I see."

"Ma—we're in your hair here, I can tell."

"Hand me a towel."

I heard splashing, feet patting against the floor, a drip-drip from Grandma Bernice's body. She used the wall as support as she walked out in a towel, Mom following into the bedroom. The door wide open.

"And what does Barry plan on doing for work?" Grandma Bernice asked, flinging off her towel and giving me a show. I looked away but had the ingrained image of her wrinkled tits seared into my brain.

"He has a plan."

"*Sekhel*, Judy. You need to have common sense. He's a *schmuck*. A *schmuck* of all *schmucks*. A knock-off watch. Gold that turns green. A *fugazi*."

"Ma, where did you learn that word?"

"First time I saw him, hair everywhere with curls like a clown, a young Elliot Gould, I thought—*oy-yoy-yoy*. This *nudnik* she chooses? You could've had a nice doctor, a stable man. Herb was not the best looking of men out there, that's why I chose him. 'He'll be good to me,' I said, yes. It's the good-looking ones you need to worry about, the Barrys of the world, who think they are owed something. Herb, he made money honestly, a tailor, a fine profession especially back then. It's how I learned to survive by sewing after he passed."

"Barry made his money honestly."

"If you say so..."

"Wait, Ma, what are you implying?"

"The house you lived in, the clothes you wore, that's not just from his salary."

"He invested well."

"If you say so..."

"Stop saying that!"

"I've said many *brachots* for him, for your whole family, especially after what I overheard once when he was on the phone."

Mom's voice dropped. "What did you overhear?"

"When I stayed with you. He was talking on that giant phone with the antennae. To a man. Mr. Bianchi. An I-talian."

"What does him being Italian have to do with anything?"

Grandma Bernice wrapped herself in a caftan and then her head in a scarf like a rich cancer patient.

"You know."

She was either winking or something had gotten stuck in her eye.

"Mob," she whispered, as if she was being wiretapped.

Mom let out a chortle. "Ma, that's ridiculous."

"I was *fermisht*. He owed this Mr. Bianchi money. He kept saying, 'I'll have the money for you.' Real panic in his voice."

"Ma, Barry's a stockbroker, it probably had to do with an investment."

"No, no, this man was a *gonif*. Barry was saying, 'Don't do anything rash.'"

Mom pinched the bridge of her nose, a headache forming like usual around Grandma Bernice. "Again, Ma, that could be about an investment."

"When he got off the phone, I asked him if anything was wrong. He acted like it was *gornisht*, nothing, tried to change the subject. Asked how my sewing was going—I think I was making mittens for Jenny, like he would care about that. Your husband's always been a *macher*, scheming with a side hustle."

"Barry has no side hustle."

"Oh really? So, on that same trip, I'm reading your local newspaper and who gets mentioned but a Gianni Bianchi involved in some racketeering conspiracy."

"There must be a million people in Jersey with the last name Bianchi."

"Wake up, Judith, your husband has mob ties!"

This was when Mom walked out of the bedroom in a huff, nearly running into me.

"Oh, Aaron, I thought you had gone—"

Grandma Bernice came charging out. "You can leave him, we'll change the locks, the kids could go to school in Florida."

My ears perked up at that. A wild fantasy entering my mind of being at the same school as Heidi, holding hands in the hallways, making out by our lockers, her watching me play basketball from the bleachers as I landed a jump shot.

"You never gave Barry a shot," Mom said, swiveling around with an accusatory finger in Grandma Bernice's face.

"You weren't yourself when you met him. Your father—God bless him—had just died, I couldn't control you. And he swooped in. He took advantage."

"We fell in love."

"You fell in lust, there's a difference."

"We made three beautiful children."

Grandma Bernice gave a look that said, *The jury's still out on that.*

"The truth is, Ma, you joined this Orthodox cult, and I wasn't good enough for you anymore. Nothing I would've done, save joining myself, would've been sufficient."

Without her makeup on, Grandma Bernice looked like a cadaver. She was speechless, maybe for the first time in her life.

"Dad is the best Dad there is," I said, piping up. Grandma Bernice held onto her heart in shock. She clearly hadn't seen me there. "It's *not* okay for you to talk bad about him."

I felt Mom put her hand on my shoulder and give a light squeeze that told me to continue.

"He wants only the best for us," I continued, as if I was convincing myself. "He goes out of his way to give us everything we want. You're just old and jealous because you have no one."

"You *chaya*, how dare you speak to your grandmother like that."

"That's why you fill your place up with cats," I said, kicking one aside that tried to curl around my leg. "They're the only things that will put up with you."

"Okay, Aaron, thank you," Mom whispered into my ear and gave me a little push away. "Ma," she said, because Grandma Bernice was quivering. For a second, I worried I'd given the woman a heart attack. "Ma, he didn't mean that."

"Yeah, I did."

"Aaron!" Mom said, but I knew she wasn't angry.

"I'm sorry, Grandma Bernice," I said, twisting my toe into the ground.

"In my time, we respected our elders," she said, as Mom led her over to a chair. She took a big gulp of a breath as she sat down. "My meds," she said, pointing to a side table.

"Do you need water?"

Grandma Bernice shook her head and swallowed them whole. Impressive.

"You can't talk like that about a boy's father," Mom said. "Barry's on a pedestal."

"This will not end well."

Mom chuckled. "What do you mean?"

"Your RV excursion, whatever it is you have planned," she hissed, and then spit-up into a tissue curled into her sleeve. "If you don't leave him now..."

"Ma, stop that!"

"You'll have turned your back on God for good," Grandma Bernice said. "That's what I foresee. There'll be no chance of finding Him again."

Mom glanced at me and spun her finger around her ear to indicate that Grandma was crazy.

"Go on, make fun of your *alter kaker* mother. You have the power to save the rest of your family and you still choose lust with that *shlimazel.* Only a tragedy will get you to see I'm right."

"Fine, you can say, 'I told you so' then."

"I don't have to, I'm telling you now."

Mom grabbed my arm and yanked me toward the front door. We could hear Grandma Bernice carrying on about a *meesa machee af deer* that would visit us, which I gleaned was some type of curse. Then she coughed up a pool of phlegm. Outside, Johnny Cash was barking in the RV. Mom lit a cigarette she pulled from her jeans pocket, the pack crumpled. She inhaled like it was the only thing keeping her sane.

"She's wrong," she said, shaking now like Grandma Bernice was earlier.

"I know."

"She deserved what you said to her, even though it wasn't nice."

"I didn't like the way she was talking about Dad."

I made a signal for her to hand me a cigarette. She shrugged like she'd given up and passed one over, lit it hesitantly. We puffed together. She laughed, but it was hollow sounding, as if the laugh was masking something much worse.

"We're not cursed," she said, quietly. I wasn't sure if she was only telling it to herself.

"No, definitely not."

"We're *not*," she said again, and this time I knew it was Hashem she was speaking to.

We waited for a sign from Him, but on a hot Florida day, there wasn't even a breeze, no answer, so we kept smoking down to the filters, and I hugged her hip.

"I think I need to take a walk," she said.

"All right—"

"Myself," she said, giving a slight bow like she was apologizing, backing away and then turning around. I was losing her, she was losing it, the Mom I knew—lost.

In my mind, a big score would bring her back.

Yes, that was all she needed.

26

The next day, Mom took off with Barry early morning. They left in the RV with Johnny Cash; I heard the engine churning and saw a spit of exhaust as it barreled away. For one second, I worried that they wouldn't come back. Free on the road without children bogging them down. But I knew they needed us for the bank job, that they couldn't make it on their own from only knocking off liquor stores. I imagined them high and making love on the side of the road, pretending they were young again. They deserved that momentary fantasy.

As for Steph and me, we had plans to be picked up by Troy and hang out at his grandfather's place. I couldn't leave Jenny alone with Grandma Bernice, who herself had gotten up early and was meeting a few of her cronies for breakfast. Jenny didn't want to get up, so Steph and I pulled her out of bed and propped her up in front of the bathroom mirror to brush her teeth. She got like that sometimes, Jenny's moods. Mom shrugged them off, Barry was always working so he didn't really notice. It was like she didn't want to do anything, just lie there like a blob. We combed her nest of hair and were grabbing a box of egg matzo to munch on when Troy honked the horn outside.

Heidi wasn't in the car, but Jenny was acting so weird it was probably for the best. We had forgotten Seymour, but it was too late now to turn back so she moaned and growled like a stray dog.

"What's wrong with your sister?" Troy asked, fiddling with the radio and settling on "Fast Car."

"What isn't?" Steph snorted.

"I got a fast car," Troy said, singing along and revving up the engine. "You guys ready to do some practice shooting?"

"FUCK YES," Jenny screamed, and we all looked at each other uncomfortably.

Their home was a sad little, yellow-painted thing on a weedy lawn, the foundation tilting when you looked at it for too long. Metal roof and vinyl siding, a deck with a rusted bicycle and two wicker chairs with a wicker table between them holding an overflowing ashtray.

"C'mon," Troy said, waving us inside.

The place was a mess. Old magazines piled in stacks, *Hunter's Quarterly* and *Bait & Tackle* going back to the 70s. The air somehow more humid than outside, another old Floridian who refused to use air conditioning. Fishing rods tossed aside, buckets of hooks, a tangy fish smell.

"Grandpa used to fish," Troy said.

"Troy?" we heard from the TV room. Grandpa in his boxers and black slippers with old socks, a sleeveless undershirt and a can of Schlitz. *Cheers* on the TV with warped reception, a rainbow line cutting through Shelley Long's head.

"These are my friends," Troy said. "We're gonna borrow your guns."

"Eh," was all Grandpa replied. He blinked behind coke-bottle glasses but didn't acknowledge our presence.

A room off to the side held Grandpa's guns encased in a glass cabinet and kept cleaner than the rest of the house.

"He's waiting for the apocalypse," Troy said. "Although, he can barely get out of his chair so I'm not sure who he could shoot."

Heidi popped her head in.

"Hey, shit sandwich," she said to Troy. She wore a bathing suit top and short-shorts, her hair slick.

"Hey, crackhead," he said back to her, and she mimed taking a big hit of crack. Some inside joke between them, I guessed.

"Hey, Heidi," I said, with a goofy wave. I literally thought I must've looked like Goofy doing it.

"Yo," she replied.

"We're going shooting out back," Troy said, and we followed him through a dark hallway that led to a busted screen door and their backyard. Cans had been set up along a moldy fallen tree that seemed like a feast for bacteria.

"It's really not hard," Heidi said, grabbing one of the pistols from Troy. "You aim like you're certain you'll hit the target. Don't second-guess."

She fired once, narrowly missing. She fired again, the bullet pinging off the can.

"See?" she said. "What's this all for anyway?"

I couldn't believe Troy hadn't told her about our planned bank heist. I wondered why. To protect her? No, he didn't seem the type. There had to be some other reason.

"Never can hurt to know how to shoot," Troy said, putting on his charm. Even Heidi seemed to fall for it.

"My turn, my turn," Jenny said, pushing Heidi aside and grabbing the gun.

"Jenny, I don't think—" Steph began.

"I don't remember asking what you thought," Jenny said. "Ever! Just stand aside and look pretty."

Jenny closed one eye and lined up the can. She fired and hit it dead-on, the can zinging off of the tree.

"Holy shit," Troy said, clapping, but somehow, I wasn't surprised.

Jenny blew the smoke from the gun like she was in a Western and passed it over to Steph.

"Your turn, big mouth."

Steph barely grasped the gun and passed it back to Troy like it was a loaded diaper. "I don't want it."

"She doesn't need to know how to shoot," I said, grabbing it from Steph. I wouldn't be shown up by my little sister. The steel cool in my hands, heavier than I expected. When I shot, it had a kick back, the bullet spiraling into the grass. I shot again, missing by miles. Maybe I wasn't cut out for this.

"You suck," Jenny said, and Heidi laughed.

"She got in your head," Heidi said.

Troy had plopped in a plastic chair with Steph on his lap, canoodling.

"Who's gonna take care of the men in the cubicles now, Aaron?" Jenny said and started clucking like a chicken. "Mom and Dad might have to assign new roles?"

"Shut up, Jenny."

"You guys are so weird," Heidi said.

I closed one eye and lined up the shot, feeling the can, willing the bullet to come into contact. *I will hit this target*, I told myself, like I did when I willed myself that I'd kiss Heidi. I pictured her whispering softly into my ear, the sound soothing like listening inside a seashell. I fired and heard a brilliant *ping!* The can flying off the dead tree, Troy hollering.

"That's how you do it," he said, lifting Steph off his lap so he could tousle my hair. "Looks like the Gimmelmans are all crack shots."

We went back inside and ate Keebler Cheese & Sandwich Crackers around a table in their "dining area" that mostly held more magazines. Troy and Steph couldn't keep their hands off of one another and soon migrated into his bedroom. Since we were pulling off the job tomorrow, this could be my last chance with Heidi. I wanted to make the most of it.

She sipped Capri Sun and eyed me.

"What do you guys and my brother have planned?"

I choked on my cheese crackers. "What? Nothing?"

"Jenny, could you give us a moment?" Heidi asked, sweetly petting Jenny's hand.

Jenny stuffed her face with more crackers. "No."

"I heard you like animals. I have a guinea pig in my room—"

"Bye," Jenny said, darting away.

"Kids," Heidi said, throwing up her hands, then she got serious. She grabbed my arm and dug her nails into my wrist.

"Oww."

"Spill it, Aaron."

I managed to yank my arm away. "Nothing, we're not doing nothing."

"That's a lot of negatives. My brother'll do anything to get out of Boca.

But he's got no options. He dropped out of school."

"Who hasn't?"

She got up and slammed her chair into the table.

"Playing with guns, do you think I'm stupid?" Her eye makeup started to run. "I know it's not just for fun."

I bit into my lip and caused it to bleed.

Jenny emerged from Heidi's bedroom with a beige guinea pig trapped in her hands.

"We're going outside," she said, giving a whistle and scurrying out to the backyard.

"She's gonna murder your guinea pig, you know," I said.

"Fuck you."

Heidi tore away and bolted to her room. Slammed the door and turned up music, "Heaven Knows I'm Miserable Now" by The Smiths. I tried knocking.

"Go away, Aaron."

"Let me in, I'll—okay, I'll tell you what's happening."

The door unlocked and she left it open. I went inside. Wall-to-wall carpeting that squished when I stepped. A tiny room with a twin bed shoved against the wall, a desk with books, and posters of Depeche Mode, The Cure. Morrissey watched over her bed with bedroom eyes. She was lying down, hugging her thin pillow.

"You don't understand my family," I said, sitting down next to her. I picked up a Jean Nate after-bath spritz from the bed stand and sprayed it into the air. "We're not who you think we are."

"So, who are you?"

"We're robbers," I said, proud. Likely, I was beaming. That was who we were—no mincing words. It felt good to have an identity. I used to say, *I'm Aaron, I love the Knicks, I hate milk*, but that didn't really define me. *Hey, I'm Aaron, I've robbed two convenience stores and hit a bank where we netted thousands, all at the ripe age of twelve. Didn't expect that one, did you?*

Heidi was intrigued. She tried to play it cool, nodded like, *sure, sure.*

"Why do you rob?"

I made sure to close her door, as if her grandpa could overhear us.

"We lost all our money in the stock market."

She shrugged, not making the obvious connection.

"The RV is all we own right now, *every*thing else was repossessed. Do you know what that means?"

She crossed her arms. "Yes, Aaron, we've had plenty of stuff repossessed. Look at this shithole I live in." She knocked on her wall to a hollow sound. "It's practically plywood!"

"We started with convenience stores, liquor stores, all of us, Jenny included."

"*That* child has issues."

"Tell me about it. But this is actually giving her a focus. You might not have a living guinea pig in a few minutes, but that would be the first animal she's killed since we started our trip. That's progress."

"Are you joking?"

"Of...course I'm joking."

"Okay, you rob stores, fine. Big deal."

I blew on my fingernails. "The last job was a bank."

Her mouth formed an O.

"In Virginia. We were on the news. I mean, we wore masks, so no one knew it was us."

Heidi slinked off her bed and turned down the music on her portable cassette player.

"And now you've roped my brother into robbing a bank here?"

"Well, roped is a strong word. He was all for it."

"Because he needs cash to get out of here. Like, goodbye Boca forever."

"So, go with him."

"It's not as easy as that. I'm a minor, he'd have to adopt me from my grandpa. And, he's not gonna do that. He wants a new life."

She rubbed her eyes until they were painted black. Now I saw where this was going. If this bank got hit, her life would be ruined.

"Heidi, I hate to break it to you, but nothing is gonna stop us from robbing this bank tomorrow."

The silence was deadly. She burned me with her eyes. Vicious thoughts of her maiming my body churned. The tiny whisper of "The Boy with the Thorn in His Side" slicing through the tension.

"Get out," she said, quietly at first and then when I tried to reason, she roared. Fists were upon me, punching and clawing. I took the brunt. Made sure not to fight back. Let her have this final say. I was destroying the little she had left of her family, but what she didn't realize was that if Troy wanted to leave, some other opportunity would come along to help him go.

"You could come with us," I said, as she was pushing me out.

"I'm a minor, idiot. That's kidnapping. And your parents don't want me, I barely know you."

I wanted to say that she was my first kiss and that for the rest of time, I would know her. Remember the taste, the swell in my toes.

"Everyone fucking leaves me, everyone disappoints."

We were nose to nose. I'd seen in movies where the heat of an argument caused the lovers to embrace. Not here, not with that dagger gaze.

"You won't tell anyone, will you?" I asked, a nervous ball lodged in my throat.

"God, fuck you. Your stupid floppy hair and your dumb basketball shorts. The three hairs on your upper lip you think is a mustache. Your rich life. You all don't know what it's like to be poor. You were poor for two seconds and couldn't handle it. I've always had nothing. Spaghetti-O dinners and hand-me-down clothes from Troy. A grandpa on dialysis that I have to look after because we can't afford a caretaker. Parents dead before I went to kindergarten. And your family loses money in the stock market and can't handle getting a normal job like anyone else? You asshole." She pushed me into the wall. "Asshole, asshole, asshole."

"Okay, okay," I said, throwing up my hands and making for the door.

She gave a final push and I landed on my ass in the hallway. The door slammed. The music turned back up, "How Soon Is Now?"

You shut your mouth.

How can you say?

I go about things the wrong way.

"I am human," I said, as Morrissey continued with, *And I need to be loved, just like everybody else does.*

My first girlfriend and I torpedoed the relationship before it could even begin.

I slouched into the living area, the laugh track from the TV reaching full tilt. Their grandpa staring dead at the screen. Through the window, Jenny in the backyard, hands blood red. I ran outside.

She was sobbing over a ball of matted fur. A bloody rock the culprit.

"What did you do?" I asked, wrenching the mushed guinea pig from her hands.

"It was squirming."

"Jesus Christ, Jenny. Don't you know that's wrong? Don't you know right from wrong?"

She blinked without a response.

"C'mon," I said, yanking her back into the house. Through the hallway to Troy's room—I could still hear the sound of The Smiths pumping from Heidi's. From outside Troy's, a bed squeaking. I slammed into the door until it banged open. Troy and my sister under the covers as she screeched and cursed at our arrival.

"What the hell are you doing, Aaron? Get out!"

I showed them Jenny's bloody hands.

"Jenny killed Heidi's guinea pig. We have to go."

Jenny wiped a bloody hand on the carpet, making it look like a crime scene.

I stared at the little red handprint, looking like the tiniest murder.

27

After Jenny killed Heidi's guinea pig, we got outta there fast. Heidi lost her ever-lovin' mind. I didn't think she could care about a rodent that much, but she was likely more pissed off that we'd be responsible for her brother having the funds to flee their crap life. My stomach did that lurching thing as we were driving away. Heidi had locked herself in her room with the dead guinea pig and wouldn't even say goodbye. Troy said she was over-emotional, and it was best to leave her alone when she got like that. The worst part was, I figured I'd never see her again.

"Aaron, we need to talk about Jenny," Steph said, facing the backseat in the car as we drove back to Grandma Bernice. We often spoke about Jenny like she wasn't there. Clutching Seymour, Jenny leaned against the window, lost in a never-ending mumble. "Do we tell Mom and Dad?"

"No," I quickly said. Troy eyed me through the rearview with a look that said, *Right answer.* "We can't have anything distract us from tomorrow."

Steph crossed her arms in a huff, clearly unhappy with my response. Troy tried to tickle her ear, but she wasn't having that either.

When we got back, Barry and Mom weren't home yet. Around a warped color TV, we watched *The Facts of Life*. Grandma Bernice shuffled by in her house slippers.

"What are you watching?" She put on her glasses hanging around her neck. "Feh, none of them Jewish."

"The actress who plays Natalie is named Mindy Cohn," I said, as Tootie roller skated around.

"I'm not convinced," said Grandma Bernice, as she coughed her way into the kitchen.

Jenny was munching on egg matzo, Seymour in her lap.

"Jenny, do you wanna talk about what happened today?" I asked.

"About what?" Jenny asked, so sweetly you'd never know she was a murderer.

"Killing the guinea pig."

"Feh," Jenny said, mimicking Grandma Bernice. "I freed that pig from its stupid life."

Steph shot up on the couch. "Jenny!"

"It lived in a cage," Jenny pleaded. "How would you like living in a cage? It's like a jail."

Steph dialed down her tone. "So, that's why you killed it?"

"Sure," Jenny said, petting Seymour. "Let's go with that."

I wasn't convinced, but for now it would have to do.

"You can't decide which living creatures should die," I said. "You're not God."

"God doesn't exist."

With that, Grandma Bernice marched back into the living area and gave Jenny a pinch on her cheek hard enough to leave a red mark. Jenny swatted her away with a shrill cry.

"The *nerve* of this child, forsaking Hashem in my very own house." She pointed a shaking finger at the door. "You deserve to stay outside like that mutt."

"Fine!" Jenny said, jumping up and stomping her feet. "Your house smells like old crotch anyway. C'mon, Seymour."

She bolted for the door and slammed it behind her.

Exhausted, Grandma Bernice sat on the Barcalounger, fanning herself with a *TV Guide*.

"Oh, I'm *ferdrayt*," she said, looking whiter than ever. "Tell me you both don't believe in Hashem as well." Her eyes begged us, hopeful we were not like Jenny.

"Like, sometimes it's hard—" Steph began to say, but I talked over her.

"I do, Grandma Bernice." Her eyes now lit up. She didn't really have the ability to smile, but a semblance of one formed, her mouth like a wrinkle. "Like, I talk to Him sometimes when I feel like there's no one else to listen."

"Aaron..." Steph butted in, but I kept going.

"Like, not because I want a cassette tape or nothing, but whether what I'm doing is right or wrong. To help guide me."

Grandma Bernice nodded along while Steph blew a raspberry.

"I can't..." Steph said, getting up and heading into the kitchen.

"*Boychick*, you were always my favorite."

"You say that to all the *boychicks*."

A laugh weaseled its way out of Grandma Bernice's mouth.

"I made someone really angry recently," I said, watching the TV where Mrs. Garrett was soothing the girls. "I'm responsible for hurting them."

"Well, did you apologize?"

"Yes, but I will still hurt them."

Grandma Bernice twisted her face in confusion. "What does Hashem say?"

"I haven't asked Him yet."

"Then I'll leave you to it." Her bones cracked as she rose, gave me a light pinch on the cheek, and shuffled away. She was in the kitchen, talking to Steph. I could hear her murmured accusations of "bad Jew."

The door burst open, and Barry and Mom galloped inside like they'd come from a rodeo. Red-faced and high, giddy with one another, the energy between them electrifying, like none of us were able to enter their sphere. Didn't even notice I was there. She licked his chin, his five-o'clock stubble. He dabbed out the vial of coke onto his index finger, gave her a sniff. Mom woo-hooed. Acknowledged my presence. Danced over with a curl of her fingers and some song about "Me and Bobby McGee." Her shirt had fringes and she glided them through the air, like it was fucking magic or something.

"Judith," Grandma Bernice hissed while walking over, her voice like glass being cut. Mom withered. "*Don't* let them see you like this."

If Grandma Bernice had been referring to us, I'd already seen Mom lit, especially on this trip.

"Bernice, we were just having a good time." Barry pointed his finger in the air like John Travolta in that old movie *Saturday Night Fever*. "Don't be a spoil sport."

"Get into the bathroom," Grandma Bernice ordered Judith. "I'm running you a shower. You need to soak."

Grandma Bernice always with the firm belief that one could wash their problems away. She mumbled some Yiddish stuff under her breath, likely curses, while Mom hung her head and followed her down the hallway. Grandma Bernice looked over her shoulder and gave Barry evil eyes.

"God," Barry said, flopping on the couch. "That woman is just..." He took off his shoes and socks, beat the sock against his sweaty foot to air it out. "Always tries to diminish your Mom's greatness." He sniffed and then sniffed some more, shrugged and took another toot of blow. "You didn't see that," he said, but then laughed.

I was simmering. "What are you doing?"

He shrugged and ripped a long fart.

"Barry!" I shouted, causing him to glance up. His face all twisted and mean.

"What the fuck did you call me?"

"We have a job to do tomorrow."

He was on me fast, lifting me up off the floor by squeezing my neck. We tumbled onto the Barcalounger that bounced us into the coffee table, knocking over a menorah.

"What the hell," Barry said, picking up the menorah. "It's not even close to Chanukah, that woman's nuts."

"Why did you have to get high tonight?" I hate-whispered under my breath. Steph was lurking outside of the kitchen, hanging back and debating whether to reveal herself.

Barry drew a square in the air. "You're so square, man. Five-oh. Pig. Drugs bad. Buzzkill. Be a circle. Be complete." He finished by drawing a circle in the air and sat back, satisfied.

"We need to be on our game tomorrow."

He pushed my face, causing me to fall on my butt. A pain traveled up my spine, nearly knocked the air out of my lungs. Barry cackled.

"I really didn't think you were gonna go down so hard."

I managed to stand. "What's wrong with you?"

"Losing inhibitions, man. That'll be the key."

"Fuck your hippie bullshit."

"You're so serious, Aaron. Lighten up."

"Your mind needs to be clear—"

He got in my face again, his breath full of alcohol and coke drip.

"It's clearer than it's ever been. I go in tomorrow all Sober Sally, my mind will mess with me. This'll take the edge off, for Mom too. We go in tomorrow with our dicks swinging. Soldiers do the same, jacked up on invincibility. I don't want any doubts in your skull, ya hear?" He knocked on my head and made a clucking sound with his tongue. "I want you all to be free and unencumbered. So, don't give me no lecture, you zygote." He huh-huh-huhed. "Zygote."

"I have a real gun." I'd been keeping it tucked in my waistband, the bullets separate in my pocket. I whipped it out, laid it on the coffee table by the menorah.

He poked his tongue into his cheek. "You get that from Troy?"

"I'm bringing it tomorrow."

He wagged his finger, followed by a wink. "Don't tell Mama."

We heard the water running in the bathroom and Grandma Bernice stepped out. I put the gun back in my waistband, causing my pants to sag. She came at Barry as fast as she could, a whirling Yiddish dervish.

"Whoa, Grandma Bernice," Barry said, backing up, a nervous laugh gurgling with his coke phlegm.

"Utter *dreck.*" Grandma Bernice gave a spitless spit Barry's way. "My Judy was a good girl before she met you."

"That was a thousand years ago. That wasn't who she really was. I lit a flame in that beautiful soul."

Grandma Bernice's eyes rolled to the top of her skull.

"You should be afraid of me," she said, giving another spitless spit.

"And why is that?"

"Because I'll find a way to wrench her from you. Your whole family. They deserve better than a *momzer* like you. I know who you do business with."

Barry's face got small, like all his features were moving toward the center, huddling close out of fear.

"What do you know?"

"Exactly who you are. *A shanda fur die goy.* These I-talians you mess around with."

Barry chomped his teeth. "What Italians?"

"These horrible *goys.* They'll come after what's theirs."

Barry grabbed Grandma Bernice by the neck just like he had done to me. I felt a twist in my insides when he did it. Nearly barfed. Grandma Bernice let out a wail to compete with the sound of the *shofar,* the ram's horn they blew into at Rosh Hashanah services. He directed her over to the Barcalounger, thumped her down. She deflated like a tire.

With his finger in her face, he unleashed. "You don't know nothin', you puny old bat. Nothing of my business, of my love for my family and what I wouldn't do for them. I'd give my arms, my legs, my very being."

"Hashem will have consequences for your sins. He will condemn you. In this world and in *gehinom.* You will not be absolved, no matter how much you regret what you've done. It's too late for you, but for Judy and the children—"

He roared in her face so loud she had to block it with her shaking hands. She shut her eyes tight, hoping to make him go away. And I guessed that Hashem listened to her prayers because Barry sauntered down the hall, tossing a "see you as early as can be" to me before he shut the bedroom door. Steph crept out, lingered behind Grandma Bernice. We both felt like we wanted to comfort her but didn't know how and hadn't wanted to defy Barry and show any other allegiance. Grandma Bernice waved us away, turned so she wouldn't have to look at us as she cried, nothing sadder than an old woman's dry tears.

Since I didn't have a room and wasn't in the mood to couch surf that night, I made my way to the Gas-Guzzler. Jenny was inside with Johnny

Cash, telling a secret in the dog's floppy ear. She froze when I entered. Not wanting to deal with her, I retreated to my nook and shut the curtain, got on my knees with my hands locked together and prayed, for a bank heist tomorrow without glitches, for us Gimmelmans to be kinder to one another, and then my prayers found Heidi. I knew she and I were a lost cause, so I prayed that things would turn out well for her. That if Troy left Boca, he'd take her with him because everyone deserves to be cared for, however tough she might make herself out to be. And that sometime later in life, after our thieving ways were done and we'd hang up our masks, that I could find her again and truly apologize because I'd never known anything of love until our first kiss.

"Are you listening, Hashem?" I asked, out the window at the stars.

Pray for us.

28

I couldn't sleep for shit thanks to the dueling snores of Jenny and Johnny Cash making my life hell in tandem. If I was honest with myself, there were a million other reasons preventing any shuteye. For one, we were totally unequipped to rob a bank tomorrow. Especially since it wasn't just a rinky-dink bank run by some hee-haws like we'd hit before, but an actual one with huge safes, and multiple security guards and cameras, and a ton of other ways our asses could wind up in jail. If I was doubly honest with myself, Heidi also wouldn't leave my skull, rattling around and making me feel guilty for the way things ended. I'd been a class-A dick, no respect for what she was going through, and she probably had a voodoo doll with pins in its eyes and my name on it.

Jenny choked on another snore, and I'd had enough. I flung off my sheets and bolted out of the RV, marching back into Grandma Bernice's place. I needed something to help me get some winks, Ovaltine or whatever she'd have in her cupboards besides stale matzo.

The condo was soupy and humid, a tiny fan doing nothing to circulate air around. The lights off in Grandma Bernice's room, but not in Barry and Mom's. I tiptoed up and put my ear flush against the door. Luckily, the walls were thin and easy to hear through.

"I'm coming down finally," Mom said. I pictured her running her hands through her brown hair, massaging her scalp.

"Me too." He was likely rubbing her neck. She always had a sore neck.

"Barry, I don't know—"

"Wait, did your mother get in your head? Tell me she didn't."

"It's not just her. I feel...untethered, like the wind could blow us any which way."

"Which way do you want it to blow?"

She blew her nose, it sounded extra snotty .

"Back to our old lives."

He gave a sigh, one that made me feel for the guy, the sigh coming from the depths of his stomach.

"They don't exist anymore."

"I'm scared."

"What of?"

"What if tomorrow doesn't turn out like we want it to?"

"Impossible."

She was crying now, softly, tears she tried to hide.

"Judy, my Judy... It's your mother, her evil hooks."

"She's not evil."

"She's a danger to us. To what we believe in. What we're trying to accomplish."

"What is that?"

"Freedom, baby. From the preordained prison we'd been stuck in. I didn't see it then, but I was miserable...not, not with you and the kiddos, but with my own acceleration. Life had lost its spark, but I feel it again, in my loins—"

"Barry."

"In my loins, Judith. You above all people can attest to that. Our nookie sessions, they'd been struggling before this jaunt. Tell me that the sex hasn't been on another level since we left."

I puked up in my mouth and swallowed it back down.

"We *have* been connecting," Mom said, in a sing-song way.

"I predict we do this job, and if it goes well—which it *will*, then we do an even bigger one and we're done. We go out on a high note before it catches up with us. That's the biggest problem with a lot of the greats—"

"The who?"

"The greats! The robbers we're aspiring to be, well even more than that, that we're aspiring *not* to be *exactly* like. Take the best of 'em and discard the rest. Don't get greedy. Pull in just enough to live comfortably for the rest of our lives. Never rely on your fucking mother or my shitty brother, disappear off the grid. We could live internationally. *Gay Paree?*"

"Ooh la la," Mom said. She was starting to come around like she always did with Barry, his ability to persuade knowing no limits.

"A little apartment along the Champs-Élysées, or Spain! Gazpachos every day, a balcony in Barcelona overlooking Park Güell?"

She said something so low I couldn't make it out.

"Yes, with the kids, of course with the kids," he replied, and I froze in place. The very thought of the two of them considering life without us, even if it was only bringing up the fact that they would *never* consider life without us, got me scared. That simply being a family didn't mean we were locked together forever. These relationships, fleeting. There would be a time in my life when I didn't see them all day. And then days would pass without contact, even months. I'd have to find my own new family, maybe with Heidi if she could ever forgive me.

"My point is, *we* create our destiny, Judy. We write these next chapters. And tell me you didn't get wet when we robbed that bank in Virginia?"

She snickered. I'd heard enough.

As I was about to turn around, Steph blocked my way, a shadow in the hallway in Slouch socks. An oversized T-shirt of a melting boom box in rainbow colors. Blonde hair in a side ponytail that reached toward the ceiling. A scowl on her face.

"Thanks for throwing me under the bus with Grandma," she yell-whispered.

"What are you talking about?"

We heard giggling coming from Barry and Mom's room, and an "I'm gonna get ya," growl coming from him.

"Gross," she said, and grabbed my hand to whisk me down the hallway. We reconvened in the kitchen, which was the furthest away from the bedrooms. She got down a box of egg matzo and munched.

"This really does taste like wallpaper dipped in ass," she said, but kept munching.

"You're pissed from when I told Grandma I believed in God?" I asked.

"Yeah, that's exactly what I'm fucking pissed about."

"I don't not *not* believe in God."

"What?"

"I mean, I don't know what I believe. Like I believe in something."

She took out the rubber band holding her ponytail high and shook out her hair.

"Bullshit."

"It's not bullshit."

"You believe in God like I have a dick."

"Well, so nice to meet you, *Mister* Gimmelman."

She threw an egg matzo at me.

"It's true, I do believe in... I mean, not so much a God, like some higher power with a big flowing beard that sits up in heaven and judges all of us, but *something* to look up to. Makes me feel less alone and shit. I just prayed before I went to bed."

She let out a snort. "You prayed?"

"For a successful day tomorrow. Do we really want to get into this now? Shouldn't we be getting some sleep?"

"I don't think Mom and Dad are. Besides, we have Troy with us this time." Her voice tickled over his name. "The two of us are gonna run away together."

An anchor dropped in my stomach. What little this poor peasant knew. Troy had sold her a tall tale. I must have been making a face.

"Fuck you, Aaron. He loves me."

"You've known him all of two minutes. What about Kent?"

"Kent and I... We weren't meant for one another. Kent is beige, he's khaki pants, he's boat shoes, he's white-painted walls, I'm vibrant, and shining, and Troy makes me feel like there's a firecracker in my vagina."

"Okay," I said, plugging up my ears. Between Mom and Dad's coitus and now picturing Steph's nether-regions, I'd had enough. "Just don't fall for him too hard. You're sixteen."

"And you're twelve, Aaron. As smart as you think you are, you don't know anything about love."

I could've slapped her.

"Hey! I kissed Heidi and felt it in my toes and if it wasn't for this stupid family, I could be with her."

I made my way out of the kitchen, but Steph caught my arm.

"You made out with Heidi?"

I wrenched out of her grasp. "Yes."

Steph's eyes danced. "Was that your first kiss?"

"No. Well, yes. It was."

"Awwwwww."

She took my hands, and led me in a dance.

"Baby's all grown up, baby's all grown up."

"Stop."

She kissed me on the cheek. "Truce. Please? I don't want to fight with you."

I touched my nose with the tip of my tongue. "I don't want to fight with you either."

"We're the two sanest ones in this bunch of apples," she said, winking. "We're all we got."

This 'twas true.

"I hope things work out with Troy," I said, holding back the truth I sadly knew. "He's a really good guy."

"The best."

She hugged herself, this deluded bird. Troy was set to love her and leave her.

"Promise you'll invite me to the wedding," I said, and she picked up a couch pillow to whap me.

From out of Barry and Mom's room, their lovemaking reached a crescendo, like they wanted us to hear. Always the stars of their own show. Steph made a retch sign, then turned glum.

"You think it's okay they got so high earlier?" she asked, as Mom's wail rattled the foundation. I shook my head and went outside, Steph following in her socks.

"Dad says he needs it to take the edge off."

She nibbled on her bottom lip. "They seemed more out of it than ever before."

"Yeah."

"Like not just pot. Or coke."

"What else is there?"

"A lot, Aaron. Like, a real lot."

Tucking her arms into her T-shirt, she blew at her bangs. "It's like you and me are the mom and dad."

"Jeez," I said. "That's kinda true."

"And what about Jenny? She killed that guinea pig."

"They kill guinea pigs all the time in South America. Eat them too."

"That's so grody."

"Maybe we could pay more attention to her. Like after tomorrow, figure out a game she likes to play?"

"She likes to play murder, Aaron."

"I dunno, maybe hunting? Dad would actually be all for that."

"I'm—"

"Don't be worried."

Her teeth were chattering. "What if you all don't make it out of the bank? What do I do then?"

"You drive. No matter who isn't there. You're our closer. You get us out of there."

She tugged her lip even more. "Okay."

I went to hug her because I could see she needed it, and because it had been a long time since we hugged. She put out her hand like, *no, thank you. I'm good.*

"I'll see you in the morning."

She spun into the condo, the screen door flapping.

I went back in the RV where Jenny's snores still reigned. It was that weird time of night, when the sky looks blue-black. Morning not too far away.

The chaos of tomorrow, like a thrum in my bones. I could eat my excitement with a spoon. Despite everything going on, the thrill of it, still a delicious cherry pie. I gravitated toward the glove compartment, as if what might be inside called out. Popped it open and there sat a vial half filled with white powder. Like Barry left it for me. So I could get on his wavelength. To not believe in his genius meant we'd fail. If I didn't continue with stars in my eyes, we were headed for surefire destruction.

The first shot up my nose, a carnival: freaks and ghouls and tilt-a-whirls. I whipped the gun out of my waistband, let my eyes roll to the clouds and entered a trance where the entire heist spilled out before me, in all its wretched glory. The cool steel in my hands and drool dripping down my chin. Ready to wake with the birds first thing and explode.

29

Not even sun-up and Barry was already pounding at the door yelling, "Wakey wakey, eggs and bakey!" This got Johnny Cash howling as Jenny let out a ream of curses at the mutt. I'd just fallen asleep because of the coke rush. This was my third time ingesting the drug and therefore I was now a full-on cokehead. But Barry had been right. The nerves were gone, only impulse remaining. I squeezed toothpaste in my mouth, brushed my teeth with my tongue, stuck the gun in my sweatpants, and I was out the door.

Barry waited, pinching a cigarette between two fingers, his pupils doing a samba. He flicked the cigarette to the ground followed by a hock of spit. Even at such an early hour, the sweat clung to his forehead, the sun brutal. His glasses fogged from condensation. He took my face in his hands.

"You ready?"

He asked, almost afraid of my answer. At least that was how it seemed. My defiance could spread. How much power did I have with the others? Steph under Troy's sway, Jenny a lone island, the two of us only battling for Mom's allegiance. He didn't have to worry since she'd always lean toward him.

"Of course I'm ready." I gave an extra sniff to prove it.

Jenny slammed open the RV's door, a growl coming from her Mama Cass mask.

"There's my Jenny Henny," Barry said, clapping his hands.

"I'm not your fucking Jenny Henny." She pointed to her face. "You call me Mama."

"Mama, of course, Mama," Barry said, winking at me.

I winked back, still in awe of him. Looking back there'd been a nagging doubt starting to fester. That my once emperor might not have clothes. But we were supposed to idolize our fathers. Who could blame me for being naïve?

"Your mother's getting Steph up, Troy's taking the bus over. Don't want his car out front."

I wanted to find out whether Heidi had asked Troy about me but hearing it in my brain sounded stupid. If that girl wasn't throwing darts at my face, she had forgotten about me entirely.

We waited in the pool area for Troy because Grandma Bernice might be up with her hearing aid turned on high. The sun peeking over the horizon, an orange flame mixed with purple dust. I swatted mosquitoes on my arm as one dug in.

"Where's my hunka hunka burning love?" Troy asked upon entering, and Steph smooched him on the mask's lips. Mom gave them an *ah, young love* look. I have to admit I was eager for Steph's heart to be broken. If I couldn't have Heidi, I didn't want her to find happiness with Heidi's brother, even after our heart-to-heart last night.

Barry unrolled the blueprints for the bank. We went over our assigned rolls three times. Barry taking care of the managers, Troy focused on the tellers, Mom on the security guard and the door, me on the advisers, and Jenny on the customers. He wanted us to say what we were doing seamlessly. Any blip caused us to start over again.

"This is the precision part of the plan," he said, as Troy "yeah yeahed" in agreement, "but we leave ourselves open to chance, that's where impulse comes in."

The butt of the gun felt cold in my sweatpants, jammed against my ass crack. There could very well be a scenario where after today, I not only shot a gun, but hit someone with a bullet.

"Can I get a, Whoa Gimmelmans?" Barry asked, all shining teeth. Our guarantor that everything would go smoothly. Those teeth grinding, revealing the fear within if I looked hard enough.

We all gave an absurdly soft, "Whoa Gimmelmans," since everyone in the Orthodox complex was still sleeping.

Except on our way to the RV, from out of Grandma Bernice's bedroom—which I didn't even know faced the pool area—the old woman stood in curlers at the window, gumming her lips. What were we all doing by the pool area so early in the morning? Her antennae raised.

But I didn't mention it to Barry, not when he seemed so gung-ho, directing his troops to the Gas-Guzzler. Mom at his side, gently running her finger up and down his arm. He whispered in her ear, and she nodded like a robot over and over, receiving whatever information he gave. When she saw me, she smiled, trying to assure me that nothing would go wrong. I pretended not to notice her trembling lips.

Inside the Gas-Guzzler we were quiet. Masks donned as Steph drove, searching the radio and deciding on Michael Jackson's "Wanna Be Startin' Something?" My coke high, had turned into a numbness. I guessed that was good too. Like this was our normal. The clock said just after seven a.m. We'd go in at nine sharp, time enough for the managers to settle in, but there wouldn't be too big a crowd, only enough to add some wallets and jewelry to our bounty, in case the safe turned out to be a bust like last time.

We waited on the corner, barely anyone on the street. The sun, hot through the window, burning my face. Steph flicked to another station, "Don't Dream It's Over" by Crowded House. Right before eight a.m. one of the managers came up to the doors with a ring of keys. He wore a top hat like he was Russian and had *payot* , strings of curls instead of sideburns, since it was against their beliefs to shave the corners of their head. He wasn't too old but walked with a limp. Before he entered, he paused, and I felt the food I consumed last night rushing through my guts. Was he aware of us? His head tilted toward the RV, the sun a laser reflecting off his eyeglasses. But he only stopped to sneeze, which he caught in a handkerchief and stuffed back in his front pocket.

No one else showed up for another ten minutes until his doppelgänger walked up to the doors and got out a ring of keys too. After another ten minutes, two of the yarmulkes in the cubicles showed up together, seeming to have an intense conversation. One pointed to the sky and the other shook his head. Probably about God or something.

"Okay, that means there's probably only two managers, since any others should have arrived already," Barry said. Then something caught his eye down the street. "The security guard," he said, and we all watched the security guard huff and puff his way up to the door. The man very overweight, his stomach doing circles as he ran, everything jiggling. He caught his breath at the door, his cheeks bright red, his shirt soaked from that one-block run.

"We hold off until nine," Barry said, calmly. "That's our witching hour."

At eight thirty, the bank officially opened. The few tellers had arrived with the third adviser with a yarmulke and a few customers: an Orthodox woman with a stroller and two men, one old and the other young and bald under his yarmulke.

"We wait until the mother leaves," Barry said. "I don't want to deal with babies."

Mom agreed with a light sigh like she wanted to say something but wouldn't. When nine o'clock arrived, the woman with the baby in the stroller still hadn't exited the building. A heavyset Orthodox woman was the only other one who entered. She had an air about her like she was annoyed with everything. A real sourpuss.

"We can't wait any longer," Barry said, speaking only to Mom.

"But—"

"Judy, honey, baby, people will be filling up the streets. We'll have to move it to tomorrow."

"Oh," she said, like she swallowed a bug.

"Street is clear," Steph said, her eyes in the rearview. "Welcome to the Jungle" playing softly from the radio.

"Showtime," Barry said, donning his Jerry Garcia mask, white teeth flashing through the mouth hole.

Troy opened up the RV's door and we filed out. I nearly tripped over my feet but managed to maintain. Barry gave a glare that said *hold your shit together*. He got out and led us across the street. The sky clear, the pavement scorching. My heart doing double-time as my view spun and righted itself. Barry pulled open the door to the bank and we raced inside.

"Everybody be cool," he said. "Keep on truckin'."

I didn't know if he was talking to us but then saw him pointing the gun around the bank. A woman let out a scream. I wasn't sure if it was the woman with a baby or the heavyset one.

"Give me your gun," Mom said, a noticeable quiver in her voice as she rammed her gun into the security guard's cheek. He blew out a gust of air and handed it over. She pocketed it without taking her gun off the guard.

"All of you, hand over the cash," Troy said to the tellers, three of them pissing their pants. "And don't try tripping any alarms. We don't want to hurt anyone." Troy gave his Elvis an accent that didn't sound so much like Elvis.

Barry was already gone down the hall.

"All right, out of the cubicles," I said, to the three advisers. I tried to make my voice sound more adult, but I was high in the throes of puberty. They followed in a line. "Kneel down," I continued, watching them all obey. "Now lie down." Once they were on the floor, I checked all of their pockets, pilfering wallets and tossing them to Jenny. She was dealing with the heavyset woman, who had been the one to scream. The woman's knees were knocking together and she was in full cry mode. She blubbered and wailed.

"Quiet," Jenny said, kicking her in the knee. The heavyset woman folded to the ground in shifts. I went to tell Jenny to be easy on her when Troy got in my face.

"The cameras," he said, passing me the can of spray paint.

"Right."

With one eye on the three advisers on the floor, I hauled out a chair and jumped on top. By the time I sprayed all three cameras, Mom had blockaded the front door with the security guard's folding chair, Jenny was getting the wallet from an old guy waiting in line, Troy was yelling at a teller who couldn't think straight to open the cash register, and Barry came out of the hallway pushing the two managers.

"Which one of you has the keys to open the safe?" he asked, and with shaking hands they both raised their ring of keys. One muttered under his breath, "May God punish you," which Barry answered by slapping the man across the face. A dab of blood appeared at the man's lip. "You," Barry said, picking up the other one. "Lead me to the safe."

"Okay, okay," the other man muttered. He was very skinny, his legs like sticks. They disappeared through a door with a key code.

A knock rapped against the front door. Everyone hushed. The glass door cloudy. A vision of a blurry person outside. I didn't see any red lights or hear police sirens.

"Garcia?" Mom asked, but Barry had already gone. "What should we do?"

"Stay there," Troy said, to the tellers. He pointed the gun at each of them. "Do you like your faces? Keep quiet and I won't ruin yours." I could hear an audible gulp coming from each of them.

Jenny was now dealing with the woman with the baby in a stroller. The baby miraculously sleeping. The woman handed over her purse.

Troy leaped to the door saying, "I got this, I got this." He clapped his hands by the security guard's face. "Get up, get up." The overweight guard took his time. "Faster tubby, faster."

When the security guard finally rose, he was sweating so much he had full moon pit stains under his arms.

"You tell whoever it is to come back later," Troy said to the security guard, whose chins all bounced as he nodded. Troy jammed the gun in the guard's squishy back. They moved the chair, and the guard opened the door and poked his head out.

"Repairs," Troy whispered in the guard's ear.

"We're closed for repairs right now," the security guard said.

"But there's no sign." The voice, shrill enough to make my goosebumps rise.

"I apologize for that, ma'am."

"What is this *bobbemyseh*?" the voice squawked.

Holy shit, could it be...?

"I need to cash my social security check," the voice squawked again.

If it wasn't Grandma Bernice, then she had someone else running around Boca Raton who had stolen her exact voice.

"Grandma Bernice," I said out loud, and then swallowed the word. Had anyone heard? One of the adviser's eyebrows rose, but Mom and Troy were too preoccupied.

"Tell her thank you and to come back later," Troy whispered in the guard's ear.

"Thank you and come back later," the guard blubbered.

"Now shut the door," Troy whispered.

The guard shut the door. I could see the outline of Grandma Bernice, crossing her arms and refusing to leave. She held up her hand to knock again, and then seemed to think twice and turned away. Surely, she had noticed our RV. We needed to get walkie-talkies for the future so Steph could contact us for emergencies. Finally, Grandma Bernice left.

"Hendrix," Mom said, her tone flat and unbothered. "Check on Garcia."

I thrust my gun at the three advisers one last time—the one Mom thought was fake—then skipped through the door left open by Barry. Down a long hallway that smelled of cleaning fluids, I entered a vault. Barry had his gun pressed against the manager's ear as the manager turned a combination lock.

"How's it going here?" I asked.

Jerry Garcia regarded me and turned his attention back on the manager. "This slow poke needs to hurry up."

"I have arthritis," the manager said.

"We all got something," Barry replied, and pressed the gun harder against the guy's ear. The lock finally clicked, and the vault opened. Barry had a shoulder bag he tossed my way and indicated to grab the loot. There were freakin' shelves of stacked cash! I saw hundred-dollar bills filed in about thirty separate stacks. All of it went in the shoulder bag. "Now the valuables," Barry ordered the manager.

"They are all in separate lock boxes," he said, very deliberately like we were slow. "We don't keep those keys on our ring."

The wheels turned in Barry's skull. Would he order the manager to get them no matter what? That would take a ridiculous amount of time.

"Forget it," I said, hoping to bring him back down to reality. The manager curled into himself, anticipating an attack. He held up his hands in defeat.

"Yeah, yeah," Barry said. "Forget it. Any certificates too. Someone else's stocks or bonds are no good to us."

"Right," the manager said, like he was trying to suture the wound of this robbery.

Barry swatted him with the gun. "Don't tell me what's right and what's not, that's for me to decide. In fact, let's put everyone in the vault."

"What?" me and the manager said at the same time.

"So they don't come after us. So we have a head start."

From out of his waistband, he removed some cords. I hadn't seen him bring them, probably because they would have scared us. But he was right. This did give us a better shot at escaping.

"Hendrix, start bringing people here," he told me.

As he was tying the manager up, I ran back out to the main room. I did a quick glance to make sure nothing had gotten out of hand since I left. The tellers had laid on the ground. Troy pacing in front of them, a full bag slung over his arm. Jenny's bag filled up as well.

"Garcia wants them locked in the vault," I said to Troy, who pondered it for a second.

"Yeah, yeah," he said. "All right, let's go."

He clapped for the three tellers to get up and poked them in the back, directing them down the hallway. Without him or Barry there in the main room, I felt vulnerable, like things could go sideways easily.

"I have to use the bathroom," the heavyset lady said out loud.

"So, go in your pants," the older man in line said.

"I absolutely will not," the heavyset lady declared.

"Shut it," Jenny said, whapping her with the bag of purses and wallets.

"Ohhh," the lady said. "Ohhhh, ohhh, ohhh, my head."

"Lady, shut it!" Jenny yelled, causing the baby in the stroller to wake with a cough. The baby gurgled for one long second before letting out a deafening scream.

"Jesus, Jen—Mama," I quickly corrected.

"My baby," the baby's mother whined. She had tears in her eyes as well, her hands clasped together. "Don't hurt my baby."

"We're not hurting your baby," I told her.

"Don't hurt my baby," she wailed again.

"No one's hurting your baby," Jenny yelled at her too.

"Let me quiet him down," the mother said.

I looked to Mom for answers, who shrugged. Then she made a snap decision and picked up the baby from the stroller. The mother gasped as Mom rocked the baby in her arms while still holding the gun.

"Yes, sweetheart," Mom cooed. "It's okay, you're okay."

She started singing "Piece of My Heart." She used to sing this to me when I couldn't sleep, Barry would too. Janis Joplin with the mask singing her most known song. The baby still cried but softer. "We don't want to hurt anyone," Mom told the mother.

"Well, you have," the heavyset woman said.

"Quiet," the older man told her.

Troy returned with Barry, who made the three advisers get up. In a single file, they were pushed down the hallway.

"Let's get the rest," Troy said. "Up, up."

He picked up the two men in line and nodded for Mom to do the same to the two women. Mom gently placed the baby back down in the stroller.

"I'm sorry," Mom whispered in the mother's ear. But the woman didn't respond. She clasped her hands around the stroller and pushed it down the hallway.

"You too," I said, to the guard, since he was the last one.

The vault was stuffed with people once we got to it. Barry had tied up the tellers and was working on the final adviser.

"Oh no, I'm claustrophobic," the heavyset woman yelled. "Oh no, oh no." She waved her arms around like she was directing a plane.

"Be quiet," Barry muttered.

"Oh no, oh no, no, no, no, no."

Her face had turned red, and she was squirming around so as not to be crammed in the vault. The baby started crying again.

"Look what you did!" Jenny yelled in the heavyset woman's ear. She bit the woman's hand.

"Owww," the heavyset woman wailed, flailing around and nursing her hand.

"Mama," I said, moving Jenny aside. "Go in the corner."

Jenny stuck her tongue out through the Mama Cass mask.

That was when I saw a very tiny gun being raised. It took me a moment to decipher who held it, since the person was not wearing a mask. It came from out of a sock, held in a quivering hand.

"No, no, no," the older man in line said, who had seen it too.

"What's going on?" Barry asked, swiveling around.

"Bear-bear!" Mom screamed.

The gun fired, a loud blast that caused me to cover my ears. The security guard flung back from the recoil, his face pinched and tomato red. Troy was upon him instantly, wrenching the smoking gun from his hand. They wrestled on the ground until Troy freed the tiny gun and proceeded to punch the man in the face with it. My eyes followed the path of its trajectory, Barry on the floor with blood leaking out of him. Mom ran over, scooping him up.

"My ass," Barry cried, poking his ass in the air where the bullet lodged in good.

"We have to go," Troy demanded, throwing the security guard into the vault.

"Bear-bear," Mom said, bathing him all over in kisses.

"Fuck, he shot me in the ass," Barry said, trying to get up off the floor and falling back down. "This fucker shot me in the..."

Barry lunged into the vault on top of the guard, screeching at the guy. He punched him hard over and over until the guard was a bloody pulp and I couldn't even look that way anymore. The heavyset woman started carrying on louder than before, so I cocked my gun, almost wanting to put a bullet in her brain. The baby still cried, and everything seemed like it was unraveling.

"No, no, no," Mom said, swatting my gun away. It skittered across the floor. Did she know it was real?

"Garcia, c'mon," Troy yelled, dancing over the people in the vault and yanking Barry off of the guard. The guard's shirt painted red, him moaning like he was dying. I ran across the room and grabbed my gun, poking it at the last two people to get in the vault. They complied, both of them eyeing the beaten guard.

"*Guy avek*," the heavyset woman said, waving us away. "*Kinehora*," she said, over and over. "You're evil in God's eye. God watches. He sees you. He sees you all."

I got close to her, had to stand on my tiptoes to do so.

"You're lucky you didn't eat this bullet," I said.

"A curse," she belted out. "A curse upon you all, you nonbelievers."

Barry limped by her and put his bloody hand in her face pushing her over. She fell hard, I could hear her tailbone hit against the ground. She cursed at us in Yiddish as we slammed the vault door, hurried out of the room.

"Bear-bear, are you...?" Mom asked.

"I'm okay, I'm—it smarts, but let's get out of here."

We emerged from the bank like a band of wounded warriors, a trail of blood left in our wake. The street, still blissfully empty as we hurried to the RV. Steph opened the door in shock as we leaped inside, the shock radiating on her face even through the Debbie Gibson mask.

"What happened, what happened?" she asked.

"Drive, you drive," Barry ordered.

She blinked in response.

"Stephie, get behind that fucking wheel!"

The force of his yells blew her back into her seat. Pedal on the gas as we flew out of there. We sat back, all of us panting, Barry wrenching off the mask and wincing from the pain.

"What's that blood?" Steph asked, radiating pure fear as we turned off the street and headed toward the highway.

"Hospital," Mom said, her mask still on, not wanting to show any of us how scared she was.

"No hospitals!" Barry ordered.

"Barry," she said, sopping up the blood with her blouse.

I blinked and saw the security guard in my vision. At least what was left of him after Barry's assault. I shook it away.

"A hospital equals prison," Barry said. "You can't just walk in with a gunshot wound. They'll want to know what happened."

"We'll make up a story," Mom said, but it was too soft to resonate.

"My grandpa," Troy said, taking off Elvis. "He was in World War Two, he could remove a bullet."

I thought of Troy's grandpa who seemed firmly fixated to his recliner, likely already drunk this early in the morning.

"You heard the man, Stephie," Barry said.

Troy went up to the shotgun seat to direct Steph, who was lightly sobbing.

"What's with the glum faces?" Barry asked. "We scored big. This is nothing. A graze."

Mom was petting his hair, tears leaking through Janis Joplin's eyes.

"I thought..."

"Judy, stop."

"...I lost you, Bear-Bear."

"Now, now," he said, taking her in his arms, squeezing her tightly. She began heaving, trying to catch her breath, overwhelmed. He tucked her closer, comforting but also so none of us would see her collapse, as they lay together in a puddle of his blood.

"Sssshh, sssshh," he repeated over and over, his eyes firmly on me. I had to stay strong, couldn't falter like the rest of the Gimmelmans, sans Jenny who seemed perfectly content pulling on the dog's ears.

"Count the cash," he said to me, kicking at the bag. In a hushed voice, he added, "To keep everyone's spirits up."

I nodded, fully understanding. Got the bag in my lap and began to count. When we arrived at Troy's place, I had gotten up to fifty thousand dollars and there were still some stacks left plus the tellers and customers' haul. Could be double that, almost a hundred grand. I shouted it out to Barry so we could revel in our bounty, but he had passed out by then as Mom's screams earthquaked the RV.

30

After parking the RV in their backyard to keep it out of sight, we carried Barry into Troy's house, Mom and I getting his arms and Troy and Steph getting his legs. He was coming to a little bit, focused on the trail of blood from the RV and letting out these moans that sounded like a goat bleating. Jenny followed, with Johnny Cash, who nipped at her heels. Heidi stepped out of her room and dropped the glass of milk she was drinking. She had a milk mustache, I'd never been so attracted and repulsed by a human before.

"Take his leg while I go get Grandpa," Troy said.

She'd frozen in place, her mouth in a perpetual O.

"C'mon, Heidi," he shouted, waking her up. She stepped over the spilled milk and grabbed Barry's leg from Troy, who ran into the TV room. I couldn't imagine what he'd tell his grandpa.

I tried to glance Heidi's way, but she was clearly avoiding me.

"Shot in the ass, huh?" she said, to the room. Mom responded with a death wail.

"Mom," Steph said, reining her in. "He's gonna make it."

"It's not worth it," Mom said. "He should be in a hospital."

"No hospitals," Barry wheezed.

Their grandpa emerged in the doorframe. A tall son-of-a-bitch with a rock-hard beer gut and coke-bottle glasses. He stifled a belch, scratched his ass. Mom wailed more.

"So, you need a bullet removed?" he asked, and gave a snort that rattled around some phlegm.

"Where should we put him?" Mom asked. I could see she wanted to take charge, but she seemed so fragile, unable to function without Barry.

"Heidi, clear the table," their grandpa said between belches.

Heidi let go of Barry as Steph grabbed his other leg, straining to hold him up. Heidi shoved aside a dining room table filled with yellowing magazines and half-broken knickknacks. Troy hopped out.

"I'm sterilizing the instruments, towels, and gloves in a pressure cooker," Troy said, like they did this every Tuesday. He zipped into the kitchen.

"Grandpa was an Army medic," Heidi said. She started nodding until eventually Mom nodded too, but Heidi still wouldn't look my way.

"I've taken many bullets out of ass cheeks," their grandpa said. "Best place to get shot."

"Tell that to my *tuchus*," Barry said, going in and out of consciousness.

Mom patted his cheek. "Bear-Bear, wake up."

Once everything was sterilized and laid out on a towel, Grandpa Army Medic washed his hands thoroughly and donned sterile gloves. He was wearing a sleeveless shirt so nothing would get in the way.

"Pull down his pants," he said, and when no one moved forward to do so, he cocked his head toward me.

"O-kay." I pulled down Barry's pants and tighty-whities, treated to the most unfortunate sight of Barry's hairy, bloody ass. The blood had mixed with his voluptuous ass hair that might as well have been a carpet.

"Grody," Steph said.

"Too many cooks in the kitchen," their grandpa said. "Men only, women in the other room."

"But I want to be by my Barry," Mom said.

"Sweetie, if you want this man to live, you'll scoot that caboose into the kitchen. Now get."

Mom seemed like she wanted to fight, but gave in, sulking to the kitchen while hugging Steph and Jenny at her side. Heidi kept close behind telling them what a different era her grandpa came from.

"Now without all the hysterics, let's get down to business." He turned to me, eyeing the gauze on the table. "Have the gauze ready to mop up the blood."

I gave a gulp.

He squinted. "Okay, I can see how it went in. Troy, get him liquored up."

Troy returned with what looked like moonshine and started pouring it in Barry's mouth, making him look like a gerbil at its water bottle. Then their grandpa doused the ass cheek with the rest of the liquor, causing Barry to scream like he was in labor. The flesh around the wound got spread open and their grandpa went for the bullet using a Q-tip and a tweezer.

"It's a tiny bullet so we don't need no knife," he said. "Lucky it didn't break apart neither." Once the bullet was out, it was no bigger than a dime. Their grandpa left it on the table. "Now, we stitch him up. He's gonna live. Get me a cig."

Troy returned with a Doral 100 he shoved in his grandpa's mouth and lit. Their grandpa puffed without removing the cigarette from his lips. I figured I didn't need to stay and watch the rest.

In the kitchen, everyone sat around a table, Mom hugging a cup of steaming coffee in a mug that said *Florida*, except the O was shaped like a sun with cool sunglasses, and the L was a palm tree.

"He's gonna be okay," I said, and Mom looked toward the ceiling, whispering, "Thank you." She jumped up and hugged me hard, going on about how she thought she'd lost him and that she wouldn't know what to do without him.

"You didn't lose him," I said, annoyed at her reaction.

"But I could've."

"Okay, Mom." I wrenched away as she still reached out, needing to remain comforted. My parents, both exhausting in their own way, at least that day. Mom had made it her business to attempt to soothe all of us when this whole trip started, except she really depended on us to assuage her. As for Barry, I wondered what if Jenny or me had been shot? Would he have taken us to a hospital, or gambled with our lives like he did his own? I hated that I probably knew the answer.

"You know Grandma Bernice was that lady who came to the front door,"

I said. Mom made a face like she had diarrhea.

"What?" Steph asked, nearly spitting out her coffee.

"At the bank, some lady tried to get in after we blocked the doors. It was Grandma Bernice."

Mom took a cool sip from her mug. "No, it wasn't."

"Mom, it was her exact voice."

She let out a shriek. "Stop it, Aaron, just stop it." Pulling her hair through her fingers, she seemed to inspect for grey roots.

"Is anyone wondering if she eyed the Gas-Guzzler?" I asked, gobsmacked at their lack of reality.

"Your father is fighting for his life out there, that should be your only worry." She tapped her fingernails against the mug, then stood in a trance. "Excuse me? The bathroom?"

Heidi woke from her slumber, likely choosing to ignore our chaos.

"Down the hall, first door on the left."

"Thank you." Mom actually sneered at me as she passed by. Clearly, she was frazzled and needed an easy target.

"Steph, how did you not see Grandma from the RV?" I asked.

"I-I don't know. There was an old woman that went up to the bank. She wore a housecoat."

I looked over at Heidi so someone could be on my side at the ridiculousness that was my life. But *nada*, the girl frigid as Antarctica.

"I love your nails," Heidi said to Steph, who basked in the attention and showcased them, each painted a different neon color.

"It's Natural Wonder with airbrushing," Steph said, as if we should all bow down.

I ran out to the backyard, frustrated that Heidi wouldn't acknowledge me. Back in the RV, I saw what looked like a gory mess of blood-stained floors. With paper towels, I started to clean, getting a good amount done when there was a knock on the door.

"Come in."

For a second, my heart skipped. What if it was the police? None of us even considered that we might've been tailed, too wrapped up in Barry to think clearly. Or that Grandma Bernice might've narced on us. But Heidi entered. She'd thankfully cleaned off the milk mustache and wore a Mötley Crüe *Girls, Girls, Girls* T-shirt with cutoff denim shorts. Her legs, the kind of tan one could only get in Florida.

"Wow," I said, tossing aside the bloody paper towels. "Did you just change outfits?"

She shrugged like she couldn't care less. "Maybe. It's a Troy hand-me-down."

"I'm really sorry about your guinea pig."

"*That's* only what you're sorry about?"

"And for my dad bleeding all over your house."

She inspected the RV, running a finger through a line of dust on a counter. "So, this is your getaway ride?"

I went to respond, but she talked over me.

"Why did you have to get my brother involved?"

"It was my dad's doing. And really, Troy helped us out. He's gonna get a lot of money."

"Yeah, *he's* gonna get the money."

"I'm sorry if he leaves you here, but like, your grandpa seems cool."

"He's a drunk, Aaron. He barely exists outside of his recliner. Fine, he saved your dad's life today, but he's not a real parent."

"I'm sorry."

"Like, don't be sorry, okay? I hate when people pity me. It's phony. No one really cares. They say they're sorry, so they feel like they're saying the right thing."

She stuck her tongue into her cheek, pissed off to no end. I wanted to hug her but had a better idea. I grabbed the bag that Jenny used to collect the purses and wallets.

"What are you doing?"

Pilfering through the wallets and purses, I found about six hundred dollars.

"Here, it's yours."

She eyed it like it was a snake about to attack. "This is from the bank?"

"Yeah, from customers in line. Go on, take it."

She snatched it fast, as if I might change my mind. I dumped out the bag. "There's jewelry too if you want it."

She began rooting through the loot, trying on a ring and a necklace.

"It looks good on you."

"It looks like old lady jewelry, but maybe I can pawn it." She observed the ring in the light. "This ring actually doesn't suck... If it's a diamond and not a cubic zirconia."

"I'm sorry we're responsible for taking your brother away from you."

She shrugged again. "He's kinda a dick, so... And he's really into your sister. Usually, he like sleeps with a girl and doesn't call her back."

"She's into him too."

"Yeah, they're both pretty simple people. Pretty on the outside, kinda dumb on the inside. They're made for each other."

"Steph's gonna lose her mind when my dad won't let Troy come with us," I said, and then covered my mouth. "That's a secret, don't tell her."

I thought I noticed the tiniest of smiles. "Only because you gave me jewels."

"It's too bad you can't come with us."

"Huh, no thanks. I think your spree is over anyway."

I was baffled. "No way, José."

"Aaron," she laughed, a cruel cackle. "Your dad was shot in the ass. You think he's gonna want to rob again?"

"Uh, I'm sure he's planning the next heist right as we speak."

"Well, that's fucked up." She stuffed the money in her jean shorts. "You think you can just keep robbing banks over and over and get away with it?"

I twisted my toe into the ground. "I dunno."

"The police will catch up with you. Name me one famous robber who got away with it, completely? It's impossible. You guys could be on the news right now."

I held up my Jimi Hendrix mask. "We do it incognito!"

"You think you're the first to ever hide your faces? Your dad was shot, his blood is all over the bank. Did you use gloves? Your fingerprints are everywhere."

"Yeah, but how would the police know our fingerprints? None of us have been arrested, we wouldn't be in their system."

"All of your DNA will be in the system now, it's a new thing with crimes so it's only a matter of time."

"You're wrong."

"Look, I hope you get away with it. Really. Like, I'm not wishing anything bad to happen. But pros get caught and you guys aren't pros."

I unzipped the shoulder bag with the real loot. "There's almost a hundred thousand dollars there."

She reached in and caressed a bill, a dollop of saliva forming on the corner of her mouth. She then came out from her spell, hands on her hips. "You should have an exit strategy."

"A what?"

"I thought you were a brainiac. It's a way of looking out for yourself when all of this goes south."

Maybe I wasn't as smart as I made myself out to be. Even though I didn't really buy into what she was saying, I could play along.

"Like how?"

"I dunno, write down anything you remember that shows how it was all your parents' idea, and you had no choice."

"That's not entirely true—"

"Doesn't matter. Look, they are adults and will be tried as adults and go to prison for a long time. But it's up in the air what could happen to the rest of you. If it seemed like you couldn't go against them, you might avoid juvie."

"Juvie?" I had to laugh, although my laughs died down as I thought about it more.

"This is a lot of money, Aaron. It's grand theft."

"How do you know all of this?"

"*L.A. Law*, it's like my favorite show. I'm obsessed. And with Harry Hamlin. There was an episode recently about a kid being tried, and he got off because he blamed his parents."

"I don't blame them, I mean, like we're really good at what we do."

"You're in a cult."

"What?"

"A cult. You can't say anything bad about them. You can't see them for who they really are. Your little sister murdered my guinea pig. It's all because of bad influences."

"Whoa, Jenny was always like that. Born psychotic."

"The apple doesn't fall far from—"

"Okay, they're not perfect, no debate there, but like, what do you even know? You never had parents really."

She let out a huff, and I immediately wanted to take it back. Sometimes I could say the stupidest things. Tears welled in her eyes, and they came hard. Her fist, directed squarely at my jaw, an uppercut that would rival Mike Tyson in *Punch-Out!!*

My knees buckled as I fell over, my cheek against the sticky, bloody floor. Heidi stormed off with a "Fuck you" tossed over her shoulder. I deserved nothing less, subconsciously wanting to push her away so it'd be easier to eventually say goodbye. I'd often heard that people come into your life for a reason, a season, or a lifetime. Heidi would be a reason. She put the bug in my ear to document Mom and Barry's worst impulses, my only chance at a Get Out of Jail card, so I sat up, found a notepad, and started writing down my vilest memories. It began with the most recent—Barry pummeling the security guard and leaving him a bloody pulp. Did he have to destroy him so completely, or had he enjoyed it? A blinding white smile, all the proof I needed.

Then I hid the notepad under my couch/bed, a first offense documented, but definitely not the last.

31

When I got back inside their house, Barry had splayed himself on the couch with his ass in an ice bucket. Mom was feeding him grapes and Hi-C. Troy and Heidi's grandpa had gotten himself a Michelob, sipping with fervor, while Troy flipped through the channels on the TV with the remote. Steph hung on his arm as everyone expected us to be on the local news.

Finally, a newscaster appeared on Channel 4. The reception wasn't great, so their grandpa went over and gave the TV a good slap. He fiddled with the antennae as a rainbow line cut through the newscaster, but then evened out.

"Boca Raton is rocked by a high-stakes bank robbery that left the security guard in the hospital and almost a dozen people locked in a vault all day. It wasn't until Rose Schwartz, who tried to enter the bank around noon, noticed something was wrong."

The camera cut to Rose Schwartz, big curly hair and purple-framed glasses.

"I had an appointment with my financial advisor and was surprised when the door was just open. No one on the floor. I was about to leave when I heard a knocking, from down a hall. I was horrified to find all those people stuck in a vault."

The camera panned back to the newscaster. "Rose called the police who arrived immediately to let everyone out. Mr. Samuel Myles was taken to Boca Raton Regional for bruises all over his face and internal bleeding due to a severe beating from one of the robbers."

I turned to Barry, who viewed it all on the edge of his ice bucket, rubbing his hands together in anticipation.

"We spoke to Mr. Myles's mother while he was getting tests done."

"A shame," the woman says, dabbing her eyes with a tissue kept up her sleeve. "My Samuel is a good boy. A shame, whoever did this to him. May these thieves be locked up for good."

A picture of Samuel Myles on a rollercoaster filled the screen.

"Apparently, Mr. Myles fired a second gun he kept for emergencies at one of the robbers, shooting the man in his...butt." The newscaster seemed embarrassed to say the word. "After the robber was shot, he attacked Mr. Myles."

The camera switched to the heavyset Orthodox woman. "It was a tragedy. We were all afraid for our lives. I thought I was going to be his next victim. How could people be so cruel?"

The newscaster stared seriously into the camera. "We have early footage of these robbers before the bank's cameras were sprayed with some kind of paint."

With the sound off, we saw us burst into the bank. Janis Joplin sticking the gun in the security guard's face. Elvis, going for the tellers, Jerry Garcia after the managers. Everyone inside going crazy. I watched myself get a chair and climb on top to spray the cameras, the last image the viewers seeing was of me as Jimi Hendrix.

It cut back to the newscaster. "Apparently, this gang of thieves, wears masks of musicians. We've identified Jerry Garcia as the ringleader."

An image of Jerry Garcia playing guitar on a stage took up the screen.

"The others are Jimi Hendrix, Janis Joplin, Elvis Presley, and Mama Cass."

The camera switched to the heavyset Orthodox woman. "That Mama Cass. She was the meanest of them all!" She displayed her hand with a bite mark. "Bit my hand, and she was littler than everyone else. One of those...little people."

The newscaster butted in. "There are two little people police are reporting in the gang."

They showed the video of Jimi Hendrix spraying the camera again.

"Jimi Hendrix seems to be little as well," the newscaster continued. "And police are linking this crime to a bank robbery last week in Virginia that wasn't caught on tape but had witnesses describing similar masks used."

It switched to the newscast from Virginia with the old cast of characters dragging our names through the mud.

"There were no witnesses of a getaway car, and the county is on high alert for anyone with information. The bank estimates that the robbers made off with almost a hundred grand. We spoke to a Bernice Finkelstein who luckily was not allowed to enter during the robbery."

" A *Shanda*," Grandma Bernice said, pointing at the camera. "These *nudniks* taking what isn't theirs. They had barricaded the door and wouldn't let me inside, but I knew something was going on. I was supposed to cash my social security check. If I had gone a little earlier, I could be dead."

The newscaster looked back into the camera. "Thank you. More on this story as it breaks."

"See," I said, leaping up. "I told you Grandma Bernice was there."

Barry blew a raspberry. "It's not like she knew it was us."

"We don't know that," I said. "She might not have told the newscaster everything."

"Where's your phone?" Mom asked their grandpa, who pointed to one hanging on the wall.

"Wait, Judy, what are you doing?" Barry asked.

"I need to call Ma, make sure she's all right."

She went toward the phone on the wall. Barry rolled over on his side and kept rolling off the couch, crashing to the floor. "Ow, for Jesus's sake. Judy, do not call that woman."

Mom had already picked up the receiver. "She has a heart condition."

"She can't know where we are, or our plans."

Mom had a finger on the rotary dial. "What are our plans?"

"Okay, okay," Barry said, hoisting himself back on the couch. "For one, they don't know about our RV, so that means we're safe...for now."

"Your DNA is all over the bank," I said.

"Right," Barry said. "Wait, what?"

"When you were shot in the ass," I said. "You bled everywhere. It's a new thing with crimes. They're putting it in the system."

"God, you're so smart," Barry said. "Fuck. Well, no. I've never been arrested."

Mom hung up the phone hard. "I have."

"Judy...?"

"Before I met you, we were protesting the Vietnam War."

"Okay, okay, but you didn't bleed anywhere, right?"

"What about her fingerprints?" I asked, as Mom chewed on one of those fingerprints.

"Chill, chill," Troy said, standing up and waving his hands like a conductor in an orchestra. "There is nothing we can do about anything in the past, right?" He looked around the room until we all began to nod. "And fingerprints don't mean much. You could've been at the bank a different day and left fingerprints. So even if you do come up, it won't prove anything."

Mom let out an exhale. "Right."

"The blood is a different story, but since you're not in the system, we're good. I would say we shouldn't stay in Boca too long in case they start canvasing house to house."

Steph jumped up and gave him a strangling hug. "What would we do without you, Troy?"

"You're about to find out," I said, but no one heard.

Their grandpa finished his beer with a rocking belch and went to get another in the kitchen.

"So, what's the next step?" Troy asked, flipping his bangs out of his eyes.

Barry shifted in place. "I think this ice is starting to melt. Anyway, I'm out of commission for a bit while my ass feels like someone took a bite out of it. But I say we head west, Texas or something like that. Houston where there's big oil money and we hit a Federal Reserve bank there for our last haul. We score there and we can retire for good."

"And then what?" Mom asked. She was back by the phone, like she was willing herself to pick it up.

"My brother in California. We hide out there until the heat is off and they all forget about us. Then we go wherever we want. Paris, Spain, like we talked about?"

Heidi appeared in the doorway, cutting me a look. She thought it nuts that we would even continue. I went to speak up, but everyone started talking over me about where they wanted to live.

"Mexico," Jenny said, singing "La Cucaracha" and shaking her hips.

"That's so messed up," Steph said. "The first thing that pops in your mind with Mexico is cockroaches?"

Jenny stuck out her tongue. "It's a famous song!"

Barry snapped his fingers at me. "Kid, kid," he said. "Can you get me that vial from the glove compartment?"

I didn't move.

"Go on, go on." He cocked his head toward the door.

I wanted to argue with him, but it was easier to get him the vial. On the way, I did a bump myself because it had been a while. My nerves sated. Inside, I stealthily slid it into his palm, but it wouldn't have mattered because no one was paying attention to me anyway.

32

Barry decided we should all stay the night, since it was getting dark, and he was as high as the sky. Wanting some privacy, Mom helped carry Barry back to the RV and they set up in the overhead nook. When I went to go to sleep in my couch/bed, they shooed me away.

"It's not that we don't want you here," Barry said.

"Your father and I need some alone time," Mom said, with her hand in Barry's shirt, tweaking his nipple.

"Let me get a change of clothes." I went behind the sheet partition and grabbed whatever smelled the cleanest.

"Hey, c'mere," Barry called out, and I crawled up in bed with them. He had a bottle of alcohol clamped in his hand, sharing sips with Mom, who giggled after each swallow. "I was really impressed with you today."

I thought of the notepad where I'd written his most gruesome act and instantly felt guilty. "Oh yeah?"

"With everyone. This hiccup was no one's fault."

"You had a real gun," Mom said, swaying in place and having trouble propping herself up on her arm.

Barry and I gave each other a quick glance. "No..." we both said simultaneously.

"It's okay." She took another strong sip. "I mean, it's not, but what's it matter anymore?"

"Sweetie, he's capable of handling it," Barry said.

"Well, good." She was looking out the window. "Look at the moon, so big, makes you do crazy things. I can't even call my own mother."

"Jude, we talked about this—"

"Did we? Because I don't remember coming to a consensus. We're leaving tomorrow and you won't let me tell her we've gone."

He brushed away a strand of hair blocking her sight. "It's too dangerous."

She hiccupped. "You think she'll call the cops? She wouldn't do that to us, at least not to her grandchildren."

"She already knows we've gone. We can call from the road once we're far enough away."

Mom buried her head in a pillow. "I'm never seeing her again, am I?"

"Sweetness, your relationship was not a healthy one."

"You lost your parents so early," she said. "You never had an adult relationship with them. For all her faults, she's still been my mother for thirty-seven years."

She began weeping loud enough for Johnny Cash to dart over and mewl too.

"Come here, puppy, come here." She patted the bed and Johnny Cash leaped up, licking her face and blues away.

"We have to be smart, Judy," he said. "Not let emotions get the best of us. Otherwise, we're done for."

Mom wasn't listening anymore, caught up in Johnny Cash's love. Barry cocked his head to the side, telling me he wanted a chat. He winced as he made his way down.

"This is seriously a pain in my ass," he said, as he collapsed onto my couch/bed. He patted for me to sit next to him. "I made a decision."

"Yeah, I heard. Texas."

"Right. But another decision. I want Troy to come with us."

"Why?"

"Son, we wouldn't have been able to pull off that heist without him. We'll need him for a bigger score. Besides, your sister will go bonkers if we don't bring him along. She carried on for an hour earlier today about how she'd *die* without him."

As much as I hated to admit it, he was right. But I didn't want Troy around, my connection with Barry lessened. My role sidelined.

"Can Heidi come along too?" I asked, the real reason why this news bothered me.

"Who?"

"Heidi. His sister. She has a great shot—"

He poked me in the spleen. "Look who's got a little girlfriend."

"I do not."

"Get to second base yet?"

"I don't even know what that is."

He mimed the action of squeezing a breast. I shook my head.

"Ah," he said. "Don't get stranded on first."

"Why can't she come?"

"Son, does this look like a motel on wheels? Where would she sleep?"

"Troy's sleeping with Steph!"

"Exactly, so he has a bed. Now, I may not win father of year, but I'm not letting my eleven-year-old shack up with a girl."

"Dad, I'm twelve."

"Whatever." He dug into his eye and removed some crust. "Hey, when did you turn twelve?"

"In January."

"Right, the sixth?" he asked, as if he wasn't sure. "Yeah, things were hectic then, what with us about to lose the house. Kinda slipped my mind." He gave me a side hug. "I'm sorry, bud."

"It's okay."

"No, it's really not. Happy birthday, man. Twelve years old, huh? Already chasing tail. I remember my first crush. Cookie Feinworth-Bucaritz."

"That's a name?"

"One you don't forget. She'd do this thing with her tongue when we kissed where she'd roll it around..."

"Okay, Dad, I get it."

"I know you want your little girlfriend to come along, but the truth is, we can't take the risk. And with Troy, it's only gonna be for this last score.

We're gonna net so much we can go buy a place somewhere international and there will be a million little Parisian girls for you to play with." He nudged me in the stomach. "Huh, I bet they French kiss well."

"So corny."

"I'm really proud of you, my man. How you're helping to lead this family, get the girls to see my way." He rubbed his nose until it was red. "I love you, bud."

"Love you too, Dad," I murmured, as he hugged me close.

"Ah, I might as well crash right here. Think those pills their grandpa gave me are starting to kick in. Woo, my dreams are about to be lit."

I got off the couch/bed so I could tuck him in, weirdly feeling like the parent and he, my child. I even left a kiss on his forehead. He closed his eyes and was snoring in seconds. Mom as well from her bed with Johnny Cash in her arms.

"Good night," I said, leaving the RV and closing the door.

* * *

Jenny was asleep on the couch when I went inside. From down the hallway, I could hear Steph and Troy bumping uglies. Their grandpa passed out on his recliner in front of a TV showing infomercials. A light shone from Heidi's door crack. I knocked as I entered.

"I didn't say come in."

She was curled on her bed, a stuffed animal clutched to her chest. For all her bombast, she was still a little girl.

"I got no place to sleep," I said, and when she didn't respond, I sat on her bed.

"Oh, just get under the covers," she said, kicking them off so I could get under them. She smelled like vanilla. On her ceiling, she'd stuck stickers of the solar system that glowed in the dark. "I put them there years ago, never have taken them down."

"I like 'em."

She shrugged, and I snuggled closer.

"What are you doing?"

"I'm cold."

"Aaron, it's like a hundred degrees."

"We're leaving tomorrow."

"So?"

"So, this may be our last night. My dad said you can't come with us."

I could hear her grinding her teeth. "But Troy can?"

"Yup."

"Once he leaves, I have a feeling he won't ever come back."

"That's not true, he will."

She turned on her back. "No, Aaron, he won't. And I told you, I don't want to come with you."

"We're hitting a big bank in Texas."

"I know, and I think you're ridiculous for doing so."

"You won't think that when we take serious dollars."

"Oh, serious dollars? They've linked you to your other robbery."

"So?"

"You really trust your dad to pull this off?"

"I...do."

"That doesn't sound convincing."

"No, I do. I mean, can we talk about something else?"

"Okay, fine, what do you want to talk about?"

"Tell me what you wanna do with your life."

"I wanna be a vet. Help animals."

"I really am sorry about your guinea pig."

"Shut up, Aaron."

"Can I write you?"

She sat up and reached over to her desk to pull out a Post-it and a pen.

"Here's my address," she said, writing it down. "And speaking of writing things down—"

"I know, I did what you said. I wrote something bad that my dad did."

"Keep doing it."

We lay in silence, nothing left to say. Her stickers catching my focus, mimicking a universe beyond our comprehension. So many possibilities. Paths to travel. Alternate versions, other than our own. Some less exciting, some safer and more well-trod. Different Aaron Gimmelmans and Heidis living in other dimensions. Maybe meeting at better times in their lives when they could be together.

"I think I love you," I said, but she was already snoring, the sound like a whistle.

Still full of coke, I wasn't getting to sleep anytime soon, so I let that whistle guide me to those other paths I'd never get to explore.

Morning came like a bruise, our reality humid and sticky, the RV already revving up.

33

We left super early in the morning. I didn't say goodbye to Heidi because she was still asleep and there was nothing left to say. Their grandpa made breakfast sausages he doled out wrapped in napkins that we munched on as we floored it out of Boca Raton. As part of the deal to come along, Troy would be the driver, especially since Barry was holed up in bed still on pain killers, Mom wrapped in his arms. It was a fifteen-hour drive to Texas, one we planned on doing in two shifts. Since Jenny was being weird with Seymour, and Barry and Mom had cordoned themselves off, I was stuck with Troy and Steph making goo-goo eyes with one another in the front.

"Got close to my sister?" Troy asked, after Steph took a break from petting his hair to paint her toenails out the window.

"We're gonna keep in touch."

"They kissed," Steph said, as the RV jerked to the right, and she left a green streak on her foot.

"She was worried you'll never come back," I said.

Troy licked his lips, flipped his bangs out of his eyes with one hand on the wheel. "Not likely."

"Who will take care of her?"

He chuckled. "She can take care of herself. Going on to high school soon. She won't miss me."

"Oh righteous," Steph said, turning up the radio. "Tiffany!"

We were bombarded with an off-key version of Steph singing along with

"I Think We're Alone Now," complete with primping her hair and aping Tiffany from the MTV video. Troy turned it up, and Steph leaped out of her seat, shimmying to the beat, her oversized jean jacket hanging from her back.

"You have a great voice, girl," Troy said, and I knew he was a big fat liar. The coke I'd ingested last night seemed to form under the bridge of my nose and cause a rousing headache. I went to shut the radio off, but she grabbed me by the collar to join in her uninhibited dance. We bounced around, even Johnny Cash got involved, while Jenny gave us the finger. When it ended, she hugged me.

"Smile, Aaron, live life."

The radio DJ came on and talked about a concert Tiffany and Debbie Gibson were doing together at a huge mall in New Orleans tomorrow, part of Tiffany's Mall Tour.

"Shut up," Steph screeched. "Shut up."

"You shut up," Jenny called out from the back.

"Tiffany AND Debbie Gibson together. It's like the two sides of World War Two uniting."

"Yeah, totally, babe," Troy said.

"No, it's not," I said.

"I've been so caught up in this RV," Steph said. "I haven't been paying attention to the news."

"That's not news," I said. "A Kuwait airliner was hijacked demanding the release of—"

"Oh Aaron, no one cares about that." Steph bolted over to Barry and Mom's bed.

"Mom! Dad!"

Barry and Mom emerged from under the covers, the smell of their body odor filling the RV.

"What is it, sweet?" Mom said, her eyes glassy and sparkling.

"Mom, Tiffany AND Debbie Gibson are doing a concert together in New Orleans."

"Wake me when it's Jim Morrison risen from the dead," Barry said, and nibbled on Mom's shoulder.

"We have to go," Steph begged. "New Orleans is on the way, and like, this is an opportunity that might never happen again. It's like the Nazis and the Americans coming together for a night of, like, amazing pop tunes."

"That makes no sense," I said. "Are you calling Tiffany or Debbie Gibson a Nazi? Because I don't think either would be pleased at the comparison."

"Neither, it's a figure of speech, and like, c'mon, I mean, Mom, you two don't have to go, I'll take Jenny and Aaron and give you guys a night off."

Barry and Mom's eyebrows rose at the offer. Barry's like thick caterpillars that had a life of their own.

"Please, don't make me go," I said, interlocking my fingers and getting on my knees.

"No, this'll be good," Barry said, swinging his legs out of the bed and showing his boner.

"Dad, what the hell?" Steph asked.

"Jesus," I said.

"Whoops," he *huh, huh, huh*ed. "Didn't realize I was exposed."

"Nothing wrong with our beautiful natural bodies," Mom said, but wisely covered him up.

"It's the meds their grandpa gave me, makes me loopy." He looked down at his tush, as if he'd forgotten the bullet happened. "Goddamn, that still smarts."

"Stephie, I think it's a lovely idea," Mom said, and Steph screeched like a banshee on crack. "You all could use a happy moment."

Mom seemed so sad when she said this, like happy moments had become a foreign concept.

"Happy happy," Barry said, kissing her neck.

Steph ran over to tell Troy, while Barry and Mom got back under the covers.

"We should be celebrating," Barry said, tickling Mom.

"Barry, stop. Stop."

Barry poked his head back out, nodding to the front. "Aaron, if you'd give us—"

"I'm gone," I said, and rejoined Troy and Steph up front. Steph was canoodling in his lap.

"Rad," Troy said. "You guys are so fucking bodacious." He rubbed Steph's cheek with his eyes still on the road.

The radio DJ came back on. "And now, our number one requested song. 'Lost in Your Eyes' by Debbie Gibson." Steph clapped like a fool. Troy began to lip sync.

I get lost in your eyes. And I feeeeeel my spirits rise.

Steph melted into a puddle.

We drove into the night where we found a rest stop in Slidell, Louisiana, near a highway that would take us across a giant lake to New Orleans. I figured I should sleep and not have a toot from Barry's vial, which was getting dangerously low. That either meant he'd been dipping in more than before, or I was guilty, for emptying it up my own nose. Sober for once, my dreams delved into violent scenarios. We were back in the bank in Boca, Barry, punching the security guard so hard in the face that it collapsed like in some poor special effects B movie. When I woke, we were crossing Lake Pontchartrain. I stumbled out of bed, made some coffee as Mom sat glued to the small TV on the counter, flipping from news station to news station. She bit her nails, now chewed to the nub. She flipped from the local news to the national covering the robbery. She had the volume on soft, so it was hard to hear, but it seemed like the police had no leads, showing the same grainy footage of the heist before I sprayed the cameras. The last image on the screen of me masked as Jimi Hendrix.

"Morning," I said to her, but she barely acknowledged, a grumpy *har-rumph* attacking me with coffee breath. I figured it was best to leave her alone.

In New Orleans, we found a park for the RV to stay, while us kids walked to the nearby mall. The concert was at noon, and it was just past nine. Secretly, while I hated the two-headed beast of Tiffany/Debbie Gibson, I was excited to let loose. Steph had told me the other day to live life, and I realized it was hard for me to ever relax enough to actually enjoy myself. Even my time with Heidi, I was so worried I'd screw everything up that I barely remembered anything we talked about or did. Just that one kiss, played over and over, each time my memory making us kiss longer. I wanted to write to her soon.

When we got to the mall, a zillion girls with braces foamed at the mouth. I had never seen anything like it before, all these girls, holding signposts with music pumping. Girls were crying, or screeching, cackling like hyenas, shouting Tiffany's and Debbie's names in a chant I could feel in my bones.

"This is fuckin' nuts," Jenny said to Seymour. I'd forgotten she was there. Seymour seemed more well-worn, like he'd been through a war and only made it through semi-intact.

"Is this line even moving?" Steph asked, after an hour of standing still in the exact same place. The doors hadn't opened yet, security guards on high alert for any little girls trying to break in.

"Some people got here at midnight," a girl in front said, dressed like a Tiffany clone: hoop earrings hanging from other hoop earrings, a jean jacket like Steph's, scrunchie socks over her tucked-in jeans.

"I have an idea," Troy said, and whipped out a stack of bills. "I had a feeling this might happen, so I brought some tubular cashola."

He had a bop to his walk as he headed to the front of the line. I could see him talking with two of the security guards who shook their heads, but then he showed them the cash, and they nodded. We were waved over past a million fans glaring at us to die, gnashing their teeth, cursing us with imagined voodoo dolls.

When we entered the cool AC of the mall, a light shone through the glass windows like we'd been sent to heaven, bathing us in shimmering bliss. A pseudo-stage had been set up, microphone stand ready, the crowd screaming until their throats became sore.

"Oh my God, oh my God, oh my God," Steph said, and linked her arms around Troy's neck. "You are so bodacious for getting us in."

"Anything for my girl."

We found a spot to plant ourselves, close enough to the stage after Troy gave a posse of little blonde girls forty bucks each to get behind us. Troy and Steph started making out, and since there was no one else to talk to...

"Hey Jenny belly."

She looked up cross-eyed. "What?"

"Nothing. How've you been?"

She was glaring at me so strong it was like her eyes had lasers.

"How've I been? What the fuck do you care?"

"I wanted to check in about the guinea pig..."

She rolled her eyes. "Everything dies, Aaron."

"What? No, I know. But you killed it. Have Mom or Dad talked to you about it?"

"Do they even know?"

I gave her a side hug. "I just want to make sure you're okay."

She looked at Seymour and then up at me. That was as much of an answer as I was gonna get.

"How's Seymour been?" I asked, trying to keep the conversation going.

"Seymour isn't real."

"Right. No, I know. And good you know that too."

"No duh, of course I do."

"Why don't we make fun of the songs when they come on, to keep us from dying of boredom?"

She petted Seymour's fur slowly. "I'm listening."

"Like let's substitute words in the song titles and sing it really loud to piss off Steph."

She put Seymour up to her ear, he was obviously telling her something. "Seymour likes your idea."

"Like instead of 'Lost in Your Eyes' we could sing, 'Lost in Your *Thighs*.'"

Seymour shot up to her ear again. "That's the best you can do?"

"You got anything better?"

Seymour poked his nose in her ear. "Seymour says instead of 'Lost in Your Eyes,' we could do 'Lost in Your *Vagina*.'"

She barked the word *vagina* loud enough for a few fans around us to swivel their necks.

"Or," she said, smiling like a devil, "instead of 'I Think We're Alone Now,' we can sing, 'I Think We *Boned* Now.'"

I burst out laughing but wagged my finger. "Tell Seymour that's crude."

"Fuck your crude."

The shrieks around us got louder and louder, deafening all other sounds. A Casio beat thumped through the mall as Tiffany burst on stage and everyone lost their ever-lovin' minds. What felt like a tall wave knocked us from behind as girls yanked each other's hair to see over one another. Tiffany was dressed in a small top hat, her red hair spilling out, and a leather jacket halfway on filled with colorful pins.

"Hello, New Orleans," she said, into the microphone, waving at the crowd who responded with "We luvvvv you Tiffany!"

"I love you all too!"

A fan next to me gripped my arm and jumped up and down screaming, "She loves me. She loves me."

"Calm the fuck down," I said, yanking my arm away.

Jenny spun her finger around her ear. If Jenny was calling someone crazy, they had mega issues.

Tiffany started singing "I Think We're Alone Now."

"*Children behave*," she began, as everyone sang along, knowing every word. Tiffany, to her credit, worked the crowd well, bopping from side to side on the stage and catering to all her adoring fanatics. Steph and Troy danced in each other's arms, and Steph looked so damn happy I couldn't hate. She'd been so miserable when we left Kent at first, now she seemed in pure love, touching Troy like she never wanted to let him go.

Trying to get away into the night
And then you put your arms around me
And we tumble to the ground
And then you say...

"I think we *boned* now," Jenny sang.

I found myself shaking my butt a little, Tiffany being infectious, I guess. The stress of the robbery pushing into the rearview as my shakes became bounces and then jumps until my arms were moving too, swinging around and nearly decapitating a little moppet.

"Sorry," I went to say, but the girl, a trooper, brushed it off and flung her arms in the air.

I closed my eyes and let Tiffany guide me to a moment of happiness. In this paradise, the police weren't currently sifting through our DNA and combing over the camera footage for any indication of who we were. We had gotten away with stealing close to a hundred thousand dollars, an amount people could take a lifetime to amass, and we had done it in a matter of hours. And yeah, I'd found true love and lost it, but at least Heidi and I left off better than we initially had. And yeah, Barry had been shot in the ass, but at least it wasn't anywhere more serious. And sure, Mom seemed depressed, but she wasn't being fake smothering anymore so that was a plus. I could also be mad at Troy for weaseling his way into the family, but he *was* keeping Steph preoccupied. Even Jenny, sure, she mutilated Heidi's guinea pig but didn't seem too affected, so it was best to just move on.

"*I think we're alone now. There doesn't seem to be anyone around,*" Tiffany sang, as I joined in.

I opened my eyes to Jenny dancing with Seymour, dropping her guard enough to become lost in the exhilaration.

"*I think we're alone now,*" I continued, singing louder. "*The beating of our FARTS is the only sound.*"

Jenny's eyebrows shot up into her hairline, and she laughed so hard she doubled over, calming herself down enough to sing, "*The beating of our FARTS is the only sound,*" when the chorus came back.

And then, like a magic rope pulled her toward us, Tiffany danced in our direction. Steph was clawing out her eyes as Tiffany got closer, mere inches, Steph's voice carrying through the microphone and blasting into the mall. Tiffany smiled, winked, and took off her little top hat, then placed it on Steph's head. Some other girls tried to grab it, but Steph stayed strong, using her shoulders to knock them all away. Tiffany bee-bopped back to the center of the stage to finish the song and punched at the air during the final chorus as the crowd chanted along, who then lost their shit even more when Debbie Gibson peeked out from the stage singing "Out of the Blue," and gave her frenemy Tiffany a nod. Girls flipped their signs to the other side with Debbie Gibson proclamations. Jenny sang "Out of the *Poo*" instead as I made fun as well, the two of us with our arms around each other, Seymour forgotten and stuffed into her jean skort.

After the concert, we were high, not a drug high like on coke, but fueled. Steph was babbling about getting Tiffany's mini top hat, and Troy said how sexy (barf bag) it was when she got to sing into the microphone. Jenny was singing "Out of the *Poo*" all the way back till we heard "Try (Just a Little Bit Harder)" pouring from the shaking RV. The inside hot-boxed with windows shut, candles melting into wax nubs, and Barry and Mom peeking from under sweaty covers, their faces long and disappointed at our return. They didn't say anything, but I could see it, while Janis Joplin wailed and they had forgotten about us for a glorious day, entwined until the buzzkills came roaring back, marching to Tiffany songs and destroying their sixties free love vibe where they had no responsibilities and recklessness reigned. Mom seemed to swallow a ball of tears at our revival, retreating under the covers while Barry chewed at his cheek, eyes spinning and wild, and I made an excuse for the rest of us to grab a bite. Johnny Cash had pissed all over the floor, so we took him out for a walk. We found a diner that let him in where we got milkshakes and burgers and tried to hold on to our day of happiness that was disappearing with the sunset and coming night.

"Out of the *Poo*," Jenny said, and we smirked but couldn't bring ourselves to a full-on laugh. The mall concert one of the last times we ever really would.

34

Now came the time for two non-Gimmelmans to enter our universe. Unbeknownst to us, they'd been orbiting for a quite a while—well, one of these non-Gimmelmans Barry knew about, but put his threat level on the backburner. Out of sight did not necessarily mean out of mind, but Barry surmised that the United States was a very big place, and we were too far away from New Jersey to be on Mr. Bianchi's radar anymore. He should have realized that when money was a part of an equation, no one, especially mobsters, ever let their radar lapse. Of course, since I wasn't actually present for these interactions, a lot has been reimagined, but one thing about me was that I always had a great imagination.

So, while Mr. Bianchi was on his way to Kent Goodyear's house, once boyfriend of Stephanie Gimmelman and heartbroken enough to sell her out for a generous donation to his church, another entity had picked up on our scent. A man on the other side of the law who had done equally despicable things in his own line of duty and off—a fine line of sadomasochism between the two.

Later on, I'd learn a lot about Special Agent Alan Terbert mostly through my own research to add to my reimagining. He might have banked on a hero's worship once he sunk his teeth into our case, never expecting he'd be reviled to such a degree that he would leave the Bureau, even go so far as to change his name and relocate to the boondocks of St. Andrews by-the-Sea, only to be outed after a drunken row at a popular bar for lobstermen, who made his life a living hell (deservedly), and caused him to go wandering on a dark night in the middle of a brutal winter when he found himself on an iced lake, dead the next morning of hypothermia. But that would be years away.

While the Gimmelmans plus Troy were on our way to Houston to hit the Federal Reserve Bank, Special Agent Terbert, a Florida resident but a Virginia native, became closely aligned with our own travels. After a messy divorce from a wife who wound up with sole custody of his two kids, Special Agent Terbert relocated to Florida to start anew. A functional alcoholic, he was good at his job and devoted himself to it with a borderline obsession. The Bureau even looked the other way at any allegations of spousal abuse by one Kimberly Terbert, who wound up settling out of court and keeping the kids instead of any further charges against her ex. Alan never cared much for kids anyway, so he accepted the terms. He couldn't go within five hundred yards of her. At first, he stayed in Virginia a few towns away, but he swore he could still smell her in the air, and when a position opened in Miami, he jumped.

An FBI office in 1980s Miami primarily dealt with drug cartels moving product from Mexico, something his colleagues had a greater interest in combating. So, he was often given, the non-drug-related offenses. He stayed connected to Virginian news by subscribing to all their major newspapers out of a force of habit, which was where he came across the first Gimmelman robbery. It had caught his eye because he had been to that very town before, thinking it a ho-hum, Bible-thumping yawn where Kimberly's sister lived. In fact, her sister's sister-in-law was one of the tellers at the bank who was interviewed for the newspaper. She described the masks of famous musicians that the robbers wore and how she was afraid for her life. Alan rolled his eyes at her overreaction; most robbers never shot the guns they held. He'd even seen heists where the guns were fake or hadn't been loaded. The sister-in-law carried on about how Jesus had been with her during this trying time and carried her to safety. He threw the newspaper across the room.

He met the woman once, but she represented the ilk his ex-wife gravitated to: pious and judgmental, quick to use the Lord as a scapegoat. Kimberly used to do it all the time. He'd never pretend that he wasn't at fault for the souring of their relationship, but she was to blame too. He had to walk on eggshells at all times for fear of Jesus frowning on him. His nightly drinking didn't please Jesus. His cussing—a word he abhorred because it made her sound like a simpleton—made Jesus weep. Every fiber of his being seemed to piss off Jesus in some type of way, so he gave up and went further to the side of the devil. Rubbed it in her face until she had more than enough. But her faults were minor in comparison. If he'd gotten his own head out of his ass for long enough, he would have understood that no one liked to go to bed with a black eye after an argument.

The Gimmelmans' first robbery irked him because it brought up shit about his ex. He spent that day swimming in a bottle of rye instead of cleaning the mulch out of the drain pipes like he'd planned. The second robbery, however, was close enough to his current home that it was blasted all over the TV. It dominated the news cycle likely because of the whimsical masks the robbers wore. The image of me as Jimi Hendrix before I sprayed the final camera became a front-page hit. After a week of killing too many bottles, Alan was glad to dry out in Boca while he followed the case.

Alan noticed one major misstep by the local police at the scene of the crime. They had taken samples of Barry's blood, only worthwhile if he ever got arrested and wound up in the system but failed to see a bit of tire track that had shot through a streak of blood during its getaway. Now most vehicles could use most tires, but ours being an RV had to use special tires, something he'd later learn. He also was wise enough not to spill that information to the media. If we knew the FBI was after an RV, we would've ditched the Gas-Guzzler. Alan understood that prey only gets caught when the predator is a few steps ahead.

He spoke to everyone in the bank. Lengthy conversations at their condos, usually over rugelach and weak tea. The managers who had mostly dealt with Barry obviously couldn't describe any facial features but found him to be gruff and impatient with a nasally voice. Samuel Myles, the security guard, was still being kept in the hospital to monitor his internal bruising.

He had a different description for Barry, a "sadomasochist." This dig hit Alan hard, since his wife Kimberly referred to him in the same way right before she packed up the kids and left him after he broke her nose. The three advisers who'd mostly dealt with me described me as short and Black. They assumed since I wore a Jimi Hendrix mask that I was Black as well. They all agreed that at around four foot five I was a little person, none of them suspecting a child. The same went for the heavyset Orthodox woman's assessment of Jenny—referred to as a "beast" for biting the woman's hand. She thought Jenny was an even shorter little person, around three feet tall. The tellers described Mom as shrill and scared, less sure of herself than the rest of us, especially Troy, who seemed in his element.

Alan wrote down in his notebook, *A mixed male and female multi-cultural gang with two little persons. How did this ragtag group of people come together?*

Meeting with his boss, Alan surmised that we would be hitting an even bigger bank for our next haul. Robbers got greedy, not content with the amount they'd amassed. Since the first bank had been in Virginia and the next Florida, around eight hundred miles separated the two. This meant if we continued in a similar way, we might wind up somewhere around the edge of Louisiana and Texas, since we'd be unlikely to head back up north toward Virginia. While this was pure speculation, police in Louisiana and Texas were notified to keep their eyes peeled. This would be around the time we planned to strike the Federal Reserve Bank in Houston, except Alan never expected us to try such a ludicrous gamble. With all of his obsessive tendencies to ferret out hunches and clues, he never once imagined he was dealing with someone like Barry, a madman who never saw losing as a possibility, even in the most wildly impossible scenarios.

35

While one threat in Florida was creeping our way, looking back, the other was probably gleaning info about us around the same time in New Jersey. Mr. Bianchi, aka Bananas Bianchi, aka The Strangler, was a John Gotti worshipping "pool man" from Tenafly. If you needed a new pool, he was your guy in the Tri-State area, except everyone who really knew Mr. Bianchi understood that pools were his cover. He was many things to many people, but to Barry he was a client and a loan shark. Mr. Bianchi fronted the money for some under-the-table investments that went belly-up when the stock market crashed. Since Mr. Bianchi also lost some of his own personal money on tips from Barry, he was doubly pissed. The fact everyone lost money didn't matter to Mr. Bianchi because Mr. Bianchi was not like everyone. From some digging, I found out that while Mr. Bianchi grew up in a three-family house and shared a room with his brother and sister kicking him every night in their one bed while he tried to sleep, he swore he'd find a way to break free from his Jersey wretchedness. His father, a garbage man, always smelled like garbage, his mother suffered from terrible migraines, always laid up with a washcloth over her face. No one paid attention, if he was around or not. He stole in junior high, sold enough drugs by high school to keep him cash heavy, and founded his own school with a roving gang of other thugs to rough up those who defaulted on any loan payments. The market for drugs in the sixties was high and Mr. Bianchi ran the neighborhood, then the town, and soon the surrounding ones until he was pretty well known in

New Jersey if you needed quick cash or a score, despite any caveat that came along with it. Once you were in Mr. Bianchi's circle, good luck leaving.

Barry had worked with some low-level mobsters before. During the mid-eighties boon, he made a shit ton of moolah for many of them, enough to come across Mr. Bianchi's lizard lips. At first, Mr. Bianchi was rolling in it from Barry's tips, up until the crash when Mr. Bianchi lost an amount so astronomical, he took it personal. Barry swore the money would come back and that the market ebbed and flowed, but Mr. Bianchi wasn't seeing any upticks. Barry borrowed more cash against what he lost, which caused Mr. Bianchi to become even more inflamed. And while Barry was able to pay off other investors he owed he got in deeper with Mr. Bianchi. By the time Mr. Bianchi showed up to their house expecting a payment, a new family had already taken over, no clue where Barry went. He'd have to do some detective work to find out.

In terms of immediate family outside of his wife and kids, Barry had little. A brother on the West Coast he'd not seen in years. Few colleagues, since most had been fired after that fateful Black Monday. His mother-in-law lived down in Florida so Mr. Bianchi figured he'd save her as a last resort. Asking around at Barry's kids' school led him to discover the oldest daughter had a pretty serious boyfriend named Kent Goodyear.

Now some of this was retold to me a long time afterwards, and I filled in the rest through the eyes of those involved. The Goodyears' doorbell played "Blessed Assurance" when rung. Mr. Bianchi's father had been a staunch Catholic, and he'd been confirmed, and his children confirmed as well. They went to church every Sunday. He believed in God but did not fear Him. He'd already tilted too far along the spectrum to wind up in heaven and figured all bets were off for the rest of his time on Earth.

Kent opened the door, one eyebrow raised in suspicion. Mr. Bianchi lied and said he was a good friend of the Gimmelman family and had been worried sick ever since they disappeared. Kent's mother was lurking in the background. She could either be a pest or try to help him out of the goodness of her heart.

"Please, come in," she said, a meek lady with a bouffant hairdo and wide, spooky eyes. A cross hanging from her neck weighed more than her. No makeup, no other jewelry, plain clothes and sensible shoes. "Kent was so upset when Steph first left, but I was always..."

Her spooky eyes circled around the room.

"Always what, ma'am?"

She had a tea kettle on and offered him a cup along with a plate of wafers that tasted like paint chips.

"Well, they were...*Jewish* for one."

She said it quickly, as if it was a secret. I'd never liked her, the quiet ones the most suspiciously prejudiced.

"Just the kind of clothes she wore," Mrs. Goodyear continued.

"Mom," Kent said, in a whine.

"I don't think she was right for you," she said, and then nodded for Mr. Bianchi to nod too, so he did, just to satisfy her.

"So, you and Stephanie Gimmelman were going steady?" Mr. Bianchi asked.

Mrs. Goodyear made a birdlike sound that was sort of a hiccup. "Steady? No, no, no."

"Mom," Kent whined again.

"Mrs. Goodyear," Mr. Bianchi began, turning on the charm. "What church do you go to?"

"Trinity Church," she said, as if he should know.

"Beautiful." He wasn't about to admit his Catholicism to this WASP, even though he reeked of it. Still, he went on about how lovely her pastor and the services were, even their choir.

"Yes, like angels singing."

"I would love to give a sizable donation," he said. She pressed against her heart, which must've been fluttering. "Would you have the precise information about who I should send any checks to?"

She jumped up, more alive than he'd seen her thus far. "Yes, let me get it for you."

Darting from the room like a squirrel, she was gone in a flash.

"Now," Mr. Bianchi said, shedding any polite skin he maintained with the mother, "Do you have any idea where Stephanie might be?"

Kent thought about the week after Steph left when he waited by his phone for hours: not sleeping, not eating, simply existing for her. At first, her calls were a wonderful song, the ringer stirring his heart, but when they stopped, he came to resent the phone, sitting there all smug and silent, and soon he came to resent her. Steph didn't care about him. She never cared about him. She'd been with him because he was a good Christian boy, the opposite of what her mother wanted. They could never have a life together. He'd die before converting to Judaism and even if she'd convert, she didn't really care about the Lord. She always yawned every time he brought up Jesus, making fun of him the time she put her hand down his pants and he recoiled when the tip of her fingernail touched his dick. He kept picturing how the Lord would be frowning as they moved toward intercourse. Even the songs he made up for her never seemed to excite as much as her idols, Tiffany and Debbie Gibson. Through this lens looking back, he now viewed their entire relationship as a sham.

"She went down to Florida," he said. "In her family's RV. To her Grandma Bernice in Boca Raton."

Mr. Bianchi whipped out a checkbook and proceeded to write out two thousand dollars. He ripped off the check and handed it over.

"May your church do wonderful things with this gift."

He was gone before Mrs. Goodyear returned, already contacting his right-hand man to book him a ticket to Boca Raton.

36

Back in our reality, I woke up to Steph puking before dawn, heavy heaves that sounded as if she was trying to bring up a swallowed elephant. We'd parked the RV at a truck stop on the outskirts of Baton Rouge, Troy too tired to drive anymore and Mom and Barry not offering to exit from under their covers. Steph came out of the bathroom wiping her mouth with her sleeve, her face mashed with tears. Troy went to comfort her but she pushed him away and got into the top bunk in the back where she curled up in a fetal position and cried some more.

"What gives?" his eyes seemed to say to me, and I shrugged. He went to go after her, but I shook my head.

"She can get in a mood," I said. "Best to let her be."

"'Let Her Be,' like the Beatles."

I gave a polite laugh even though I didn't find it funny because that wasn't the title of the song.

"Let's get breakfast," he said, and I threw on a hoodie over a Spuds MacKenzie shirt that smelled of BO. We migrated to an all-night diner at the rest stop and ate this dish called coush-coush, cornmeal with bacon drippings.

"You don't like me much, do you?" he asked.

I was on my first cup of coffee and hadn't fully woken yet. All I could give was a shrug.

"I'm not trying to muscle in on your family," he said, while checking out a waitress's butt. "I really am into your sister."

I tilted my head toward the waitress whose butt he just ogled.

"Nothing wrong with a little lookin'. Your sister isn't like any other girl I've met before. She, like, sparkles."

"That's cause she's gassy."

"What?"

I downed the cup of coffee and flagged the waitress over for another. "Keep 'em comin'," I said.

"Well, aren't you a little man," she said in her thick Louisiana twang and shuffled off.

"I know your dad wants me to do one last job with you guys, but I'd like to stick around."

I blew my bangs out of my eyes. "I haven't seen Steph this happy. Don't break her heart."

He chuckled out of the corner of his mouth. "Oh yeah? Is that a threat?"

"Total threat. I'll kill you if you hurt her."

He patted the table with a drumbeat. "Respect, man. I hear you. I have the best intentions."

"I'll believe it when I see it."

From out of the window, I watched Steph leave the RV in an oversized sweatshirt, the sleeves long like a straitjacket. We'd left a note for everyone that we'd gone to the diner, so she ran over.

"Coffee," she said, to the waitress, once she slumped into the booth. "Must have a stomach bug or something. I haven't puked like that since the night I did Goldschläger shots. What the hell are you guys eating?"

"It's kinda like grits," Troy said.

"Barf city."

She ordered a bagel with peanut butter.

"Are you feeling better?" Troy asked, running his fingers through her hair.

"I might puke again. But yeah, a little better."

"Mom and Dad get up yet?" I asked, and Steph gave me a look like, *what do you think?*

"Does anyone else think this Houston plan is ridiculous?" she asked.

I didn't want to say anything, but I'd been thinking that too.

"I know, a Federal Reserve Bank," I said, and Steph interrupted.

"I don't even know what that is, but it sounds like it's out of our league," she added.

"We haven't made enough to stop now," Troy said. "Less than twenty thousand each, that's decent money but not life-changing."

"Why do we need life-changing money?" Steph asked. "When Mom was my age, she'd dropped out of school to follow bands. She had, like, no pressure. When you guys..." She lowered her voice. "...*rob*, it's all on me to get us away. Like, I'm waking up from nightmares of a bloody Dad jumping into the RV. Maybe that's why I've been puking?"

"Something's different with him," I said, then wanted to swallow it back, but Steph gave a cool nod.

"He's mega lost it," Steph said. "I don't think he can see past dollar signs."

"I thought about what would've happened if either of us were shot," I said. "Would he have taken us to a hospital?"

No one responded. I hated talking bad about Barry, but it felt good to get this off my chest. I would never tell him this, at least not at this time. I was glad to hear that Steph had the same concerns.

"Listen, listen," Troy said, his arm around Steph. "We do this last job and then quit. Go to a foreign city, wherever we want. Me and you," he said, into her eyes. "We can leave your family."

A twitch traveled up my spine when he said this.

"Sorry, Aaron," he said, as if he'd forgotten I was there. "I meant, away from your parents. You can come with us?"

The thought of being trapped with the two lovebirds for the rest of my life, too nauseating to imagine.

"Point is, none of you are bound to them," Troy continued. "Once we net a certain amount of money, you don't need them anymore."

Steph nuzzled into his shoulder. He lifted up her chin to kiss.

"I have pukey breath," she said.

"I don't care."

They swapped spit and I spun out of the booth. Outside the hot sun melted over the pavement. I sat on the burning cement, knees tucked to my face. I had never imagined a world without my parents before, one where I could be free. I would miss them, sure, but life might be easier without their narcissistic drama. It didn't mean I never had to see them again, we simply didn't have to live together.

"No," I said, shaking my head. These thoughts had only crept in because we were stuck in such close quarters. That wouldn't be for too much longer. And if the next job was a success, we'd kick ourselves for not going along with Barry's plan. I had to be his good soldier for a little bit longer, get everyone else on board. Then when we were rolling in it, I could decide what my future would be.

I went back inside the diner to convince Steph. And because she had such a simple brain, it wasn't hard to sway, especially after she got up to run to the bathroom again and I told Troy he had to help convince her too. It was too early to go against Barry and Mom, we didn't have enough of a justifying reason yet.

That would come later.

37

On our way back to the RV, Mom cut us off. She appeared out of the Gas-Guzzler in an oversized shirt that looked like a Mondrian painting, hair messy and covering her face in curls, dark Ray-Bans. She'd lost weight since we began our adventure, knees jutting from her legs like doorknobs, toenails semi-polished as if she'd given up halfway.

"Babies," she said, the rum on her breath oppressive. She captured us all in a hug, held on for long enough for it to feel awkward. Steph and Troy peeled away, sensing her neediness. "Stephie," she said, reaching out as Steph and Troy scurried back in the RV. She kept holding out her arms even after the door slammed. "Your father isn't awake yet," she told me like it was a secret. She wasn't even wearing any shoes. "I have to make a call."

At a pay phone, she opened her palm revealing a stack of quarters. From her other pocket, she removed a crumpled-up pack of cigarettes. She took one between her lips and lit it fast, inhaling nearly half the cigarette in one suck, her bare foot tapping against the pavement.

She took my hand, hers slick with sweat. "I'm calling Grandma Bernice."

"Does Dad—?"

She cut me with an evil glance. I backed down immediately. "I'm here for you," is all I said. "It's going to be all right."

She inhaled the rest of the cigarette, tossed it into the lot, dialed.

"Hello?" Grandma Bernice asked, her near-deafness allowing me to hear her shouting on the other end.

"Ma?"

"Judy?"

"Ma." The tears came, hot and spewing.

"Judy, where are you? You just disappeared. I've been worried sick."

"We had to go—"

"No note, nothing. I wake up and you're gone. I almost called the police."

Mom squeezed my hand, rubbing my finger bones against one another.

"No, no police. It wasn't...it wasn't working staying with you. Ma, we were all miserable."

"I'm sorry I bring you such misery."

"No, Ma, it's..." She let go of me to shake another cigarette out of the packet.

"Judy, I don't like what you've gotten yourself mixed up in."

"I'm fine," Mom said, but no one was buying that, not even herself.

"A man came to see me," Grandma Bernice said.

"What man?"

Please deposit a quarter to continue your call.

Mom shoved more quarters into the coin slot.

"Ma, what man?"

"Judy, I..."

"Ma, what man!"

"You must think I'm some *schlemiel*. Judy, I was at the bank that day—"

Mom hung the receiver against her shoulder while she lit her other cigarette.

"Nothing I ever did was good enough for you," Mom screeched, attacking the air with the cigarette.

"I didn't raise you to be like this. I lost you long ago."

I could hear Grandma Bernice weeping, and my heart hurt for that old woman's tears.

"Ma, what man came?"

Grandma Bernice sniffed back her tears. "FBI."

Mom grabbed for my hand again, squeezing the bones even harder. "What did he want?"

Silence over the receiver.

"Ma, what did he want?"

And then, quietly: "Judy, you know what he wanted."

It was out in the open now, obvious that Grandma Bernice had connected us to the bank heist, but Mom was in firm denial. Her hand holding the receiver started shaking, the cigarette spilling from her lips. She crouched to the ground, the phone tucked into her neck.

"Ma," she said, as an elongated spitball formed in her mouth.

"What you're putting those grandchildren of mine through is *tsuris*, suffering, and for what? What? That no good *shtunk* husband of yours? He was never worth any more than a common *shnorrer*."

"He didn't..." Mom got her breathing under control. "I wanted to do it as much as him."

"I don't believe that for a second. You're a follower, Judith, you have no mind of your own."

"Ma, stop."

"I will not stop, not until you get it into that thick skull of yours. And if anything happens to my grandbabies because of your foolishness, a *shanda* on you. You are no daughter of mine."

Mom melted, barely coherent.

"You selfish, rotten child," Grandma Bernice carried on. "Your father would spit on you. He's spinning in his tomb, oh my Herb, the only silver lining is he'll never know what a *loch in kop*, a hole you have in your head! A *shanda, a shanda, a shanda, a shanda.*"

Please deposit a quarter to continue your call.

"The FBI man?" Mom asked, quivering like she was having a seizure. "What did you tell him?"

"What do you think I told him? I told him nothing. And let God strike me down for my silence, I will not put my grandchildren in harm's way. But Judy, you must stop this *narishkeit*, or Hashem will punish. He won't stand..."

Please deposit a quarter to continue your call.

Mom tried to add more coins into the slot but her shaking fingers caused the quarters to fall to the pavement. Instead, like a spirit had goosed her body, she rose up and slammed down the receiver, again and again until the cord broke and the receiver went flying. Next, she attacked with her fists until they were red and raw and sliced open.

"Mom, Mom!"

I yanked her away from the phone booth. We skittered along the pavement as she fought against me.

"Mom, stop. Stop it!"

Snot poured from her nose, and she began speaking in tongues. I'd later realize this was a panic attack, but I didn't know what one was at the time. I pinned down her arms so she wouldn't hurt herself anymore. We cried together. I held her close and whispered into her ear that everything would be okay, even though I knew it would not. We were unraveling and no amount of money could get us back to who we were.

Barry emerged from the RV, hair in shock mode, barefoot and only wearing a bathrobe. He waltzed over like he had all the time in the world. He opened his fist revealing two white pills that he shoved in Mom's mouth and made her crunch down. He kept her mouth shut until he was sure she had swallowed. Slowly, she numbed, a moan escaping from her lips like a tire losing air.

"What the fuck?" I asked, scooting off of her to catch my breath.

"She's fine."

"She's not fine!"

He pinched the bridge of his nose. "Fuckin' kid, get her in the RV and let's get the fuck out of here before any of these rubberneckers call the cops."

I looked up at an audience of half a dozen people surrounding us with gaping mouths.

"Night terrors, she has night terrors," Barry told them, as he hoisted her to her feet and carried her toward the RV. Once they went inside, I had a brief moment where I thought to run, plead for a new family to take me in, one that lived in a sensible house with a school down the road who let me go to basketball practice every afternoon. I could see these strangers' mouths moving, calling me to join them, to be protected, secure.

Barry bust his head out of the window, Creedence's "Bad Moon Rising" pouring from the speakers as he screamed for me to get in. And I did, because I guess I was a follower like Mom. I often wished I had been more of a leader, or that Grandma Bernice gave us up, or a million other scenarios other than the road we actually traveled, with hazard signs aplenty.

38

Somewhere in Louisiana, we lost Johnny Cash. One of us had left the RV door open a smidge and he likely bolted to his freedom. None of us would realize until we were driving far away. At first, I worried that Jenny might have a meltdown, but she didn't really care. She had Seymour and all of us had other things on our minds other than the dog's welfare. If I'd have thought about it more, it should've concerned me that us Gimmelmans could be so nonchalant to lose a family member, even one with four legs.

In Baton Rouge, Barry got up early in the morning with the grand idea for the two of us to spend the day together. "Male bonding," he called it. Mom was holed up under the covers, licking her wounds. Steph and Troy were tasked to watch her and Jenny. He slid the coke vial into his front pocket, and we took a taxi to the downtown area. Some old buildings and plantations, I wasn't impressed. I knew he needed me on his side and could sense a separation. To lose me meant our whole carefully stacked Jenga operation might fall apart.

"What do you want?" he said, all teeth, whipping out a stack of bills. "Anything."

I wanted him to comb his hair, his 'do out of control. I picked out one of Mom's cigarettes, wrapped in a curl.

"Maybe I was saving that," he said, laughing way too hard. Had he taken a toot from the vial without me noticing, I couldn't tell. "How about a suit like those guys wear on *Miami Vice*?"

"Okay."

We went to a store where I chose a pastel blue suit, tailored to my size. Trying it on in the mirror, I had to admit I looked rad.

"You look rad," Barry said.

"I know."

He bought me Ray-Bans too, the whole outfit running over a thousand dollars.

"Somebody earned good grades," the saleswoman said, shaking her finger.

"I don't believe in school," Barry said, as she frowned. "I'm my own school."

I tugged on his sleeve to get us out of there before he could embarrass us more. We stopped at a café and got beignets dusted with powdered sugar.

"Your mother," he said, halfway through a beer. "She's really okay."

I took a hit of sweet tea, the sugar overload rocking my brain.

"Her relationship with Grandma Bernice was not a good one," he said. "It's better for them to be apart."

"Are you saying that because it's true, or because it's something you want me to hear?"

"Goddamn, you're a smart fuck." He drained the beer. "She doesn't realize it yet, but it *is* better. That woman is all negativity and brimstone."

"She knows about the bank."

He looked to the left, then the right. Customers having conversations around us, none of them listening. Inching forward in his seat, he talked close. "She cares about you kids too much to rat. Your lives would be destroyed."

"Do you want our lives to be destroyed?"

A bird landed on our table, small like a swallow. It cocked its head, waiting for his answer too.

"Of course I don't—"

"How do you see this ending?"

His eyes bugged. "The plan we had. International. Paris, maybe? Spain."

"What if we went there now?"

He shook his head. "This troubles me to hear. You're my gung-ho soldier. I'm saying we don't have enough cash yet."

"We don't have to live fancy." I tossed my hand in the air like that was what fancy people did.

"I owe money. You know this. You know this, right? I'm buying myself time."

"How much do you owe?"

He rubbed his nose as if he had an itch he couldn't scratch. "A lot. A lot a lot. Too much."

"Mob?" I asked, mouthing the word.

"It's not for you to worry about."

"But if we went to France, they wouldn't find us."

"They would. Eventually. So, this last job...it'll solve all our problems."

The sparrow flew away, unsatisfied with his answer. Part of me wanted to follow it wherever it went. After our bite, Barry got the wild idea to get me a better gun, a Bren Ten like they used on *Miami Vice*. He decided this gift would make me stop questioning his ways. We went to a gun store. A man with neck hair manned the counter. He showed us the Bren Ten, cool steel like Crockett and Tubbs used. The catch, there would be a wait. But hold on! Barry had another wad of bills hidden in his shorts. The man with neck hair was delighted. Bought off so easily. We left with the gun, and along with the suit and the Ray-Bans, I should've been ecstatic. But a sense of dread rumbled through my belly. I had awful diarrhea. Had to run into a shoddy restaurant and squat over a rusty toilet. In the mirror, I was pissed at how simply I could be bought. Outside Barry was whistling on the corner, "Friend of the Devil" by the Grateful Dead. I wondered if he'd firmly made the shift to becoming Jerry Garcia, a laser focus honed on our next job. He put his arm around me, yellow pit stains gaping from his undershirt, pulling me close. Kissing the top of my head.

"I'm giving you life experience," he said. "Worth more than any cash we'll steal. A story to tell your grandchildren. No one on this planet has had a childhood like you."

"That's a good thing?"

He winked. "A very good thing. What is life if not for experiences? We might as well be dead then."

I had a chill when he said the word "dead." Maybe it was because he walked with a terrible limp from being shot in the ass, and I had almost lost him. Maybe it was because the night before, he came to me bloody in my dreams. Maybe because I envisioned that he'd never survive this job. That an ominous cloud hung over our world, wanting retribution for the last time he escaped by the skin of his teeth. He continued singing "Friend of the Devil," not surprising because he'd been hoodwinked by the other side a long time ago, like I had too. I was his son after all. We shared the same blood.

There was no denying who I was. A Gimmelman through and through.

Great only in our warped delusions.

39

Grandma Bernice had gotten over the *fertummelt* ordeal of the FBI man visiting her condo when a very different threat rang her doorbell. She would tell this story over and over later on as a way to prove her stoic nature. She hadn't slept the night before, beside herself about the conversation she'd had with her daughter. Had she been too harsh? No, Judith had always been a *luftmensch*, her head in the clouds. Only a fool like her would have ever married a con artist like Barry. Grandma Bernice didn't trust him the first time she saw his mustache. So bushy. And he'd twirl it like a comic book villain. His baby blue eyes, suspicious too. She was of the mindset that husbands should be ugly, or at least not attractive. Her Herb wasn't deformed, but no one would ever call him a prize in the looks department. His bulbous nose full of cracks and fissures. His face mushed as if a giant pressed the features too close together. Teeth twisted from never wearing braces. A gut that hung over his belt. An oddly shaped head like a pumpkin. Yet he treated her well. When he was alive, Herb worked hard and there was always food on the table. In the old country, that was never a given for her family. She recalled one dinner when she was a child that consisted of a potato and onion sliced in bits for her parents and her brother too, before he died as a soldier in World War I. Her parents were strict and quite religious. Shabbat sacred, every holiday spent in temple, even after they migrated to America. Living on Essex Street, her father worked as a pickler. After school, she would hang out at the pickle stand. By the time she finished high school, he had passed, her mother never fully recovering. Grandma Bernice lived with her through her twenties, taking care of the woman who rarely left her room. She met Herb on the Third Avenue bus.

They had both rushed for a seat on a busy morning. She'd gotten a job as a typist for an Orthodox man and often he sent her around to pick up supplies. He was transferring his life's studies into a book. The man's father had been a rabbi and she was mesmerized by all he had learned. She found herself telling this to Herb once he insisted, she take the seat. She'd given him her number and told him to call after seven when she got home. Sure enough, at seven on the dot the phone rang, and they talked all night. He had migrated from Poland with his family and agreed that even though he'd lived in America for some time now, it still didn't feel like home. Grandma Bernice complained that people moved too fast in New York City. The other day she had a cup of coffee, and the waitress couldn't wait to rush her out. He suggested they go for a cup of coffee the next day and take all the time they wanted. On the date, she wore a new scarf she had purchased at Gimbels. It had a paisley design on it, and he commented how beautiful she looked. Grandma Bernice knew she was not a beauty but didn't think he was lying. He had rough hands and stubby fingers, but when he took her hand on the street she felt as though she'd always been meant to hold onto his. After leaving her that night with a kiss on her cheek, she stayed up all night thinking about him. They were married within six months.

He'd been on her mind after the FBI man came, mostly because she wondered what he might say at this whole *meshugge*. Much like her own mother, she was a single parent for most of Judith's life. From an early age Judith was wild and reckless. She'd refuse to eat her meals except for plain pasta and rarely listened. When Judith dropped out of school at sixteen to follow rock bands, Grandma Bernice prayed that Hashem would guide her right. At first, when Mom met Barry and got pregnant with Steph, Grandma Bernice hoped it would calm her down, her new keeping up with Joneses lifestyle even seemed to occupy her days, but Grandma Bernice knew that soon enough Judith would grow restless again. Although, she never would've imagined her daughter would become a bank robber.

With the FBI man, Grandma Bernice acted cool, clearly the opposite of her personality. She made him a cup of Nescafe and described exactly what happened. She was going to the bank to cash her social security check when the door was locked. The security guard poked his head out to say that they were doing renovations, but something seemed fishy. She knocked again and when no one answered she got back in her car and drove away. He didn't ask about the RV so technically she didn't have to lie. In fact, it appeared as if the police didn't know the RV was involved. And Grandma Bernice didn't either at first. She'd seen the RV but assumed it was simply parked and the family was downtown for the day. It wasn't until later watching the news when she saw the footage of the bank heist and put two and two together. She nearly choked on her babka seeing me as Jimi Hendrix spray-painting the cameras.

While the FBI man questioned, she went over the options of confessing what she knew or staying mum. And perhaps, if she warmed to him more, she might have. But instantly he made a comment about the picture of Herb on display. He said that Herb "looked like a good man," and when he talked his thin lips barely moved and she hadn't seen him smile once. There would be no way for the FBI man to know from the picture of Herb whether or not he was a good man, but it did prove to her that he was a liar. As much as it killed Grandma Bernice that we had become criminals, she'd rather us get away with it than be in prison forever. As long as no one knew we were actually the crooks, she could still show her face at temple and remain in good graces with Rabbi Moshe Drebelbaum.

So, when the doorbell rang the day after her fight with Judith over the phone, the last time they would speak, she thought she was done with our nonsense. But since she rarely received visitors, a ringing doorbell usually meant doom. Opening the door, she said "*goy*" under breath, since Mr. Bianchi was the *goy*est man she'd ever seen. He had a thin mustache, these fat sausage hands, and a fake tan. His wool suit out of place in hot Florida, and she reasoned that he had the kind of slicked-back hair only Italian men had. She imagined if she touched it, her fingers would be greasy all day.

"Mrs. Finkelstein?" he asked, extending one sausage hand. "How do you do today?"

She left his hand hanging, drummed her fingers against the door.

"I am an associate of your son-in-law's," he said, taking a further step inside. She stuck her tongue out at the mention of Barry. "Excuse me for bothering, but I was wondering if you knew where he was?"

"He doesn't live here," she said, going to close the door but his big foot was in the way.

"Yes, I know this." Mr. Bianchi took off his hat and spun it around in his hands. "But the family seems to have left New Jersey and I have urgent business to discuss with him."

She focused on a white crusted ball that formed on the corner of his lips. When he opened his mouth, it elongated.

"I'm parched, you wouldn't have a glass of water?"

"The pipes are rusty."

"Or a cold glass of milk. I've been traveling for some while."

Against her gut, she allowed him inside. Maybe that was for the best. Had she denied him entry, who knew what he might've done? Pushed her aside and ransacked the condo for any evidence of us? As I'd learn, he knew that we'd been here very recently. And he'd knocked down old women before—his nonexistent conscience didn't distinguish.

Once she closed the door, a chill ran up her legs. She had awful pains in her thighs for the last few years, usually the worst in the mornings. She had forgotten to stretch. She came out of the kitchen with two tall glasses of whole milk and handed him one. He was looking at the picture of Herb displayed like a shrine on the mantel.

"That's my Herb," she said.

He had nothing to say to that, already inside and done with small talk. He placed the glass of milk down without taking a sip.

"Mrs. Finkelstein," he said.

"Ms.," she said. "My husband is long dead."

He didn't correct himself. "Your son-in-law owes me a lot of money."

Two cats darted over, weaving past each other in an oval shape. The man scooped one up.

"Oh," Grandma Bernice said, caught off guard. Yakob was her favorite cat, a tabby. She had him the longest. He seemed so serene in this Italian man's arms. *Fool*, she wanted to say. The way the man petted him was menacing.

"They left Jersey in an RV, this I know."

How he talked reminded her of men in the 1950s with cigarette packs folded into their T-shirt sleeves.

"So?"

"I don't see no RV parked by this complex."

"That's because they've gone."

He petted Yakob harder, and Yakob purred.

"Where did they go?"

He stepped toward her, and she had trouble swallowing. A pocket of phlegm trapped in her throat. She blamed the milk she had just sipped.

"We had a fight and they left without telling me."

Again, she had not lied. She told herself not to look the other way and show any uncertainty. He gazed deep into her soul for any inconsistencies, held the cat tighter.

"I believe you."

"I think it's time for you to leave," Grandma Bernice said. She wasn't afraid of this man. If he struck her down and this was to be the end of her life, no one would find her body for days and the cats would eat her face. But she had too much faith in Hashem to have this be it. This man needed her, the only link he had to that *nudnik* Barry. He wouldn't have come all the way down to Boca Raton if he had other options.

He handed the cat to Grandma Bernice who held onto the soft fur as if for dear life. She had told herself she wasn't afraid, her body betraying her mind. When he leaned in closer, his breath smelled of cured pork. She'd never been so physically disgusted with a person and had to restrain herself from spitting in his face.

He removed a card from his front pocket that said, *Gianni Bianchi*. It had a picture of a pool.

"I'm in the pool business," he said. "If you hear from your son-in-law, please notify me. Otherwise, I'm going to have to return."

Grabbing the glass of milk, he gulped it down and then let go. The glass crashed to the floor.

"Oh," she said, jumping in fright as he laughed and sounded like a foghorn. She shooed the cats away from stepping on the glass, and by the time she did, Mr. Bianchi had gone, a faint whiff of cured pork still in the air. She clutched her bathrobe to her neck and sat down on the plastic-cushioned couch. She didn't clean up the glass, too shocked to move. Once the sun went down, she stirred back to reality and got a broom to sweep up the mess.

40

Yee-haw, we hit Texas finally reaching Beaumont at night, a sleepy city with only a few lights blinking. Off the highway, a Motel 6 called out, and Barry suggested we all take a break from the RV (and each other) by renting three separate rooms. The 'rents in one, Troy and Steph in one, and Jenny and I bunking up in the third. Our room had thin walls, bookended by both couples, and I knew I'd have to wear my headphones to drown out their lovemaking. Jenny got Bonkers candies and Mambas from the vending machine, and we had ourselves a late sugar dinner.

"How you doing?" I asked, lying on my bed, glad to not have a converted couch for once this trip.

"This room smells like death."

I looked over at Seymour, but she shook her head and pointed at a suspect stain on the carpet. I got up and covered it with a towel.

"Let's forget that we saw it. TV?"

She shrugged, and I flipped through the channels, coming across us again on the news.

"Leave it," Jenny said, sitting up on her knees. She watched in fascination when she came up on the screen and the Orthodox woman described Mama Cass again as a terror.

"I love it," she whispered to Seymour, in a creepy voice.

"Uh, let's watch something else."

I flicked through until we found an episode of *Growing Pains* where Mike

Seaver got in trouble for writing the notes from a test on the bottom of his sneakers. But then he never actually wound up cheating, learning so much from copying it down so intricately. Everyone hugged in the end. Fucking bullshit simplistic family. I turned it off.

"Hey," Jenny said, lobbing a Bonkers into my eye. I joined her on her bed.

"Listen, I'm gonna take care of you."

"O...kay."

"No really, no matter what. Even if Mom and Dad aren't here anymore."

"Why wouldn't they be?" she asked Seymour.

"Look at me," I said, and took Seymour away. She scratched my arm. "Jesus, Jenny, ow."

"Don't fuck with Seymour."

She hugged him so tightly, smushing his little fuzzy face. Seymour, a calm in the center of her crazy storm.

"I'm sorry, but if you love animals so much, why do you hurt them?"

She bounced out of the bed, eyeing the window as if PETA could be eavesdropping. Her little shoulders stayed up by her ears.

"I dunno."

"It's not what normal little girls do."

"Who said I ever wanted to be fucking normal?" She did a cartwheel. Stood in front of the mirror and made her hair into even more of a lion's mane. "You're like smart, and Steph's so pretty, what am I?"

"You're Jenny."

"I'm weird, like I never remember not being weird. Seymour listens to me when no one else does, when the animals don't either. That's why I've hurt them."

"What do you want them to hear?"

She did another cartwheel. "Okay, I'll...I'll get real angry sometimes. Like there's a *tick, tick, tick* inside of me. Gonna explode. Pow. So, I do."

"Do we make you angry?"

Through one of the walls, we could hear moaning, and the squeaking from a bedframe. Jenny banged on the wall.

"I'm not here, Aaron," Jenny said, her teeth chattering like she was cold.

"What do you mean you're not—"

"Like I'm a ghost, right? I pop up here and there, say boo, but usually no one notices."

The hairs on the back of my neck got all prickly.

"It's been a nutso time lately, Jenny."

She held up her tiny palm for me to stop talking. "That's how it's always been. No one has ever noticed me."

My heart nearly broke, I could feel it fracturing in two. Eyes watering.

"Jeez, I'm so... You know we all love you."

She shrugged her baby shoulders again. "Because you have to. But do you really?"

I sucked up a big ball of snot. "Yeah, you're my Jenny belly."

"You haven't called me that in years."

"I'm calling you that now."

She let out a child's sigh, one even sadder than an adult's because children shouldn't have the kind of problems that would make them sigh. She went back to her bed and picked up Seymour.

"I heard Mom and Dad once talking about me. They were fighting in their room, I guess I'd done something pretty bad, killed a bird or something and they said I was a mistake. They weren't trying to have me, but I happened anyway, and they thought about getting an abortion."

I wanted to hug her right there but was afraid she'd push me away.

"Hey, a lot of kids are unplanned. Like Drake at my school, his parents didn't want kids but then they had him."

"But they were glad they had him," she sang.

"So are Mom and Dad."

She cocked her head to the side. "That's not what they said that night. They called me the Exorcist."

"Wow, Jenny, I mean they were probably drunk or something and just upset. You know, people, adults especially, say a lot of things they don't really mean. It's called venting."

She held up her little palm again. "I know what the fuck venting means, Aaron. I'm not slow."

"No, I know—"

"Look, I'm freaky, I get it. I would be weirded out by me too."

"You're unique."

"Ugh, grody, you're such a cheesehead. Like, it's fine. Mom and Dad aren't that great themselves."

It was the first time one of us had really said it out loud. The motel got super quiet, even the moans from the adjoining rooms, as if they were listening to our secret truth session.

"No, they're not," I whispered, wanting to swallow the words back immediately after they escaped. This actually got Jenny to smile.

"Oooh, I've never heard you say bad things about Dad."

"Shut up, I didn't—"

"You hate Dad, you hate Dad," she shouted.

I leaped over and clamped my hand over her mouth as she still tried to shout my disloyalty.

"Stop it, listen, stop it. Can I take my hand away?"

She nodded for me to do so. Once I did, she shouted again.

"You hate Dad, you hate Dad!" she screamed, so I flung open the door and ran out into the night. The Texas air, smelling different, like leather, cotton, and sage. The motel lights glinting along the interstate. A semi roaring by, tooting its horn. I dug into my pocket and ate the last Bonkers. I didn't hate Barry, far from it. I still needed his acceptance like a junkie to a hit. Fuck Jenny for allowing any doubts to circulate. I looked up at a show of stars that twinkled. Those stars knew of our future because they existed so many light years away. They could see whether we'd be successful in Houston, whether Barry would remain a star like them in my eyes, or fall swiftly, become Barry eventually, and no longer Dad.

I spat out the Bonkers because it was cloyingly sweet, and I was getting too old for that kind of sugary shit.

41

We left the motel early and made Houston by the late morning, just in time for a pit stop at a local BBQ called The Pig Feast. On picnic tables outside, we tried their grub: slathered ribs, beef brisket, pork sausage, BBQ taters, and bourbon banana pudding. We ate like we might never eat again, focusing on the food rather than talking, until we finished our plates and were forced to make conversation.

"I feel ill," Steph said, rubbing her stomach. Sitting next to her, Troy bent down to kiss it. "Stop," she said, and then threw her greasy napkin down and mumbled about "going to the bathroom." She'd been in a foul mood ever since we left New Orleans.

Troy twiddled his thumbs and then got up as well. "Ima go check on her."

I wondered if their relationship was starting to sour, like it had with her last boyfriend.

No one seemed to acknowledge they had gone. Mom was dipping her spoon into her last bit of pudding, watching the yellow glob stick before slowly oozing off. Jenny, in Jenny land like usual, tried to feed Seymour a bit of sausage. Only Barry seemed to rise above the glum, licking the remnants of BBQ sauce off his fingers.

"After this we'll scope out the Federal Reserve," he said into the air. "You and Jenny," he continued, pointing a rib bone at me. "Just a mild-mannered dad giving his two kids a tour of the bank."

Both Jenny and I murmured "okay." I wondered if he had heard us last night when she screamed that I hated him. It pissed me off because it was far from the truth, so I perked up and gave him a second, "Okay!" He seemed to enjoy that one more and gave me a fist pump of solidarity. At least until he noticed Mom zoning out on the pudding.

"Hey, Judy, let's take away that puddin'. Looks like you're done."

Sometime since entering Texas, he'd developed a wavering Southern accent. She didn't respond until he took it from her, and she started grunting.

"Okay, okay, love," he said. "It's comin' back at ya."

He zoomed the spoon through the air like an airplane before directing it into her mouth. She barely opened and it remained on the corner of her lips.

"Bear-bear, I'm not in the mood."

He threw up his hands. "All right, all right. Sue me for trying to have some fun. Is it your mother? You laid next to me last night like a cadaver."

She nodded our way. "Bear, the kids."

"Oh, fuck the kids."

Our ears burned. I could literally see Jenny's turn red, even though she tried to play it off by whispering to Seymour.

"I don't mean..." he began. "Look, we work the best as a Gimmelman unit. A great Gimmelman unit. And we are. But not if one of our spokes is loose."

"So, I'm a spoke?"

"Judy, c'mon, your mother will understand someday."

"That I'm a criminal?"

His eye twitched, looking like he was about to snap. For a second, I cased the table for any weapons, glad that we were only eating with plastic utensils. He eased closer to her in a way that caused a chill to hang at the top of my spine.

"Judy, baby, that's a loaded word. The money we took..."

"It's not about the money."

"Then what? What, love?"

She titled her head toward us. "Not in front of them."

"But you wouldn't even talk to me last night."

She crossed her arms and stood up, walked off in the distance, but she stopped close enough away. She wanted him to follow. He rolled his eyes to the top of his glasses and went after her. I could hear them anyway.

"The security guard…" was all she said, and I knew it was because she'd seen on television what he did to him and coupled with not being allowed to speak to Grandma Bernice anymore, made Barry into a different man than she thought she knew.

He cupped her face in his hands, fed her something, not banana pudding this time, more like a pill. I could see him mouth, "It'll calm you down."

She rocked in his arms. They stayed there like that for a while, the love between them strong, even when they couldn't stand one another. Troy returned and lit a smoke.

"Steph doesn't feel well," he said, blowing an O.

My stomach rumbled. "I think the food's gotten to me too."

"What's up with your parents?"

A car drove by blaring "Everybody's Working for the Weekend," parked in the lot by us, and shut off the radio. It had a siren on the dashboard, like an undercover cop vehicle I saw all too often on *Miami Vice*. My stomach rumbled again but in a worse way. We all watched a man get out of the vehicle like we were trying not to watch him. As he went into the Pig Feast, he gave us all a polite nod.

"Pig," Jenny said, under her breath.

I kicked her leg under the table. "Jenny, stop it."

"I'm not afraid of that ass sandwich," she mumbled again.

Barry and Mom stopped rocking. Just as the guy was about to go inside, Steph ran out, colliding into him. He apologized, she apologized. He was chewing on a toothpick and the toothpick had plopped to the floor. Like an idiot, she bent down to get it for him, and he told her it was okay. She apologized again, but by then he had already gone inside.

"What a weirdo," she said, flopping back down on our bench.

"He is a cop," I said, pointing at the siren behind his dashboard.

"Oh," she said, looking like she wanted to vomit.

"Let's get the fuck out of here," Barry said, rushing over and grabbing all the paper plates and utensils and stuffing them in the trash. He whistled over his shoulder while booking it to the RV.

"That was a coincidence, right?" Mom said, gliding her hands through the air like she was swimming in glitter.

Barry gave a "hrmph."

"I mean, how could he know?" Mom asked. "They have no idea who to look for. And we're far out of Florida. Far out." She stretched out the word and sucked it under her tongue like she was tasting wine.

Behind the wheel, Barry got out the map and spread it over his lap. "Federal Reserve, people. No time for dilly-dallying." He whistled me over and whapped the map. "Aaron, my boy. Feed me the directions." He pointed to shotgun, and I sat beside him, flipping on the oldies station where CCR hummed, causing Mom to sway. "You ready?" he asked, as "Who Will Stop the Rain?" played. I swallowed and could feel the saliva as a lump. I nodded, too eagerly, maybe to convince myself.

"You ready?" he asked again, and I believed he was trying to convince himself as well.

42

Driving past the Federal Reserve Bank, I knew there was no way in hell we had a chance at robbing it. A giant brick exterior with blue glazed tile and a statue of an eagle at its center, not to mention its hefty fence surrounding it like a moat. Guards with guns patrolling around the circumference let alone a security station in the front.

"Fuckeroni," I heard Jenny say.

Barry parked and took Jenny and I by the hand as we exited the RV. Steph still wasn't feeling well so Troy stayed to rub her feet. The pill Mom had taken knocked her out, so she was lying down. The goal was to enter as unsuspecting as possible. A dad giving his two kids a tour.

"Dad," I said, yanking his hand. "There's no way."

"No way to what?"

He walked us closer until we could see the guard posted at the security station watching us behind a pair of mirror shades.

"Like, no way we'll be able to..." I lowered my voice as much as I could. "Rob."

He let go of my hand to wave away my insecurity. "All their bombast is for show."

We signed up for the tour, the highlight being to look at a giant vault. Inside was said to house millions of dollars. Barry's eyes sparkled.

"Did you hear that, millions?" he said, nudging me.

"Yes," I replied, hoping the tone of my voice would get him to stop acting weird.

"How can people trust that their money is safe here?" Barry asked the tour guide. She was dressed in a smart suit with a helmet of blonde hair sprayed rock-hard with mousse. She explained about all the video cameras, some of which were hidden, and the round-the-clock security guards. The vaults were also impenetrable, even by dynamite. No one had ever attempted to rob it before, and they would be very foolish to try. I could see her wisdom going in one of Barry's ears and out the other.

When we got outside, Barry started carrying on. "That's a lot of baloney. They make it seem impossible, so no one bothers. I see right through them."

"Dad," I said, pinching the bridge of my nose.

"Ah, my ass," he said, rubbing his butt. "I need a new cold compress to go in my pants."

Back in the RV, I kept trying to dissuade him while he sat on an iced ring. "There's plenty of other banks in Houston to hit."

"No, this is the one."

I looked to Troy to help. Steph had gone down for a nap, so he was just sitting around.

"It does seem pretty...what's the word I'm looking for?" Troy asked. "Fortified."

"But there's millions," Barry said, as if it was the only defense needed.

Troy tossed his bangs out of his eyes. "Listen, man, a tubular idea, but I think your boy is right."

"Eh, fuck you." Taking the iced ring, Barry got behind the wheel and put the RV in drive. Switching on some tunes, he hummed The Byrds' "Turn! Turn! Turn!"

"He's a stubborn fuck," Troy said.

"It's a suicide mission," I said.

Troy went over to sit shotgun.

"Listen, man," Troy began, but Barry turned up The Byrds.

"I can't hear you."

Troy turned the music off, and Barry's mouth dropped.

"Way harsh."

"Barry, look," Troy said, as we drove past a bank called Trust Savings, bigger than any we hit so far but not Federal Reserve level. "The goal is to get out of this alive."

"I know."

"There's just no way we can hit the Federal Reserve only with guns. You can't walk in that door. Maybe tunnel in, but we don't have the resources for that. Trust Savings," he said, pointing out of the window. The sky blue and the sun beaming a halo on the bank. "Trust that this might be our calling."

Barry started to ease off of the gas until we sat across from the bank.

"See this street," Troy said. "Major avenue. Leads right into Interstate Sixty Nine."

"Ah, sweet sixty-nine," Barry said, following the line of the avenue.

"Good shot out of here. Let's go take a look. Just to humor me."

Barry shut the engine off. "All right. Just to humor."

I didn't even ask if I could come, and followed behind them. When we stepped inside, Trust Savings was certainly a huge bank. Two security guards, one at the doors and another by the tellers. About twenty people milling about. A dozen tellers plus about the same amount behind cubicles. Tall ceiling, like the woman wear their hair in Texas, closer to God. Marble floors and wide windows letting in the sun.

"This place has to hold millions as well," Troy said, in Barry's ear. "Maybe not hundreds of millions, but enough to keep us set for life."

Barry's white teeth peeked through his lips. The gears turning in his mind.

"Hmmm," he said again, stroking his chin. All of a sudden, his eyes lit up, the pupils going wide. "What if...what if we hit it at night?"

"Yeah, man," Troy said, slapping him on the back. "Now you're talking."

"No patrons to worry about. No tellers, managers, simply the security guards. And what if...?" He snapped his fingers. "What if we use Jenny as bait?"

"Where you going with this?" I asked, skeptical.

"No, no, hear me out. Yes, Jenny'll knock on the door, tell the security guard she's lost, can't find her parents, and then we burst in. Me, Aaron, and Troy."

"Wait, Jenny won't have a mask?" I asked.

"She doesn't need one, she's a little fucking girl. The news thinks she's a little person anyway, no one's suspecting a child."

I didn't answer right away. Barry grabbed me by the collar.

"Listen," he said, pulling me. "We were this close...*this close* to hitting that Federal Reserve, which I still think we could do, but you two pansy-asses believe it's out of our range. Okay, okay, democracy rules..."

I guessed he'd taken a few toots before this speech.

"So, I'm list-en-ing to y'all, hearing y'all out, changing our plans." He sucked in a deep breath. "And I feel this bank. I feel good and righteous energy here. It's speaking to me, these walls. Listen...they're telling me the plan, Jenny as bait, the three of us as muscle, we leave Mom out of this one, let her rest some, Steph can still drive. We were meant to pass over the Federal Reserve. Troy, you were meant to come into our lives so we could be brought to this path, this bank, these whispering walls. Do you hear them?"

Troy and I eyed each other and gave a couple of nods.

"Brilliant," Barry said, kissing the top of my head. "Tomorrow night. Let's take the time to locate all the cameras and any nooks and crannies that might cause trouble. Can I get a soft, Whoa Gimmelmans?"

"Right here?" I asked.

"Right here, baby." He put out his palm. "Let's go."

We stealthily put our palms over his and gave the softest murmur of a "Whoa Gimmelmans" that we possibly could. When we broke up to case the joint, Troy elbowed me in the ribs.

"Does that count since I'm technically not a Gimmelman?"

He laughed while I took assessment of five cameras in my line of sight. With an attached pen on a counter, I scribbled on my hand exactly where they were.

43

I couldn't sleep, going over in my mind the plan Barry dictated. It would've been too rushed to do it that night; Barry wanted one more day of going over all the steps. Also, Steph still felt crummy so he wanted to give her another day to recover, and I figured he was hoping Mom might come around.

I sat up and listened to the two couples talking softly from their nooks. Jenny already in dreamland, her snores loud enough to call sailors back to land in a fog.

"You feel worse or a little better?" Troy asked Steph, barely above a whisper.

"The same, like I ate something bad."

"I think it's nerves."

"Maybe."

"How would it make you feel to tell you I am falling in love with you?"

I nearly retched out loud.

"Awww, Troy. Really?"

"I mean, with other girls it never was like this. The circumstances were different, we weren't robbing banks and evading the law."

She giggled at that.

"Actually, this is the first I've lived with a girl before," he said. "Besides my sister. And it's been cool. Like, I love how you hum when you're eating something you really like."

"I do?"

"You never knew that? Yeah, you do. It's super cute."

"I like that you get these wrinkle lines around your eyes when you smile. Like an old man."

"I am old compared to you."

I couldn't hear what they said next, but it sounded like he was biting her shoulder playfully.

"Stop making me laugh, it hurts," she said.

"Your stomach?"

"Yeah."

"What do you think about what we talked about?" he asked.

My ears perked up.

"You mean...leaving after this next one?"

"Yeah."

"I dunno."

"Do you really want to stay with them?"

"Mom and Dad?"

"All of them?"

"No. Well, I dunno. Maybe it would be good to leave for a while, get some space. Mom's been crazy lately, she's barely coherent, and Dad, he's like a different person."

"We'd have enough money if we pull off this job, to go anywhere."

"We don't have to decide now."

"Okay, I don't want to give you more anxiety."

"Hey, Troy. I love you too."

The sound of them kissing made me turn my focus to Barry and Mom. While I was upset that Steph might be ditching us, I really couldn't blame her. Why not take an out if she had one? But what would that mean for the remaining Gimmelmans? With one kid gone, I wondered if Barry and Mom would want Jenny and me to follow suit.

"I need you to get out of this funk," Barry said to Mom, as if it was an order.

"It's not as easy..." She sighed. "It's not like flipping a light switch."

"Let's get to the root of it, baby."

"Bear," Mom hissed. "My mother said I'm not her daughter anymore."
Audible tears.

"Okay, okay, Judy, calm down. Listen, your mother is reactive. She says things she doesn't mean. Always been like that."

Sniffle. "Yeah?"

"Yeah. You're still her only daughter, that will never change. And she still loves you, even if she's angry with you. You can call her again when the time is right. Let's give her a moment to calm down."

Mom blew her nose.

"Now we're not hitting the Federal Reserve, I made the decision. This will be our last bank and we'll head up to my brother's until there's no heat on us whatsoever, then we can decide our future. Whether that's Paris, or...wherever you want, baby."

He talked to her in a soothing, laconic way, still maintaining the Texan accent.

"Your brother's," she said, far from happy.

"I don't want to make any rash decisions about leaving the country. And California is far enough away from where we've caused some chaos. We'll still keep the RV if we need to flee, but we can regroup there."

"I hate Connie. And their kids. Your brother ain't a peach either."

"No, he isn't, but he's blood, and working for the travel industry might come in handy. Get us to the right place, ya know?"

"I guess."

"What if we choose Spain and it's not right? I don't want to be bouncing around. I want to take our time to think about our next home. And maybe we wind up in California, not necessarily San Bernardino where Mort is, but anywhere we want. This bank tomorrow night, Judy... It's huge, I figure we'll pull in major coin."

"Are you mad I won't be part of the heist?"

"Naw, you are, you'll be in the RV with Steph. Making her feel better too. Being her mom."

"Am I a good mom?" she asked, so hopeless. I wanted to hug her right there, even though I should be telling her that she had things to work on in the mom department.

"Hey, hey, baby, the best mom there is. Those kids love you like crazy, and I know how much you're nuts about them."

"You don't think we've been..."

"Been what, Jude?"

"Selfish," she said, swallowing the word like it was a sin.

"No, no, selfish would've been being complacent. Not giving our kids the best. We got almost a hundred thousand bucks in just a couple of weeks and we're about to net a whole lot more. We'll give those kids anything they want. And we've given them adventure. Life is about adventure. Didn't we used to say that when we were young and free? All we wanted were adventures, one after the other, so we never felt stuck."

"I love you, Bear."

"And I'm madly in love with you, Jude. Through all our ups and downs, I never stopped. Never will."

Smooch. Smooch. Smooch. Their kisses, growing more intense. I knew where this was heading so I threw on headphones, an old Bangles tape with "Walk Like an Egyptian." I listened to it over and over, rewinding and catching right when the song would begin again until eventually sleep came.

44

Fate was a funny thing, depending on how much you believed in it. I, for one, did. Maybe not completely at the tender age of twelve, but my twelve-year-old eyes had seen more than most pre-teens to grasp that not everything in the universe could be explained. I assumed Special Agent Alan Terbert believed in it in spades. While the majority of lawmen relied on facts and figures, I imagined that Terbert looked to his gut, which had stayed rather trim for a forty-four-year-old who had a hankering for BBQ.

From some intel I did in the future, I discovered he'd sent in the tire prints from our bloody getaway and found a match issued mostly to RVs, since they used bigger tires than regular cars. Trucks, however, used larger tires so they could be ruled out. Better to remain a step ahead of the perpetrators.

With his stomach grumbling, fate took him to the Pig Feast at the same time we were chowing down on a bench outside. Luck would have it that we left the Gas-Guzzler in the lot out back, which he didn't see, and therefore saved us from an earlier meeting. He would remember Steph and her side-ponytail from when they bumped into one another, and curse himself later on, but really, he couldn't be blamed. How was he to see an Americana family like the Gimmelmans stuffing our faces with dripping pork and assume we were notorious? At that time, he was still looking for two little people in the gang, one of them Black.

He hung around Houston though for a bit and would be there when we hit the Trust Savings, except on the other side of town and therefore, useless.

This would haunt him. That he would've been so close, yet powerless. His drinking had already been getting worse, his anger pushed in more menacing directions. We were the criminals, but Terbert had evil in him, just ask his wife.

During a moment of frustration on the night that we'd hit the Trust Savings, he wound up at a bar nursing his wounds. Started talking to a pretty girl on the adjacent stool. Inebriated, he thought she was interested, ratcheted up his flirting, even grabbed her arm. When she squealed, the bartender got involved and they started tussling. The bouncer was gonna call the cops until Terbert flashed his badge. He stumbled out and got into his vehicle, drove on the highway and nearly veered into the wrong lane, the flash of another car's headlights guiding him back. In his hotel room, he lay on the bed punching his head, thinking about us even though he didn't know exactly who we were. This wouldn't be a case he'd fuck up. He had too many fuck-ups in his life already. Was a joke in his precinct in Miami, since he avoided the drug-related crimes. We would make him a star. He wandered out to the hotel balcony, took in flat Houston, and asked his gut where we were. Even prayed to God in the sky to guide him.

When no answers came to his gut, except for it rumbling dramatically, he puked a river onto the street below.

* * *

While one threat was in the throes of what was about to be a monumental hangover, I pictured Gianni Bianchi being a step ahead since he knew the prey he targeted. The connection to the robbery hadn't been made...yet. That would change as he and his goon, a man simply called Fingers, watched the news in their hotel room and saw the Gimmelmans at the top of the hour. Gianni Bianchi hadn't left Florida yet, which still ran the story like gangbusters. Now we were dubbed the Woodstock Thieves from Barry yelling "Woodstock" when it was time to flee our first heist.

Seeing the robber with a Jerry Garcia mask sparked a memory of when Mr. Bianchi had gone down to Barry's office for some under-the-table stock tips. Barry had been playing a cassette tape of Terrapin Station, and while sharing lines of coke, gave Mr. Bianchi a fucking dissertation of the song. How it was about a hero's quest. A sailor had a chance at love and inspiration and didn't take it. The sailor knew better now. Terrapin Station was the path to enlightenment, which everyone reaches in their own way. Gianni Bianchi thought this wonderful, since he was about to propose to his love, Carlotta, even though his family didn't like her so much. He thought *fuck them*, and Barry told him how his wife's mother hated him too. "It didn't stop us," Barry said. "And I think about that every time I hear this beautiful song." "Who's the singer?" Mr. Bianchi asked. And Barry replied that it was Jerry Garcia, then gave another dissertation about the legend. Coked-up, Mr. Bianchi went to a Sam Goody and bought the tape, played it in his Sports Walkman as he got in his limo on the way back to New Jersey.

By the time he got home, the coke had worn off and the Grateful Dead sounded like a bunch of noise, but he wouldn't forget the conversation he had with Barry about the man's love for the band. When he had this aha moment in the hotel room, he knocked the pizza slice resting on his chest and it splat on the carpet. Fingers thought he had gone crazy, but Mr. Bianchi didn't care. He figured we'd be hitting another bank, not content with our take from the one in Boca, but then after that, we would need a safe place to hide out. And if we hit a bank by one of our loved ones in Florida, maybe our next heist would be near San Bernardino, California where Barry's brother Mort resided with his family. It was as good a shot as any to drive there, so even though Fingers was tired and a few shots in, Mr. Bianchi had him take his cherry-red Iroc-Z from one coast to another and kicked off the drive by blasting Duran Duran's "View to a Kill."

45

I had the fidgets waiting for Barry to give us the go-ahead. We parked kitty-corner to the Trust Savings, close enough to eye the two lumbering security guards fighting off sleep inside. Barry's idea was to hit the bank when one left to take a leak. With our masks on except for Jenny, guns in hand, Steph at the wheel feeling better, and Mom sitting shotgun, the hours ticked down until finally one of the security guards signaled to the other that he was heading out back, and we made our move.

Barry, Troy, and I crept behind Jenny while hiding in the shadows, the street thankfully empty since it was past midnight. We told Jenny to start crying and she turned on those waterworks faster than if she was Meryl Streep, her little fist knocking on the glass door.

The security guard perked up, squinted his eyes, which softened when he noticed Jenny. He got out of his seat and headed toward the door while waving. Jenny heightened the tears, a loud wail he was sure to hear behind the glass doors. He hurried out, removed his keys, and opened the door a crack.

"What is it, little girl?"

"My-my...I'm lost," she cried.

"Where are your parents?"

"I dunno."

That was when we left the shadows and burst toward the door, Barry nearly knocking Jenny over as he thrust the gun in the guard's pale face.

Troy used the shock to ram into the door, sending the guard to the floor. Barry got on top of him as Jenny and I coolly waltzed inside and left it open a smidge for easy access out.

"Shut the fuck up," Barry said, because the guard was murmuring. Troy had duct tape ready and ripped off a piece to cover the guard's mouth. "The other guy in the bathroom?"

The guard gave a nervous nod that wiggled his few chins.

"Elvis, be on watch for him," Barry said. "You too, Hendrix."

We peered in the direction the guard had gone. In the distance, a hallway led to the bathroom. We'd learned that from scoping the place out the other day. No sign of the other guard.

"Keys," Barry ordered, as the guard fumbled around and passed over a ring of keys.

"Which one is for the safe?"

"Mmagrmsonleehavthatttt."

"What the fuck did you say?"

Barry ripped off the tape enough for the guy to speak.

"Only managers have those, not security."

Barry taped up the guy's mouth again. "Lucky, I have a Plan B."

I went about collecting chairs to stand on to spray the cameras. Since there were five in total, it would take some time.

"Any sign of the other guard?" Barry shout-whispered.

Troy had his eyes down the hallway but shook his Elvis head.

"What's he taking a shi—"

Troy didn't finish the sentence because a bullet came from out of nowhere and got him in the stomach. He doubled-back, lost his balance, and keeled over.

"Troy," I yelled, as Jenny screeched. "Fuck," I said, realizing I said his actual name.

The guard who shot Troy was shaking as he held the gun at us. He moved it from me, to Barry, then to Jenny, still screeching.

"Ah shit," Troy said, taking his hand away from the bloody wound. The bullet staying in and not exiting, the blood spilling out at an alarming rate.

"I'm calling the police," the other guard said. "Don't move, don't try any—"

Just as Troy had been cut off mid-sentence, Barry ran closer and fired a shot at the guard right in the head, his brain exploding like I was watching some Nickelodeon show where green slime should've been oozing out. Jenny screeched again.

"Stop," Barry said, catching her eye through Jerry Garcia. "Just stop." He leaped up and pulled the living guard to his feet. "You take me to the safe."

"Itoluonleemnrgshavthekey."

Barry gave him a push. "And I told you I have a Plan B."

"Jerry," I yelled, almost saying "Dad."

"Hendrix, make a tourniquet. Use your shirt, keep the blood from spilling."

"Shouldn't we make a run for it?" I pleaded.

"No, no way." Through the mask, his eyes were full of fire. "Do what I say."

I jumped down from the chair, nearly slipping, in the blood, tiptoeing around the guard with the exploded brain while wrenching off my shirt, and got down on my knees. I wrapped it around Troy's stomach, but since I was small, it didn't do much.

"Give me your jacket," I screamed at Jenny.

She was frozen, taking a second for it to sink in, then threw her jacket on Troy. Blood kept squirting in a stream like a little kid pissing while getting his diaper changed. Troy didn't look good. His face turned blue, then purple, his eyes receding into his skull.

"Jerry, he's dying," I said, unable to understand the words coming out of my mouth. How we'd react in this moment meant saving Troy's life.

But Barry had already gone with the other guard to the safe. I could've tried to drag Troy out of the bank with Jenny's help, but Troy was six foot and probably weighed two bucks, there'd be no way.

Jenny and I observed one another, silently asking what we should do. We could go to the RV and try to get Steph or Mom to help, but I knew that both of them right now couldn't save Troy. Mom too out of it and Steph too blinded by love. So we shrugged like dumb fools while he bled out.

"What's happening?" Troy managed to ask, as his eyes rolled back into place.

"You're okay, buddy," I said, because that was what people did on TV and movies when someone was shot. Lies, lies, lies.

"I feel like a cannonball has been shot into my stomach," he said, his eyes glancing down. Fear exploded in them. "Oh fuck, oh shit, oh damn." The blood seemed to pour at an even more alarming rate once he noticed his fate. Even Jenny shook her head and whispered, "Dude isn't making it out of this bank."

And then an explosion rocked from downstairs. I wondered if it was an earthquake, having never felt one before. We could smell smoke.

"What was that...?" Troy asked, before passing out entirely. I went to feel his pulse like I had learned in health class. It didn't sound good. We watched the far away darkness where Barry had gone, praying for him to return. Seconds passed like years. We were on camera all this time. Had the police been alerted? Did someone else in an undisclosed location monitor the security cam? I didn't even know. Why hadn't we done more reconnaissance?

I turned from Troy to the dead security guard, never experiencing seeing a body drained of its life in such a short amount of time. He no longer had a face, bits of it flung across the marbled floor. This man could've had a family who had no idea they'd never see him again. And then I nearly lost it because I thought of Heidi.

Troy's breaths had gone short, he didn't have much time. She was sleeping in bed right now with no idea her brother was about to die, all because of us. I knew whatever happened after this, she would never want anything to do with me again. And then I felt shitty for being so selfish. I didn't deserve a girl as magical as her. In the grand scheme of good and evil, I'd toed the line already, but now there would be no chance of ever veering toward good again.

"Wooooooo," we finally heard an echo, and Barry emerged with two weighted gym bags. The guard wasn't with him. I wondered if he had killed him too. Even though I couldn't see Barry's face, I knew he was smiling, a wicked grin.

"Let's get the fuck outta here," he said, passing us.

"What about Troy?" I asked.

The fire in his eyes grew dull, two dead marbles appearing in its place. His sigh full of sorrow, but did he actually care?

"There's nothing we can do for him, Hendrix. He's a liability."

"We can take him to a…"

"Hospital? Fuck no. I just set off dynamite and I'm guessing we have about two minutes to get away." He motioned for Jenny to get up. She hung beside him as they ran toward the front door.

"Hendrix!" he shouted. To not follow them would be suicide. I rose on shaking legs and peered back for one last look at Troy. He was reaching out his arms, begging for us to show any kind of humanity. I had to turn away.

"We minimize the fallout with Steph," Barry said, as we burst out of the door. "She won't drive away without Troy. You two pull her from behind the wheel, and I'll put pedal to the metal."

From many streets away, in the flat Houston darkness, a red light blipped, the cops close. Barry kicked open the Gas-Guzzler's door and threw the two gym bags inside. Jenny hopped in. She reached out her hand, and I jumped in too.

"Where is Troy?" Steph said, swiveling her head around. She turned back to the bank. "*Where* is Troy?" Her cries so loud my eardrums hurt as I flung toward her, ripping her away from the driver's seat as Barry took her place, and we shot out of there fast enough to rattle everything inside like we were on a rocking boat headed into a violent storm.

46

Steph beat and thrashed against me on the floor, surprisingly stronger than I expected. Jenny waited, teeth bared, chomping as a threat. Beneath me, I could feel us pushing the speed limit, making hard turns. I couldn't hear the police sirens anymore, hoping we were far enough away. I pinned her arms down, yelled for her to calm down, but she wasn't human anymore. In her mind, we had left Troy, betrayed him. Little did she know he was dead.

"Aaron!" she bleated, face red with rage, a vein on her neck pumping. "Let go of me. We have to go back."

I got in her face, nose-to-nose. "We can't."

The anger turned to tears. "I love him. How could you leave him?"

"I know, I know."

I changed my tactics to more of a soothing tone, shushing her like a baby. She wriggled out from under me, kicked me in the balls.

"Oof."

"Hey!" Jenny snapped, picking up the gun next to me. She pointed it in Steph's face.

"Mom!" Steph yelled.

Mom's face turned in shifts, clearly on some major narcotics. Barry must have plugged her up. Even as she watched us, it was clear she wasn't taking in the situation, her face radiating nothing more than blankness.

"Listen," Jenny said, poking Steph's cheek with the gun. "Your boyfriend is dead. Do you understand? He was shot by a guard. There is no one for us to go back to."

"Nooooooo," Steph wailed. "No, no, no, no, no."

"Yes, yes, yes, yes, yes," Jenny said.

"Nothing can be done," I said, taking the gun away from Jenny and reaching for a drawer in the kitchen. "A guard came out of nowhere."

Steph went far within, mumbling incoherently.

"A little help here!" I barked, toward the front.

"Don't distract me right now," Barry called back.

"Do you have something we can give Steph?" When he didn't answer, I asked in a different way. "Something like you gave Mom?"

"Glove compartment. Dilaudid in an RX bottle."

"Jenny," I said, cocking my head toward the glove compartment.

I petted Steph's hair while we waited. She still thrashed around but with less fight. Jenny returned and shoved some pills in Steph's mouth. She worked Steph's jaw up and down until Steph swallowed the pills. When I asked if she did, Steph held out her chalky white tongue. I took off her Debbie Gibson mask. She was breathing heavily. I crumpled up the mask until it was unrecognizable.

"Come, sit up," I said, and Jenny and I helped her until she was leaning against the kitchen sink. Steph's hair in shock mode, looking like she'd been electrocuted, her mouth hanging open. She'd cried so much her eyes were stained with mascara.

"I was gonna marry him," she murmured. I wanted to say that they only knew each other for like a week and a half and she had said the same thing about Kent not too long ago, but kept my trap shut.

Even Jenny was feeling bad and curled up against Steph, rubbing her arm.

"Do you want candy?" Jenny asked.

It took a second, but Steph finally nodded.

Jenny returned with a row of Dots on a strip of paper. She ripped them off, not being too careful, and fed the Dots to Steph with bits of paper attached to the ends. Then the Dilaudid must have kicked in even more because Steph stuck her finger in her mouth and just sat there like a zombie.

I got my Walkman and her Tiffany cassette and placed the headphones over her ears. When I pushed play, she seemed to smile a little, nothing to write home about, but enough to let me know she was at least on the way to her semi-happy place.

"C'mon," I motioned to Jenny, so we could leave her alone. We went to the front of the RV where we could see Barry was getting on a highway.

"Looks like we're in the clear," he said, upbeat as ever. He even reached over to tousle my hair. Didn't he realize that not only was Troy dead, but he had killed a guard too? I was afraid to even ask about the other one and found myself pulling away. He turned on the radio that played an Aerosmith song and began humming along to Stephen Tyler.

"You did good," he said, still wearing the Jerry Garcia mask, eyeing us through the rearview. I removed Hendrix, never wanting to see it again. "Both of you."

Jenny grinned at that.

"Man, Jenny, can you turn on those waterworks. What a talent!"

Jenny started sniffling and tears shot out of her eyes. A few seconds later she stopped.

"Beautiful," Barry said, taking his hand off the wheel to kiss his fingers.

Jenny was enamored with him, or at least faking it well. I didn't want to look at her, or zombie Mom, or zombie Steph. I retreated to my nook, pulled the curtain, and shut my eyes. A flash of the dead guard rocked my brain. His own brain exploding and bits and pieces flung all over the bank. I wondered if there would ever be a time in life again where I'd see darkness and not replay that image. So, to avoid torturing myself anymore, I got out my journal and began scribbling. I wrote into the night, long after I could hear everyone had gone to bed, yet Barry still drove. I knew he wanted to put as much distance between us and the scene as possible. The trip to California would take almost twenty-four hours if he did it straight. I figured he'd probably coked himself up enough to do it.

I wrote about what he did to the guard and how I wanted to save Troy but couldn't. I wrote about how afraid and uncertain I was, despite whatever windfall we amassed. No longer were we just criminals, we were murderers now, and I had to really take Heidi's advice to separate myself as much from

Barry Gimmelman as possible. He would be to blame if it all went south, so that was exactly the picture I'd paint.

When I finished, the sun hung over the lip of the horizon. We were just past Odessa, entering Lea County, New Mexico. The RV was slowing down at a rest stop and a tiny restaurant called the Bug Café.

"Wakey, wakey eggs and bakey!" I heard Barry screaming, as he tore through the RV. I stuffed the journal under my mattress and rubbed my eyes when he pulled back the curtain, as if I had just woken from sleep, and not a night of treachery.

47

The Bug Café had a dirt patio with rusty red benches for the take-out orders. Barry wanted to eat outside to soak up the air, but also to be able to make a quick escape in the RV if need be. Right when we sat down, Steph wasn't feeling well, and the waitress overheard. She said there was a pharmacy across the way and angled her face into the wind.

"I don't know," Barry said once the waitress left, as he dug into a Tex-Mex frittata.

"Barry," Mom said sharply, like there would be no discussion. The pills he gave her, and Steph must've worn off, the zombies vanished in the night.

Supporting Steph, Mom walked her down a trail ending at the pharmacy. Barry agreed because it was close enough to see. If necessary, he would honk outside its doors and no matter what, they had to come out, or be left behind. Mom didn't seem too happy when he said that, and he tried to make like he was kidding, but it was hard to tell. I occupied myself with a fresh-squeezed glass of orange juice while Jenny munched on syrupy French toast.

"How you two spuds doing?" he asked.

Jenny shrugged and stuffed her face with more syrup until her lips stuck together.

"And you, bud?"

I hated when he gave me nicknames so I shrugged like Jenny did hoping that would end it. Fat chance. He smacked the fork out of my hands, and I watched it bounce on the hard dirt. Five-second rule, so I was bending down to pick it up when he grabbed my arm.

"Listen," he said, staring me down more intently than ever before. I'd spent the night thinking about how what happened in that bank would change me, but it had to affect Barry worse. I was only an accessory to murder.

He softened, maybe because he could see he'd scared me. He loosened his grip on my arm, apologized. Whether half-hearted or legit, it was hard to tell.

"Look, things happened at that bank which I didn't intend." His voice, still low and with a bit of a Southern twang. Maybe the accent helped him to cope with this new Barry whose skin he'd have to wear forever. "And I'm sorry about it."

"The other guard?" I asked, my voice quavering. That other guard didn't need to die, and I prayed that Barry hadn't killed him.

Barry was about to answer when the waitress wandered out. Big shoulder pads and crimped hair, acid-washed jean shorts with cowboy boots up to her knees. Frosted eye shadow and hot pink lipstick. She saw my fork on the ground.

"Ooh, lemme get you another," she said, and was gone before we could say no.

Barry eyed the door as he continued: "I left him down in the vault, didn't touch a hair."

I breathed a sigh of relief. I could hear Jenny doing the same.

"Is that what you wanted to hear?"

I nodded as the waitress returned and handed over a new fork with a "Here ya go, sugar."

"Can I get y'all anything else?" she asked. Barry shook his head. She turned on her heels and went back inside. I continued eating my now cold eggs.

"I'm not..." he began. "I did *not* enjoy killing that man." He looked to the sky, possibly for absolution. Never believing in God before, I wondered if this would change that. "But he would've been the end of us. You see? And he should not have fired on Troy. He should've given us all a chance to lower our weapons."

"Would you have?"

"That's not the point, Aaron. He did not do his job correctly and therefore I had to make a split-second decision." He took a strong sip of coffee. "But for some good news. Perk them ears up. From that haul, we netted about eight hundred thou."

I choked on my eggs. "Are you serious?"

"As a heart attack during a blizzard. Meaning our sum total is closing in on a cool mil. All for a couple of weeks' work. Now I'm gonna do some research, and hopefully with my brother Morty's advice, figure out the place where that money will go the furthest and I'll never have to work again."

"No more robbing?" Jenny asked, unsticking her mouth.

"No, pumpkin, as they'd say in Texas, we're hanging up our spurs."

"Even when we get to Uncle Mort's in California?" I asked.

"Mort's is a rest stop, that's all it will be. My brother owes me. They'll be monitoring the airports right now, but in a week or two, things'll settle. New criminals will surface, the tide will shift."

"Have you seen the news yet?" I asked.

"Only listened to the radio through the night, and they mentioned us, certainly did, but nothing about an RV, nothing about us as a family. They hadn't released Troy's name yet, but that's probably changed. In fact, you might wanna head inside and grab today's newspaper, see if we're the headline." He winked. "Also, gives me some time with my little Jen Jen." He tweaked her on the cheek.

I spun off the bench and went inside the Bug Café, typical diner except for ladybug wallpaper throughout. I sat on a stool at the counter.

"Something I can get for ya?" the waitress asked. She was kind and I felt like I wanted to bathe in that kindness for a while.

"Do you guys sell newspapers?"

She pointed a purple Lee Press-On nail to a rack by the cashier.

"So, you on a trip with your family?" she asked, smacking gum.

"Uh yeah, for spring break."

"That's so nice, on your way to the Grand Canyon?"

I was about to say California but bit my tongue. I couldn't be honest with strangers, never again. This almost made me cry. Everything I'd say from here on out would have to be thoroughly vetted.

"We sure are," I replied, way too excited.

"It's amazing there. Seeing how big nature can be. Will change your life, really."

"My life will have definitely changed when this trip is done."

She held up a spray-painted finger. "Here's some lemon pies, on the house. They were from yesterday so usually the kitchen crew takes 'em home." She placed a few slices with plastic forks in a Styrofoam box. "Y'all enjoy now."

"We will," I said. "And here's for the newspaper." I left a JFK half dollar on the counter, tucked the pies under my arm, and took a paper off the rack.

My stomach instantly dropped. On the front page, not only Troy's name in bold—I never knew Heidi's last name was Kingelton—but there was a picture of the security camera footage. No big deal for Barry and I with our masks on, but a tiny pixelated image of Jenny was about to be introduced to the world.

I shot out of there and thrust the newspaper in Barry's face.

"We *have* to fucking go."

His eyebrows rose like they were being pulled by a puppeteer's strings.

"Yes, that we do."

48

Back in the RV we read through the newspaper to get a gist of what the authorities knew. Troy was identified as the man behind the Elvis mask, who hadn't been present for the first robbery. The reporter speculated that he was picked up along the way. His grandfather, Marty, had not issued any comment. There was no mention of Heidi. I pictured a circus tent of reporters camped in her front yard, Heidi refusing to go outside. She had warned me that things wouldn't end well, and I was too stupid to listen.

On the bright side, there was no mention of the Gas-Guzzler. The street had been empty, so no witnesses could've seen our getaway. By the time the police arrived, we were already gone. The bank had a camera outside, but it only captured us coming up to the door. That was the photo of Jenny with hair like a scarecrow wearing OshKosh B'gosh overalls. The photo they captured had been too pixelated to perfectly make out her face, but it was clear this was a little girl. A cop interviewed surmised that we had kidnapped a child to use as bait. Another charge to add to our laundry list.

There was mention of Janis Joplin not being present for this robbery, leading to a belief that she was the getaway driver. Mama Cass was not present either, but since she was a little person, she likely wasn't the driver. No one put two-and-two together about Jenny being Mama Cass. Nothing about a Debbie Gibson, so Steph didn't even exist to the public. The guard Barry had killed was Kevin Lurante, twenty-five, no kids thankfully. He left behind his boxer dog, Bugles.

The surviving security guard, Michael Bedloast, thirty-one, described the ordeal as a "harrowing experience. [He] did not know whether he'd live or die. When Jerry Garcia brought out the dynamite, [he] prayed for God to see him through ." The dynamite blew out the vault and destroyed the basement of the bank where clients kept locked boxes. We were thought to have made off with more than a million in cash, and we were mentioned along with the likes of John Dillinger, Bonnie and Clyde, Robert LeRoy Parker, "Pretty Boy" Floyd, and "Slick Willie." This made Barry beam, flashing his pearly chompers.

"We're legends," he yelled, shaking the newspaper in his fists.

"Says the *Albuquerque Journal*."

"Aaron, I guarantee you, we're front page everywhere."

"Meaning the FBI is now fully involved."

"You mean the Foolish Bumblefuck Idiots? I ain't worried."

"Where's Mom and Steph?"

"Must still be at the pharmacy."

He switched on the TV, and sure enough on the news, we were everywhere. The newscaster warning that what we were about to see wasn't "for the faint of heart." Watching Troy take a bullet made my insides roll around, and I ran to the window, sticking my head out and trying to hurl. Nothing came up. I could hear Jenny's cackles. She was loving it, the little psychopath. Turning back, I saw Barry firing on the guard, the guy's head exploding like it'd done every time I closed my eyes. I stuck my head out and this time hurled, my vomit dripping down the side of the RV. In the distance, Mom and Steph were making their way back.

"They're here," I said, popping my head back in and wiping my sleeve. Barry wasn't listening, too caught up in being the center of the news.

The door banged open as they came inside, both of their heads down. Steph scurried into the bathroom with a plastic bag clutched between two fingers.

"What's going on?" I asked, as Mom sat down on my couch/bed and ran her fingers through my hair.

"Nothing, nothing at all."

It was the sing-song way she said it that made me call bogus.

"What's going on here?" she asked, with a ten-dollar smile.

I threw the paper in her lap. "We're front-page news."

She ran her finger over the image of Jenny, then quickly tossed it aside. "I'll read it later."

Barry danced over, took her by the hands and swung her arms from side-to-side. "Baby, they are speaking about us in the same sentence as Dillinger."

"Oooh, Dillinger."

Had she taken more pills? Her dilated pupils said she had.

"Dance with me, baby."

He pulled her up and they swayed to non-music.

"Jenny, turn on the radio," he barked. "We should always be dancing to music."

Jenny turned on the radio to Cutting Crew's "(I Just) Died in Your Arms," not exactly the best choice, but Barry and Mom danced like it was the most romantic song on the planet. He dipped her and they kissed with tongues.

"Barf," Jenny said, powering through them on the way to her room.

"Hold on, little lady," Barry said. "When Steph comes out of the bathroom, we're gonna need to cut your hair."

Jenny stamped her foot. "What?"

"The world sees this little girl with big hair. Oh no, no. We can't have that. Buzz cut city."

"Like in the military?" Jenny asked.

"Pretty much."

She pumped her fist. "Cooooooool."

The bathroom door opened a crack. "Mom?" Steph warbled.

"Honey, I'm busy," Mom said, with an evil laugh as she got dipped again.

"Mom!"

Mom rolled her eyes as Barry brought her back to her feet.

"Stephie, anything that's going on you can tell the whole family," Barry said. "Just take some Pepto if you're having tummy troubles."

"This isn't that," Steph said, sounding like a wounded bird. The door opened more. She held a white stick in her hand, tears dripping, mouth agape.

"What?" Barry asked. "What, baby?"

"I'm...pregnant," she screamed, and then slammed herself back into the bathroom.

The three of us eyed one another, no one knowing how to respond, only aware that this was in no way good.

49

"Who's the father?" Barry asked, far from the right thing to say, which sent Steph back into the bathroom, wailing.

"Bear-Bear," Mom said, in the most scolding way she could still do.

"Duh, it's Troy," I said.

Steph's wails got louder.

"Anyway, we can't dilly-dally," Barry said, running his fingers through his curly hair. He pulled out a tiny tuft, looked at it. "Shit."

Barry got behind the wheel and we left Lea County, New Mexico, winding our way up the state. I sat in front doing yo-yo tricks to keep me distracted. Steph still hadn't left the bathroom, her cries only drowned out by Barry's CCR tape. Jenny was playing with Seymour, and since Mom just seemed to be staring into oblivion, I nudged her.

"Go talk to her," I said, indicating the bathroom.

The frown lines on her forehead deepened. "I don't know what to say."

"When did you stop being a mom?"

She looked like I'd shot her, and I was glad. Ever since Florida, frankly ever since we left New Jersey, she'd lost all authority. She'd become a child needing care. Between her fingers, she rubbed a tiny pill.

"No," I said, making sure Barry wasn't paying attention. He was busy singing "Lookin' Out My Back Door."

Her eyes told me how much she wanted it.

"Go talk to her," I said, reaching out my palm. She debated before she placed the pill in my hand. For a second, it seemed like she'd grab it again, so I made a fist. Finally, she rose and headed to the back.

"Jesus Fucking Christ on a cob," I said, heading up front and was met with the back of Barry's hand. He'd never hit me like this before. This blow had heft. I'd nearly been knocked off my seat, my cheek stinging.

"Don't talk to your mother like that," he said, eyes still on the road. "She's still your mother."

I was about to say that was debatable but feared the back of his hand again. Neither of us spoke all the way to Roswell when Mom emerged from the bathroom and slunk over to Barry.

"Stephie wants to see a doctor," she told him.

"But we're making such great time!"

"Bear-Bear, please. I think she wants to..." Mom mimed scooping something out of her stomach, which I guessed referred to an abortion.

"Ah," Barry said. "She can't wait till California?"

And then Mom whispered into his ear, "I don't want her to change her mind."

"Good thinking, Judy."

A giant green alien welcomed us to the town, holding up a sign that said Dunkin' Donuts in his three-fingered hand. Barry went to the drive thru, ordered some donut holes and asked for the nearest doctor. The employee, obviously a gawky teenager from the sound of his voice not hitting puberty, directed us to a clinic a mile away. Once we parked, Steph came out of the bathroom, which was good because I had to take a monster piss, and she went into the clinic with Mom. Through the tiny window, I could see Mom take Steph's hand, and I hoped that she was taking what I said to heart and acting like a mom again. When I opened the door, Jenny burst in with a pair of scissors.

"Move, I'm cutting my hair," Jenny said, already in front of the mirror and hacking off a giant chunk.

"Good luck with that."

Inside the RV, Barry was nowhere to be found. I saw him outside smoking a rolled joint and pacing. I hopped out and paced with him, feeling like I didn't want to be alone.

"I'm sorry for smacking you," he said, between drags.

I motioned for him to pass it over and took a toke. "It's okay."

But it wasn't. Tears were forming and I couldn't stop them. Maybe it was the grass making me sentimental, maybe the insanity of the last few days, weeks, months. It was hard to remember when life had been normal. Playing basketball in my front yard with Drake and Liam, H-O-R-S-E or Twenty-One, going to the Tenafly Mall, and eating Hardee's beef sandwiches, watching a Knicks game on TV, dancing around in my Underoos to "Mony Mony" in my old bedroom, where someone else lived now. All of that a part of a different life I'd never get back again.

"Stop crying," Barry said.

"I'm not."

"You are, you're tougher than that."

You killed someone, I wanted to scream. *You took a life. And I'm responsible too. Forever. This man doesn't exist anymore because of us.* But I stayed silent.

"My parents," Barry said, the pot likely kicking in. He watched a cloud float above as if it carried their memory. "I don't speak of them much."

"No."

"I was so young when they died, in college."

"I know that."

He sniffed, making me wonder if he'd done a line too. "They didn't have a very happy life."

"I knew that too."

"The camps. They barely spoke of those times. But it was also where they met. And fell in love. Or, maybe they just clung to one another to get them through it and then that became love. They weren't really loving. I think life had beat that out of them. The horrors they saw. And yet with God, they never stopped believing."

I wanted to say something like, I wish I'd met them, but I let him talk because he rarely spoke like this, so vulnerably.

"I had Hebrew school twice a week, and I hated it, oh how I hated it. Imagine regular school and you finish for the day and have another school to go to? But it would've been unfathomable for me not to go. God had saved them, where many others were not as lucky, and I and my brother Mort were given life. To learn, to study the Talmud, it was a repayment in their eyes. And so, I went. I soaked up very little, but my mother never smiled like she did during our bar mitzvahs. When we read the Torah, she came alive." He blew out the last hit and flicked the joint into the dirt. "What would she think of me now? And her God...?" He choked when saying God, could barely get the word out. "What would He say?"

I gulped. "I thought you didn't believe in Him."

He rubbed his eyes under his fogged glasses. "I don't. But they did. And therefore, He existed to them. That's the God I'm thinking about. What would He say?"

I shrugged because to say what I really felt would mean that this God had the same opinion of me too.

"In Virginia, I could say He'd think us resourceful, in Florida, steadfast, but after Houston, whether I believe in Him or not, we are no longer in His favor."

I felt a buzz on the back of my neck like when you walk into a room and an appliance has been left on.

"No, we're not," I said.

He studied a bitten-down fingernail. "I'm not sure if it matters. At least in the here and now, this life, right, Aaron? What we have left of it."

The pot was making me fuzzy too. I pressed against my temple to wave off a headache.

"And afterwards, if I truly don't believe and there is only dirt to look forward to, then nothing we do in this life matters. It's a free-for-all, and to regret anything, to feel guilt, is the biggest con there is. My parents felt guilty their whole lives, even after what the shit God had put them through..." A piece of angry spit launched from his lips. "And then cut down when they were still young, in their forties, after worshipping Him, it's a fucking con is what it is. And I am not going down that road of guilt, Aaron."

He thrust his finger at me, his glasses so fogged up I couldn't see his eyes.

"Okay," was all I could say, taking a few steps back.

"What's done is done, you hear? And we don't mention it again. That guard did not follow proper procedure. He put himself in the ground."

I nodded like a bobblehead. "Yes."

Barry picked up a stone and launched it. "He put himself in that fucking ground." He looked over toward the clinic. "Let's hope your Mom and Steph get outta there quick. The sooner I'm not a grandfather yet, the better."

He stomped back in the RV as I watched a cloud sail overhead that could resemble the shape of a man with a long flowing beard if I wanted it to be, before it floated away, lost in the horizon.

I pressed a knuckle into my temple, but it was no use, a headache like a marching band had formed.

50

When Mom and Steph returned, Barry immediately drove out of Roswell. If Steph had been looking for a father/daughter bonding moment, she wasn't about to get one then. But she seemed at peace with what happened. I left her alone for a while after she retreated to the back. Jenny had finally finished cutting her hair, at best a disaster. She looked as if she'd caught on fire. A few clumps sticking up amidst patches of bald skin so pink you would've thought it belonged to a baby pig.

"I think it looks punk," she said, catching a glimpse in the mirror from outside the bathroom.

"All you need is a paper clip nose ring."

Her eyes got wide.

"Don't get any ideas," I said.

"Mom," Jenny cried, running to the front. "Look at me!"

Mom instantly burst into tears, bemoaning the loss of her baby's once wondrous hair.

"But why...?"

"Judith," Barry said, chewing the hell out of a toothpick. "It's so she can be incognito. Remember the newspaper?"

"Oh yes," Mom said, ripping off a fingernail between two teeth.

"So, how did it go at the clinic?" he asked.

We were reaching Albuquerque, a city tucked behind a mountain bed, the peaks sprinkled with snow.

"I think I should tell you," Mom began.

Barry's caterpillar eyebrows rose to the sky. "Yes?

"Stephie didn't go through with it."

"What?" The steering wheel spun between Barry's hands, veering us into the next lane. He righted the RV, wiped the sweat from his brow.

"She didn't want to, Barry. I can't force her."

"She's sixteen." He slammed on the horn. "She's goddamn sixteen."

"We let her bunk with her boyfriend."

"Just a few years ago she wanted to be carried on my shoulders," he said, as if to an imaginary audience.

"We'll help her." She reached over and rubbed the back of his neck. A weak spot. He gave into the massage. "A new baby in the family. Remember baby life? The smell of the top of their little heads?"

I left them up front to go to the back and see how Steph was doing. She lay on the top bunk with her knees up to her chin, headphones on her ears. I hopped up and sat beside her, motioned for her to remove the headphones.

"What are you listening to?" I asked.

"Lisa Lisa and Cult Jam."

She passed it over, but I shook my head. She stopped the tape.

"So, you're keeping it?"

She blew her bangs from her eyes. "Uh, yeah. I mean, it's a piece of Troy, ya know?" She chewed her lip as if it could stop her from crying. No chance. "I really loved him."

I rubbed her arm. "I know."

"Not like it ever was with Kent. I mean, like real true love. Like, I wanted to share his blood, and like find a way to be inside his skin. Weird shit like that."

I never thought about those things with Heidi, but I guessed it was different for girls.

"I'd dream about him, and when I was awake it felt like a dream to be with him. I can't get rid of the baby."

"You don't have to make that decision now, right? In health class, they said you can do it up until—"

"I won't change my mind. Troy would talk about fate and destiny a lot. He was the kind of soul who believed in things that couldn't be explained. The universe's secrets. He would have said that this was always how it was meant to be. For us to meet him and for him to die so a new him could be born."

I wondered if she'd gotten into Barry's stash of grass too.

She inched closer to me. "I don't want Mom and Dad raising it, though."

"Oh."

Lowering her voice even more, she said, "By the time I give birth, I'll emancipate. Get away from them, from this. I won't raise a child in this."

"But he said we won't rob anymore."

She gave a hoarse laugh under her breath. "Don't believe him."

"This last heist spooked him. He was talking about his parents, and the camps, I mean, he killed someone..."

"Fuck, Aaron."

We swiveled our heads out of the nook to make sure the 'rents weren't listening. Sure enough, they were caught up in an argument, oblivious to us as usual.

"When we get to California," she said, "we have to feel out Uncle Mort and Aunt Connie, see if they can help us."

"I barely even remember them. I was a kid when we saw them last."

"You still *are* a kid, Aaron. Don't you understand? We've been abused."

"No."

But my cheek stung in a déjà vu sense when I said it.

"Well..."

"Yes, Aaron, and I'm not talking physical abuse besides a slap or two, forget that. We've been mentally abused to follow this insanity."

I shut my eyes and saw that guard's head explode. I shot them back open, saw the world again through a wall of tears.

"It's okay," she said, giving me her shoulder. I rested my head, let out my anguish. "I realized all this when I was on the doctor's table, right before they were about to... And it was Mom, she was coaxing him to abort."

The venom in Steph's voice was apparent.

"We've done everything they've wanted. That's being brainwashed. And it cost me my boyfriend's life. So, fuck them. We'll get away. I'll take care of you...and Jenny," she said, rolling her eyes. "I don't care what happens to them anymore."

"I've been writing everything down."

"What?"

"In a journal. Heidi told me to do it. She said if we ever got caught, it could save us kids, put the blame on them."

"The blame *is* on them," she hissed. "Me keeping this baby is a big fuck you to both Barry and Judith—"

"So we could avoid juvie. That's why I've been doing it. We say we had no choice."

"We *didn't* have a choice."

I picked a piece of lint from my sock. "We did. We started it all."

"They are the fucking parents. They're the ones who should've known better. It's not on us. That guard, Troy, it's fucking on Dad, and Mom's his enabler, she's just as bad. So fine, you keep writing everything they've done down, Aaron. You've always had a flair for words. Jenny and I will be counting on you."

I swallowed the last of my tears. "I'm glad you're keeping the baby."

"Oh yeah?"

"Yeah. Uncle Aaron. It has a nice ring."

She gave me a rare hug.

"It does." She pressed her forehead against mine. "And I know you'll be a great uncle."

Jenny popped in as Steph's mouth dropped.

"What are you guys doing?" Jenny asked.

"Oh my God, your hair!" Steph screeched.

"Why are you hugging?"

"Just get in here Jenny," Steph said, gesturing.

Jenny thought about it for a second and lumbered up on the bed. She dove into the three-way hug as if she hadn't had one in too long. Over her prickly skull, Steph mouthed: *What in the fuck?* And I mouthed back, *I know. This kid doesn't stand a chance without us.*

This made Steph smile. And me too a little bit. Our family was changing, but the core, stronger than ever.

51

Though I didn't know it at the time, **S**pecial Agent Terbert would find out about the Trust Savings bank heist the morning everyone else did. In a Houston motel, he woke up, to a breakfast of Marlboro Reds and a swig of Three Fingers, turned on the TV, and spit out the drink in a spray. When he checked his beeper, he saw a flurry of 911 messages about the case from his superior. He'd been on too much of a bender to hear it through the night. By morning, the criminals were likely far away, no use patrolling the streets looking for an RV. He still thought it best to keep that information to himself, so he got in his car and drove to Delray Beach to speak with the family of Troy Kingelton.

Reaching Delray by nighttime, the Kingelton's front lawn was filled with reporters waiting in their parked vans. The family still hadn't given an interview to the press . The police hadn't obtained a warrant yet to search the premises. Evidently the only two people who lived there were Troy's grandfather and his little sister in junior high school. Terbert knew that they didn't have to speak to him if they didn't want to, the question remaining was whether either of them knew that too.

"Go away," a voice barked from inside, followed by a string of wet coughs.

"Mr. Kingelton, this is the FBI," Terbert said. He was tired, hungry, but wouldn't let himself stop at all along the way.

"I do not give a hog's ass," the grandfather shouted.

"Mr. Kingelton, please, just a few questions. What if I helped get the press off your lawn?"

The blinds opened by a window and an eye appeared.

"Yes, get the cockroaches away," the grandfather said and shut the blinds.

Terbert turned toward the weary reporters. "There's no use staying. He's not gonna come out and talk to you. I'll make a statement when I get back to my station, but for now, go home until morning."

It took a lot more convincing, but finally they all left with their tails between their legs.

"See, Mr. Kingelton? I'm a man of my word. You don't have to answer anything you don't want to. I want to help you."

"How?"

"Make sure you have no part of this."

"Po-lice already brought me in to speak," he said, stammering.

"Well, I'm in charge of the case. I drove all the way from Houston."

"I don't give a rip where you drove from."

"The faster you talk to me, the faster this ordeal can end for you. We know you had nothing to do with it since you were in Florida when the robbery occurred, but—"

The lock opened and the grandfather peeked through a crack in the door.

"That so? Your colleagues were a might nastier."

"It's local cops, don't worry about them. Can I?"

Terbert gestured to the door. The grandfather left it open a crack.

Inside, he sat at a round table smoking a cigarette over an overflowing ashtray. A few empties stacked on the table in a line sat as a barrier between them.

"Thank you," Terbert said, sitting down. The grandfather shrugged. "Did you have any idea your grandson was involved in anything like this?"

He coughed into his fist. "He lived in his world and I live in mine. Two rarely crossed."

"The man in the Jerry Garcia mask, you have no idea who that may be?"

"Nope."

I'd never learn why their grandfather covered for us. He certainly didn't owe us anything. Not only had he saved Barry's life, but we were responsible for the loss of his grandson. And yet, he still kept mum. Rather honorable. Maybe he hated law enforcement enough not to bow down to their pressure. Maybe he also figured it would be a better way to keep him uninvolved.

Terbert pointed to the cigarette box and the grandfather passed him one.

"Marty, right?"

"Yep."

"Alan here, you can call me Alan."

"Don't give a fuck what I call you as long as you finish up what you need here soon."

"Fair. So. Tell me about Troy."

"What do you want to know?"

Terbert lit the cigarette, took a puff. "Kind of guy was he, a leader, a follower?"

"Parents died when he was just a little squirt, so I raised 'em. Let him do a lot of his own thing. I think he wanted outta here."

Terbert ashed in the tray. "Oh yeah?"

"Far away, guessing he got caught up with people that promised him that."

"Not locals?"

"No, definitely not locals."

"You ever see an RV around your place?"

The grandfather sucked the top of his lip. For Terbert, it was hard to say whether that was a tell. He was usually good at reading people.

"RV? No."

None of his other questions proved fruitful, and the grandfather was starting to get a sleeping buzz on.

Down the hallway, Heidi opened her door to watch them, only her eye visible.

"Can I talk to your granddaughter?"

"I don't give a cat's piss—"

"Yeah, yeah, I get it."

Terbert put the cigarette out and went down the hallway to knock on Heidi's door. The Cure's "Disintegration" played from under the doorjamb.

"What is it?" she called out.

"It's the police, sweetie—"

She opened the door before he could finish. She hadn't cried yet. This would bother her. In one of the few interviews she would ever give, she'd expected the tears to come right away after hearing of Troy's death, but she couldn't squeeze them out, hard as she tried. She hoped he wasn't watching from above, angry that it might've seemed like she didn't care. Truthfully, she was still mad at him for being so foolish.

"Cool tunes," Terbert said, coming inside. She gave him a side-eye. "Now, I know this must be hard for you."

"I don't know anything." She plopped on her bed, picked up an Etch A Sketch and started doodling. "Me and my brother weren't, like, close."

"Your grandpa said he wanted to get out of Delray?"

"Yeah, probably, I mean, who wouldn't?" She knocked on her wall that seemed made of paper. "Like, our house is a shitbox."

"You ever see him hang with anyone who owns an RV?"

She tossed the Etch A Sketch aside. "Like I said, we weren't close. He was a shitty brother. He didn't care about me."

Terbert looked her deep in the eyes to ascertain whether she was lying. All she radiated back to him was pissed off.

"He was barely home anyway, so you can check his room but—"

"We're waiting on a warrant. Do you know what that is?"

"Yeah, I know what that is."

"I hope you aren't keeping anything from me." He hiccupped, a waft of booze filling the air. She turned her nose, but wouldn't break her stare. "Here's my card if you think of anything."

Barely holding it in her hands, she nodded. He rose, his knees popping.

"I'm sorry for your loss."

She shrugged one shoulder and left it hanging up by her ear. His gut told him neither the grandfather nor the sister was lying, just part of a family that wasn't too close. When I'd learn of their interaction later, I wondered why Heidi didn't give us up either and whether I was the reason. But I'd never find out from her. And I didn't deserve the truth. She and her grandfather likely forming a solidified front against the rest of the world. The less they outwardly connected themselves to Troy, the better. She said in one press interview that she always saw a sad end for Troy. Her brother too reckless to live forever, some shiny object would catch him in its snare. I figured she really believed that. So maybe it was a relief that it finally happened. The worrying could end. Only the grieving to deal with.

Terbert drove back to his station, reaching Miami by midnight, not any closer to catching us but with a renewed zest and feeling in his gut he would take us down. Through sips of Three Fingers in the car, an oracle appeared in the form of the moon and told him so. He would not be completely victorious, the oracle warned with its crescent shine, but he would end our spree, he alone, and this was enough for him, this fervent belief.

He toasted the moon and killed the bottle.

52

Albuquerque to San Bernardino would be a straight shot west across I-40. Barry decided to drive right through so we would reach Uncle Mort's by morning. A rainbow welcomed us outside of Gallup, New Mexico, arced over the craggy red-brown cliffs. The sun a setting fireball as we ate tuna from cans to avoid stopping. Nothing new on the news regarding us, except our story still took center stage. Steph and Jenny retreating into their nook. Steph trying to salvage Jenny's hair with some clips. Barry and Mom listening to "Everybody's Talkin'" by Harry Nilsson up front. She'd stuck her feet out the side window, drying her painted toenails. He chugged coffee after coffee to keep himself alert. I leaned with my cheek against the window and wrote to Heidi.

Dear Heidi.

I crossed it out. *Dear* sounding stupid. What was I, forty-five years old?

Hey girl.

I crossed that out too.

Heidi,

I'm probably the last person you want to hear from, and I'm sure the last few days have been horrible for you. I'm so sorry for what happened to Troy. And I'm sorry we got your family involved. I know the words I write can't make up for what we did, and I don't deserve for you to forgive me. The truth is, the Gimmelmans are a selfish fucking bunch.

We always have been. My dad, and it's tough to even call him that anymore, because he hasn't felt like a dad in a while, but he was a stockbroker and all about money. Our house, the things we owned, this was what became important. And I'm guilty for that too. My Nintendo, the basketball I had signed by The Knicks, our big screen TV, a Laserdisc player, that was what mattered to me. I thought money would be something we always made, but I don't like how we made it recently. It's far from honest.

I know you saw that Troy wasn't the only one who died in this last heist. My dad, Barry, he shot the guard that shot Troy. I don't know if you were mad at that guard too, but he really isn't to blame. He might have done his job wrong by firing at Troy before giving us a chance to lower our weapons, but the truth is it wouldn't have mattered. Barry wouldn't have lowered his gun for nothing. And the fact that he killed the guard over what amounted to some money is disgusting. The truth is I don't want anything to do with this money. And I'm starting to think I don't want anything to do with my parents anymore either.

I doubt you'll even read this whole letter. You'll probably rip it up and throw it away when you see who's it from. But you should know that you were right all along. We were stupid to keep this up after the Boca heist. We were greedy and now we're paying for it. Or, well, Troy paid for it. And that's really fucked up. But I have a bad feeling. It sits in my gut and hangs out there like I ate too much McDonald's. This is gonna catch up with us. And you know what, it probably should. We don't deserve to get away with it, not anymore, not after what we've done.

I did like you said and started writing everything bad down. My sisters are starting to feel this way too so I'm hoping it can help us when we get caught. I know I'm responsible because I was the first one who stole, but that was just a couple of bucks from a convenience store. I did it to help my family because we were running real low on cash and that's never something we had to deal with before. I never expected it would come to this, even though it was exciting at first, especially because we were all really good at it, and it brought us together in a way we never had been before.

We'd never really been a close family. Everyone tended to do their own thing. And I didn't realize how much that sucked until we began doing things together on this trip. Families are weird things. You're stuck with these people without a *say in it, and I know you probably feel really alone now with just your grandpa. I wish I could be there for you. I wish I could be your family. But I'm probably no good for you. You wouldn't have done the things that I've done, and therefore, you should be with someone great who really takes care of you. I hope you find that. I hope you get out of Delray Beach someday too if that's what you want. And I hope you can forgive me, even if you never tell me you do. I hope you forgive me because I'm not worth the time spent on being angry. You're so wonderful and cool that you shouldn't spend any time focused on me. So forgive me only because it's the best thing you can do for yourself.*

I'll always think of the time we hung out as one of the best times of my life.

–Aaron Nicholas Gimmelman

I couldn't mail it right away, since we weren't stopping. It would have to be done once we reached Uncle Mort's without Barry knowing. Too much of a chance at giving away our location, but I didn't care anymore. Let Heidi rat us out if it made her feel better. Would kinda be poetic justice.

When I finished writing, we were passing through Flagstaff. It was fully nighttime and there were few other cars besides some semis on the road. Mom snoring up in her nook, Steph and Jenny asleep in the back. A few days ago, I would've used this as a time to get Barry's vial from the glove compartment, but I didn't want that shit anymore. If coke was something he liked, I wanted nothing to do with it, nothing that could make me similar to him. A hatred was bubbling, it festered in my stomach, looking at the back of his wild hair poking up over the seat. To hit him would feel so good, cause him pain like the pain he caused all of us.

As if he could sense my pulsating anger, his eyes clocked over to the rearview, made me jump in place. Through his glasses they told me I better stay in line, remain loyal, not go rogue, ruin everything. When they glanced back at the road, I could breathe again and shut the sheet blocking off my area. I tried to sleep, quiet my spinning mind. But it wasn't working. A lifetime of insomnia to look forward to, that would be my penance. I would accept that. It made me feel better to know my charge, since no verdict could ever be fair.

So I stayed flush against the window, watching the highway roll by as hours passed and the darkness turned a twinkling purple before the sun fizzled between two faraway mountains and we drove through the Mojave Preserve. I had no clue that in a short time, we'd be driving back this way in an attempt to flee our pursuers, only for our lives to be shattered.

Right then, the Mojave exuded a whistling calm, the mountain breeze in my face, nature's one last caress before the inevitable shitshow.

53

I had my Lady Macbeth moment of waking up thinking I had blood all over my hands and trying to wash them in the kitchen sink, only for the bloodstains to remain. I scrubbed so hard the skin started peeling off, my palms underneath pink and raw. Waking up again, I realized I was dreaming, my hands back to normal. I shook like I was caught in a downpour, my sheets soaked. I ran into the bathroom, turned the water on hot and stuck my face under. The scalding stream, like needles on my face. I gulped a few breaths before my heartbeat got back to normal. Closed my eyes praying I didn't see the blood anymore. A minute passed and nothing but wonderful darkness. When I opened them, I didn't want to stare in the mirror, so I looked out the window.

We had stopped, parking the RV in Uncle Mort's driveway, my family already stepping out. Uncle Mort stood at his front door with his hefty arm around his wife Connie and their two kids Andy and Randy squinting into the sun.

Uncle Mort had gotten beefier since I last saw him, which must've been years ago. He swept what was left of his hair across his skull in an attempt to stave off baldness. His body, shaped like Grimace from the McDonald's gang. He wore a Lacoste shirt, two sizes too small, the alligator looking like it was about to pop off his man breast. A bushy mustache dusted his top lip as his mouth opened wide with a "Helloooooooo." Connie was a plump woman in a Day-Glo jumpsuit with dyed red hair and skin so pale you could see her veins. She'd grown up Irish Catholic and converted to Judaism when she married Mort. They kept Sabbath and were pretty serious about it all. Andy and Randy were a mix of the two of them. Roly-poly , Randy red-headed and Andy with dark hair, the equivalent of Jewish choir boys. The last time they were over at our house I wanted to shoot firecrackers and they were too chicken shit and nearly crapped their pants before telling on me. I hoped we wouldn't be spending too long here.

When I got out of the Gas-Guzzler, Uncle Mort did this stupid thing he always did where he would mime holding a fishing pole and pretend to reel me in. I didn't want to do it but played along. We all hugged one another and went inside.

Their house smelled clean, too clean, but it was nice after being cooped up in the hot-boxed Gas-Guzzler. Connie was OCD and scrubbed everything until it gleamed, even as we were walking in, she had Handi Wipes and was wiping down Andy and Randy's grubby hands. A few things were noticeable at first glance. The giant portrait of Ronald Reagan as a cowboy that sat over the mantle, and the myna birds they had caged that squawked like crazy. Also, all the pictures of the family vacations adorning the walls: Lake Tahoe, Israel, Vegas at the Trump International Hotel, their illustrious stay at the Milford Plaza in New York City, the lullaby of all Broadway. In each one they had cheese grins that made me equally annoyed and jealous.

"Good to see you, brother," Mort said, slapping Barry on the back, as they half-hugged. But it was all for show. The brothers really hated one another. Never got along. Connie also once called Mom a "loose woman," and Mom never forgave her. We couldn't stand Andy and Randy because they smelled of farts.

"Please take off your shoes," Connie said, beaming a smile when it was clear she was angry at us for tracking in dirt from outside. We all obliged. "I laid out some bagels and lox spread if you're hungry."

In the dining room, a platter awaited, along with orange juice and fruit salads. Andy and Randy sat down and began stuffing their faces, smearing an inch-thick layer of cream cheese on their bagels and shoveling it in their pie holes. I wanted to sit near Steph, but Jenny got there first, forcing me to be next to the fart brothers.

"So, you saw some of America?" Mort asked.

"Beautiful country," Barry said, going into a long-winded lie about the Grand Canyon.

"You'll have to show us pictures," Connie beamed.

"When they develop," Mom said, picking at a fruit salad like an anorexic.

"Judy, can I get you something else?" Connie asked.

Mom shook her head. "It's lovely, Connie."

"You know," Mort said, with a cream cheese blob on the edge of his lip, "your industry's not the only one hurting. The travel business is getting hard-hit too. I haven't had nearly as many bookings since the crash."

"People are scrimping and saving," Connie added, unnecessarily.

"Mom, is there strawberry cream cheese?" Andy asked, after devouring his bagel in about three bites.

"Or Strawberry Quik?" Randy asked.

"Strawberry Quik I have," Connie said, getting up and going into the kitchen.

"Gross," Jenny said.

"Aren't you old for stuffed animals?" Andy asked.

"This is Seymour, and he is an *actual* stuffed animal, meaning he was once alive."

"That's gross," Randy said, as Connie returned and scooped Strawberry Quik powder into his glass with some milk, making it look like Pepto Bismol. She did the same for Andy and they gulped it down, their tongues looking like they had a bad disease.

"Funny you should mention travel," Barry said.

"Well, it's not funny because it's my job," Mort replied.

"We want to go somewhere international. Somewhere a little off the beaten path maybe." He glanced over at Mom who still picked at her fruit salad but managed to nod. "Love to give you the business."

Mort talked through munching on his lox. "Well, I don't *need* your business. Bookings have been less, but we're weathering the storm pretty well."

"Morty," Connie said, rubbing his arm.

"It's not like a charity case," Barry said. "If we're already booking it, why not give you the business?"

Now I realized Barry's reason for coming here. The money we stole, could potentially be traced, I'd seen it before on *Miami Vice*. But if he paid his brother in cash out right, it might give us enough time to leave before Mort took it to the bank. I counted the days to Saturday, three away. So, that would be the plan. Get Uncle Mort the money over the weekend so he wouldn't put it in the bank until Monday. And by then we'd be gone. This meant I had precious few days to make a decision about the next step for the Gimmelman kids.

Andy or Randy let a fart rip and it smelled like strawberry sewage.

"Oh Jesus," Steph said, waving her hand in front of her nose.

"Oh no, young lady," Uncle Mort said, wagging his finger. "We don't say that in this house."

"Oh...Moses?"

"Fresh," I heard Connie mumble under her breath.

"We can go over some travel recommendations later," Barry said, working on biting his tongue. "We really appreciate you letting us stay for a few days."

"Anything for my little brother," Mort said, picking the lox from his twisted teeth. "You don't turn your back on family."

Connie just continued beaming.

I doubted they'd think the same if they knew of our infamous aliases.

54

Since the adults needed to talk, they sent us kids up to Andy and Randy's playroom in the attic. For a second I was excited it might have a basketball hoop so I could pretend to be Patrick Ewing after not practicing my jump shot for so long, but their toys were fucking lame. First, they wanted to show off their Lite-Brite set where one of them made a basic heart. Even nine-year-old Jenny was unimpressed. Then we had to listen to their Teddy Ruxpin, a dumb stuffed bear who asked, "Can you and I be friends?"

"Weren't you just making fun of stuffed animals?" I asked.

"Teddy Ruxpin is not a stuffed animal," Randy roared, as if possessed by a demon.

Then we played some Simon while Steph lit a cigarette out the window.

"What are you doing?" Andy asked.

"I'm smoking."

Andy and Randy looked at one another in fright.

"Smoking is bad for you," they both said in eerie tandem.

"Go tell on me," Steph said.

"We will," they said again at the same time.

Steph gave them the finger.

"You guys are mean," Andy said, almost in tears. Jenny went over and pushed him to the floor. He hit his head on the edge of an easel. "Owww."

"Andy!" Randy shouted and ran over to him. "Where does it hurt?"

"My *keppe*," Andy said, rubbing his head. Randy started rubbing it too.

"Bunch of pussies," Jenny said to Seymour.

"That's a bad word," Randy scolded her.

"Jesus Christ on a Ritz cracker," I said, wanting away from them. My bloodied hands dream from last night still rattled. I needed a moment to clear my thoughts. I burst down the stairs and heard Barry and Uncle Mort talking softly in Mort's den. I stayed outside the doorframe and listened.

"Level with me," Mort said. "How bad are the finances?"

"They're not," Barry stuttered. "I converted a bunch of stocks to cash before the crash."

"Lucky you."

From down the hall the myna birds said, "Lucky you, lucky you."

"What about you?" Barry asked.

Mort let out a sigh that sounded like a deflating balloon. "Well, Bar, made some less-than-stellar investments. Gold, silver, and oil. Who'da thunk they'd tank? Then we got a timeshare in Florida I can't get rid of. And my mortgage interest rate is sky high. Don't tell Connie this. She thinks everything's rosy."

"Why don't you let me give you the business for a trip? We couldn't maintain our house, but I wanted to give the kids one last hurrah. Somewhere special. Before I go back and figure out the next step in my life."

"Do you think it's wise to splurge like that?" Mort asked.

"I'll make the money again. Stockbrokers will be needed. I'm letting the market ride out right now."

"You love it, don't you?"

"What?"

"Having a hold over me. Here I thought you're the one who needed charity, losing your house and your job, and I was happy to do it, Bar, but no, you're just peachy keen, money out the wahzoo."

"Morty, that's not the case. I'm planning a long vacation, you work for a travel business, that's all."

"You were like that as a kid, always undermining me. Making me look bad to our parents."

"At my worst, I was just a bratty younger brother."

"Hogwash, you pit them against me. Made up lies."

"I think you're remembering things differently—"

"When they were dying, Bar, they asked for you. Not me. You. While you were traipsing around with Judith up at Columbia and I took care of them."

"Is that what this is about, Mort? I was a fucking kid still. I was a teenager."

"You've always been a selfish prick, Bar. You didn't care about them."

"You keep fucking talking like that..."

"Or what? What are you gonna do? You gonna hit me?"

"No, I'm not gonna hit you, Mort. But don't tell me I didn't love them."

"You loved them, I'm not saying that, but you didn't care. You never respected the religion."

"Okay, so I'm an asshole because I was never Jewish enough for you? I don't see you with a yarmulke."

"We hold Shabbat, my kids go to Hebrew school."

"Aaron, will be bar mitzvahed."

My neck prickled at the mention of my name.

"But it won't mean anything to you, to him. You've never had the ability to see what is beyond your sphere. The world revolves around Barry's orbit and nothing outside of it matters. You never gave into any Jewish beliefs because it is something bigger than you and therefore not worthy enough."

"Okay, Mort, you win. What do you want me say?"

"I want you to take responsibility."

"For what?"

"For the wool you pulled over our parents' eyes. That you were this God child born out of all the anguish they went through."

"That's ridiculous."

"They saw greatness in you. They truly believed their suffering was for your creation. That you would do such great things to make it all worthwhile. They never spoke of me that way."

"I think you have what is called selective memory. They loved us both the same."

"Barry is so talented. Barry is a whiz with numbers."

"They wanted me to be a doctor, or at least a lawyer."

"Because they saw your potential. They couldn't care less what I did with my life."

"Look, if you want to torture yourself with alternative history, be my guest. I wanted to come here to give my kids a breather from the RV, and frankly, Mort, I worked fucking hard for the cash I have now. We were dealt a blow—my family lost their home. As far as I see you still have yours. And these weeks have been trying, very trying. Exhilarating but I've also lost myself a little. I have. It's not the same world it was when we left New Jersey."

"I don't know what you're talking about, Barry."

"You think I'm great, you think I'm destined for greatness? My name in lights? Not if I can fucking help it, man. I'm torturing myself right now to just burrow down in a hole and never surface, and I want to, believe me I do, but I don't know if I'm capable of settling, if my need for recognition will be the end of me. And so maybe you're right? Maybe our parents did put unrealistic expectations on me. Maybe the horrors of the Holocaust made me fight to not be ordinary, so their plight could have a greater meaning. And maybe you were meant to be plain, in your basic house with your basic kids and your birds, and like soothsayers our parents saw that end for you. They knew you'd accept your drudgery. But not me, you fuck-o. I know that years from now I'll still be mentioned, whispered with the greats..."

"What greats?"

"My brother, my lughead brother, you could never realize in your wildest dreams the things I've done and achieved. In some ways, our folks would curse my fall, but in other ways, deep down in the places they could never admit, they would have been in awe. Trust me."

Barry stormed out of the room, nearly knocking into me, his face puffing and on fire. He barely acknowledged my presence, not ready to spiral back down to reality. Down the hall, he reached in his front pocket and removed his vial, taking a sharp snort, then shook his head back and forth and floated into the shadows.

When I peered back into Uncle Mort's den, the man was crying, not with deep sobs but the kind of tears one releases out of shame.

Shame for his small stature in this giant universe.

"Lucky you, lucky you," the myna birds continued squawking.

55

Once again, I got shafted with rooms. Steph and Jenny taking the guest quarters while I was stuck with the Fart Brothers farting away in their sleep. Both of them were also afraid of the dark so a giant nightlight would've kept me up anyway despite the flatulence. Sometime after four in the morning, I knew sleep was a lost cause and made my way downstairs for a snack. If I'd been honest with myself, I was afraid I'd dream of the bloody hands again. And a vice felt like it was gripping around my throat.

One benefit of insomnia is the ability to witness the secrets of others. And so, after finding some egg salad in the fridge to munch on, I discovered Barry in the living room. Mort and Connie had a glass case full of old photographs and keepsakes. Barry had opened it and was holding a picture of his parents. We all had seen very few pictures of them young. I guessed they had lost most of their photos when they went to the camps. But this photo might've been from their wedding afterwards because they looked happy, or at least relieved. My grandma was a beauty, short curly hair like Barry's, a dot of lipstick. It was the only picture I ever really saw of her smiling. And she had one of those smiles that drew you in. Maybe because it happened so infrequently that there was a specialness in witnessing its charm. My grandfather had slicked-back black hair and a thin mustache of the era. He was dressed in a suit and she in a dress, the photo sepia-toned. Barry held it close to him.

"I'm sorry," he said, so softly. The magnitude of the silence in the house allowed me to hear. "Forgive me."

I felt like I was privy to a private moment I shouldn't be watching, and it was stunning to see him so exposed. This would never be the Barry he'd reveal to anyone: apologetic, lost. He stared at the photo as if he needed answers, a sign from above. He looked around. A towel had been draped over the myna birds' cage and even they were quiet.

"I could believe if you would forgive," he pleaded, the desperation in his voice making it crack. But believe in what? Was he referring to God? Would he give himself over to a higher power if he knew he'd be absolved? Or was he saying only what he wanted his parents' spirits to hear? "I believed in Him before. Before I became old enough to question."

I pictured a young Barry learning about the ways of God's existence and taking it as a fact. Maybe his parents told him how God had saved them during the dark times and that they stayed alive by not turning their back on Him. So what changed? In our house, the idea of God had never been brought up. We were Jews only in tradition. Had bar and bat mitzvahs because that was what you did in our New Jersey community. Parties with DJs playing "YMCA" and the Chicken Dance and relatives giving hundred-dollar checks. Half my class was Jewish, and we sat through their readings of Haftorahs and Torahs waiting for it to end, making fun of the crazy tone-deaf old lady in temple who always sat in the front and whose voice echoed. And then we'd have cake and think of it no more. Barry would say he did it all for his folks, even with my upcoming bar mitzvah—although those plans were likely sidetracked now. It was doing the bare minimum so as not to feel guilty. Uncle Mort truly lived spiritually, and maybe Barry was realizing now that in the afterlife he could never match up.

He kissed the photo of them, placed it back behind the glass case. More of a show of emotion than I'd ever seen him give, even to Mom. He truly loved his parents, even though they'd passed so long ago, their memories feeling like, from other lifetimes. I would know how that would be. Soon enough and for the rest of my life. That when you lose someone close to you those memories are all you have of their existence. And as time passes, and you lose more and more of those remembrances, they fade further away, only photographs igniting their presence again. I would be destroyed to not have enough of those photos, my own mind becoming unreliable.

But then I was still young, for the next few days at least. I wished that I could whisper that to myself, to treasure the last moments, but I was too preoccupied. I was figuring out our next plan, monitoring Barry, monitoring Mom, making sure that they still were on track to head somewhere international while us kids could decide our own fate.

I heard Barry's slippers shuffling out of the room. Once he had gone, I lay down on the couch and had a moment of rest before I heard someone on the phone in the kitchen. Looking at the time, I saw it was six in the morning. The voice belonged to Mom. "Ma," she said, into the receiver. She didn't notice I was on the couch. She paced while wrapping the long cord of the hanging rotary phone around her index finger. "Ma," she said again. Quietly, I picked up the phone on the TV stand, listened in. The sound of Grandma Bernice's breathing on the other end. "Ma, please forgive me," Mom said, just as desperate as Barry, equally as tortured too. But Grandma Bernice held firm. She let Mom talk out all of her despair, apologize for every misgiving. She at least gave her that. But she wouldn't respond. My broken mom couldn't take it anymore and finally hung up. She collapsed in a ball in the kitchen, heaving. A light turned on. Connie came in wearing a fuzzy bathrobe and leopard slippers.

"What's wrong, Judy?" she asked, but Mom couldn't catch her breath. "Judy?" she asked again, before giving up and just hugging Mom, the two of them rocking in the corner.

"My mother hates me," Mom finally admitted, but Connie shushed her.

"Whatever fight you are having, it will pass, dear." Mom refused to listen. "It will," Connie said again. "As mad as I get with Andy and Randy, they are my children, and I would love them even if they were serial killers."

"You would?" Mom asked, the hopefulness in her voice reaching a pitch.

"Of course, they're my babies. Always will be. And you'll always be her baby."

"I will?" Mom asked, and Connie shushed her again, let her cry the rest of these dark feelings out. The sun slanted into the house, a bright California morning.

"Lemme get you some fresh-squeezed OJ, hon," Connie said, and Mom thanked her. I could hear Connie getting to work on the OJ. I rolled off the couch and made my way upstairs so Mom wouldn't know of my spying.

I went into Steph and Jenny's room. Steph, already awake.

"Morning sickness," she whispered, rubbing her stomach.

"They're still human," I told her. She cocked her head to the side.

"So what does that mean in terms of what we should do?" she asked.

"I dunno. Let's think about it more. Whether we run or not. It's a big decision."

"It is."

"We can decide over the weekend. They won't leave before then."

"How do you know?" she asked.

"Barry has a plan that involves Uncle Mort and his travel company. He won't go until they've picked a place."

Steph blew her bangs out of her eyes. "Okay."

"Okay," I said.

And then we linked hands and blew on them like we used to do when we were little kids and shared a secret we promised not to tell .

56

The day proved busy since Jenny got into a fight with the Fart Brothers over Seymour and ran off. Apparently, they decided Seymour and Teddy Ruxpin should host a tea party but hadn't told Jenny. She frantically tore up the house looking. When she found it in Andy and Randy's room, she proceeded to beat them up. At first, they thought she was kidding but she split Andy's lip and gave Randy a black eye. Uncle Mort screamed at her and then at Barry and Mom for raising such an unruly child. She took off down the block like a feral cat, and Steph and I were tasked to find her.

Anything to get out of the house. We walked the suburban streets and used it as a good excuse to go over the pros and cons about what our next step might be. The first choice was obviously remaining with Barry and Mom wherever they might decide to go.

"If they've given up thieving, it may just be the easiest thing to do," Steph said, chewing grape Hubba Bubba gum and blowing a huge bubble.

"But do you *really* think Barry will never try to rob again?" I countered.

"...No, but maybe he's done with big heists at least."

"We'll always be on edge thinking we might get caught. Do you want that for Little Troy?"

She caressed her stomach. "That name has a nice ring."

"How are you doing?"

"Okay. I mean, I have my moments. I cried today already. Usually once a day I just sob. And then like, I think, what's the point of crying anymore?"

"True." I kicked a stone. "Leaving with them also means we're stuck wherever they decide. It could be Paris, but what if it's somewhere grody?"

"We can wait until they pick a place?"

"That might be too late."

She blew another bubble and popped it. "Okay, so we don't go with them. What are our options?"

"Hmm. Stay with Uncle Mort and Connie."

Steph gave me a look like she saw the Terminator coming after her.

"Right, right, I'm not into that either," I said.

"I'd rather be with Grandma Bernice," she said, and we both let that hang in the air.

"I mean, if we took enough of their money, at least all our cuts, and honestly Troy's because it's not like—well, you know what I mean?"

"We *would* have a lot to last us," Steph said, getting kind of excited. "Like L.A. might be fun. I could get a car. Could we rent an apartment at our age?"

"In L.A., I'm sure we could. Like, if we have money that's all that matters."

"We could try that, and if it doesn't work out have Grandma Bernice be a last resort?"

"God, the thought of living with all those cats."

"Jenny would hate it."

"Right, we still have to find Jenny."

We started calling out her name, the area devoid of people like in some weird science fiction movie that zapped up everyone in the suburban enclave.

"Okay, another option that we probably won't do, but we could tell Uncle Mort and Aunt Connie what's been happening—"

"They would for *sure* call child protective services," Steph said. "Hold on, lemme fix my sneaker." She took off her Keds and popped a pebble out from the heel. "So that's a no-go. We could put out an anonymous tip to the cops? No, then they'd be after us too."

"If we split up from Barry and Mom, we don't rat on them. I don't want to do that."

"I don't either."

"We would go in the middle of the night. Leave them a note."

"Hey, Aaron?"

"Yeah?"

"Do you think they'd...actually be pleased? I mean, not to have to worry about us, not to have us as a burden?"

"I don't know. I really can't answer that."

"I'm not saying they wouldn't miss us, but that secretly, they'd be relieved."

I sucked in a hit of cool air. "Yeah, I think they would."

"Then we have our answer."

The two of us walked without speaking for a while, letting the truth hang between us in all its reeking glory. We would leave our parents, never look back. And it would be better for everyone.

"We could do it tomorrow," I said. "Tomorrow night. Give us a chance to sleep on it."

"Yeah, I need a night," Steph quickly said. She re-ponytailed her hair, tightening it with a scrunchie.

"Okay, tomorrow we make a definite decision."

"I see Jenny," she said, and started running.

Jenny was sitting on the curb with Seymour in her lap smushing ants with her thumb.

"Everyone is worried sick," Steph said, as Jenny looked up with a scowl.

"No, they're not."

"Fine, everyone is pissed, and we've been sent to find you," I said.

"I hate it there," she said, wiping a dead ant on her Rainbow Brite shirt.

"Everyone does. But we have a plan. Are you a big enough girl to listen?" Steph asked.

"Don't talk to me like I'm a fucking goo goo gaga baby!"

"Okay, okay, Jenny, calm down," I said, sitting next to her. "Listen, tomorrow night we can all take our cuts of the money and go away somewhere, away from them."

"Mom and Dad?"

"Yeah, like we talked about, but we can really do it. We'd have enough money. We can go to L.A. and get an apartment."

She put Seymour up to her ear and listened for almost a minute of crazy.

"Seymour's in," she said, giving a smile with a missing front tooth.

"Jenny, when did you lose your tooth?"

"I dunno. I yanked it out yesterday or something."

"And no one noticed?" Steph asked.

Jenny shrugged.

"This child is growing up and no one is paying attention," Steph said. "All the more reason we need to do what we need to do."

"Jenny, you can't say anything and let on," I said.

"Who am I gonna fucking tell?"

"Barry! Or Mom. Just keep your mouth shut."

"Why are you calling Dad 'Barry'?" she asked.

"Why?" I thought about it for a sec. "I–I don't even know. I just started doing it. Honestly both of them don't deserve to be called Mom or Dad. But like, you saw what he did, Jenny. To that guard?"

"I know, Aaron. Jeez, beat a dead horse some more."

She got to her feet and marched away.

"Where does she even learn these expressions?" I asked.

"Beats me," Steph said. "Probably TV."

When we got back, Jenny stayed in the RV and Uncle Mort and Aunt Connie thought that was a good idea, since Andy and Randy were still frightened of her. Barry groaned at that. This erupted into another fight between the brothers that no one wanted to hear. Steph was feeling queasy, so she went upstairs to rest, and Connie was tending to Andy and Randy's wounds, so that left me with Mom. In a short amount of time, the two of us had nothing to say to one another anymore. I found a tin of Cheez Balls and parked myself on the couch to watch TV. She joined me and we watched an episode of *Mr. Belvedere* before *A Current Affair* came on. Sure enough, we were the top story. A reporter talked about our newly dubbed name, the Wild Woodstock Gang, like we were outlaws or something. Mom grabbed the remote and shut it off. She ran her hands through her hair that looked like a ball of mess.

"Do you really think I haven't been a good mom lately?" she asked, still facing the television.

Here she went tugging at my heartstrings just as we were deciding to leave. As if she knew our separate futures. As if she was doing anything to keep us close.

"Yes," I flat-out said, no pussyfooting around.

She covered her mouth, not expecting me to be so harsh.

"I remember when I learned that my mother was human too. It's hard to wrap your mind around. That your parents aren't perfect."

I gave a huff of a laugh under my breath.

"Maybe we got carried away?"

I turned to her. "Is that a question?"

"My babies are safe right now, that's all that matters." She nodded to convince herself. "That's all I asked for."

"No, that's not enough." She still wouldn't face me, so I physically turned her face. Although, she still wouldn't look at me. I guessed it hurt too much. "You put us in danger."

"I followed your father."

"That's no excuse."

We were talking under our breaths so as not to raise our voices, call attention.

"This was his idea," she said. "His show."

"You're no better for going along with it."

Her eyes turned to ice. "Neither are you."

I crossed my arms. "*You* are the parent. I'm the child. You're supposed to teach us right from wrong."

"Aaron, you started all of this. You got the bug in Bear-Bear's head."

I stood up and stamped my foot.

"I stole three hundred bucks from a convenience store!"

"He's been more alive in these past few weeks than I've seen him in years. That job consumed him. The money for your Nintendo, your basketball hoop. He broke his back."

"Fine, and he could've found another job."

"It's not that simple. We're in a recession. There was no telling when—"

"We would have survived. In a smaller house. In a shittier neighborhood.

298

And if us kids would've complained—"

"Oh, you would have."

"Fine, we would have because you raised us to be spoiled. But we would've dealt with it, and maybe you would've had to get a job, or Steph and I would work at the Tenafly Mall and help out. There would've been food to eat and a roof..."

She scrunched her face, a migraine forming. I knew when she got like this she'd be out of commission for a while.

"You want me to say you're right and I'm wrong. Is that it, Aaron?"

"Yes! I want you to apologize for—"

"Well, I'm not going to. There's a million dollars in that RV and we can go anywhere. And we will. And we'll start over. And you kids *are* safe, so there was no harm."

"That guard? Troy?"

She stuck her fingers in her ears like a petulant child, then composed herself. "I'm not saying there was no harm overall. There was no harm to you. But..." She took a deep breath through her nose. "If you need that *sorry*, I'm giving it to you, baby. I'm sorry. I'm very sorry. Okay? We'll never do anything like this again. But it gives us a start. It gives us something."

I longed to say that her start would wind up being five hundred thousand less, but I couldn't tip her off in any way.

"Okay?" she asked, spreading out her arms, motioning for a hug. "Okay, baby?"

It was easier to agree and fall into her hug, let her cry out her guilt. When she was finished, she rubbed away the last tears and went into the kitchen for an ice pack before covering her face and heading upstairs. In a way, I knew right then it would be the last conversation we'd truly have.

And I was okay with that.

I turned *A Current Affair* back on to remind myself why.

57

In solidarity with Jenny, Steph and I agreed to stay in The Gas-Guzzler too. It was also more of a statement against not only Uncle Mort and Connie, but Barry and Mom as well. That we didn't even want to be under the same roof as them. Andy and Randy were still going through PTSD after Jenny's attack, so Connie was busy with calming them down, and Barry and Uncle Mort were locking horns over who was the better son. If Mom were less self-absorbed, she'd realize why we chose not to stay in the house, but the back-to-back disappointing conversation with Grandma Bernice and then me kept her spiraling. She'd taken to staying under the covers and emerging only for meals with her hair in shock mode.

For us kids it gave us a chance to see what life might be like without them around. We found that it wasn't so bad. Nothing seemed ramped up to ten anymore, and we could hear ourselves think. We had a dance party tape that mixed all of our favorite music together: Debbie Gibson's "Out of the Blue" for Steph, Springsteen's "Born to Run" for me (hey, I was a Jersey boy after all), and death metal for Jenny, which wasn't too big a surprise. We feasted on Mallomars and Corn Nuts to avoid eating inside and rode our sugar highs. Jenny would do this funny thing where she pretended to be Johnny Carson interviewing Seymour. She had Carson's voice and mannerisms down perfect, and I laughed so hard I got a stomachache. Steph even mentioned that this made her realize we were making the right decision by leaving. She suggested driving away with the RV, but I said that was too risky. We would leave tomorrow night, and call a cab to take us to L.A. She wanted to live on the beach so we thought about Venice because it was grungy and affordable. She wanted to get rollerblades and glide down the boardwalk. I had to admit I was getting excited.

Barry was still deciding where we would go internationally, but it really didn't matter. Staying in the RV, I barely encountered him. I wasn't even sure if I'd say goodbye. Part of me loved him like crazy, always would, but he had a way of getting his hooks in. If we said goodbye, he could turn it around, convince us to stay. It wasn't worth it. After Steph and Jenny went to bed, I divided our cuts fairly. The money was being kept in the kitchen cabinets, and I chose to just split it fifty-fifty, leaving us with almost five hundred thousand smackeroos. I'd be lying if I said the money didn't feel good in my hands.

* * *

While we had a semi-solid plan for the cash, picking up with Gianni Bianchi, he did as well. He'd traveled all the way to California with Fingers driving his cherry-red Iroc-Z. Fingers had worked for Mr. Bianchi since Fingers dropped out of high school. He was selling nickel bags of weed when Mr. Bianchi took him under his wing. Mostly, Fingers was good at threatening men who owed money. He used to be a boxer and had such a rapid-fire punch you didn't even see it coming. He'd catch a target when they were least expecting it and leave their face a bloody pulp. Mr. Bianchi was a fan of keeping his pin-striped suits clean, so he had his underlings do his dirty work.

An East Coast man, Mr. Bianchi had been to California before but never the middle of America. They passed through flat plains as house music pumped from their car windows. Got slack-jawed looks in gas stations. All the while, he pictured Fingers wailing on Barry Gimmelman's face, and the money he hoped he'd get to make this journey worthwhile. They arrived in San Bernardino before us Gimmelmans, staking out Mort Gimmelman's house in the Iroc-Z across the street. When they saw an RV finally arrive a day later, they wanted to wait for the right time. But Barry didn't leave the house. Us kids came out. Barry's fat brother and their stupid kids too, but not Barry. Mr. Bianchi and Fingers could break in in the middle of the night and drag Barry outside, but they figured it might be better to be patient. Then they saw us three kids enter the RV one day and not leave when it turned nighttime.

"They're sleeping there?" Mr. Bianchi asked Fingers.

"Looks like."

"I think we found our in."

Wearing entirely black, they crept up to the RV in the dead of night, ski masks over their faces. Fingers put his finger to his lips. Both of them heard rustling inside. The plan would be to use one of us kids to lure Barry out.

I had locked the RV door, but it was easy for a pro like Fingers to pick. I was in the kitchen stuffing the cash into separate bags when the door creaked open. At first, I thought it was Barry and my heart sank. He would *not* be pleased that I was messing with his cash. When I saw two men in all black step inside, my butterfingers caused a bag of cash to fall to the floor, bills everywhere.

"What the f—?"

One of them grabbed me, the other (Fingers) wrapping his long fingers around my mouth.

"Shut up," Fingers said. He had a gun that poked my back. I nearly shit myself. "Boss, look at the money on the floor."

"I see it," Mr. Bianchi said, although I didn't know either of their names at the time. If I thought about it, I would've remembered Grandma Bernice going on about a mobster named Mr. Bianchi who she'd heard Barry talking to once, but my mind was too jumbled to focus. I thought of the gun pressed into my spine. My sisters snoozing in the back. All the money we worked so hard for about to get vacuumed out the door.

"Okay, this is how it's gonna work," Mr. Bianchi said. With the ski mask on, he only existed as a mouth. "I'm guessing this is all the money you stole." His eyes locked in on the open cabinets. "I was gonna have you get your no-good father, but this is even better. I'm just gonna take the cash."

I raced through the list of options I had. Go along and hope to live through this. Bite Fingers's fingers and see what happens. As I was about to make a decision, Steph came out of her nook, rubbing her eyes.

"What's that noise?"

She took in the men in black, probably wondered if she was still dreaming. Then let out a scream.

"Keep fucking quiet," Mr. Bianchi said, running over to her and clamping his palm over her mouth. We all eyed the house to see if any lights came on. After a few seconds of nothing, we realized her screams probably had been muffled by the RV. Mr. Bianchi stuck a gun in Steph's temple and I wanted to murder him. I wanted to yell that my sister was pregnant, and I would torture him if he hurt her at all. She was sniveling, face flushed and red, tears building.

"Sweetie, if you don't keep quiet, I'm gonna knock you out, ya hear?" She nodded. "Okay, this is how it's gonna go. Sweetie, you're gonna get me the bags of cash and we'll be gone. If you don't do this, we will hurt you, maybe even kill you, we don't care. Your fuckin' father owes us a shit ton of money, and we've come all the way to Cali-fuckin'-fornia to get it. So, you're gonna get us that money, honey?" Steph nodded again. "Good, sweetie." He let her go. We all probably held our breath wondering if she would scream again. But she didn't. She started stuffing the cash that fell back into the bag, her hands shaking but still doing a good job under the circumstances. When she was done, she handed over the bags.

"Good, good girl," Mr. Bianchi said.

"Now, you forget you saw us, all right?" Fingers said, both of them giddy. He removed his hand from over my mouth.

"Yous stay back, ya hear?" Mr. Bianchi said, as they inched toward the door. All of a sudden, a shot rang out. I wondered if they had fired. I checked myself for a wound I might've been too shocked to feel. Steph did the same. Nothing. We looked at each other, confused.

Fingers collapsed to the floor, the bag of money spilling out again. He clutched his stomach that spat up blood like a gaping mouth. Jenny walked in holding a smoking gun.

"Drop it!" she said, as Fingers let go of the gun as well, his eyes turning white.

"What in the fuck?" Mr. Bianchi asked.

"I said, fucking drop it, big nose," Jenny insisted, barreling into him and knocking him to the ground. The cash bags and the gun flew out of his hands. I ran over and grabbed the gun, pointed it at Mr. Bianchi.

"Jenny, how did you...?" Steph asked.

"I saw them from the bedroom. Had the gun under my bed and jumped out of the window."

"Uhhhhhhh," Fingers said.

"Your man doesn't look too good," Jenny said. "Who are you?"

"Little bitch I ain't telling you nothing," Mr. Bianchi said, so Jenny whacked him on the skull with the butt of her gun, causing Mr. Bianchi to pass out.

We all stared at each other, befuddled.

"I think we need to get Barry," I finally said, although we all were thinking it.

Jenny, as if she'd been elevated to running the crew, gave a firm nod.

I ran out of the RV and into the house.

58

Bursting inside, I ran into the blinking eyes of Uncle Mort and Aunt Connie looking like owls in the darkness. Connie, her hair in curlers and cold cream slathered all over her face, resembled more of a snow owl. Mort's comb-over standing straight at attention. He held a Louisville Slugger.

"What was that?"

"Uh, truck backfiring," I said, impressed by my quick thinking.

Connie put her hand over her heart. "Oh, thank God."

"And the scream?" Uncle Mort asked, still gripping the bat.

"That was...Jenny. She scares easily."

They both didn't seemed convinced by the last lie. Thankfully, I was saved by Barry in slippers and a bathrobe rushing down the stairs.

"Truck backfired," I said, but was raising my eyebrows in a way that told him I was slinging some bullshit. "I think you should come and check on Jenny. She's spooked."

"Uh, yeah," Barry said, weaving past Mort and Connie and flying down the stairs. "That kid, she has a thing about trucks."

"About trucks?" Connie asked.

"It's a fear. She was almost hit by a truck as a child... I mean, when she was younger, and so it...explains a lot of her behavior."

"She is a strange one," Connie said to Mort.

"I'm going back to bed," Mort said, the slugger slack at his side.

Mom was on the top of the stairs now, her hair tied up with a bandana.

"What's happening?" she asked, her voice shrill.

I wanted to tell her nothing, knowing it would make it worse if she knew and came along. But Barry opened his big mouth and told her that "Jenny needs you."

"Jenny," she whispered to herself, as if she'd forgotten her child's name. Mort and Connie went up the stairs.

"What's really going on?" Barry asked, his hand on my collar.

"We got company," I said, as we all scurried out of the house.

Mom held on to Barry's bathrobe, frightened. The RV's door already open, revealing the horror of a puddle of blood when we stepped inside.

"Fuck," Barry said, pushing Mom in and slamming the door. He checked out the window to make sure Mort and Connie weren't watching. "What happened?"

"This man came looking for money you owe him," I said, pointing at the sleeping Mr. Bianchi.

"Bear-Bear," Mom said, clutching her neck.

"Jenny shot this other man who must be his sidekick."

"Oh, my baby," Mom said, going over to hug her but Jenny pushed her away.

"I'm fine," she mumbled.

"I'm not," Steph said.

"None of us are fine!" I shout-whispered.

"Okay, okay, okay," Barry said, picking at his curls and pacing. "Okay." He shot his finger in the air and made his way to the driver's seat, turned on the ignition, and drove out of the driveway.

"Where are we going?" I asked, running to the front.

"We gotta get rid of these bodies. Empty streets, empty streets," he repeated. "Kid," he pointed at me. "Get the map."

I opened the glove compartment as the map spilled out.

"We're looking for a body of water."

I flipped the map from upside down to right side up. "Here, Silverwood Lake, it's about twenty miles away."

"Okay, good."

"Dad," Steph called out.

"What, Stephie? We're kind of busy."

"I think the man who got shot is dead. He's not moving."

I could see her poking Fingers through the rearview mirror and recoiling in disgust.

"What about the other one?" Barry called back.

Steph poked him too, his breathing audible due to a deviated septum. "Still alive."

"Let's tie him up," Barry said. "Judy, use the bedsheets."

Mom stood frozen.

"Judith!" he shouted, causing her to jump.

"I'll help you, Mom," Steph said, guiding Mom over to my bed where they began removing the sheets.

Barry wiped the sweat from his brow. "Phew, this was close."

"Did you know these men were coming?" I asked, but he just kept wiping away sweat. "Barry!"

He whipped a finger in my face. "Don't call me that. I'm your father. The lack of respect—"

"Did you know these men were coming?" I asked, more forcefully.

"Look, in the kind of business I do you come across an unsavory lot at times. When the stock market was rolling, I was their best friend, couldn't make them enough money, and when it tanked, they needed a scapegoat. Hence, me."

"They said you owed them money. Were these the guys you were talking about before?"

"It's complicated, kid. You wouldn't get—"

"I could be taking calculus for my age, *Barry*, I think I fucking could."

"Don't call me Barry!"

"Stop changing the subject. How much money did you borrow from them?"

"I mean, some, I mean, a lot, well, what's your definition of borrowing?"

"Them lending you... I'm not gonna do this. Is this why we were robbing banks, to just pay back these thugs?"

"Look, I had house payments, and I was gonna buy us a boat, a nice boat to take on the Hudson, and lemme tell you, boats do not come cheap. And banks are assholes, you don't need me to tell you that, right? So, they were finicky about a loan, and I was talking to Mr. Bianchi, and—"

I could barely contain my rage. "All of this was because of a boat you never even bought?"

"Oh, I bought the boat. And we're minimizing it by using the word *boat* by the way. This was a beaut. Really more of a mini yacht. It was called *The Judy*, written in a script right on the masthead. And I was gonna surprise you guys—"

"What did the boat cost?"

"The thing about a yacht, even a mini one, is the cost is not a one-time payment, there's insurance and so...yeah we were lookin' around a million, maybe two."

"You are a piece of shit."

"Hey, watch it there."

"No, Barry, no. You risked our lives for a mini yacht?"

"Again, *you* were the one that started this robbing thing."

"God, you and Mom are exactly alike. You take no ownership for your fucked-up choices. And I'm not even talking about the robbing, you borrowed two million dollars from mobsters."

"Again, the market was soaring, I'd have done it a couple of months earlier and it would've been fine."

"You don't live in reality, it's your own version of how things go. And people are dead."

Barry's eyes shifting to the rearview. "Well, no real loss there."

"That could've been us! I can't. I can't anymore. I live in crazy town and you're the mayor and..."

"Settle down, Aaron. You having a titty attack right now, is not doing us any good." His eyes shifted back to the road. "Ah, I think we're approaching the lake."

"What are you gonna do there?"

"Son, we're gonna do what must be done."

"Jesus Christ, Jesus Christ, Jesus Christ," I said, looking back at Mr. Bianchi and wondering which one of us was going to do the deed.

59

In the middle of the night, the Gimmelmans were luckily the only ones on Silverwood Lake. Barry and I took separate turns dragging out the bodies from the RV and lining them up by the water. The girls stood over them like we were at some weird Viking funeral. Mom and Steph in stunned silence, Jenny rubbing her grubby hands together in delight.

"Okay, this guy," Barry said. "Fingers. We fill him up with rocks so he'll sink."

We proceeded to stick rocks in his clothing. A meditative aspect to the ritual. The stones, cold in our hands. Jenny stuffed some bigger ones in his gaping wound.

"Good idea, Jenny," Barry said.

"Jesus," I muttered.

"Stop saying Jesus, Aaron. You are a Jew."

"Don't tell me what the fuck I am."

He raised the back of his hand to hit me, but then thought better.

"Just keep stuffing him with rocks, then we'll push him out and see what happens."

We finished with a giant rock that was hefty for Barry to lift and place on Fingers's chest. Then we pushed him out, and watched as he began to sink.

"See, it's working."

All our eyes went to Mr. Bianchi.

"Here's the thing, troops," Barry said, getting us in a strange huddle.

"We've come this far, right? This stain on the Earth, this Guido mobster, is better off gone. If it wouldn't be us he was harassing, it'd be someone else, the loop continuing. We're stopping him, and I believe that's rather heroic."

"Save it," I said.

"No, I will not *save it*, Mr. Sarcastic. Your attitude has been totally in the toilet lately."

"Bear-Bear," Mom said, coming out of her coma.

"Mr. Bigshot thinks his shit doesn't stink as big as the rest of us, and let me tell you, sonny, that shit is just as foul."

"Are you done?" I asked.

"We're about to head wherever your heart's desire. And this sourpuss wants to take a dump in my coffee."

"Let's just call a spade a spade," I said. "We're killing this man."

Mom covered her mouth in shock.

"Oh, save it," I said. "You've been complicit in all this too. We all have. We're going to hell."

"Lucky Jews don't believe in hell," Barry said, showing off his white teeth.

"Less talking, more killin'," Jenny said, picking up another rock. "I've already got one notch on my belt."

"No, no," Mom said, "Bear-Bear, let's keep them innocent. Don't make them do it."

"In no way are we innocent, or ever will be innocent again," I said, right in her face. "You've destroyed our childhoods. There's no getting them back."

Mom looked at Barry to refute.

"All right, all right," he said, and picked up another big rock.

"They don't have to watch," Mom said, holding her arms out as a shield and attempting to keep us spared. Steph turned into Mom's shoulder at the sound of the first thwack. Jenny of course watched, as did I, so I'd be able to describe every detail in my journal for the judge and jury. With the second thwack, Barry's glasses went askew, and he huffed and puffed, the out-of-shape bastard. Mr. Bianchi had come to a little, just enough to hold out his palms for the beating to cease. But Barry whacked again. And again. Blood painting the rock. A piece of flesh flew into the dirt.

In silence, we repeated the ritual of filling the body with rocks and then sending Mr. Bianchi out for a final swim. The body bubbled before sinking. We kicked dirt over the bloodstains, and Barry ordered us to remove any clothing with blood on it as well. In our underwear, we made our way back into the RV, trading turns over the sink to clean up with harsh pink soap. We changed into the clothes we had left in the Gas-Guzzler, and Barry got on the road again, the sound of our heavy breathing all that was audible until it became too unbearable to listen anymore.

"We repeat none of this," Barry said, one hand on the wheel, the other holding a dangling cigarette out of the window. The cherry alive, as he brought it to his lips. "I convince my asshole brother tomorrow to sell us a trip somewhere and we're gone. Tomorrow."

He passed the cigarette to Mom who took a suck as well with quivering fingers, then got tired of the cigarette and threw it out the window. She brushed the hair from her face under the bandana and played with the radio station until she found Kate Bush's "Running Up That Hill." Barry was still talking about his plan, but she cranked up the music until the RV shook, and I loved her for a moment again. She mouthed the words to the song, "Been running up that road, been running up that hill, been running up that building, see if I only could."

Steph was swallowing her tears, and I reached over and held her hand. She squeezed me so tight my knuckles cracked. Barry still talked as if any of us were listening, but no one was anymore. We lived in that Kate Bush song, the only thing keeping us clinging to sanity. Mom stopped mouthing the words, singing now, her voice calling us. "You don't want to hurt me, but see how deep the bullet lies, unaware I'm tearing you asunder, oooh there's thunder in our hearts." Her voice full of menace now, pupils red and pulsing, fang teeth bared in the flashes from the headlights, Barry yammering on, Steph squeezing harder until I gasped from the pain, Jenny now howling like a wolf along to the music, our demonic vehicle barreling down that road—something needed to stop us, break the chaos before it broke us.

"Say, if I only could," Mom sang, the timbre of her voice a birdsong, so beautiful it made me weep. The blood of those men we killed stuck to my Velcro sneakers, tunneling into the grooves. "I'd make a deal with God and get him to swap our places."

And then Mom shut off the radio with a snap before the song ended, the music still hanging in the air, escaping through the open windows, and my heart burst, never to be repaired again, leaking out of me, left behind on the road.

60

Barry ordered us to sleep in Uncle Mort's house and not the Gas-Guzzler that night. I'd later learn that he used the opportunity to lock up the bags of cash and hide the RV keys in case we were planning an escape. Exhausted, I went up to Andy and Randy's room, which smelled of hotboxed farts, and covered my nose as I got in my sleeping bag. When I woke the clock said noon. No dreams of bloody hands, no dreams of anything really, as if I wasn't even alive enough to dream anymore. I brushed my teeth and made my way down, where everyone was eating lunch. Aunt Connie had made hot dogs on the grill in buns with potato chip toppings.

"There's our sleepyhead," Barry said, pulling out a chair next to him.

Mom was nibbling on a bun, barely coherent, likely plied with pills. Steph poked at some baked beans on the side of her plate. Jenny ate ravenously with ketchup around her mouth. Uncle Mort read the paper while Connie was cutting the hot dogs into bite-sized pieces for Andy and Randy.

"I'm not hungry," I said, going into the kitchen. I just wanted something to drink. I imagined if I found a beer in the fridge, I would have that.

Barry leaped up and pushed his chair into the table before following me to the kitchen. He waited until the swinging door stopped , then got in my face.

"Don't act suspicious."

"Leave me alone."

He grabbed my arm. "You have some hot dogs with your family."

I wiggled out of his grasp.

"Now look, Morty is about to sell me some trip. I'm thinking Malaga. That's Spain, but the bottom of Spain. *Andalucía*," he said, using an accent that wasn't quite Spanish. "But it gives us easy access to North Africa if we need it."

I made my way to the fridge, saw a Bud Light and popped the cap. I took a strong sip.

Barry yanked the bottle from my hand. "What do you think you're doing?"

"Give it back."

"So Mort can see I allow you to drink beer? I think not, bud."

"Oh, so the cocaine and weed is fine?"

"Watch it." He removed the vial from his front pocket and took a toot. I pushed the vial into his face causing the white powder to fly out, his nose covered like a clown that hadn't put on the rest of its makeup. "You shit."

He whacked me across the face. Instead of crying like I'd done before, I stood firm.

"Do it again."

"Aaron, don't get me started."

We were whisper-shouting, but I was ready to amp it up.

"Do it again. Hit me. Spend the rest of your life hitting me."

"I can't win with you." He latched onto my chin, squeezing. "And don't you even think about taking my money. It's locked up now and only I have the key." He jutted out his neck where the key hung from a chain. "I have the RV's keys too, so if you were thinking of running away—"

"I wasn't."

"Bullshit you weren't. The three of you plotting, that's what you were doing in the RV when the mobsters came. There's no escaping us, Aaron. You'll always be a Gimmelman."

I charged at him, knocking him into the counter, spilling some flour and a case of dried pasta. He got me in a headlock, gave me a noogie. "Don't fuck this up," he said, under his breath. "Not when we're this close. Mind your fucking Ps and Qs."

The kitchen door swung open, and Uncle Mort entered, scratching his belly.

"What are you two doing?"

"Wrestling," Barry said, tousling my hair. "Sorry about the flour. Me and the boy do this from time to—"

I punched him hard in the stomach, felt the air get knocked out of him.

"Right," I said, weaseling out of his grasp. Mom stepped in.

"Are you two all right?" the space case asked.

I gave her a *talk to the hand* gesture. "No," I said, passing by. I booked it upstairs, a full panic attack coming on. I never had one before and didn't realize what was happening, but I couldn't catch my breath. It scared me, this loss of control. I wondered if I was dying. There was no chance for us Gimmelman kids anymore. Barry had taken away our only glimmer of hope in the cash bounty, now we were forced to follow him. Running away would mean living on the streets. However, I could still tell Uncle Mort and Aunt Connie about everything. I should've used that as a threat, but Barry knew I wouldn't. I may have hated him then, but I wouldn't betray him. I couldn't.

Back in Andy and Randy's room, I found my Walkman, threw on the headphones, and hit play. "Wanted Dead or Alive" by my Jersey boy Bon Jovi came on. The lyrics in sync with my own fate. I listened with the volume at the max, but my breathing still stayed out of whack. Jenny came in the room, her hair such a goddamn mess it looked like she'd escaped from an insane asylum. She saw me melting and took off my headphones. She placed her little hands on my cheeks. They were warm.

"It's gonna be okay," she said, eyes locked.

"No, it's not."

I was crying now. I'd never cried in front of her, my big brother cred shot to hell.

"Even if it's not, there's no use being upset. Right?"

She nodded her little head until I nodded too.

"He locked up the money, Jenny. We can't run away."

She shrugged one shoulder. "I don't think we would've ever left."

"No, I—"

"What's gonna happen is what's gonna happen. That's the way it goes."

My teeth chattered. "W–what's gonna happen?"

"Who knows? But there's no stopping what's meant to be. That's life."

"What the fuck, Jenny? What the fuck are you talking about?

"Just accept it." She sounded hollow, like there was nothing left in her. "I have."

"Accepted what?"

She petted the top of my head like I was a sad, stupid child, not wise enough to understand the depth of the universe. This baby Buddha telling my fortune. I had chills like I was going through the flu, my tears hot against my cheeks. And through it she remained calm, as if she saw whatever path lay ahead for all of us, and good or bad, realized that there could be no other way. Our fate ready at the next turn, tapping its long fingernails in wait. She placed the headphones back on my ears as Bon Jovi's chorus reached a crescendo, then backed up out of the room into the shadows like a tiny monk.

"I'm a cowboy," I mumbled, tasting my rancid spit. "And we're wanted, dead or alive."

I hit rewind and played it again at the highest volume possible until I blasted out my eardrums.

61

How Uncle Mort became involved in our downfall would be replayed during his court deposition. Barry shouldn't have trusted a brother who'd been jealous of him from birth. Before Barry was born, Morty was the center of their parents' universe, then he got shuttled to side-saddle. Barry was cuter, and wittier, and generally more pleasant to be around. Mort was moody and lumpy, the kind of child who already looked like a middle-aged man. Barry excelled in sports, in academics, in social life, while Mort spent all his time studying for lesser grades and was unable to devote any time to friends or girlfriends, not that anyone was really barking up his tree. After Mort had been labeled as the sole reason for his parents' surviving the camps, as an adolescent and teenager, he was often forgotten. Even in their small apartment, he managed to go unnoticed, relegated to the top of a bunk bed that became his world while Barry got all the fanfare.

As an adult, his job put food on the table, and he had a nice marriage with Connie. He loved his sons fiercely but longed for more than mediocrity. Barry lived this posh life, and even though Barry had taken a hit, he was talking about taking his family on an international trip when he didn't know what his next job would be. It was unfathomable. Still, Mort needed the business, so he booked the Gimmelmans an open-ended vacation to Malaga. Barry didn't want return flights in case they decided to stay longer. He sprung for a nice hotel in the center of the city. The trip came to ten thousand in total for the entire family. And Barry had cash ready! He handed it right over. Mort was embarrassed that he'd never held that much cash at one time, the money feeling alien in his palms. It was too late on a Friday afternoon to make it to the bank before it closed, so he'd hold onto the money through the weekend and deposit it on Monday, his cut coming out to eight hundred dollars, enough to fix a leak in the attic, nothing more than that.

He was most excited for the Gimmelmans to be on our way. Our presence upset the fine-tuned machinery of his own family. Andy and Randy were still beside themselves about Jenny's attack. The kitchen was a mess after Barry and I "wrestled," and Connie confessed that she had to "talk Judith down from a ledge the other night" when Mom devolved into a mess of tears. Normally, Mort ran the roost and there was little drama with his brood. Connie was a doting wife, and Andy and Randy were weird children, but they always listened and didn't cause trouble. The Gimmelman kids were polar opposites. Steph was turning into a full-fledged woman and Mort admitted to himself that it was hard not to stare at her newfound breasts. Jenny was a nightmare wrapped up in wildcat, and I was sarcastic, snotty, and the last time we stayed with them he caught me having a Bud Light.

So, the fact that by Sunday we'd be out of his hair added an extra hop in his step the night that precipitated everything turning to shit for us. It was late and everyone had gone to bed. Connie had put on her cold cream and was already snoring like a tugboat. I was holding my nose in Andy and Randy's room. Mom had been on a pill flight all day and had passed out after dinner. Mort had just finished up the transaction with his brother and placed the ten thousand in a safe in the basement. Of course, Barry had to joke how meaningless the money was to him, knowing that would prickle Mort. He boasted of this chapter of their lives closing and a new one on the horizon that would be even more fruitful. "I fall into money," he told Mort. "It's just the kind of luck I have."

Mort didn't respond. He knew that earlier the flour on Barry's nose was actually cocaine. It peeved him how Barry partied through life and seemed to come out on top. Mort had never indulged in any vices other than a beer and sweets, practically a Mormon, and he dreamed of going to a place like

Malaga, Spain, but the biggest trip they ever did besides once to NYC was a drive down to the Grand Canyon, which Barry had just come from and barely seemed to care about.

Mort tried to get into a fight with Barry about the way he casually spent his money, but Barry wasn't into it that night. He'd gotten what he needed from his brother and therefore didn't need to give him any more attention. This inflamed Mort more than anything else his brother had ever done. He even considered figuring out a way to cancel the Malaga trip but had already placed a call into his office and they had closed for the weekend. Barry practically skipped up the stairs, the clear winner in their dogfight.

When Mort finally went up too, the myna birds were squawking. Their newspapers needed to be changed. Mort found the latest edition of the *L.A. Times*, which he finished and began lining the cage. He'd read about the Wild Woodstock Gang and even mentioned it briefly to Connie after seeing an episode of *A Current Affair*. But he hadn't thought twice about it. Still, something drew him to the photo of the little girl in the bank in Houston. The grainy image difficult to make out a face, but the light of the full moon streaming through the blinds seemed to illuminate more than ever before. The pinched little face of the little girl, her crazy hair like a scarecrow's. The tiny button nose causing his mind to travel to Jenny. He took her image and placed it in the confines of the little girl in the photo and it was an exact match.

His stomach dropped like he was descending on a roller coaster. His knees quivered. He wrenched the newspaper from out of the myna birds' cage, making them squawk even more. If you took away the hair of the little girl in the photo and replaced it with Jenny's burn-victim 'do, he was looking at her doppelgänger.

"Holy moly," he said, stroking his bushy mustache. "Oh Mylanta," he said. "Oh no. Oh no." He resisted having to puke. Reading through the article, the reporter called the little girl a kidnap victim, but it was clear Jenny was in on the whole shebang. He recalled the other heists that had been on the news. Barry as Jerry Garcia. How could he not have seen it before? How many times had he had to cover his ears while Barry played the terrible noodling songs of The Grateful Dead? Jerry Garcia was the kid's idol. Mort woke up every day to a poster of Jerry Garcia, high as the sky and tacked up in their shared bedroom. Janis Joplin must've been Judith. He snapped his fingers. This had been why Judith was acting so strangely. From breaking down in tears to numbing herself with pills. And the two members of gang who were referred to as little people were not little people, it was his nephew as Jimi Hendrix and Jenny as Mama Cass.

"That's how Barry had all that money," Mort said aloud. The myna birds repeated.

"All that money, all that money," they squawked.

"Shut up you," he said, his brow a pool of sweat dripping into his eyes. "What do I do? What do I do?"

He paced back and forth, clutching the newspaper article in his fist.

"I must protect my family first."

"Protect family first, protect family first," the myna birds squawked again until Mort threw a towel over the cage, so they'd fall asleep.

He read the article again, drops of sweat blurring the typeface. At the end of the article was the number for the FBI agent assigned to the case. Mort crept into his study where he'd have the most privacy. He stared at the phone on his desk, picking up the receiver and hanging up again. If he let Barry and his family get away, he could be in trouble for being an accessory to the crime. Since he knew about it now, he worried he'd fail any polygraph test. This made the decision for him. There was no way in h-e-double hockey sticks that he would go down for Barry's crimes. He picked the phone up and dialed.

"Yes, I'd like to speak with Special Agent Alan Terbert," he said to a woman who answered.

"What is this regarding?"

He cleared his thoughts, felt the power surge through his body, a new-found experience.

"The Wild Woodstock Gang is currently at my house."

62

Waking up the next morning, I was aware I'd lost it, all the screws leaving my brain. Again, I didn't dream, a blessing but also a curse. I was hollow, a scooped-out shell, a body going through the motions. In the bathroom, I stared into the mirror. Who was Aaron Nicholas Gimmelman? I went through all the things that were guarantees about myself. I loved the Knicks, and still did. I hated milk. Sometimes I touched things in threes when I was agitated. Once at the Westchester County Fair a goat sneezed on me, and I thought I was dying. When I was little, I threw up spaghetti and meatballs and the meatballs looked like eyes and the spaghetti a smiling mouth. None of this had changed, but I had. I'd stolen money, I was responsible for people dying. I'd done hardcore drugs. Because I'd gone this far at the age of twelve, if I didn't wind up in jail, then death would be the only other outcome.

I thought about criminals who had sinned, and how after they did their time they came out of prison with a newfound appreciation for God. They would swear to be better. Give back to the homeless. Never sin again. I could make that promise, but was it enough? Had I already gone too far? I didn't even feel like brushing my teeth.

Back in Andy and Randy's room, I went through my suitcase and realized I didn't have any clean clothes. The only outfit I hadn't worn yet was the pastel *Miami Vice* suit Barry bought me after the Boca heist. I put it on, thinking how normally it would've gotten me so excited, but I could barely muster a grin.

I slouched down to breakfast.

Everyone was eating Eggo waffles, a plate already set for me. Connie gave me a strange look, likely because of my get-up, but squeezed my shoulder and squirted some Mrs. Butterworth's on the waffles.

"Coffee please," I said, with a frog in my throat.

She glanced over at Barry who gave the okay. Then he looked at me like, *see I'm still your cool Dad, I let you have coffee.* When Aunt Connie poured me a cup, I wanted to throw it scalding hot in his face.

No one was talking, but Uncle Mort couldn't sit still. He kept squirming in his seat like he had a bug up his ass.

"Morty, are you all right?" Aunt Connie asked, her French manicured fingernails tapping his shoulder.

"Fine."

"So restless. He was like that all night too. Tossing and turning up a storm."

"Excuse me," he said, dabbing his mustache with a napkin and leaving the dining area.

Andy and Randy made sour faces. "What's wrong with Dad?"

Barry's chewing slowed down, his eyebrows slanting, a radiator of worry lines appearing on his forehead. He caught my eye. *What's going on?*

"Excuse me," Aunt Connie said, and followed her husband out of the room.

"So, our trip is all booked," Barry said to the table. "We leave tomorrow. Malaga, Spain."

Steph and Jenny barely managed a shrug. Mom focused on chewing her waffle.

"Spain, guys! Can I get a Whoa Gimmelmans?"

Silence answered him back.

"C'mon, Spain! Paella, the Flamenco, Judy."

He tickled Mom's neck and she managed to grin.

"Jenny, we'll get you an animal there. How's that sound, bug?"

"A tiger would be acceptable," Jenny responded.

"A tiger it is!"

"Seriously?" Steph said, slamming her fork down. She held her hand over her mouth. "I'm gonna be sick."

Steph took off while Andy and Randy pushed their chairs into the table like two polite butlers and left the room as well.

"Those kids creep me out," Barry said. He pointed a syrupy fork at me. "Nice suit."

"It's the only thing I had that wasn't dirty."

He stuffed a massive amount of Eggo waffle in his pie hole. "Suits you," he said, laughing at his own joke.

Uncle Mort and Aunt Connie returned. Aunt Connie looked frayed, like she'd aged ten years in ten minutes.

"Mort just told me about your trip," she said, her voice shaking.

Uncle Mort had his arm around her, bringing her close to him. They were acting weirder than normal. She tried to smile, but it was as if her lips couldn't stretch wide enough without shaking. Soon they gave up and devolved into a frown. A big drop of sweat was making its way down Uncle Mort's face and hiding out in a groove in his neck. They stood there, wrapped up in one another, forcing smiles.

"Guess you'll be spending the day packing up," she said.

"Packing up, packing up," the myna birds squawked from the living room, causing Aunt Connie to jump in place. She held her hand over her heart.

"What's going on?" Barry said, rising and clutching his fork like he was ready to use it as a weapon.

"Nothing, nothing at all," Uncle Mort sang.

"Nothing at all," the myna birds squawked.

Even Mom now was darting her eyes from Barry to Uncle Mort and Aunt Connie, her pupils involved in an intense tennis match. My stomach turned. I pushed aside my plate of food.

The silence became deafening, piercing our eardrums, just the tick-tock of a grandfather clock and the myna birds shuffling in their cage. Outside someone turned on their leaf blower, causing me to almost crap my pants. Something was up, the tension in the air vibrating. I could barely swallow my last bite.

"Morty, what's going on?"

"Nothing, baby bro." He let out a laugh that sounded like a wheeze. It nearly made me cry. Aunt Connie joined along as Mom stuck a piece of her long hair in her mouth and chewed. I tapped the table once, twice, and a third time, my OCD at a heightened pitch.

"Morty!"

The fork was now being used as a threat, the prongs pointed at Uncle Mort.

"I'm sorry," Uncle Mort said, looking like he was about to lose his lunch.

"Sorry about what?" Barry yelled.

"I'm so sorry. I-I didn't know what else to do."

"Bear-Bear?" Mom yelped.

"What is fucking happening?" I said, and Connie's eyes cut me like I shouldn't be cursing.

"I had to," Uncle Mort said, twiddling his thumbs. "My family. I needed to protect—"

"What did you do you son-of-a-bitch?" Barry asked.

"Now, you listen," Aunt Connie said, wagging her finger.

"They're coming," Uncle Mort whispered.

"Who is coming?"

Uncle Mort gulped, his Adam's apple bobbing up and down.

"The FBI."

* * *

I'd find out that Special Agent Terbert had received many calls about the Wild Woodstock Gang all filtered through his secretary Mona, a no-nonsense woman in her sixties who'd been fielding calls at their Miami station since post World War II.

She smoked a Benson & Hedges, her fingers yellowed from years of puffing. Through the fog of smoke, she told Agent Terbert about the call she received. A man in San Bernardino who claimed his brother was the Jerry Garcia of the gang and was staying with his family at their house. The brother bought a one-way ticket for the whole family to Malaga, Spain and would be departing on Sunday. It was almost three in the morning Saturday then Eastern Standard Time. Agent Terbert got on the phone.

"I'm going to ask you an important question," he said to Mort. "What type of vehicle were they driving when they arrived?"

No one had mentioned an RV yet, and he still hadn't told the field office, keeping that break in the case mum.

"Uh, it's an RV, sir."

He felt a shimmer pass through his body, like he'd been lit from within.

"Can you keep them there?"

"Yes, yes. I can. They're not leaving until Sunday morning."

Agent Terbert weighed notifying the local authorities, but they would probably fuck things up like they always did. This was his case, and he alone would be the one to bring the Wild Woodstock Gang to justice.

"I'm getting on a plane."

After getting the address and having the office book an immediate flight, he reasoned that since it was the middle of the night, there was a good chance the family was sleeping and not fleeing. It was a risk, but he'd rather muck-up the case because of his own failings rather than be pissed that someone else did. An hour later, he was on a direct flight to Los Angeles. Five hours later, he landed at six a.m. Pacific Time and got a car the FBI rented for him. He phoned Mort Gimmelman, who answered after the first ring. Mort relayed that everyone was sleeping. He hadn't told anyone in his family yet. Around seven in the morning, they would likely have breakfast. Mort promised to stretch out the meal. Agent Terbert stressed to the man not to let on in any way, shape, or form that something was amiss. Pedal to the metal Agent Terbert sped to San Bernardino, the local authorities notified he was in town in case he needed backup.

When he arrived at the residence, there was no RV in their front driveway.

The Gimmelmans had already blasted off.

63

Shooting down the highway toward the Mojave Desert, it seemed to Barry that the Gimmelmans might be in the clear. He didn't realize that Agent Terbert knew we were driving an RV and had put out an APB for miles. We left with the clothes on our backs, Jenny grabbing Seymour, Mom wrapping herself in a pashmina, Steph wiping the puke from her mouth, Barry taking a snort to get us through this last leg. But where could we really go? Barry had our plane tickets but LAX would be heavily monitored. Now that our identities were revealed, there were no more hiding places. This would be the end.

But you wouldn't have known that according to Barry. He played Debbie Gibson's *Electric Youth*, since Steph had left it in the tape deck. He sang along, not knowing the words but making up his own. The rest of us looked at each other with suspicion. I was tasked to watch out the window for any "pigs" as he called them. He had shoved a Bren Ten stainless steel in my hand and told me to shoot at anyone trying to take our livelihood. There was no reasoning with the man and my anger vacillated to concern. I had lost the dad I knew somewhere in Virginia when this all began. To simply be enraged was missing the point. We weren't dealing with someone who was well.

"How's your eye look?" Barry called out over his shoulder, maintaining a steady speed so as to not tick off any naïve patrolmen.

By "eye" he meant my sights on the FBI. Before we left, Uncle Mort gave a blubbering rundown of what we were dealing with, a special agent all the way from Miami to bring us down. He'd been following our heists from the start, us Gimmelmans his brass ring. Mort apologized more but Barry just slapped him across the face. I wanted to do the same. It would've been one thing for us kids to turn ourselves in, it was another for an outsider to tempt our fates. On the way out, I went ahead and slapped Uncle Mort across the face anyway and gave the finger to Aunt Connie, our tires hitting the road as they wandered out to the front lawn with hands on their hips.

Before I was tasked to be the spotter, Barry planted me in the shotgun seat, spoke to me more like a man than he ever had before.

"This is war we're entering," he said, as the RV turned down suburban streets, past neighbors without a clue of what was unfolding.

"What's your endgame?" I asked, hoping he might face reality. The potential of escape so miniscule it veered toward impossible. The best we could do was minimize the damage.

"I won't go out like a chump." He rubbed his five o'clock shadow. "In all the great movies, they go out in a blaze of glory. *Butch Cassidy, Bonnie and Clyde.*"

"They die," I said, the words hanging in a lump in my throat.

"We're writing this story. We can choose the ending. You fire that great gun of yours on any fucker who tries to bring us down, break up our family. You understand me?"

"I do."

I felt it was better to agree for everyone's safety. Barry had to be handled just right. I imagined the RV rearing off the road and us all dying in a fiery crash.

"Then get to work, soldier," he said, slapping me on the back and pushing me toward the side window. I cocked the gun.

"What are you doing?" Steph asked, at my ear.

"It's called defusing the situation," I said, under my breath. "He's likely to drive us into a ditch."

I eyed the highway spilling out behind us, so far, no sign of any police.

"You're not gonna...?"

"Steph, what is our other option? You wanna wrestle the steering wheel from his hands?"

From the speakers, Debbie's Gibson's "Lost in Your Eyes" blared.

"Go take care of Mom."

We looked over at Mom, who had huddled in the corner, her pashmina a security blanket. "This has gone too far," she said, over and over. She glanced up, pleading, but Steph shook her head.

"Not my problem."

"Okay, watch Jenny."

Jenny, in Jenny land, surfed in the middle of the RV with Seymour, dancing along to the song.

"Okay, she's fine," I said. "Keep your eyes peeled for police out the window on the other side."

Steph bit her lip, drew blood, but listened and pressed her face against the opposite window.

I monitored my breathing, keeping my anxiety level low. The Bren Ten maintained in my grasp, still wearing my fucking pastel suit. A vision of everything us Gimmelmans had gone through playing like a movie in my mind. Leaving Jersey, the adrenaline of robbing that first convenience store, when we ate that meal in Virginia and all decided to team up for a bank heist. The first success, hiding out in Boca Raton, meeting Troy, and Heidi of course. I had never sent that letter I wrote, didn't think I ever would. If a news channel was playing this chase, she'd be spitting at the TV. Rooting for the police to bring us in and justify her brother's death. We should have stayed in Boca Raton and let Barry and Mom plunge toward their own doom. We didn't need to get greedy in Houston, take a security guard's life, lose Troy, get hunted by mobsters here, dump their bodies in a lake.

And then, a blip of a siren piercing the air. The hairs on the back of my neck getting fuzzy. Barry's gaze caught me in the rearview.

"Aaron, talk to me."

Out the window, a few car lengths down the road we were being pursued by a vehicle with a spinning siren on the roof. The man driving had aviator sunglasses and was gnashing his teeth. I leaned out, all Crockett and Tubbs cool, eating bugs as the wind whipped my face.

"Do it, Aaron," Barry called out. "Shoot him."

Mom screamed so loud it felt like it rocked the RV, but it was just because Barry slammed on the gas, and we were pushing eighty miles per hour. My finger on the trigger. "Electric Youth" coming on, the police vehicle speeding closer, a few feet away.

"Aaron!" Barry roared. "C'mon, boy. Aim for his tires. He's the only pig on the road. You can save us, you can save us..."

I wanted this all to end. I really did. Swear to everything, but I likened it to those cult leaders taking hold. You couldn't defy them. You had gone too far under their teachings. You were one and the same with them. To break away was impossible to compute. I was Barry Gimmelman's son more than ever right there, his right-hand man, his loyal solider ready to go down with the ship. Or maybe I was just too much of a pussy to truly stand up to him.

"Aaron, fucking pull that trigger," the demon at the wheel ordered. My fingers separating from the rest of my body, my mind breaking from reality, as I pulled the trigger and the bullet spiraled into the FBI man's windshield, shattering it upon impact.

"That's my boy!" Barry thundered, and I hated to admit it but at that moment, a shred of me felt complete.

The FBI man had not been hit and whipped out a gun. He brushed away the loose shards of glass and aimed.

"Oh fuck," I said. "I didn't hit him, he's about to fire."

"Shoot again, shoot again," Barry cried.

The gun slipped from my hand. I watched it tumble down the road. The FBI man fired at the RV, a few bullets missing but one shooting through the back window zooming past my face. Mom's screams erupted again. Glass shards fell in a pool by the back window. I didn't hear the bullet ping off of anything in the RV. I had no idea where it landed.

Mom's screams morphed from shrieks to something much darker, deeper, sadder, a cry from within that no one should ever have to utter. I craned my neck around and saw the reason for her torment. Jenny lay on the floor, blood pumping from her chest.

"Jenny!"

I ran over as Steph followed. We squatted at her side. Jenny's eyes wide in shock as she touched the wound. Little hands so red and bloody.

Another shot came through the back window, pinging off the kitchen stove. Like a wraith, Mom crawled over to Jenny.

"No, no, no, no," she wailed, heaving for breath.

"Barry!" I yelled. No response. "Barry, Jenny's been shot."

I didn't want to look over at him. If I saw his face, I would've mauled it like a bear, but Jenny needed my attention.

"Cover the wound," I said, bringing Steph's hands over the wound. "Stop the blood."

"It's okay," Jenny whispered, like she had a secret.

I wrenched off my suit jacket and pressed it over where the bullet hit, trying to recall everything I'd learned in health class.

"Make it stop, make it stop," Mom cried. She flung herself on top of Jenny, hugging her close.

"It's okay," Jenny said, softer this time. "Seymour?"

I could barely see through a wall of tears. My heart a torpedo that kept firing into my chest.

"You want Seymour?" I asked, scanning the floor and seeing a bloody Seymour. "Here, here."

I grabbed Seymour and pressed him close to Jenny's face. A trickle of a smile emerged. She brought him to her lips. Said something indecipherable into his tiny ear.

"Stop the RV!" I screamed out, but it seemed like we were going faster. Another bullet shot in, pinging off of the cabinets that held our dirty money.

"Jenny belly," I said, taking her hand and squeezing. "Hold on, hold on."

She shook her head in a way that gave me chills.

"No, Jenny belly, you hold on, you hold on."

Steph and Mom echoed my cries, but Jenny kept shaking her head.

"It's okay," she said, but it didn't come from her mouth, as if she was already gone. She'd stopped shaking her head. Eyes locked on Seymour, no longer blinking. Her final words, dissipating through the RV until they were heard no more.

"Jenny?" I yelled. "Jenny!"

I shook her body, limp like a doll in my arms. I backed away, stunned. The war had taken its first casualty, my baby sister, my Jenny belly.

I left my body as I flew up to the front seat, clawing at Barry's face, digging into flesh. The RV swerved from lane to lane as Steph ran over to stop me, Mom still collapsed on Jenny.

"You killed her, you killed her," I said, over and over as fear stared back at me. Barry let go of the steering wheel murmuring, "My baby." Like a ghost, he floated away from my attack, hovering over Jenny and trying to grasp onto any last sliver of life remaining. He seemed emptied out. Stabbed in the heart. A dark cloud exhaled from his lips. He and Mom locked limbs, lost in mourning.

Steph jumped into the driver's seat and slammed the brakes causing us all to topple over, diverting the RV to the shoulder before we stopped completely. The FBI car braked beside us, Agent Terbert jumping out with his gun trained. We heard him yelling. The door swung open as he burst inside. I ran over to my nook, where I hid the journal I'd written down everything in. I yanked it from under the mattress, held it close. I caught Barry's stare. Through a veil of endless tears, a confused look appeared. What was so important in that journal that I had to grab it at that moment, when an FBI agent was getting out handcuffs and reading us all our rights? Barry could be called many things, but he wasn't dumb. He understood exactly what was on those pages. And that Jenny's death would be the impetus I needed to turn on him.

I should've done it a long time ago.

Any one of us Gimmelmans could've been brave.

All of us with blood on our hands.

Now and forever.

Good night, Jenny belly.

Good night.

64

In the back of a patrol car, I understood what hitting rock bottom must be like to an addict. I didn't worry about what might happen to me at all, my only thoughts were of Jenny. All the times I wished we'd done more things together. How I took her for granted. Always assumed she'd be around. I remembered the last good day we had at the Tiffany mall concert when we were making fun of all the crazy fans and changed the lyrics to her songs. Recently, it seemed like Jenny knew her end was near. She'd been calmer these last few days than ever before, as if she'd come to peace with her fate. I would blame Barry and Mom forever. Nothing they'd ever do would get me to forgive them. But the biggest blame should be directed toward myself. If we ran away from them sooner, if I wouldn't have listened to Barry and fired the gun at the FBI agent, maybe the guy wouldn't have fired back. Maybe Jenny would still be here. I deserved all that guilt, which was like a tumor festering in my stomach. If they wanted to lock me up for the rest of my life, I was fine with that. Maybe only then would the rot within go away.

The next few months of my life were a whirlwind to say the least. Not that it hadn't been a shitshow already, but we were thrust into the spotlight, our faces on every magazine, newspaper, every reporter weighing in. Barry and Mom were vilified, the worst parents on the planet. Steph and I received mixed reviews. To some we were forced into this life of crime and shouldn't be to blame, too young to understand the gravity of what we were doing. To others, we were Satan incarnate, evidenced by me as Jimi Hendrix on all the camera footage. Steph admitted to being the getaway driver and there were multiple discussions as to how we all would be tried.

Robbing a bank was a federal crime and the murder a federal case. They never found out about Mr. Bianchi and Fingers, their bodies coming to surface years too late to make a connection to us. Since the security guard had been killed in Houston, Barry and Mom were being charged by the DOJ in Texas, but they were also tried by Virginia, Florida, and California on the state level. With Steph and I it was more complicated. The police submitted the evidence from my journal and our public defenders used it as leverage. Steph, at sixteen going on seventeen, was originally going be tried as an adult. Evidently if someone got murdered and you drove the getaway car, you could be tried for murder too.

We were kept at juvenile detention centers in our home state of New Jersey while we waited for our separate trials. Because the FBI bungled our arrest and shot our little sister, the DA didn't want to bring further charges against us kids. The thought being that we had been through enough trauma. We would be used as leverage against Barry and Mom. If we testified against them, each of us was offered a plea deal to avoid juvie, or possibly worse, and would wind up with community service. Between the relatives we had left, Mort and Connie wanted nothing to do with us, but Grandma Bernice stepped up for us to be remanded to her care should the judge rule in our favor.

The narrative of our story in the media began to veer toward us. The innocent children prey to our greedy parents. My journal held evidence of every time Barry struck me, or threatened if I didn't follow instructions. In tandem with our own trials, we became witnesses against our parents. For Mom's trial, I described how she was Barry's follower. None of this was her idea, but she failed to protect us, especially Jenny. Mom cried through it all. She looked like she had lost a ton of weight, her cheeks gaunt. The DA laid into her for being so negligent. Her trial was the first time I saw Steph since the arrest, because we were kept in different detention centers and our own trials were separate. The only person I was able to speak to on the phone was Grandma Bernice, who would tell me of Steph's welfare.

As the trials progressed, Steph started showing more, and I believed that her being pregnant softened us in the jury's eyes. She looked hardened too. No longer the bubbly sister with her hair in a side-ponytail, both of us pale and wan, grizzled from time spent in the detention centers with horrible criminal kids and bare-bones comforts. But it was Mom who seemed like she really was about to crumble. After our testimonies, against the advice of her lawyer, Mom spoke. She said she deserved life in prison for what she'd done. She and Barry had forced us kids in their heists. When we first started, it appeared to be innocent, small robberies just to get by after her husband lost his job and savings. Then it got out of hand. She couldn't reckon with Barry, who wouldn't hear of giving up. She saw something terrible happening on the horizon but was powerless to stop the freight train. For this, she did not want to be let off, nor should that happen to Barry as well. Only for us kids. We deserved a life after this with her mother in Florida. We should not be punished for our parents' abuse.

The judge and jury ruled fifteen years, since Mom hadn't personally killed anyone. She got off getting a life sentence for that reason only. There were still state charges to deal with, which would likely add years to her sentence. She would be an old woman when she'd be free. She didn't want it any other way.

She pleaded sorry to both of us, but Steph and I held firm. We wouldn't give her that satisfaction, or at least we weren't ready yet. Frail Mom was led away by the guards and it could be the last time we'd see her if, we so chose. At that moment, I was convinced I'd never see her again. None of this made the pain in my stomach over Jenny any better. The only saving grace was reuniting with Steph, and we were allowed to hug. I never wanted to let go. I felt her stomach as the baby kicked. We cried together.

Barry's trial was a whole other headache. There was more evidence against him, so it took much longer. Mom had already been sentenced when his trial had barely started. We were still kept in the detention centers because our trials were on pause until we delivered what the DA wanted against Barry: a full-court press against him that would include Mom's testimony too. During his trials, he didn't look at any of us. He seemed a whittled-down version of himself too. It was hard to tell what emotions were going through his thick skull. He had shaved his head, no longer sprouting curls, and grown a beard. I didn't know if he was angry at us for turning on him to save our own skin, upset at Mom for testifying when she wasn't even getting anything in return, pissed at me for keeping a journal of his wrongdoings, or simply mad at being responsible for Jenny's death. Did he weep himself to sleep every night, tossing and turning until cruel morning arrived? Like Mom, did he welcome a sentence, believing he deserved nothing less? His poker face wouldn't say.

Similar to Mom's trial, we testified, going through every grueling incident of our haphazard journey. Hearing me say it out loud made me realize that we really were abused. There were the multiple times he had hit me, used us kids as pawns in the robberies, the judge flabbergasted from never having dealt with such an insane case before. After every day, the media exploded outside of the courtroom, me and Steph's lawyers not letting us speak. Barry had hired a souped-up defense that tried every trick in the book, but it seemed like the judge wasn't leaning in his favor. Mom's testimony, a gut punch as well. He may have thought that us kids would turn, but never Judith. She did it for us, whether to gain favor, or for her own culpability. It was why I still thought of her as Mom, while Barry would never be Dad again. She was ashamed for what she did but didn't just put the blame on him. In front of the jury, she held herself responsible and encouraged Barry to do the same. He didn't. There was no speech at the end to me or Steph. Again, he never even looked our way. When I read from my journal about the worst of his crimes, I thought I saw a glimmer of his gaze shifting my way, a pin sticking into his tough exterior. If he felt bad for a moment, he quickly hid it deep down. He wouldn't even give me the satisfaction of shooting me with dagger eyes.

The only time his lawyer spoke up against any accusations that were actually false was related to Special Agent Terbert. When Agent Terbert was on the stand, he was convinced that Barry was the one who fired the gun at him, causing the retaliation that killed Jenny. Maybe it was easier for him not to admit it was just a kid. Neither Mom, Steph nor I refuted it, and when Barry's lawyer tried to sell me down the river, it became the nail in Barry's defense. Newspapers ran with that juicy morsel, and the hatred toward Barry skyrocketed. Finally, when the jury read the verdict, all our assholes clenched. He was given a life sentence, not the death penalty so he could spend the rest of his time on Earth thinking about what he'd done. To kill him would be too kind. On the way out of the courtroom, he turned his bearded face away from us as he passed. There were things I wanted to say, shout, curse, attack even, claw out those eyes, make him bleed. I let myself imagine the torture against him. I let that be enough.

Because Steph and I cooperated and the big fish got caught, we weren't sentenced to juvie until we were eighteen, or even worse, adult prison for Steph since she was closer in age. We got hundreds of hours of community service in Boca Raton with Grandma Bernice as our guardian. I was glad to have a home outside of the detention center because it had been eight months since we arrived. Steph was about to give birth and her judge wanted it to be in Florida with her family.

A car came to pick us up from our separate facilities and take us to the airport where we sat next to one another on the plane holding hands. We were out of tears. Thankful but also spent. Neither of us had anything to say. We munched on peanuts, avoided the whispers from people who knew who we were. I closed my eyes and actually slept for a few hours, which was something I hadn't done since this whole mess began.

Steph woke me up as we touched down in Florida. She was so big she looked about to pop. In my grogginess, I placed my palm against her enlarged stomach.

"Jenny belly," I said, still attached to my dreams. I'd been chasing Jenny down an endless hill, never able to catch her as her cackles echoed.

Steph cocked her head to the side confused, but then her lips turned upwards for a semi-smile. She nodded. Rubbed her stomach.

"Jenny belly," she agreed, and we exited the plane.

65

If we expected Grandma Bernice to welcome us with open arms, we were sorely mistaken. No whispers from her that *bubbe* would make everything okay. To offset her new financial responsibility, she made us do a thousand chores. Well, more like I had to do them since Steph was weeks away from giving birth and on bedrest. Grandma Bernice had a zillion little projects around the condo that needed to be done. I dusted and mopped, built a cordoned-off area in the foyer for her cats to use their litterbox, defrosted the freezer by chipping at it with a screwdriver, and ironed all her old dresses and Herb's mothball-eaten suits. In addition, I had community service to start. School would begin again after winter break, but my first two weeks consisted of waking at dawn to go clean trash off the highway with other derelicts: a kid who put another in a coma, a girl who set off a mini bomb in her school, a guy who robbed liquor stores.

"Holy shit, you're him," the liquor store robber said. He snapped his finger to remember my name.

"Aaron."

"The Wild Woodstock Gang. Man, I idolized you guys."

"That's pathetic."

He wasn't expecting that response. "What did you say to me?"

"I said you're pathetic."

He swung and gave me a black eye. Free from the detention center, I was still used to getting into scraps. Over that year, I'd shot up a few inches and put on some pounds, going from scrawny to normal-sized. More importantly, I knew that to win most tussles you entered, you had to make sure you scrapped with someone you had a fighting chance to beat. I wound up giving that liquor store robber kid a bloody nose.

"*Bupkas*," Grandma Bernice said, when I got home that day. "You're fighting over *bupkas*."

She yanked me to the kitchen, placed an ice cube in a paper towel and dabbed it under my eye.

"I'm not gonna let someone speak to me—"

"*Gay avek*, get outta here. This is *hakn a tshaynik*, nonsense. Do you want to end up in prison? They're watching you closely, little mister. Don't give them any reason to lock you up."

Grandma Bernice didn't realize that it was hard to shake the detention facility mentality. You had to act like you'd spar with everyone, even if you wouldn't.

"Ah, your eye is *fercockt*, there's nothing I can do."

She threw up her hands and left the kitchen. I held the ice against my eye for a while, but decided I'd rather show off my war wounds.

Steph was eating a bowl of Cookie Crisp in bed and watching *Who's the Boss* when I went in her bedroom.

"You look terrible," she said.

I crawled in bed next to her. "Grandma Bernice said I'm gonna wind up in prison if I don't watch myself."

"She's right."

She found the remote and turned off the TV. A cat popped its head out from from under the sheets too.

"Jesus, these cats are everywhere," I said.

"Every day I'm coughing up hairballs. It's still better we're here."

"I know." I lay down and stared at the popcorn ceiling.

"You'll start school in a week or so," she said. "You're smart, you love school."

"If I tell you something, promise not to judge?"

Steph put down the bowl of cereal. "Cross my heart."

"I'm thinking of going to see Heidi."

She slapped her hand on her forehead. "That's a disaster move."

"There are things I wanna tell her."

"You'll wind up with another black eye."

"Good. That would make me feel better."

I was becoming a masochist, chasing pain to hide my own.

"Mom sent a letter."

I sat up and leaned against my elbow. "What did she say?"

"I haven't read it. Grandma Bernice has it. It's up to us if we wanna see it."

"I don't."

"Me neither."

"Let her keep writing letters forever. Let her write a fucking book," I said. "What is she gonna say, she's sorry? Like, I don't fucking care. They were both narcissists."

"You're preaching to the choir."

"Look, I'm glad she owned up to her shit in court. There's no denying in a head-to-head match off who's better, she beats Barry hands down. But that doesn't mean I want a relationship with her right now."

"That's what Grandma Bernice said. She didn't think it was healthy for us. I have the new baby to worry about..."

"Exactly, our lives are moving on. It's been like a couple of weeks, maybe I'll respond in a couple of years."

"I just wanted to let you know. It's your choice."

"Thank you."

"Don't go see Heidi."

"Don't tell me what to do, narc."

I left and took the remote just to piss her off. Grandma Bernice was in the hallway with a cat in her arms.

"Your sister told you, didn't she?"

"Yeah, she did."

"Family will always be *mishpocha*. She will always be your mother. Just as she will always be my daughter."

"Okay."

Grandma Bernice let the cat leap from her arms. "The Torah says, forgiveness is a duty, a *mitzvah*. But the time needs to be right. When you are ready to forgive, you must."

I scratched at a piece of peeling wallpaper. "What if I'm never ready?"

"*Pish*. You're a child, you know nothing of time. You will be ready."

"I'll always blame her. And him."

Grandma Bernice pursed her lips. Her eyes always watery, but extra watery at that moment.

"*Oh vey*, the sorrow we've been through. The death of a little one, it's a curse that we'll have to bear. There is no coming back from it."

I twisted my toe into the floor. "I miss her."

"*Tsoriss*. Us Jews know that better than anyone. Our people's difficult plights throughout many ages. And yet, we live on. Death takes a piece of us, but not all of us for we are still here. We carry along her memory. Come with me, come with *bubbe*."

She took me by the hand and led me into the living room where she got out a photo album. She flipped through until she took out the picture she wanted. A newborn Jenny in her crib and me standing on my tippy-toes, wide-eyed just to see her.

"Oh, did that child scream when she was a baby," Grandma Bernice said, smoothing down the picture.

I sniffed back a big ball of snot. "Really?"

"Oh, like no other. A banshee in the night. Scream, scream, scream, your mother was beside herself. That little girl always was a *vilda chaye*, a wild animal. Children like that don't normally live too long. They burn out young."

She kissed the top of my head.

"We keep her memory alive, yes, *boychick*. Once in a while we talk about her. Someone is only truly dead where there is no one left to remember them."

I went into my room. Grandma Bernice had actually set one up for me. On my desk, I kept Seymour, a little worse for the wear after what he'd been through, but always enough to help me remember Jenny. I thought of a time when she was about three and we decided to make cookies in the middle of night. Neither of us knew exactly what to put in the cookie batter so we added everything: chocolate chips, peanut butter, orange slices, sprinkles, salt, pepper, garlic powder. We stuck them in the oven and then forgot about it. The smoke alarm waking everyone up after we went to bed. Mom pulled out a sheet of scorched cookies. They looked disgusting, but Jenny insisted on eating one. She said it was "yummy in the tummy" and ate the whole thing, this charred crisp of a dessert. Just to check, I took a bite too and it was the worst thing I'd ever tasted.

Sucking on my tongue, I could taste it again, the charred chocolate garlic-ness. The sweet Jenny memory.

* * *

I had one day off a week from community service along the highway, so I found all the change in Grandma Bernice's cushions and got a taxi to Heidi's house. I'd brought along my Walkman and Def Leppard's *Hysteria*. Outside, I listened to the song while getting up the nerve to knock on the door. I planned to apologize profusely first, and hope she didn't slam the door in my face.

"I gotta know tonight, if you're alone tonight. Can't stop this feeling," I sang to myself. "Can't stop this fight."

At the door, I knocked with a shaking fist. Heard the sound of steps from inside. Swallowed the bit of puke creeping up my throat. The door swung open as I began my apology tour, but it was an older woman in house slippers, a bathrobe, a lion's mane of hair, and a cigarette dangling from her lips.

"Whattaya want?"

I recalibrated. "Uh, Heidi, I'm looking for Heidi."

She took a puff that erased half the cigarette with one suck. "Don't know no Heidi."

"She lived here...with her grandpa..."

The woman waved me away. "Oh right, yeah bought the place from them six months ago."

She began to shut the door. I put my foot in the gap.

"Do you know where they moved to?"

She looked like I'd bitten the head off of a bat like Ozzy Osbourne.

"How the hell am I supposed to know that?"

"Oh...I thought...I dunno."

"Right." She took a final suck and flicked the cigarette my way before shutting the door.

I stood there, gobsmacked. I never would've expected that Heidi had moved, but she and her grandpa probably found it too tough to stay in town with all the media scrutiny. Maybe it was better this way. Unlikely she would've accepted my apologies, or even been kind enough to give me another black eye.

I put back on my headphones, picked up where the song left off.

"Oh, I get hysterical, hysteria when you're near," I hummed, thinking about our first kiss while watching *Gremlins* atop Troy's car. Like Grandma Bernice said, memories keep a person alive. Even though Heidi wasn't dead, she was dead to me. So, I remembered that night, the queasiness in my stomach, the melted Sno-Caps we shared, the way she smelled like sunflowers. I walked all the way back to Grandma Bernice's condo, all five or so miles, the memory on repeat, stopping the tape when the song ended and rewinding back to the beginning.

I did it so many times I could pinpoint exactly how long it would take, escaping more into that night with each rewind.

"'Cause it's a miracle, hysteria when you're near. Get closer, get closer to me."

When I arrived at the condo's shared space, I popped the cassette out of the Walkman and ripped out the magnetic tape, tossed it in the pool so I'd never be able to hear it again.

66

Jenny Troy Gimmelman was born on January 12, 1989, Steph's water breaking while I was playing a game of Q*bert. She was in labor for thirty-six hours and when I first saw my baby niece, she had a full head of dark hair and a smushed red face. Like Grandma Bernice had described Jenny when she was baby, new Jenny wailed like a banshee for the first few months, all of us up throughout the night to help Steph until Grandma Bernice convinced an old Orthodox former nurse to ease the burden. I was starting high school, and while back in the day I would've been nervous to not know anyone, after making it through the detention center and coming out in one piece, a Boca Raton high school was a breeze.

I got really into journalism and began writing for the newspaper, which led to an internship at the *Boca Raton Tribune*. I typed up copy for the crime beat reporters after school as they fed cigarettes into ashtrays and spoke of war wounds on the job. I had a small group of friends who also worked at the school newspaper, and we'd hang out at the mall or get forties and lounge in each other's backyards. They all knew who I was, but none of them cared. I actually think they were impressed, but I never talked about it. The less I thought about what we had done, the further away it became. At night, I helped Steph bathe Jenny and read books to her before going to bed. As she grew up, her favorites were *Amelia Bedelia* and *Euphonia and the Flood* and *Miss Nelson is Missing*. By the age of two she knew how to read a little, or at least had memorized the books enough to get by. She was a smart child, sweet, precocious, and a bit of a troublemaker, just like the aunt she was named after.

Working for two newspapers and writing all the time, I really didn't pay much attention to other studies and did just what I needed to get by. I tried out for the JV basketball team and made it playing point guard, since I'd grown a bit but not enough to be a forward or center. I got so busy I barely had time to think any more about how insane our lives had been. Occasionally someone brought it up, or I was hounded by the press for an interview, but Steph and I made a decision not to do any. We had moved on and wanted the world to move on as well.

Mom still sent letters on the dot every week. We never answered any, but after a while I started to read them. After about a year in prison, she decided to become an Orthodox Jew. Every day she studied the Talmud and the Torah, searching for an explanation as to why she'd allowed herself to become so lost. The root of it began when her father Herb died, and she tried drugs and followed bands on tour. Drugs had always been a negative influence, even more so when we were pulling off heists and she was stoned on pills most of the time. She was aware that Barry wanted her to be this way, but that wasn't completely an excuse because she wanted it too. The more she dissociated with reality, the better she felt. She'd been an addict, and it was hard to wean off in prison, but Hashem helped her. Without the pull of drugs, she found something new to attach herself to. For the past year, God had been guiding her to deal with the torturous guilt. Because her Jenny was dead, this would be the grief she must bear for the rest of her life. Now it would be up to her to discover how to allow that to make her into a better Jew, devote her time to His teachings, to His devotion. At first, Grandma Bernice pursed her lips when she read this, but as the letters kept coming and the dedication for Hashem continued, she stopped judging. She could not condemn someone for finding God, even though Mom had taken a roundabout path. She could only hope Mom continued to be as good a Jew as she could possibly be now, despite the pitfalls in her past.

Senior year I turned eighteen and was a starter for the varsity squad when

I fractured my kneecap. This ended the season for me, and I was crushed because we were in line to win the league. The guys at the *Tribune* felt bad and asked if I wanted to write an article from home instead of just typing up copy. While they couldn't put me on a current crime beat, they wondered if I wanted to write about my time as a criminal (har, har, har)? I didn't think they were serious, but they were and so I began to write. The journal I kept during the ordeal had gone into police evidence, and I hadn't written a word about it since.

I didn't know if it would be difficult to access those memories from years ago, but they flowed out of me like lava. I had pages and pages after an all-night bender, way too long for an article, but I eventually cut it down and sent it to them. I called it "I Was a Kid Bank Robber," and the article received more calls and letters than any other op-ed piece in the newspaper's history. The media had lost interest in our case. Barry and Mom were in prison and not allowed to make any money off their appearances, so they hadn't done any. Steph and I refused, and only once in a while a bit player would pop up somewhere: a waitress who served us, someone we held hostage, obviously when Special Agent Terbert died frozen on the lake in Maine. It had been a while since we were thrust in the spotlight and media outlets started picking up on the article. I was encouraged to write another, which I did to even more fanfare, and then I got a call from some big literary agent in New York City who was impressed by my writing and asked if I would author a book. They told me I could get big money for doing it.

I didn't say yes immediately, wanting to go over it with Steph and Grandma Bernice, but we were kind of struggling money-wise. Grandma Bernice received social security and Steph got her GED while working a job at the mall at an Orange Julius while Jenny was in pre-school. When they asked how much the agent thought I could get, they said I was nuts if I didn't do it. I called back the agent who clarified that the book would really sell if I got my parents' side of the story too. I told her I hadn't spoken to my parents since they were locked up, and she said for the kind of money she'd be asking for, it was crucial to have their perspective to give the book a round appeal. I didn't know what the fuck that meant, but she told me the difference could be upwards of five hundred thousand dollars and so that was when I first responded to Mom's letter and said I would be visiting her at the Texas State Penitentiary in Huntsville.

67

I knew Mom had become Orthodox, but I wasn't expecting a shaved head when I saw her behind the glass partition. She was a duller version of who she used to be, her light muted. Prison made her ropey and gaunt, in the few years apart it looked as if she aged ten. She motioned for me to pick up the phone receiver on my end. When I did, a smile made tears pour from her eyes.

"Thank you for coming."

Her voice had changed too. She used to have a sing-song tone, everything airy and breezy. This new voice had been through too much to ever return to that naivety.

"You've gotten so big."

She hadn't seen me since I was fourteen so I guess I must've been a shock. By eighteen I was six feet tall, thin muscles, I was a man. I had curtained hair in the style of Jordan Catalano from *My So-Called Life*, not because of him but kids at school started to call me that. I wore baggy jeans hanging around my ass crack and an oversized flannel shirt. I'd gotten into hip-hop like Naughty by Nature, Digable Planets, Onyx, and Wreckx-N-Effect. Neither of us, the same person we once knew.

"I never thought you'd come."

I wanted to say the only reason I showed up was to get info out of her for my new big book deal. But then I imagined she wouldn't be so forthcoming.

"It was time."

She placed her hand on her heart. It was a sudden gesture, one that embarrassed her a little.

"I sent you a letter every week—"

"I know."

"Did you read them?"

"I started to."

"And your sister?"

"Yeah, she started to as well. Jenny's doing good."

The name hit Mom like a gut punch, she deflated before my eyes.

"I mean, her daughter Jenny. That's what she named her."

"Oh," Mom said, still reeling.

"After her, I mean, we thought—"

"All I knew was that she had the baby. Your grandmother, well, she allows me to talk to her on the phone every once in a while, but she refuses to talk back. How is she?"

"Fine. Everyone's fine. I mean, considering."

Mom shook away her sadness. "So, tell me about yourself. Tell me everything."

"Uh, I'm a senior. Applying to college. Probably Florida State. Like, my grades aren't great."

"But you were so smart."

"Ya know school's kinda boring and shit. I mean, I work at the newspaper and have had an internship at the *Boca Raton Tribune* since freshman year, so that's my focus."

And I have a giant book deal and potential movie offers based on our lives, I wanted to add. *So, I might even wind up skipping college.*

"Sounds like you're busy. Sounds like you're well."

"I am, ya know Grandma Bernice has really been great. I mean, she can be a pain in the ass and there are still a million cats in the condo..."

I managed to make Mom laugh, a tiny titter. It was good to hear.

"But she stepped up. Someone needed to."

Her shoulders slumped. "Right."

"And you, so you're Ortho now?"

She sat up straight. "Yes, I follow Orthodox teachings."

"Like?"

She pointed to her buzzed scalp. "For one the shaved head, keeps me closer to God. And I study His words all day. I'm studying to become a rabbi actually."

I let out a laugh. "Really?"

She stiffened. "Yes, really. I'm making use of my time here. I want to spend the rest of my days helping others. So we do teachings in the rec room with the other women. Sometimes it's quite rough here, but other times we're a family."

"A family? Good for you."

"Now..."

"No, I'm really happy you found a new family with other criminals."

She blew a gust of air through her nostrils. "Okay, let's do this. I deserve it. Tell me everything you've wanted to say."

"Oh no, I'm past that. I really am."

"I think it might do you some good."

"Maybe another time."

"You need to know how sorry I am."

I scratched my elbow. "Yeah, sorry is just a word. It's a Get Out of Jail free card. It doesn't mean anything."

"The Torah teaches forgiveness."

"Grandma Bernice has said that. That I should forgive when I'm ready."

"And are you?"

"I don't know. I don't think it's a button you can just push. But I'm really not angry. I'm sorry for you."

"Why?"

"Because you were so weak."

She closed her eyes, nodded. "Yes, tell me."

"You were fuckin' weak. You let him walk all over you. Followed him like a lemming. He could do no wrong."

"I don't disagree." She tapped her chin, looked toward the fluorescent lights. "It's hard to recognize that woman. I remember everything, but it's as if it happened to someone else entirely."

"Does that allow you to sleep at night?"

She shook her finger, her voice now like knives. "Oh, I don't sleep at night. God hasn't granted me that peace yet. Maybe one day He will, maybe not. I've accepted that."

"Good."

"I was a terrible mother. Yes. I put my children in danger, what a mother should never do. All out of greed. I couldn't see past it. And it destroyed us."

I went to speak, but she held up a finger.

"But spiritually, I'm learning to forgive myself. If you never forgive me, Aaron, I must accept that. You would be in the right. We lost your...we lost our Jenny because of me, and that will forever be a knife in my heart, but I cannot, I *will* not beat myself up anymore. I'm so bruised it hurts to breathe, but I want the rest of my life to have meaning...rabbinical studies, giving back to a community, maybe one day forging a relationship with my actual family again, if you'll have me."

I rubbed the goatee I was growing. "I can't promise—"

"No, oh no, I wouldn't want a promise. Or for you and Steph to force anything. I don't even know if I'm fully ready to be forgiven, absolved, I need to get there with myself first. And I'm trying, I'm trying to understand why I allowed myself to do the things I did, to be so swayed, to be so hopeless. Hashem is teaching me that. Like I say, one day..."

Since there was a limited amount of time, I needed to get her talking about the heists.

"Tell me about the first time you robbed that liquor store with Barry."

Her eyebrows rose, shocked.

"It would really help me to know. To understand you better..."

She softened when she heard that I cared enough to try and understand. It allowed her to be forthcoming. Over the next few months, I returned to visit her, each time making sure she opened up more. She told me about when she and Barry met at Woodstock. The call he made to her after the stock market crashed and he debated jumping out of the window, except that the windows wouldn't open in his office. The thrill she'd gotten when they held up their first liquor store. How she had liked her life up until then, but realized she'd just been going through the motions. Us kids had gotten older, we didn't need her like we used to, she'd become obsolete, uninspired, depressed without even being aware she was.

Our adventures in the RV had woken her slumber, made her excited to be alive again, till it all came crashing down. The sad part was she always knew it would end. That we would eventually be doomed. The adrenaline of the moment made any ill-fated scenarios palatable. And we were more of a family on the road than we ever had been. Usually back in Jersey, we stuck to our own lives, barely had time for one another. Barry worked crazy hours and it felt like she was losing her husband. Us kids had our friends, after-school activities, there was no room for her anymore in our busy schedules. And yet on the road, that all melted away. Locked in an RV with the people she loved the most, endlessly winding around America. Who wouldn't have wanted to keep that going?

This had maybe been my sixth visit over the course of a year. I'd gotten most of what I needed, her chapters taking shape.

"Does that make sense at all?" she asked, clasping her hands together as if she was praying.

"Yeah, no, I get it. It's still fucked up, but my agent said it helps to walk in your shoes."

Ruh-roh.

"Your...agent?" Mom asked.

"Uh... Okay, listen I was approached to write a book."

She gathered up imaginary dust to occupy herself. "I see."

"It's a lot of money. I don't need to remind you that we were left with nothing. It's not like Grandma Bernice's social security check does much."

"You don't have to convince me, Aaron. Take whatever they give you."

I tried to see if she was being sarcastic or not. This new Ortho Mom made it hard to tell.

"Is that why you...?" She took a deep breath. "Came to see me?"

I chewed on the inside of my lip. The silence between us vibrating. She seemed as if she could shatter into a thousand pieces.

"Yeah, I mean, like I had to get your side."

Her fingers went to run through her hair, forgetting there was none.

"Oh."

"But, this has been... I don't know the words for it. I wouldn't have come back this many times just for material for the book."

"You don't have to lie to spare my feelings."

"I'm not," I shouted, not realizing I was that amped. "It's been cool getting to know things about you. Like stories from before you had us. I was gonna tell you—"

"You don't owe me an explanation."

"I mean, ultimately you would need to sign off, and not all of it would put you in a good light."

She held up her hand. "Aaron, please—"

"But some of it will. Because not all of it was bad. I mean, the Jenny stuff sure, and the...I'm not gonna get into everything, but most of our childhood was okay. I think you guys both cared about us as much as you could. Does that make sense? Like, some people are born to be parents, they just have that in them, and then for others it's not easy. It never was easy for you."

"No."

"But I know you loved us, I know both of you did. In the way that you knew how. And if that used to upset me, I've let go of any animosity. You are who you are."

She breathed heavy through her nose, possibly thinking that I would've been crueler.

"Thank you."

"I want to keep coming and seeing you, like maybe next time I could convince Steph and she could bring Jenny?"

"I would love that."

"I know, I know you would."

The next time I saw her a few months later, Steph flew down with Jenny. We stayed in a shit motel near the penitentiary, visiting her first thing in the morning. I'd never seen such tears of joy when Steph walked in carrying Jenny, a new Jenny, but with shades of the Jenny we loved and lost.

"Thank you," she said to me through the glass partition, practically convulsing.

"You're welcome, Mom."

Her mouth dropped open. I hadn't called her *Mom* yet, not for years. I didn't expect to do it, but the fact it came out naturally meant that it was time. I left Mom and Steph alone to reunite and introduce Jenny to her grandma. Outside I smoked a Newport Light satisfied that I'd finally forgiven her, the dead weight lifted.

Barry would be next when I was ready.

If I'd ever be.

68

Barry was kept at a penitentiary on the other end of Texas. Immediately I noticed the difference in the clientele: skinheads, murderers, rapists, the filth of society. It chilled my bones even just in the waiting area. When they brought him out chained at his wrists and ankles, he was a bigger, buffer Barry than the one I'd seen last. While Mom shrank from incarceration, Barry expanded. He'd shaved his head, losing his famous curls, his skin leathery with popping veins. A smirk dripping across his face when he saw it was me. I was nineteen and it had been six long years.

We sat facing each other through a wall of glass, both of us playing chicken to see who picked up the phone first. Since I was always the adult, I finally did and he followed.

"Hi, Barry," I said, in the lowest voice I could muster, maintaining toughness.

He winced at my calling him by his name.

"Always a smart-aleck," he said. "Aaron, my boy."

"Barry," I said again, wondering if I wasn't ready for this, if I ever would be.

"You've grown?"

"Children do that."

"Do they?"

I'd started school at Florida State. I partied a lot, finding a love of shotgunning beers, hooking up with co-eds, not getting as much done on the book as I wanted, even though I needed to finish to get my full advance.

"I knew you'd come one day. I would've thought a little sooner, but what's it been?"

"Six years."

"Wow, feels like fifteen. In these walls." He stuck his tongue into his cheek. Gone was his jokey persona, this Barry more serious, stoic, with spiderweb, bloodshot eyes. "Time tends to go backwards here, it's devious like that. You think it's tomorrow, but it's actually the day before. But in the real world, what are you doing?"

I filled him in on working for the *Tribune*, which I was on hiatus from. I told him about partying at Florida State.

"That's good to hear, my boy. I like that. Beers and girls. Sounds like college to me, well what it should've been. I met your mom and she got pregnant with Steph. How is your sister?"

"She's good, her daughter, Jenny..."

I waited for a reaction, but he gave me none.

"Jenny is in kindergarten. They live with Grandma Bernice, but she's thinking of getting a place on her own. She works as a paralegal at a law firm."

"Well, what a little upright member of society she's become." When he scratched at his eye, I saw his fingernails bitten down to the quick, the nerves and anxiety of the prison apparent. "I don't suppose she's going to visit me."

"No, I don't think so." I took out a photograph of Jenny, his granddaughter. She was on a tire swing at the park. She'd just lost her first tooth. "That's Jenny."

I waited for another reaction, his face unmoving.

"Cute kid."

"We named her after—"

"I know what you're doing, Aaron." He laced his fingers behind his head. "I've prepared for this meeting and what it would entail. A guilt assault."

"What's that mean?"

He unlocked his fingers and mimed a Tommy gun blasting away. "Firing on all cylinders to make me feel as shitty as possible. Blam, blam, blam, all right you hit me, I'm wounded. Are you happy?"

"Oh no, I'm far from happy."

"Is that a fact? Let's not forget who is the one in the cage between the two of us."

"You think I should be there too?"

He gritted his teeth. "In my humblest belief, and I have had much time to ponder this, I...and your mother to an extent, took the brunt of all the blame."

I tossed the bangs out of my eyes. "You're the parent."

"Yes, oh I am aware. The judge, the jury, the public, has all written that saying in harsh neon lights. I am the devil and you a sweet little cherub angel."

"Barry—"

"Don't condescend to me, do *not* fucking call me by my first name."

I cracked a knuckle, wanting to pound on him. "You're lucky I called you anything at all."

"Am I? Should I kiss your feet for this visit, Aaron. My baby boy returning to his pop. Should we try to establish a new relationship? Is that what you're doing with your mother?"

"Yes, yes I am."

"Isn't that grand? I am so glad you two were able to find yourselves again. She's written me letters about it. Oh yes, we stay in touch. She actually misses me, tells me so in juicy grandeur."

"She's a different person now. She's becoming Orthodox."

"Hmm, if I showed you some of those letters you wouldn't believe her born again lies."

"I think you're lying. She doesn't write you. She told me that."

"She and I have always had a connection grander than the family's. And I don't mean to rub salt in any wound, but the two of us were never as blissful as we were before you kids were born."

I pounded the glass. "Fuck you. Fuck you, Barry. You piece of shit."

He clapped. "There, there's the real emotion I was looking for. The hate in your eyes, I see it…I saw it…toward the end of our journey. You hated me so, Aaron."

I was trying not to cry. Summoning every shred of power I had inside of me to hold back what he craved.

"You ruined our lives."

"I gave you life."

"That doesn't give you the right to take it away."

"*You* fired at that FBI agent."

"*You* told me to."

"And because *you* missed him, well…" He cracked his neck, maybe fought himself not to shed a tear too. Maybe he cried all morning in anticipation of this tête-à-tête. "Here's a scenario, you aim for his tire, the tire blows, the car spinning off the road, and we get away."

I had to laugh. "Is that how you imagined it would go?"

"Oh, I do. Every night when darkness makes this place more miserable than during the day."

"There was an APB out on us. They had our plates. We couldn't run forever."

"I think you wanted us to get caught."

I folded my arms. "Maybe I did. To stop the madness. Is that so wrong? If we would've gotten busted earlier, Jenny would still be…"

Now my tears flowed, sharp and relentless, the dam broken.

Barry gripped his phone. "You think I don't miss her. You think that doesn't eat me up every day of my existence, and then you come here with a fucking photograph of another Jenny thrown in my face. You're cruel."

"I learned it from watching you," I said, harkening to a famous drug commercial from when I was a kid.

"I will not apologize, Aaron. I've thought about this long and hard during my time here. The day you'd show your face. And how I won't give you that."

"Why?"

"Because we all played a part."

"You think I don't feel rotten every day too? I miss her just as much as you. I know we all are to blame. Even though I'm not locked up, I'm still in my own prison. Are *you* looking for an apology? Because that's insane, Barry. You were the parent."

"Again, with this bullshit. You robbed first. You put the bug in my ear, kid. It all started with you."

"Fine, tell yourself that. If you need that fucked up kind of satisfaction so you can go to bed at night, go the fuck ahead. Yeah, I decided to steal first. I was worried that we had no money, and I wanted to help. It was a convenience store. You should have ended it right there. But it thrilled you."

"It thrilled you too, man."

"It did because of you. Because I idolized you, my whole life I wanted to make you proud. And you gave us so little..."

"We gave you everything."

"I'm not talking about fucking money. You gave us so little of you. You disappeared down on Wall Street, you made an appearance in the family when you felt like it. We were all supporting characters in your life, Mom included."

"So, this is what took you six years to say. You planned out these mini speeches to torpedo me?"

"No, I got a book deal. To tell our story."

"Fancy you. Too bad I can't profit over tragedy."

"I'm doing it to give Jenny, your granddaughter Jenny, a better life. This is gonna go to her college."

He clapped. "How noble."

"I think it is. And our story needs to be told."

He cupped his chin. "Ah, now I understand why you've come. Got your mother to be a singing canary and now it's my turn."

"They want your side of things."

"Who wants this?"

"The publisher, a big publisher, they want the book to be rounded, all of our perspectives."

He folded his arms, forearms bulging with muscles, trying to threaten.

"What if I won't give you anything?"

"Then I'll just fill in the blanks."

He blew a raspberry.

"But Barry...?"

He gave me a look like, *you call me that again and I'll snap your neck.*

"It'll be better if it's your story. You can explain yourself like I couldn't. If you're looking for empathy..."

He snapped his fingers. "Now that, *that* was planned. You practiced that in front of a mirror."

"What if I did? If you're not entirely at fault like everyone paints you out to be, then show the world, give me some of your side. Mom did it."

"Your mother is weak."

"She's not weak anymore. She's studying to be a rabbi, she found God."

"Hallelujah. The weakest people usually do."

"She's trying to be a better person."

"Are you saying I'm not?"

"Not from what I can see."

He clicked his tongue. "Fine, give me whatever papers you want me to sign. That's really why you're here. So you can use my name, my likeness, c'mon, bring them out. I'll get the guard to allow them to bring it over."

"I don't have them. I came without any weapons. I have a relationship with Mom again; it's not like what it used to be, but it's something."

"Are you saying you want that with me?"

"I'm saying the opportunity for it could exist down the road."

"Hmm, now are you saying that, so I'll go along with you, or do you really mean it?"

"Isn't it worth taking the chance? What the fuck else are you doing?"

He let out a boisterous laugh. A guard turned his head, gave him a warning stare.

"That's the vinegar I like to see, Aaron." He nodded, convincing himself. "I like that a lot. I forgot how much you used to make me laugh. Little stand-up comedian, that's what your mother and I used to say. You were such a ham." He looked off to the left, remembering. "Such a ham. How'd she look?"

"Who?"

"Your mother, all these times you saw her."

"She has a shaved head."

"Jesus, she's really taking this Ortho thing seriously."

"Yeah, she is. I dunno, she's thinner, but she seems at peace."

"Ah good, she deserves it. She does. I'm glad for her. Really."

"You honestly seem like more of a pit bull than you were."

"Ah, you gotta be like that here. Always twitchy. Always ready to snap on someone. Let me tell you, I'm the nicest guy in this hell."

"Shit."

"Yeah, daily shit. But there are moments here. I meditate. Didn't find God like Judy, or anything like that, but I have been able to shut off. Time passes so slowly like I said so some days you're able to do that. And when I don't think about anything, it's the happiest I can be. It's like wandering through nothingness. Doesn't happen often, but when it does..."

"You're free?"

A tear hid, at the corner of his eye. "Yeah, you can say that."

"Sounds pretty great."

"Barry Gimmelman," the guard called out. "Time's up."

He turned back to me as if his life force had been vacuumed out of his body. Summoned back to reality. A sigh like the world had succumbed to an apocalypse.

"My fan club awaits."

I smiled at that. "You're a stand-up comedian too."

"You got that from me. You got a lot of me in you. You know that, don't you?"

I gulped on a choked breath. "Yeah, I do."

He winked. "Tame it better than I could."

The guard came and lifted him up by his armpit.

"All right, handsy," he said to the guard.

"Zip it, Gimmelman," the guard responded, obviously not the first time they had a back and forth like this.

"Whoa Gimmelmans," he said, as if he was rocking on a boat. "Whoa

Gimmelmans."

My mouth moved to say it along with him, but I couldn't.

He fired at me with his index and his thumb. "See you again...son?"

I emerged from a fog I'd entered, shook away the cobwebs of better times.

"Uh, yeah. Maybe."

"Okay, maybe. Maybe that's enough."

The guard led him out of the room, this small man fallen from high.

"That's enough," I said out loud, before leaving too.

EPILOGUE

The End.

I hear a version of myself saying it thirty years ago for my audio book, barely twenty, already having lived a thousand lives. Never listened to it since then. I don't even realize my fingers are gripping the steering wheel so hard the skin has cracked. Roark and I stayed silent the entire time; lucky the road was empty enough to keep focused.

For the four-hour stretch, Jenny came alive, only to be destroyed again. She existed so long ago; I no longer remember the sound of her voice. I cried in parts, Roark did too, but secretly so I wouldn't know. Through the rearview, he rubbed his eyes a lot toward the end, for the aunt he never got a chance to meet. For his grandma Judy he lost a few years back around the time I departed from his life too. She'd become a rabbi in Boca Raton after being released early due to good behavior, staying close to Grandma Bernice and Steph and her daughter Jenny while I flitted in and out. The entire congregation came to her funeral, all *davening* together at the end of the *shiva* on the seventh day. Hands were washed upon arrival, candles were lit, mirrors were covered, and they all prayed during the mourner's *Kaddish*, a sea of pendulums rocking back and forth in Steph's living room. She'd become a lawyer, married a very religious lawyer who raised Jenny as his own. They lived a quiet life of *Shabbat* dinners with Grandma Bernice and Mom before Grandma Bernice passed too. Mom moved in with them into a huge eye-sore of a house, living in a converted garage. The entire Gimmelman brood turning to religion for answers. Temple every Saturday morning. A *Kosher* household. They were seeking forgiveness for our sins—Judaism as a path to absolution. And it worked for them, they found a way to avoid pulsing with anger all the time. I threw myself into my work instead—countless stories of characters being maimed, brutalized, each with the face of Barry.

A few months back, I got a call from an inmate in a penitentiary. Barry Gimmelman. The name like a knife in my gut. As I got older, I left the Gimmelmans behind, moved to Texas while they remained in Florida, and saw them on holidays. Steph and I FaceTime occasionally, Jenny as well with her own family in Tampa, but they're aware I've kept them at a distance, like I've done to most people who've tried to love me. Especially Barry. When I left the prison that day after seeing him for the first time in six years, we never spoke again. Some time ago, letters started appearing in my mailbox, then emails as the world moved to that form of communication. I never responded. I never even read them. And then, my publicist broke my heart and I found myself back in Texas: my ex, Melinda at a loss for what to do with Roark, Barry's call coming a few days later. With nausea creeping up my throat, I accepted the call.

"I have a parole date," he said, no 'Hi, how are you?'. Gave me just the facts for fear I'd likely hang up if he fed me any apologies.

"When?" I asked, in my rental apartment that lacked any personality. I wanted to fix it up for Roark when he'd come, but I had no clue what he liked.

"Four months," he said. "But it looks like I'm getting sprung."

The calls came every few days. Maybe it helped that I was feeling lonely and at my lowest. My last book hadn't been the success my publisher hoped for, my agent intimating the next deal wouldn't be a guarantee. Readers had moved on from the Gimmelmans, from *Thick as Thieves: The Untold Story of the Wild Woodstock Gang*. So, Barry and I started talking. No heartfelt apologies...yet, or screaming matches where we exorcized our demons. We spoke of bullshit, The Rangers chances that year, his roommate who sang in his sleep, and finally Roark. He called one day wanting to know all about Roark.

"He's..." I searched for what to tell him, but I barely knew what to say.

Roark liked chaos; Barry could relate to that.

"Sounds a lot like me," Barry said, with an evil laugh, one that began softly and built toward its destruction.

"The hell if he is," I said, hanging up and wishing for old school phones where you could slam the receiver down.

The next day another call.

"Barry, what do you want?"

I'd caught him off guard. He stammered, whistled in place of a response before he broke down.

"I'm scared, son," he said. He sounded like a child despite his gargling old man tone.

I swallowed hard, the butterflies in my stomach at war.

"What are you scared of?" I asked, granting him a small iota of grace.

"The world. One I haven't been a part of since 1990. Hell, prison never spooked me much. Fell in with the right crowd here. As a Jew, the skinheads don't want you, so I formed a protection early on with the rest. Us versus them, ya-know. Started doling out financial advice. I mean, at one point I was killing it down on Wall Street." He clears his throat. "Sorry, wrong choice of words."

I didn't want to have this conversation with him, but in all truth, I'd never be ready for it, so I gritted my teeth and let him wring out his soul.

"Yeah, the world has changed, Barry. We've all changed."

"I've changed," he said, the inflection in his voice rising. "Not like your mother—I'm sorry to hear about her, my condolences. She was—she was the only perfection I ever knew."

"The only?" I asked, already annoyed with how this conversation was going.

"She gave me you, and Stephie, and Jenny..."

He cracked at the mention of Jenny. Whether there were tears or not, I didn't know, but I was sure thirty years of guilt does something to you.

"You know I've never forgiven myself."

My cell phone got hot in my hand, practically burning.

"And I blamed you, Aaron, which was foolish. Put a gun in a little boy's hand and expected him to save us from that F.B.I. nut on our ass."

"You killed her," I said, practically growling. "Not him. You."

Silence hissed over the receiver. "Yes. This I've accepted. I can't tell you how sorry—"

"No, Barry. No! You don't get to say 'sorry'."

"But I am. Please, my boy, let this old man have that. I have nothing else."

I was about to throw the cell across the room.

"Will you pick me up?"

"Pick you up? What?"

"From the penitentiary. They boot us out. It's gonna be like stepping onto a new planet. My knees are already knocking. Your sister...she hasn't even accepted my call."

I could already feel him worming his way in, that mystical charisma he had like a cult leader.

"We have many, many more conversations ahead of us to get us to a place of understanding, Aaron. I'm at your mercy."

"I have no mercy for you."

"But you took my call?"

"I...don't know why."

"I'd like to meet Roark. You said he was going through a hard time. Maybe I can help?"

"You are the last person on Earth who should guide my child."

"You misunderstand. Let me be a tragic warning to him. No one should ever aspire to be me. I was rotten, son. Just rotten. Greedy. Selfish. Call me any horrible thing you need to. But I've shed that over the years. We shed our cells every seven years, right? And I've left that man behind. I've stepped into someone new. Give me a chance. Please. I don't have much left of this life. Let me spend these last years working toward some kind of good."

I let the seconds stretch before I answered. "I'll think about it...Barry."

"I'm your father, Aaron. Whether or not you want me to be. You only get one dad, and sorry to say, but I'm it. I can feel your rage through this phone, even after all this time. It's not healthy. You need to shed this skin that's been carrying around all your anger. Let me be Dad again...to you and your boy. What do you say? Give your old man something to hope for, to go on living. C'mon."

"I gotta go," I said, hanging up and rushing to the bathroom where I brought up my lunch. I flushed the toilet and lay against the cool porcelain like a madman. I had no idea what I'd decide.

The GPS now notifies us that we are a mile away from Beaumont. I shut off the audio book that's now just fizzes static. Through the rearview, Roark has moved on to a new cuticle, tearing it off with his teeth.

"So...?" I ask. "What did you think?"

I'm aware my eyes are wet, the eyelashes glued together.

He glances at the window, no more cows to distract.

"That was really messed up." He's not smirking, his eyes sad. "Your sister...and your dad. It didn't seem real."

"It was. Very real. That was my reality."

"I'm sorry your dad was such a dick."

"Yeah. Thank you. He was."

"Makes you look like a prince."

A surprised laugh pops out of me. "I'm no prince."

"No," he says. "You're not."

"Neither are you."

He has nothing to say to that.

"I see a lot of me in you, Roark. And that terrifies me."

"You don't gotta worry about me putting on a mask of a musician and hitting a bank."

I look at him carefully. "Are you sure?"

"I'm just bored," he says, swatting a bug that's flown in. "All it is."

"I fear you have my DNA—Barry's DNA."

The penitentiary looms in the distance, as if Barry heard his name being called. An American flag piercing the sky over a long building looking like a fortress. All these sinners crowded together—Barry included. But a sinner no more in the law's eyes. A free man entering society again. Fuck if I was ready for that.

"Are you angry at me?" I ask, because we know it's true. He's acting out because I wasn't there. But I'm back now, right? I'm back for good. The anti-Barry, ready to parent.

"Yes."

He doesn't mince words and I'm glad for that.

"What do you want to say to me?" I ask. "Anything. Be brutal. Tear me apart."

"Fuck you, dude."

"Good. Yeah. Fuck me. I deserve it."

He chews on his cheek. "Why did you leave?"

We lock our gaze through the rearview. He's not about to let me off the hook so easy.

"I'm restless, kid." I wince at calling him 'kid', how Barry used to refer to me, even when I wasn't a kid anymore. Even after I'd held up multiple bank tellers. "I'm sorry. You're not a kid anymore. You're becoming a man."

He puffs up his chest. "Hell yeah."

"I told you about *teshuva* before we listened to the book. What repentance means to Jews."

"Remind me again."

"Jews believe that everyone is capable of sin, but we can stop or minimize future sins by repenting, promising to never repeat that sin again."

"I don't remember you being so into religion when you lived with us."

He's right. I wasn't. My mom found Judaism, Steph too—it worked for them. For me it seemed like a cop-out. But then I found myself wandering into a synagogue after Barry's last call. Sitting in Saturday morning services surrounded by a wall of prayer. Even if I didn't want to admit it, I felt swaddled, a part of something greater than my own trauma. I started talking to the rabbi. This old man with a flowing beard, exactly how I pictured God would be, hidden in the sky behind a thicket of clouds. I told him my whole saga—he vaguely remembered it from the News in those days. I mentioned my mom's recent passing, how I'd forgiven her to an extent, but I couldn't forgive my dad. And now he was about to return.

"*Teshuva* means 'return' in Hebrew," he said, wagging a finger. "The primary purpose of repentance in Judaism is ethical self-transformation. It is for *you*, not *him*."

"Yeah, I get that," I said. "I know."

"If you have not forgiven him, it's because you need his sin to define your life."

"No," I said, way too quickly. "Like, I've moved on."

He shook his head so ominously; it gave me chills.

"No, son, you are the very definition of *stuck*. Accept his repentance, now that he will be free. Or you will never be."

I need that from Roark as well. If he can forgive, then maybe I can find that inside of myself too.

"Don't hold onto your anger toward me," I tell Roark, and his eyes flit away. His face crumples, like an old man who's faced too much anguish in his life.

"Fuck off," he says, his tongue stabbing his cheek.

"Roark—"

"Go to hell."

He's opened the car door while we're still creeping toward the penitentiary. I realize I've been delaying the inevitable. He leaps out and walks along the road, hands shoved in his hoodie pockets. I stop the car and chase after him.

"Roark!"

He swivels around, swings at me. "No, leave me alone."

"Roark, I'm sorry."

He pushes me, and I nearly topple over.

"Yeah, push me again," I say. "C'mon, you wanna hit me, hit me. Hit me hard. Make it count."

His fist comes in contact with my eye like I've been knocked with a baseball. I double back, my face throbbing. He's nursing his knuckles, blood rising to the surface.

"Okay, how'd that feel?"

He chews on this new dynamic, slowly nods. "Good, good."

"Good."

"Do you want to do it again? I got another eye."

He thinks on it, shakes his head. "Naw."

I press my palms together. "I'm sorry, Roark. I never should've left you. I was selfish and delusional."

"Yeah, keep going."

"You and your mother did nothing wrong. She loves you. She's doing the best she can. I'm the fuck-up. I'm the wreck. But this is a new me."

"Why, because you talked to some rabbi?"

"No, because I'm here now." I realize I'm yelling, my throat sore. "I'm fucking picking up Barry. After all these years. He's free and I'll be driving him away from prison. That's ludicrous, you understand that? The fact that I'm here now, the fact that I give a shit even. I'm petrified, son, I'm—"

My voice breaks, the tears building. What will be many I'll shed today. I have no idea what it'll be like when I see him, this aged Barry, so much closer to death since our last encounter thirty years ago. We've shed many cells since then. We've transformed into entirely different beings.

The penitentiary threatens in the distance like a giant monster. I could get back in the car and drive away. I could pretend I never got that call from Barry. I could remain *stuck* just like the rabbi warned.

I'm sobbing now and I know Roark has never seen me crazy like this. It's scary for a child to witness a parent at their most emotional, but I'm unable to dial it back.

"Hey, Dad," he says, his voice less accusatory than before. He hasn't called me Dad in a long time, not since I left. Another trait I passed down to him from my own fucked up relationship with Barry. "Dad," he says again, inching toward me. I crave a hug. "It's all right, like you're good."

"I'm so sorry. I wish I could take those years back. Do them over. My whole life needs a re-do, ya-know?"

"What The Fuck?" he says.

"What?"

"That band, What The Fuck? They gotta song called 'Today is the Only Day'." He starts to sing it. I never even realized he had a good voice.

Today is the only day
Fuck yesterday

Tomorrow's uncertain

Viva today

I let out a much-needed laugh. These simple lyrics. But he's singing it over and over, a penetrating mantra.

"Like, why let shit from long ago mess you up?" He shrugs his shoulders. "How about you forgive my joyride, and I'll let your departure slide, parental unit? What do they say? A clean slate."

He holds out his hand to shake.

"Just like that?"

"Yeah, screw it, just like that."

We shake hands and it's the most I've touched him in years. I want to go for a hug but shouldn't be greedy. To my surprise, he hugs me . He smells of weed and corn chips, a heavenly scent.

"I love you, Roark."

"Yeah, old man, you're all right too."

"I'm not going anywhere again. I'll be right here in Texas until you graduate."

"Uh, jury's out on that happening."

It's an expression I used to say a lot, maybe because of my own legal entanglements. It makes me smile to know he's picked up some of my slang.

"All right, enough of this sap," he says, worming out of my hug and shaking it off like it's cooties.

"Thank you," I say, and he mimes an imaginary gun and shoots me with a wink. It brings me right back to that defining moment in my life: Jenny getting shot and Barry to blame. The penitentiary is only a few steps away. My son has accepted, when I asked for *teshuva* like the lovely and kind boy he is deep inside, passing into adulthood now. I'm forty-nine years old, and it's finally my time.

"Let's do this," I say, and turn toward the prison's massive doors. Each step a lifetime, but necessary.

As we get closer, a small man awaits by the entrance. He's holding a plastic bag heavy with stuff, all his possessions. He's hunched over thanks to cruel Time, but his face has echoes of the one I remember: thick curly hair now gone stark white, wrinkles like troughs, a Sharpie dog in human form, sinewy muscles still popping out of his sleeveless shirt at seventy, skin so tan and leathery he could be a suitcase. Barry Gimmelman in the flesh. Barry Gimmelman turning my way. The thrust of feelings at war with one another: love and hate battling it out in my psyche.

We catch each other's eyes: his milky and bloodshot, mine through a covering of tears. He raises his hand to say hello, hesitant. The clouds pass over and a beam of light parts the sky. It kisses my cheek, soothes my bruised eye.

"Aaron, my boy," he says, like he's gargling rocks, his voice shot from thirty years of cigarettes being the only vice he's allowed.

"*Barry*," I'm about to say, but the name feels wrong, an alien dancing on my tongue. It morphs into something else, something a whole lot more beautiful. That rabbi at the synagogue told me that with *teshuva*, it's important to forgive as soon as there's a transgression, for death can sneak up before any kind of pardon is given. I waited over thirty years, but it's never too late.

I hold up my hand to wave.

We're frozen in place. The sun creating a perfect spotlight on this moment.

I haven't called him anything other than Barry since back in the Gas Guzzler before everything turned to fucking garbage.

But God beams down through that ray of light and digs into my throat, scoops it out of me.

"Dad," I say, as the heavens crackle, and I step out of my body into a new one.

About the Author

Lee Matthew Goldberg is the author of thirteen novels including THE ANCESTOR and THE MENTOR along with his five-book DESIRE CARD series. He has been published in multiple languages and nominated for the Prix du Polar. After graduating with an MFA from the New School, his writing has also appeared as a contributor in CrimeReads, Pipeline Artists, LitHub, The Los Angeles Review of Books, The Millions, Vol. 1 Brooklyn, LitReactor, Mystery Tribune, The Big Idea, Monkeybicycle, Fiction Writers Review, Cagibi, Necessary Fiction, Hypertext, If My Book, Past Ten, the anthology Dirty Boulevard, The Montreal Review, The Adirondack Review, The New Plains Review, Maudlin House and others. He is the co-curator of The Guerrilla Lit Reading Series and lives in New York City.

You can connect with me on:

- http://www.leematthewgoldberg.com
- https://twitter.com/LMGBooks
- https://www.facebook.com/leemgol
- https://www.instagram.com/leematthewgoldberg
- https://www.tiktok.com/@leematthewgoldberg

Also by Lee Matthew Goldberg

Slow Down
    The Mentor
    The Ancestor
    Stalker Stalked
    Orange City

The Desire Card Series:
    Immoral Origins
    Prey No More
    All Sins Fulfilled
    Vicious Ripples
    Desire's End

The Runaway Train Series:
    Runaway Train
    Grenade Bouquets
    Vanish Me